'In telling this drama, Salter gives us joy, eroticism, disgust, beauty, nostalgia, outrage, highbrow discussion and lowbrow humour. There are moments of crushing tragedy . . . followed later by lines of wry comedy . . . Throughout, the story is populated with rich and living characters who stand at the centre of our gaze'   *The Times*

'*All That Is* has a grandeur that is all its own. Its handling of time, its elliptical wisdom, and its occasional chest-tightening cruelties are masterful'   *Observer*

'If any living writer has earned the right to name a novel *All That Is*, it is James Salter . . . Salter's breathlessly simple prose is often exquisite . . . as richly sensual as anything Hemingway wrote'
Sunday Times

'Masculine, clear-cut, ravishingly sensual'
Sunday Telegraph, Books of the Year

'*All That Is* is the story of a life . . . it is a river that meanders, that surges ahead and then is becalmed. It has many tributaries; one of the great pleasures of Salter is the way he dives into the lives of minor characters, spending a few paragraphs on someone who wandered into the action for a moment, telling you everything you ever need to know about them, then leaving them be. And in all that spare, elegant, shimmering prose, those sentences long and short that seem to expand and compress time itself'   *Esquire*

'This last great book is like a tour of Salter's heavy themes – both fictional and real – of love, war, sex, divorce and, of course, what it means to write . . . spellbinding'   *GQ*

'The fast-flowing scenes that depict the forty-year passage from youth to middle age of Philip Bowman, protagonist of *All That Is*, have a burn and clarity intense even by Salter's standards. Like the densely compressed stories that cascade through the mind of the dying writer in Hemingway's *The Snows of Kilimanjaro*, they assert a bright and infectious vitality, and they evoke both an individual life in great depth, and an entire, vanishing world'

James Lasdun, *Guardian*

'Set in the golden years of post-war America . . . studded with magnificent portraits of minor characters, their whole essences captured, somehow, in a gesture and two lines of dialogue . . . Its structure is like that of memory: associative, tangential, unpatterned. Characters come at the reader as recollections do – complete and fleeting. It is an account of an existence, an attempt to forestall its oblivion. A record of a time when it was still possible to be a hero in America'

Daily Telegraph

'*All That Is* is the equal of such great novels as *A Sport and a Pastime*, *Light Years* and his memoir, *Burning the Days*. That is to say, it is delectable . . . Salter has an extraordinary gift of conveying an entire story, the huge decisions of life, in a few telling phrases . . . A story that, treated more conventionally, could have been so much longer and less affecting is refracted here into points of light, moments of intense feeling, the memories that constitute us. The way Salter writes implies an attitude to life, even down to the level of the single sentence. He is that good . . . Although Salter has never had the fame of, say, Updike or Cheever, he is their equal, at least'

David Sexton, *Evening Standard*

'A career highlight in a career of highlights . . . there isn't a young person alive now who could write anything as masterful as this'

Dazed & Confused

'One of the literary events of the year. It's a corker: a marvellous dissection of the life of one man over four decades, from his times in the US Navy during the Second World War to the flowering of his career and his passionate relationships'

Alex Clark, *Evening Standard*

'Salter at his bitter-sweet best' Michael Prodger,
New Statesman, Books of the Year

'I loved James Salter's beguiling, brilliant, worldly, sexy novel *All That Is*' Simon Sebag Montefiore,
Evening Standard, Books of the Year

'Not in my (admittedly failing) memory have I read a novel that, at its crucialest moment, made me just stand straight up out of my chair and have to walk around the room for several minutes. Laid into the customary Salterish verbal exquisiteness and vivid intelligence is such remarkable audacity and dark-hued verve about us poor humans. It's a great novel'

Richard Ford, *Guardian*, Books of the Year

ALL THAT IS

JAMES SALTER is the author of numerous books, including the novels *Solo Faces*, *Light Years*, *A Sport and a Pastime*, *The Arm of Flesh* (revised as *Cassada*), and *The Hunters*; the memoirs *Gods of Tin* and *Burning the Days*; the collections *Dusk and Other Stories*, which won the 1989 PEN/Faulkner Award, and *Last Night*, which won the Rea Award for the Short Story and the PEN/Malamud Award; and *Life Is Meals: A Food Lover's Book of Days*, written with Kay Salter. He lives in New York and Colorado.

JAMES SALTER

ALL THAT IS

PICADOR

First published 2013 as a Borzoi Book, an imprint of Alfred A. Knopf
a division of Random House, Inc., New York, and in Canada by
Random House of Canada Limited, Toronto.

First published in the UK in paperback 2013 by Picador

This edition published 2014 by Picador
an imprint of Pan Macmillan, a division of Macmillan Publishers Limited
Pan Macmillan, 20 New Wharf Road, London N1 9RR
Basingstoke and Oxford
Associated companies throughout the world
www.panmacmillan.com

ISBN 978-1-4472-3827-0

A portion of this work was originally published in *The Paris Review* No. 203 (Winter 2012).
'Comet' is reproduced from *Collected Stories* by James Salter.
Grateful acknowledgement is made to *Esquire*, where the story first appeared.

3 5 7 9 8 6 4 2

A CIP catalogue record for this book is available from the British Library.

Printed and bound by CPI Group (UK) Ltd, Croydon, CR0 4YY

Visit **www.picador.com** to read more about all our books
and to buy them. You will also find features, author interviews and
news of any author events, and you can sign up for e-newsletters
so that you're always first to hear about our new releases.

For Kay

There comes a time when you
realize that everything is a dream,
and only those things preserved in writing
have any possibility of being real.

1. BREAK OF DAY

All night in darkness the water sped past.

In tier on tier of iron bunks below deck, silent, six deep, lay hundreds of men, many faceup with their eyes still open though it was near morning. The lights were dimmed, the engines throbbing endlessly, the ventilators pulling in damp air, fifteen hundred men with their packs and weapons heavy enough to take them straight to the bottom, like an anvil dropped in the sea, part of a vast army sailing towards Okinawa, the great island that was just to the south of Japan. In truth, Okinawa *was* Japan, part of the homeland, strange and unknown. The war that had been going on for three and a half years was in its final act. In half an hour the first groups of men would file in for breakfast, standing as they ate, shoulder to shoulder, solemn, unspeaking. The ship was moving smoothly with faint sound. The steel of the hull creaked.

The war in the Pacific was not like the rest of it. The distances alone were enormous. There was nothing but days on end of empty sea and strange names of places, a thousand miles between them. It had been a war of many islands, of prying them from the Japanese, one by one. Guadalcanal, which became a legend. The Solomons and the Slot. Tarawa, where the landing craft ran aground on reefs far from shore and the men were slaughtered in enemy fire dense as bees, the horror of the beaches, swollen bodies lolling in the surf, the nation's sons, some of them beautiful.

In the beginning with frightening speed the Japanese had overrun everything, all of the Dutch East Indies, Malaya, the Philippines. Great strongholds, deep fortifications known to be impregnable, were swept over in a matter of days. There had been only one counter stroke, the first great carrier battle in the middle of the Pacific, near Midway, where four irreplaceable Japanese carriers went down with all their planes and veteran crews. A staggering blow, but still the Japanese were relentless. Their grip on the Pacific would have to be broken finger by iron finger.

The battles were endless and unpitying, in dense jungle and heat. Near the shore, afterwards, the palms stood naked, like tall stakes, every leaf shot away. The enemy were savage fighters, the strange pagoda-like structures on their warships, their secret hissing language, their stockiness and ferocity. They did not surrender. They fought to the death. They executed prisoners with razor swords, two-handed swords raised high overhead, and they were merciless in victory, arms thrust aloft in mass triumph.

By 1944, the great, final stages had begun. Their object was to bring the Japanese homeland within range of heavy bombers. Saipan was the key. It was large and heavily defended. The Japanese army had not been defeated in battle, disregarding the outposts—New Guinea, the Gilberts, places such as that—for more than 350 years. There were twenty-five thousand Japanese troops on the island of Saipan commanded to yield nothing, not an inch of ground. In the order of earthly things, the defense of Saipan was deemed a matter of life and death.

In June, the invasion began. The Japanese had dangerous naval forces in the area, heavy cruisers and battleships. Two marine divisions went ashore and an army division followed.

It became, for the Japanese, the Saipan disaster. Twenty days later, nearly all of them had perished. The Japanese general and also Admiral Nagumo, who had commanded at Midway, committed suicide, and hundreds of civilians, men and women terrified of being slaughtered, some of them mothers holding babies in their arms, leapt from the steep cliffs to their death on the sharp rocks below.

It was the knell. The bombing of the main islands of Japan was now possible, and in the most massive of the raids, a firebombing of Tokyo, more than eighty thousand people died in the huge inferno in a single night.

Next, Iwo Jima fell. The Japanese pronounced an ultimate pledge: the death of a hundred million, the entire population, rather than surrender.

In the path of it lay Okinawa.

Day was rising, a pale Pacific dawn that had no real horizon with the tops of the early clouds gathering light. The sea was empty. Slowly the sun appeared, flooding across the water and turning it white. A lieutenant jg named Bowman had come on deck and was standing at the railing, looking out. His cabinmate, Kimmel, silently joined him. It was a day Bowman would never forget. Neither would any of them.

"Anything out there?"

"Nothing."

"Not that you can see," Kimmel said.

He looked forward, then aft.

"It's too peaceful," he said.

Bowman was navigation officer and also, he had learned just two days earlier, lookout officer.

"Sir," he had asked, "what does that entail?"

"Here's the manual," the exec said. "Read it."

He began that night, turning down the corner of certain pages as he read.

"What are you doing?" Kimmel asked.

"Don't bother me right now."

"What are you studying?"

"A manual."

"Jesus, we're in the middle of enemy waters and you're sitting there reading a manual? This is no time for that. You're supposed to already know what to do."

Bowman ignored him. They had been together from the beginning, since midshipman's school, where the commandant, a navy captain whose career had collapsed when his destroyer ran aground, had a copy of *A Message to Garcia*, an inspirational text from the Spanish-American War, placed on every man's bunk. Captain McCreary had no future but he remained loyal to the standards of the past. He drank himself into a stupor every night but was always crisp and well-shaved in the morning. He knew the book of navy regulations by heart and had bought the copies of *A Message to Garcia* with money from his own pocket. Bowman had read the *Message* carefully, years later he could still recite parts of it. *Garcia was somewhere in the mountain vastness of Cuba—no one knew where* . . . The point was simple: Do your duty fully and absolutely without unnecessary questions or excuses. Kimmel had cackled as he read it.

"Aye, aye, sir. Man the guns!"

He was dark-haired and skinny and walked with a loose gait that made him seem long-legged. His uniform always looked somehow slept in. His neck was too thin for his collar. The crew, among themselves, called him the Camel, but he had a playboy's aplomb and women liked him. In San Diego he had taken up with a lively girl named Vicky whose father owned a car dealership, Palmetto Ford. She had blond hair, pulled back, and a touch of daring. She was drawn to Kimmel immediately, his indolent glamour. In the hotel room that he had gotten with two other officers and where, he explained, they would be away from the noise of the bar, they sat drinking Canadian Club and Coke.

"How did it happen?" he asked.

"How did what happen?"

"My meeting someone like you."

"You certainly didn't deserve it," she said.

He laughed.

"It was fate," he said.

She sipped her drink.

"Fate. So, am I going to marry you?"

"Jesus, are we there already? I'm not old enough to get married."

"You'd probably only deceive me about ten times in the first year," she said.

"I'd never deceive you."

"Ha ha."

She knew exactly what he was like, but she would change that. She liked his laugh. He'd have to meet her father first, she commented.

"I'd love to meet your father," Kimmel answered in seeming earnestness. "Have you told him about us?"

"Do you think I'm crazy? He'd kill me."

"What do you mean? For what?"

"For getting pregnant."

"You're pregnant?" Kimmel said, alarmed.

"Who knows?"

Vicky Hollins in her silk dress, the glances clinging to her as she passed. In heels she wasn't that short. She liked to call herself by her last name. It's Hollins, she would announce on the phone.

They were shipping out, that was what made it all real or a form of real.

"Who knows if we'll get back," he said casually.

Her letters had come in the two sackfuls of mail that Bowman had brought back from Leyte. He'd been sent there by the exec to try and find the ship's mail at the Fleet Post Office—they'd had none for ten days—and he had flown back with it, triumphant, in a TBM. Kimmel read parts of her letters aloud for the benefit, especially, of Brownell, the third man in the cabin. Brownell was intense and morally pure, with a knotted jaw that had traces of acne. Kimmel liked to bait him. He sniffed at a page of the letter. Yeah, that was her perfume, he said, he'd recognize it anywhere.

"And maybe something else," he speculated. "I wonder. You think she might have rubbed it aginst her . . . Here," he said, offering it to Brownell, "tell me what you think."

6

"I wouldn't know," Brownell said uneasily. The knots in his jaw showed.

"Oh, sure you would, an old pussy hound like you."

"Don't try and involve me in your lechery," Brownell said.

"It's not lechery, she's writing to me because we fell in love. It's something beautiful and pure."

"How would you know?"

Brownell was reading *The Prophet*.

"*The Prophet*. What's that?" Kimmel said. "Let me see it. What does it do, tell us what's going to happen?"

Brownell didn't answer.

The letters were less exciting than a page filled with feminine handwriting would suggest. Vicky was a talker and her letters were a detailed and somewhat repetitive account of her life, which consisted in part of going back to all the places she and Kimmel had been to, usually in the company of Susu, her closest friend, and also in the company of other young naval officers, but thinking always of Kimmel. The bartender remembered them, she said, a fabulous couple. Her closings were always a line from a popular song. *I didn't want to do it,* she wrote.

Bowman had no girlfriend, faithful or otherwise. He'd had no experience of love but was reluctant to admit it. He simply let the subject pass when women were discussed and acted as though Kimmel's dazzling affair was more or less familiar ground to him. His life was the ship and his duties aboard. He felt loyalty to it and to a tradition that he respected, and he felt a certain pride when the captain or exec called out, "Mr. Bowman!" He liked their reliance, offhanded though it might be, on him.

He was diligent. He had blue eyes and brown hair combed back. He'd been diligent in school. Miss Crowley had drawn him aside after class and told him he had the makings of a fine Latinist, but if she could see him now in his uniform and sea-tarnished insignia, she would have been very impressed. From the time he and Kimmel had joined the ship at Ulithi, he felt he had performed well.

How he would behave in action was weighing on his mind that morning as they stood looking out at the mysterious, foreign sea and then at the sky that was already becoming brighter. Courage and fear and how you would act under fire were not among the things you talked about. You hoped, when the time came, that you would be able to do as expected. He had faith, if not complete, in himself, then in the leadership, the seasoned names that guided the fleet. Once, in the distance he had seen, low and swift-moving, the camouflaged flagship, the *New Jersey*, with Halsey aboard. It was like seeing, from afar, the Emperor at Ratisbon. He felt a kind of pride, even fulfillment. It was enough.

The real danger would come from the sky, the suicide attacks, the kamikaze—the word meant "divine wind," the heaven-sent storms that had saved Japan from the invasion fleet of Kublai Khan centuries before. This was the same intervention from on high, this time by bomb-laden planes flying directly into the enemy ships, their pilots dying in the act.

The first such attack had been in the Philippines a few months earlier. A Japanese plane dove into a heavy cruiser and exploded, killing the captain and many more. From then on the attacks multiplied. The Japanese would come in irregular groups, appearing suddenly. Men watched with almost hypnotic fascination and fear as they came straight down towards them through dense antiaircraft fire or swept in low, skimming the water. To defend Okinawa the Japanese had planned to launch the greatest kamikaze assault of all. The loss of ships would be so heavy that the invasion would be driven back and destroyed. It was not just a dream. The outcome of great battles could hinge on resolve.

Through the morning, though, there was nothing. The swells rose and slid past, some bursting white, spooling out and breaking backwards. There was a deck of clouds. Beneath, the sky was bright.

The first warning of enemy planes came in a call from the bridge, and Bowman was running to his cabin to get his life jacket when the alarm for General Quarters sounded, overwhelming everything else, and he passed Kimmel in a helmet that looked too big for him racing up the steel steps crying, "This is it! This is it!" The firing had started and every gun on the ship and on those nearby took it up. The sound was deafening. Swarms of antiaircraft fire were floating upwards amid dark puffs. On the bridge the captain was hitting the helmsman on the arm to get him to listen. Men were still getting to their stations. It was all happening at two speeds, the noise and desperate haste of action and also at a lesser speed, that of fate, with dark specks in the sky moving through the gunfire. They were distant and it seemed the firing could not reach them when suddenly something else began, within the din a single dark plane was coming down and like a blind insect, unerring, turning towards them, red insignia on its wings and a shining black cowling. Every gun on the ship was firing and the seconds were collapsing into one another. Then with a huge explosion and geyser of water the ship lurched sideways beneath their feet—the plane had hit them or just alongside. In the smoke and confusion no one knew.

"Man overboard!"

"Where?"

"Astern, sir!"

It was Kimmel who, thinking the magazine amidship had been hit, had jumped. The noise was still terrific, they were firing at everything. In the wake of the ship and trying to swim amid the great swells and pieces of wreckage, Kimmel was vanishing from sight. They could not stop or turn back for him. He would have drowned but miraculously he was seen and picked up by a destroyer that was almost immediately sunk by another kamikaze and the crew rescued by a second destroyer that, barely an hour later, was razed to the waterline. Kimmel ended up in a naval hospital. He became a kind of legend. He'd jumped off his ship by mistake and in one day had seen more action than the rest of them would see in the entire war. Afterwards, Bowman lost track of him. Several times over the years he tried to locate him in Chicago but without any luck. More than thirty ships were sunk that day. It was the greatest ordeal of the fleet during the war.

Near the same place just a few days later, the death knell of the Imperial Navy was sounded. For more than forty years, ever since their astonishing victory over the Russians at Tsushima, the Japanese had been increasing their strength.

An island empire required a powerful fleet, and Japanese ships were designed to be superior. Because their crews were made up of shorter men, less space was needed between decks as well as fewer comforts, and this could allow heavier armor, bigger guns, and more speed. The greatest of these ships, invincible, with steel thicker than any in existence and design more advanced, bore the poetic name of the nation itself, *Yamato*. Under orders to attack the vast invasion fleet off Okinawa, it set sail along with nine accompanying ships as escort, from a port on the Inland Sea where it had lain waiting.

It was a departure of foreboding, like the eerie silence that precedes a coming storm. Through the green water of the harbor, late in the day, long, dark, and powerful, moving slowly and gravely at first, a bow wave forming, gathering speed, almost silent, the large dock cranes passing in silhouette, the shore hidden in evening mist, leaving white swirls of foam trailing behind it, the *Yamato* headed for sea. The sounds that could be heard were muted; there was a feeling of good-bye. The captain addressed the entire crew massed on the deck. They had plentiful ammunition, lockers filled with great shells the size of coffins, but not the fuel, he told them, to return. Three thousand men and a vice admiral were aboard. They had written farewell letters home to their parents and wives and were sailing to their deaths. *Find happiness with another,* they wrote. *Be proud of your son.* Life was precious to them. They were somber and fearful. Many prayed. It was known that the ship was to perish as an emblem of the undying will of the nation not to surrender.

As night fell they sailed past the coast of Kyushu, the

southernmost of the Japanese main islands, where the outline of an American battleship had once been drawn on the beach for the pilots who would attack Pearl Harbor to practice bomb. The waves shattered and swept past. There was a strange spirit, almost of joy, among the crew. In the moonlight they sang and cried *banzai!* Many of them noticed there was an unusual brightness to the sea.

They were discovered at dawn while still far from any American ships. A navy patrol plane radioed urgently, in the clear, *Enemy task force headed south. At least one battleship, many destroyers . . . Speed twenty-five knots.* The wind had risen by morning. The sea was rough with low clouds and showers. Great waves were rumbling along the side of the ship. Then, as had been foreseen the first planes appeared on the radar. It was not a single formation, it was many formations, a swarm filling the sky, 250 carrier planes.

They came from out of the clouds, dive and torpedo bombers, more than a hundred at a time. The *Yamato* had been built to be invulnerable to air attack. All of its guns were firing as the first bombs hit. One of the escort destroyers suddenly heeled over, mortally stricken and, showing the dark red of its belly, sank. Through the water torpedoes streamed towards the *Yamato*, their wakes white as string. The impregnable deck had been torn open, steel more than a foot thick, men smashed or cut in two. "Don't lose heart!" the captain called. Officers had tied themselves to their station on the bridge as more bombs hit. Others missed closely, throwing up great pillars of water, walls of water that fell across the deck, solid as stone. It was not a battle, it was a ritual, the death as of a huge beast brought down by repeated blows.

An hour had passed and still the planes came, a fourth wave of them, then a fifth and sixth. The destruction was unimaginable. The steering had been hit, the ship was turning helplessly. It had begun to list, sea was sliding over the deck. *My whole life has been the gift of your love,* they had written to their mothers. The code books were sheathed in lead so they would sink with the ship, and their ink was of a kind that dissolved in water. Near the end of the second hour, listing almost eighty degrees, with hundreds dead and more wounded, blind and ruined, the gigantic ship began to sink. Waves swept over it and men clinging to the deck were carried off by the sea in all directions. As it went under, a huge whirlpool formed around it, a fierce torrent in which men could not survive but were drawn straight down as if falling in air. And then an even worse disaster. The stores of ammunition, the great shells, tons upon tons of them slid from their racks and slammed nose first into the turret sides. From deep in the sea came an immense explosion and flash of light so intense that it was seen from as far away as Kyushu as the full magazines went. A pillar of flame a mile high rose, a biblical pillar, and the sky was filled with red-hot pieces of steel coming down like rain. As if in echo there came, from the deep, a second climactic explosion, and thick smoke came pouring up.

Some of the crew that had not been pulled down by the suction were still swimming. They were black with oil and choking in the waves. A few were singing songs.

They were the only survivors. Neither the captain nor the admiral were among them. The rest of the three thousand men were in the lifeless body of the ship that had settled to the bottom far below.

The news of the sinking of the *Yamato* spread quickly. It was the end of the war at sea.

Bowman's ship was among the many anchored in Tokyo Bay when the war ended. Afterwards it sailed down to Okinawa to pick up troops going home, but Bowman had the chance to go ashore at Yokohama and walk through part of what remained of the city. He walked through block upon empty block of nothing but foundations. The smell of scorched debris, acrid and death-filled, hung in the air. Among the only things that were not destroyed were the massive bank vaults of solid steel, although the buildings that had contained them were gone. In the gutters were bits of burnt paper, banknotes, all that remained of the Imperial dream.

2. THE GREAT CITY

"The hero!" his uncle Frank cried, stretching out his arms to hug him.

It was a welcome-home dinner.

"Not exactly a hero," Bowman said.

"Sure you are. We read all about you."

"Read about me? Where?"

"In your letters!" his uncle said.

"Frank, let me!" his aunt cried.

They had come from the Fiori, their restaurant near Fort Lee that was decorated in thin red plush and where music from *Rigoletto* and *Il Trovatore* was always playing until the last, softly talking couples left, the last melancholy couples and the few men still at the bar. Frank was the uncle of his childhood. He was dark with a rounded nose and thinning hair. Stocky and good-natured, he had gone to law school in Jersey City but dropped out with the idea of becoming a chef, and at the restaurant, when he was in the mood, sometimes went back into the kitchen to cook himself, though his real joy was music. He had taught himself to play the piano and would sit in happiness, drawn up close to the keyboard with his thick fingers, their backs richly haired, nimble on the keys.

The evening was all warmth and talk. His mother, Beatrice,

his aunt and uncle listened to the stories of where Bowman had been—where was San Pedro? had he eaten any Japanese food?—and drank champagne Frank had kept from before the war.

"You don't know how worried we were all the time you were out there," his aunt Dorothy—Dot they called her—told him. "We thought of you every day."

"Did you really?"

"We prayed for you," she said.

She and Frank had no children of their own, he was really like their son. Now their fears were over and the world was as it should be and also, it seemed to Bowman, very much as it had been, familiar and ordinary, the same houses, shops, streets, everything he remembered and had known since childhood, unremarkable, yet his alone. In some windows there were gold stars for sons or husbands who had been killed, but that and the many flags were almost the only evidence of all that had taken place. The very air, untroubled and unchanged, was familiar and the high school and grammar school with their sober facades. He felt in a way superior to it all and at the same time beholden.

His uniform hung in the closet and his cap was on the shelf above. He had worn them when he was Mr. Bowman, a junior officer but respected and even admired. Long after the uniform had lost its authenticity and glamour, the cap, strangely, would still have its power.

In dreams that were frequent for a long time, he was there again. They were at sea and under attack. The ship had been hit, it was listing, going to its knees like a dying horse. The passageways were flooded, he was trying to struggle through them to get on deck where there were crowds of men. The ship was nearly on its side and he was near the boilers that might explode at any minute, he had to find a safer place. He was at the railing, he would have to jump and get back on board further astern. In the dream he jumped, but the ship was traveling too fast. It passed as he swam, the stern rumbling by, leaving him in the wake, far behind.

"Douglas," his mother said, naming a boy slightly older that Bowman had gone to school with, "asked about you."

"How is Douglas?"

"He's going to law school."

"His father was a lawyer."

"So is yours," his mother said.

"You're not worried about my future are you? I'm going back to school. I'm applying to Harvard."

"Ah, wonderful!" his uncle cried.

"Why so far away?" said his mother.

"Mother, I was off in the Pacific. You didn't complain about that being so far away."

"Oh, didn't I?"

"Well, I'm glad to be home."

His uncle put an arm around him.

"Boy, are we glad," he said.

Harvard did not accept him. It was his first choice, but his application was turned down, they did not accept transfer students, their letter informed him. In response he sat down and wrote a carefully composed reply mentioning by name the famed professors he hoped to study under, whose knowledge and authority had no equal, and at the same time portraying himself as a young man who should not be penalized for having gone off to war. Shameless as it was, the letter succeeded.

In the fall of 1946 at Harvard he was an outsider, a year or two older than his classmates but seen as having a kind of strength of character—he'd been in the war, his life was more real because of it. He was respected and also lucky in several ways, chief among them his roommate with whom he struck it off immediately. Malcolm Pearson was from a well-to-do family. He was tall, intelligent, and mumbling, only occasionally was Bowman able to make out what he was saying, but gradually he became accustomed and could hear. Pearson treated his expensive clothing with a lordly disdain and seemed rarely to go to meals. He was majoring in history with the vague idea of becoming a professor, anything to displease his father and distance himself from the building supplies business.

As it happened, after graduation he taught for a while at a boys' school in Connecticut, then went on to get a master's degree and marry a girl named Anthea Epick, although no one at the wedding at the bride's home near New London, including the minister and Bowman, who was best man, understood him to say "I do." Anthea was also tall with dark brows and slightly knock-kneed, a thing not perceptible in her white wedding gown, but they had all been swimming in the pool the day before. She had an odd way of walking, a sort of lurch, but she shared Malcolm's tastes and they got along well.

After marriage, Malcolm did very little. Dressed like a

bohemian of the 1920s in a loose overcoat, scarf, exercise pants, and an old fedora and carrying a thorn stick, he walked his collie on his place near Rhinebeck and pursued his own interests, largely confined to the history of the Middle Ages. He and Anthea had a daughter, Alix, to whom Bowman was godfather. She, too, was eccentric. She was silent as a child and later spoke with a kind of English accent. She lived at home with her parents, which they accepted as if it had always been intended, and never married. She wasn't even promiscuous, her father complained.

The years at Harvard had as lasting an effect on Bowman as the time he had spent at sea. He stood on the steps of Widener, eyes level with the trees, looking out at the great redbrick buildings and oaks of the Yard. Late in the day the deep, resounding bells began, solemn and grand, ringing on and on almost without reason and finally fading in calm, endless strokes, soft as caresses.

He had begun with the idea of studying biology, but in his second semester he happened upon, as if rising up before him from nowhere, the great Elizabethan Age—London, Shakespeare's own city still with trees, the legendary Globe, the eloquence of people of rank, sumptuous language and dress, the Thames and its dissolute south bank with land belonging to the Bishop of Winchester and the young women who made themselves available there known as Winchester geese, the end of one tumultuous century and beginning of another—all of it seized his interest.

In the class on Jacobean drama the famed professor, an actor really who had polished his performance over decades, began gorgeously in a rich voice, "Kyd was the El Greco of the English stage."

Bowman remembered it word for word.

"Against a background of clouded landscapes and fitful lightnings, we may descry these curiously angular figures clothed in garments of unexpected richness, and animated by convulsions of somber passion."

Fitful lightnings, garments of richness. The aristocrats who were writers—the Earl of Oxford, the Countess of Pembroke—the courtiers, Raleigh and Sidney. The many playwrights of whom no likenesses existed, Kyd, arrested and tortured for irregular beliefs, Webster, Dekker, the incomparable Ben Jonson, Marlowe whose *Tamburlaine* was performed when he was twenty-three, and the unknown actor whose father was a glovemaker and mother illiterate, Shakespeare himself. It was an age of fluency and towering prose. The queen, Elizabeth, knew Latin, loved music, and played the lyre. Great monarch, great city.

Bowman, too, had been born in a great city, in the French Hospital in Manhattan, in the burning heat of August and very early in the morning when all geniuses are born, as Pearson once told him. There had been an unbreathing stillness, and near dawn faint, distant thunder. It grew slowly louder, then gusts of cooler air before a tremendous storm broke with lightning and sheets of rain, and when it was over, just rising, a gigantic summer sun. Clinging to the blanket at the foot of the bed was a one-legged grasshopper that had somehow found shelter in the room. The nurse reached to pull it off but his mother, still dazed from the birth, said don't, it was an omen. The year was 1925.

His father left them two years later. He was a lawyer at Vernon, Wells and had been sent by the firm to work with a client in Baltimore, where he met a woman, a society woman named Alicia Scott and fell in love with her and left his wife and young son. Later they married and had a daughter. He married twice more, each time to successively richer women he met at country clubs. These were Bowman's stepmothers although he never met any of them or his half sister, for that matter.

He never saw his father again, but he was fortunate in having a loving uncle, Frank, who was understanding, humorous, given to writing songs and studying nudist magazines. The Fiori did well enough, and Bowman and his mother had many dinners there when he was a boy, sometimes playing casino with his uncle, who was a good player and could do card tricks, making four kings come up in the deck after the four queens and things like that.

Over the years, Beatrice Bowman acted as if her husband were merely away, as if he might come back to them, even after the divorce and his marriage to the Baltimore woman, which somehow seemed insubstantial though she had been eager to know what the woman who had taken him away from her looked like and finally saw a photograph that was in a Baltimore newspaper. She had less curiosity about the two wives that followed, they represented only something pitiable. It was as if he were drifting further and further downward and away, and she had determined not to watch. She herself had several men who courted her, but nothing had come of it, perhaps they sensed what was equivocal in her. The two important men in her life, her father and her husband, had both abandoned her. She had her son and her job in the schools. They had little money but their own house. They were happy.

In the end Bowman decided on journalism. There was the romance of reporters like Murrow and Quentin Reynolds, at the typewriter late at night finishing their stories, the lights of the city all around, theaters emptying out, the bar at Costello's crowded and noisy. Sexual inexperience would be over with. He had not been shy at Harvard but it had simply not happened, the thing that would complete his life. He knew what the *ignudi* were but not the simply nude. He remained innocent and teeming with desire. There was Susan Hallet, the Boston girl he had gone with, slender, clear-faced, with low breasts that he associated with privilege. He had wanted her to go away for a weekend with him, to Gloucester, where there would be foghorns and the smell of the sea.

"Gloucester?"

"Any place," he said.

How could she do it, she protested, how could she explain it?

"You could say you were staying at a friend's."

"That wouldn't be true."

"Of course not. That's the whole idea."

She was looking at the ground, her arms crossed in front of her as if somehow embracing herself. She would have to say no, though she enjoyed having him persist. For him it was almost unbearable, her presence and unfeeling refusal.

She might have said yes, she thought, if there were some way of doing it, going off and . . . she was able only vaguely to imagine the rest. She had felt his hardness several times when dancing. She more or less knew what all that was.

"I wouldn't know how to keep it a secret," she said.

"I'd keep it a secret," he promised. "Of course, you would know."

She smiled a little.

"I'm serious," he said. "You know how I feel about you."

He couldn't help thinking of Kimmel and the ease with which others did this.

"I'm serious, too," she said. "There's a lot more at stake for me."

"Everything is at stake."

"Not for the man."

He understood but that meant nothing. His father, who had always had success with women, might have taught him something priceless here, but nothing was ever passed between father and son.

"I wish we could do it," she said simply. "All of it, I mean. You know how much I like you."

"Yes. Sure."

"You men are all alike."

"That's a boring thing to say."

In the mood of euphoria that was everywhere after the war it was still necessary to find a place for oneself. He applied at the *Times* but there was nothing, and it was the same at the other papers. Fortunately he had a contact, a classmate's father who was in public relations and who had virtually invented the business. He could arrange anything in newspapers and magazines—for ten thousand dollars, it was said, he could put someone on the cover of *Time*. He could pick up the phone and call anyone, the secretaries immediately put him through.

Bowman was to go and see him at his house, in the morning. He always ate breakfast at nine.

"Will he expect me?"

"Yes, yes. He knows you're coming."

Having hardly slept the night before, Bowman stood on the street in front of the house at eight-thirty. It was a mild autumn morning. The house was in the Sixties, just off Central Park West. It was broad and imposing, with tall windows and the facade almost completely covered with a deep gown of ivy. At a quarter to nine he rang at the door, which was glass with heavy iron grillwork.

He was shown into a sun-filled room on the garden. Along one wall was a long, English-style buffet with two silver trays, a crystal pitcher of orange juice, and a large silver coffee pot covered with a cloth, also butter, rolls, and jam. The butler asked how he would like his eggs. Bowman declined the eggs. He had a cup of coffee and nervously waited. He knew what Mr. Kindrigen would look like, a well-tailored man with a somewhat sinewy face and gray hair.

It was silent. There were occasional soft voices in the kitchen. He drank the coffee and went to get another cup. The garden windows were vanishing in the light.

At nine-fifteen, Kindrigen came into the room. Bowman said good morning. Kindrigen did not reply or even appear to notice him. He was in shirtsleeves, an expensive shirt with wide French cuffs. The butler brought coffee and a plate with some toast. Kindrigen stirred the coffee, opened the newspaper, and began reading it, sitting sideways to the table. Bowman had seen villains in Westerns sit this way. He said nothing and waited. Finally Kindrigen said,

"You are . . . ?"

"Philip Bowman," Bowman said. "Kevin may have mentioned me . . ."

"Are you a friend of Kevin's?"

"Yes. From school."

Kindrigen still had not looked up.

"You're from . . . ?"

"New Jersey, I live in Summit."

"What is it you want?" Kindrigen said.

"I'd like to work for the *New York Times*," Bowman said, matching the directness.

Kindrigen glanced at him for a brief moment.

"Go home," he said.

He found a job with a small company that published a theater magazine and began by selling advertising. It was not difficult, but it was dull. The world of the theater was thriving. There were scores of theaters in the West Forties, one after another, and crowds strolled along deciding which to buy tickets to. Would you like to see a musical or this thing by Noël Coward?

Before long he heard of another job, reading manuscripts at a publishing house. The salary, it turned out, was less than he'd been making, but publishing was a different kind of business, it was a gentleman's occupation, the origin of the silence and elegance of bookstores and the freshness of new pages although this was not evident from the offices, which were off Fifth Avenue in the rear of an upper floor. It was an old building with an elevator that ascended slowly past open grillwork and hallways of worn white tile uneven from the years. In the publisher's office they were drinking champagne—one of the editors had just had a son. Robert Baum, the publisher, who owned the company together with a financing partner, was in shirtsleeves, a man of about thirty, of medium height with a friendly face, a face that was alert and somewhat homely with the beginnings of pouches beneath the eyes. He talked amiably with Bowman for a couple of minutes and, having learned enough, hired him on the spot.

"The salary is modest," he explained. "You're not married?"

"No. What is the salary?"

"One sixty," Baum said. "A hundred and sixty dollars a month. What do you think?"

"Well, less than needed, more than expected," Bowman replied.

"More than expected? I made a mistake."

Baum had confidence and charm, neither of them false. Publishing salaries were traditionally low and the salary he offered was only slightly below that. It was necessary to keep overhead low in a business that was uncertain in itself as well as being in competition with larger well-established houses. They were a literary house, Baum liked to say, but only through necessity. They were not going to turn down a best-seller as a matter of principle. The idea, he said, was to pay little and sell a truckful. On the wall of his office was a framed letter from a colleague and friend, an older editor who'd been asked to read a manuscript. The letter was on a sheet of paper that had two fold marks and was very to the point. *This is a very obvious book with shallow characters described in a style that grates on one's nerves. The love affair is tawdry and of little interest, and in fact one is repelled by it. Nothing but the completely obscene is left to the imagination. It is utterly worthless.*

"It sold two hundred thousand copies," Baum said, "and they're making a movie of it. The biggest book we've ever had. I keep it there as a reminder."

He did not add that he himself had disliked the book and had only been persuaded to publish it by his wife, who said it would touch something in people. Diana Baum was an important influence on her husband though she very seldom appeared at the offices. She devoted herself to their child, a son named Julian, and to literary criticism, writing a column for a small, liberal magazine, influential beyond its numbers, and she was a figure as a result.

Baum had money, how much was uncertain. His father, a banker who had immigrated to America, had done very well. The family was Jewish and German and felt a kind of supe-riority. The city was filled with Jews, many of them poor on the Lower East Side and in the boroughs, but everywhere they were in their own world somewhat excluded from the greater one. Baum had known the experience of being an outsider and more at boarding school, where, despite his open nature, he made few friends. When the war came, rather than seeking a commission, he had served in the ranks, in intelligence, as it happened, but in combat. He had one near-death experience. They were in the flatlands of Holland at night. They were sleeping in a building where the roof had been blown away. Someone came in with a flashlight and began moving among the sleeping men. He tapped one man on the arm.

"You a sergeant?" Baum heard him ask.

The man cleared his throat.

"That's right," he said.

"Get up. We're going."

"I'm a supply sergeant. I'm a replacement."

"I know. You've got to take twenty-three men up to the front."

"What twenty-three men?"

"Come on. There's no time."

He led them along a road in the dark. There was the sickening sound of firing up ahead and the heavy thump of artillery. In a slight decline a captain was giving orders.

"Who are you?" the captain asked.

"I've got twenty-three men," the sergeant replied.

In fact there were only twenty-one, two had slipped away or become lost in the darkness. There was firing going on not far away.

"Been in combat yet, sarge?"

"No, sir."

"You will tonight."

They were supposed to cross the river in rubber boats. Almost on hands and knees they dragged the boats down to the bank. Everyone was whispering but Baum felt they were making a great amount of noise.

He went in the first boat. He was not filled with fear, he was almost paralyzed by it. He held his rifle, which he had never fired, in front of him as if it were a shield. They were making a fatal transgression. He knew he was going to be killed. He could hear the low splashing of the paddles that was going to be drowned in a sudden outbreak of machine-gun fire, the whispers he knew they could hear. Paddle with your hand, someone said. The Germans were waiting to open fire until they got halfway across, but for some reason nothing happened. It was the next wave that was caught midway. Baum was on shore by then and the entire bank above his head and further back exploded into firing. Men were shouting and falling into the water. None of those boats made it.

They were pinned down for three days. He later saw the captain who had given them orders in the ravine lying dead, a half-naked body with a bare chest and dark, swollen woman's nipples. Baum made a vow to himself, not then but when the war ended. He vowed never to be afraid of anything again.

Baum did not seem the sort of man who had been through and seen that. He was domestic and urbane, worked on Saturday and in deference to his parents appeared in synagogue on the holiest days, in deference also to those more distant in obliterated villages or mass burial pits, but at the same time he did not represent the Jewishness of black hats and suffering, the ancient ways. The war, he imagined, from which he had emerged whole and unharmed, had given him his credentials. He was almost indistinguishable from other citizens except in inner knowing. He ran his business in an English way. In his sparsely furnished office there was only a desk, an old couch, a table, and some chairs. He read everything himself and after some agreement from his wife made all the decisions. He went to lunch with agents who for a long time regarded him lightly, had dinners, and in the office made it a practice to go around and talk to everyone every day. He would sit on the corner of their desk and chat casually, what did they think about this or that, what had they read or heard? His manner was open and talking to him was easy. He sometimes seemed more like the mail clerk than the publisher, and often had tidbits himself, stories he had heard, gossip, news, feigned horror at the size of advances—how could you hope to publish good books if you went broke in the process? He seemed never to be in a hurry, though the visits were rarely lengthy. He repeated jokes he had heard and called everyone by their first name, even the elevator man, Raymont.

Bowman was not a reader long. The editor who'd had a son left to take a job at Scribner's and Bowman, taking the trouble to find out what his salary had been, took his place. He liked it. The office was a world of its own. It did not run by the clock, he was sometimes there until nine or ten at night and other times having a drink at six. He liked reading the manuscripts and talking to the writers, being responsible for bringing a book into existence, the discussions, editing, galleys, page proofs, jacket. He'd had no clear idea of it before he started but found it fulfilling.

Going home on weekends was a pleasure, sitting down to dinner with his mother—shall we have a cocktail first? she always said—telling her what he was doing. She was fifty-two that year and showing no age but somehow past the thought of remarrying. Her love and all her attention went to her family. During the week Bowman was living in a single room without a bath off Central Park West, and the comparative luxury of his old house stood in contrast.

His mother so liked talking to him, she could have talked to him every day. It was only with difficulty she resisted the impulse to hug and kiss him. She had brought him up from the day he was born and now, when he was the most beautiful, she could only smooth his hair. Even that could be awkward. The love she had given he would pass on to someone else. At the same time he was somehow still the wonderful child he had been in the years when there were just the two of them, when they went to visit Dot and Frank and have dinner at the restaurant. She would never forget the well-dressed woman who, seeing the little boy holding the fork too big for his hand and trying to pick up spaghetti, had said admiringly,

"That is the most beautiful child I have ever seen."

Making little word and picture books from folded paper that was sewn together, writing out his first words with him, the many nights that now seemed a single night, putting him to bed and hearing him say, pleading, "Leave the door open."

All of the days, all of it.

She remembered when the down had appeared on his cheeks, a faint, soft down that she pretended not to see, and then he began to shave, his hair gradually darkened and his features seemed to more resemble his father's. Looking back she could remember every bit of it, most of it with happiness, in fact with nothing but happiness. They were always close, mother and son, without end.

Beatrice had been born, the younger of two girls, in Rochester in the last year and month of the century, 1899. Their father was a teacher who died of the flu, the so-called Spanish flu that had first appeared in Spain and then broke out in America in the fall of 1918, just at the end of the war. More than half a million people died in scenes reminiscent of the plague. Her father had been stricken while walking on Clifford Avenue on a balmy afternoon, and two days later, face discolored, burning with fever and unable to breathe, he died. Afterwards they went to live with her grandparents, who ran a small hotel on Irondequoit Bay, a wooden hotel with a bar and a large, white kitchen and, during the winter, empty rooms. When she was twenty, she came down to New York City. She had distant relatives there, the Gradows, cousins of her mother, who were rich, and she was a number of times in their home.

One of the lost images of Bowman's boyhood was of the mansion—he'd been taken to see it when he was five or six—a great, ornate, gray granite building with, as he remembered it, a moat and latticed windows near the park somewhere but not to be found, like streets in that familiar city that repeatedly appears in dreams. He never bothered to ask his mother about it and if it had been torn down, but there were places along Fifth where it seemed it might have been.

Beatrice, perhaps because of her father's death, which she remembered clearly, had a certain lingering dread of the fall. There was a time, usually late in August, when summer struck the trees with dazzling power and they were rich with leaves but then became, suddenly one day, strangely still, as if in expectation and at that moment aware. They knew.

Everything knew, the beetles, the frogs, the crows solemnly walking across the lawn. The sun was at its zenith and embraced the world, but it was ending, all that one loved was at risk.

Neil Eddins, the other editor, was a southerner, smooth faced and mannerly, who wore striped shirts and made friends easily.

"You were in the navy," he said.

"Yes, were you?"

"They wouldn't have me. I couldn't get into the program. I was in the merchant marine."

"Where was that?"

"In the East River, mostly. The crew was Italian. They could never get them to sail."

"Not much danger of being sunk."

"Not by the enemy," Eddins said. "Were you ever sunk?"

"Some people thought we were."

"What do you mean?"

"It's too long a story."

Gretchen, who was the secretary, walked by as they talked. She had a good figure and an attractive face marred by three or four large inflamed blemishes, some unnameable skin trouble, on her cheeks and forehead that made her miserable though she never betrayed it. Eddins gave a slight moan when she had passed.

"Gretchen, you mean?"

It was known she had a boyfriend.

"Oh, my God," Eddins said. "Forget the acne or whatever

that is, we can clear that up. Actually I like women who look a little like boxers, high cheekbones, lips a bit thick. What a dream I had the other night! I had three cute girls, one after the other. It was in a little room, almost a stall, and I was starting in with the fourth and someone was trying to come in. No, no, damn it, not now! I was shouting. The fourth one's ass was right up against me as she bent over to take off her shoes. Am I being too disgusting?"

"No, not really."

"Do you have dreams like that?"

"I usually only dream about one at a time," Bowman said.

"Anyone in particular?" Eddins said. "What I really like is a voice, a low voice. When I get married, that's the first thing I'm going to tell her, speak in a low voice."

Gretchen passed on her way back. She gave a slight smile.

"Jaysus," Eddins said, "they know what they're doing, don't they? They love it."

After work they sometimes went up to Clarke's for a drink. Third Avenue was a street of drinkers and many local bars, always in the shadow of the elevated and the sound of it passing overhead, rocking by tenements and daylight dropping through the tracks after it had gone by.

They talked about books and writing. Eddins had had only a year of college but had read everything, he was a member of the Joyce Society and Joyce was his hero.

"But I don't normally like a writer to give me too much of a character's thoughts and feelings," he said. "I like to see them, hear what they say, and decide for myself. The appearance of things. I like dialogue. They talk and you understand everything. Do you like John O'Hara?"

"Somewhat," Bowman said. "I like some O'Hara."

"What's wrong with him?"

"He can be too nasty."

"He writes about that kind of people. *Appointment in Samarra* is a great book. It just swept me away. He was twenty-eight when he wrote it."

"Tolstoy was younger. Tolstoy was twenty-three."

"When he wrote what?"

"Childhood, Boyhood, Youth."

Eddins hadn't read it. In fact he'd never heard of it, he admitted.

"It made him famous overnight," Bowman said. "They all became famous overnight, that's the interesting thing. Fitzgerald, Maupassant, Faulkner, when he wrote *Sanctuary,* that is. You should read *Childhood*. There's a wonderful short chapter where Tolstoy describes his father, tall and bald and with just two great passions in his life, you think it's going to be his family and his lands, but it's cards and women. An amazing chapter."

"You know what she told me today?"

"Who?"

"Gretchen. She told me the Bolshoi was in town."

"I didn't know she was interested in ballet."

"She also told me what Bolshoi means. It means big, great."

"So?"

Eddins made a cupping gesture with each hand.

"Why is she doing this to me?" he said. "I wrote a little poem to her, like the one Byron wrote to Caroline Lamb, one of the many women including countesses he put it to, if I may use the term."

"He was in Dionysian flux," Bowman said.

"Flux. What is that, Chinese word? Anyway, here's my poem: 'Bolshoi, Oh, boy.' "

"Referring to what?"

"Are you kidding? She's flaunting them every minute."

"What's Byron's poem?" Bowman said. "I don't know it."

"It's said to be the shortest poem in the English language, but mine is actually shorter. 'Caro Lamb, God damn.' "

"Is she the one he married?"

"No, she was married. She was a countess. If I knew a countess or two, I'd be a better person. Especially if she were leaning a little towards beauty, the countess, I mean. In fact she doesn't even have to be a countess. That's a word that invites vulgarization, doesn't it? In high school I had a girlfriend—of course we never did anything—named Ava. Anyway a beautiful name. She also had a body. I wonder where she is now, now that we're grown up. I should get her address somehow unless she's married, ghastly thought. On the other hand, not too ghastly if you think about it a certain way."

"Where did you go to high school?"

"The last year I went to boarding school near Charlottesville. We ate our meals together in the dining hall. The headmaster used to light dollar bills to show the proper attitude toward money. He ate a hard-boiled egg every single morning, shell and all. I never quite got around to that although I was always hungry. Starving. I was probably there because of Ava and what they were afraid might happen. My folks didn't believe in sex."

"What parents do?"

They were sitting in the middle of the crowded bar. The doors to the street were open, and the noise of the train, a loud crashing like a wave, drowned out what they were saying from time to time.

"You know the one about the Hungarian count?" Eddins said. "Anyway, there was this count, and his wife said to him one day that their son was growing up and wasn't it time he learned about the birds and the bees? All right, the count said, so he took him for a walk. They went down to a stream and stood on a bridge looking down at peasant girls washing clothes. The count said, your mother wants me to talk to you about the birds and the bees, what they do. Yes, father, the son said. Well, you see the girls down there? Yes, father. You remember a few days ago when we came here, what we did with them? Yes, father. Well, that's what the birds and the bees do."

He was stylish, Eddins, wearing a pale summer suit, slightly wrinkled, though it was a little late in the year for it. At the same time he managed a carelessness about his person, the pockets of his jacket were filled with various things, his hair needed cutting in back. He spent more than he could afford for his clothes, the British American House was his favorite.

"You know, back home there was a girl in the neighborhood, good-looking girl, who was a little retarded . . ."

"Retarded," Bowman said.

"I don't know what was wrong, a little slow."

"Don't tell me anything criminal now."

"You're such a gentleman," Eddins said. "You're the type they used to have."

"Have where?"

"Everywhere. My father would have liked you. If I had your looks . . ."

"Yes, what?"

"I'd cut a swath through this town."

Bowman was feeling the drinks himself. Among the brilliant bottles in the mirror behind the bar he could see himself, jacket and tie, New York evening, people around him, faces. He looked clean, composed, somehow blended together with the naval officer he had been. He remembered the days clearly though they had already become only a shadow in his life. Days at sea. Mr. Bowman! Yes, sir! The pride he would never lose.

In the doorway then, just coming in, was the girl Eddins had tried to describe, with a boxer's face, flat-cheeked with a somewhat wide nose. He could see the upper half of her in the mirror as she passed, she was with her boyfriend or husband, wearing a light dress with orange flowers. She stood out, but Eddins hadn't seen her, he was talking to someone else. It didn't matter, the city was filled with such women, not exactly filled but you saw them at night.

Eddins had turned and caught sight of her.

"Oh, lord," he said, "I knew it. There's the girl I'd like to make love to."

"You don't even know her."

"I don't want to know her, I want to fuck her."

"What a romantic you are."

At work, though, he was a choir boy and even seemed or tried to seem unaware of Gretchen. He handed Bowman a folded sheet of paper, somewhat offhandedly, and glanced away. It was another poem, typed in the middle of the page:

> In the Plaza Hotel, to his sorrow,
> Said the love of his life, Gretchen caro,
> It may be infra dig,
> But, my God, you are big,
> Could we possibly wait till tomorrow?

"Shouldn't that be *cara*?" Bowman said.

"What do you mean?"

"The feminine."

"Here," Eddins said, "give it back, I don't want it falling into the wrong hands."

3. VIVIAN

St. Patrick's Day was sunny and unusually mild, men were in shirtsleeves and from the appearance of things work was ending at noon. The bars were full. Coming into one of them from out of the sunlight, Bowman, his eyes blinded, could barely make out the faces along the bar but found a place to stand near the back where they were all shouting and calling to one another. The bartender brought his drink and he took it and looked around. There were men and women drinking, young women mostly, two of them—he never forgot this moment—standing near him to his right, one dark-haired with dark brows and, when he could see her better, a faint down along her jawbone. The other was blond with a bare, shining forehead and wide-set eyes, instantly compelling, even in some way coarse. He was so struck by her face that it was difficult to look at her, she stood out so—on the other hand he could not keep himself from doing it. He was almost fearful of looking.

He raised his glass towards them.

"Happy St. Patrick's," he managed to say.

"Can't hear you," one of them cried.

He tried to introduce himself. The place was too noisy. It was like a raging party they were in the middle of.

"What's your name?" he called.

"Vivian," the blond girl said.

He stepped closer. Louise was the dark-haired one. She already had a secondary role, but Bowman, trying not to be too direct, included her.

"Do you live around here?" he said.

Louise answered. She lived on Fifty-Third Street. Vivian lived in Virginia.

"Virginia?" Bowman said, stupidly he felt, as if it were China.

"I live in Washington," Vivian said.

He could not keep his eyes from her. Her face was as if, somehow, it was not completely finished, with smouldering features, a mouth not eager to smile, a riveting face that God had stamped with the simple answer to life. In profile she was even more beautiful.

When they asked what he did—the noise had quieted a little—he replied he was an editor.

"An editor?"

"Yes."

"Of what? Magazines?"

"Books," he said. "I work at Braden and Baum."

They had never heard of it.

"I was thinking of going to Clarke's," he said, "but there was all this noise in here, and I just came in to see what was going on. I'll have to go back to work. What . . . what are you doing later?"

They were going to a movie.

"Want to come?" Louise said.

He suddenly liked, even loved her.

"I can't. Can I meet you later? I'll meet you back here."

"What time?"

"After work. Any time."

They agreed to meet at six.

All afternoon he was almost giddy and found it hard to keep his mind on things. Time moved with a terrible slowness, but at a quarter to six, walking quickly, almost running, he went back. He was a few minutes early, they were not there. He waited impatiently until six-fifteen, then six-thirty. They never appeared. With a sickening feeling he realized what he had done—he had let them go without asking for a telephone number or address, Fifty-Third Street was all he knew and he would never see them, her, again. Hating his ineptness, he stayed for nearly an hour, towards the end striking up a conversation with the man next to him so that if by chance they did finally come, he would not seem foolish and doglike standing there.

What was it, he wondered, that had betrayed him and made them decide not to come back? Had they been approached by someone else after he left? He was miserable. He felt the terrible emptiness of men who are ruined, who see everything collapse in a single day.

He went to work in the morning still feeling anguish. He could not talk about it to Eddins. It was in him like a deep splinter together with a sense of failure. Gretchen was at her desk. Eddins smelled of talcum or cologne, something suspicious. Bowman sat silently reading when Baum came in.

"How are you this morning?" Baum said easily, the usual overture when he had nothing particular in mind.

They talked for a bit and had just finished when Gretchen came over.

"There's someone on the phone for you."

Bowman picked up his phone and said, somewhat curtly, "Hello."

It was her. He felt a moment of insane happiness. She was apologizing. They had come back at six the night before but hadn't been able to find the bar, they couldn't remember the street.

"Yes, of course," Bowman said. "I'm so sorry, but that's all right."

"We even went to Clarke's," she said. "I remembered you said that."

"I'm so glad you called."

"I just wanted you to know. That we tried to come back and meet you."

"No, no, that's all right, that's fine. Look, give me your address, will you?"

"In Washington?"

"Yes, anywhere."

She gave it and Louise's as well. She was going back to Washington that afternoon, she said.

"Do you . . . what time is the train? Do you have time for lunch?"

Not really. The train was at one.

"That's too bad. Maybe another time," he said foolishly.

"Well, bye," she said after a pause.

"Good-bye," he somehow agreed.

But he had her address, he looked at it after hanging up. It was precious beyond words. He didn't know her last name.

In the great vault of Penn Station with the light in wide blocks coming down through the glass and onto the crowd that was always waiting, Bowman made his way. He was nervous but then caught sight of her standing unaware.

"Vivian!"

She looked around and then saw him.

"Oh. It's you. What a surprise. What are you doing here?"

"I wanted to say good-bye," he said and added, "I brought you a book I thought you might like."

Vivian had had books as a child, she and her sister, children's books, they had even fought over them. She had read Nancy Drew and some others, but to be honest, she said, she didn't read that much. *Forever Amber*. Her skin was luminous.

"Well, thank you."

"It's one of ours," he said.

She read the title. It was very sweet of him. It was not something she would ever expect or that boys she knew would do or even grown-ups. She was twenty years old but not yet ready to think of herself as a woman, probably because she was still largely supported by her father and because of her devotion to him. She had gone to junior college and gotten a job. The women she knew were known for their style, their riding ability, and their husbands. Also their nerve. She had an aunt who had been robbed in her home at gunpoint by two black men and had said to them coolly, "We've been too good to you people."

The Virginia of Vivian Amussen was Anglo, privileged, and inbred. It was made up of rolling, wooded country, beautiful country, rich at heart, with low stone walls and narrow roads that had preserved it. The old houses were stone and often one room deep so the windows on both sides could be opened and allow a breeze to come through in the very hot summers. Originally the land had been given in royal grants, huge tracts, before the Revolution and put to farming, tobacco first and then dairy. In the 1920s or '30s, Paul Mellon, who liked to hunt, came and bought great amounts of land and friends joined him and bought places for themselves. It became a country for horses and hunts, the hounds baying in disorder as they ran, while after them, from around the trees, came the galloping horses and their riders jumping stone walls and ditches, uphill and down, slowing a little in places, galloping again.

It was a place of order and style, the Kingdom, from Middleburg to Upperville, a place and life apart, much of it intensely beautiful, the broad fields soft in the rain or gentle and bright in the sun. In the spring were the races, the Gold Cup in May, over the steeplechase hills, the crowd distractedly watching from the rows of parked cars with food and drink laid out. In the fall were the hunts that went on into the winter until February when the ground was hard and the streams frozen. Everyone had dogs. If you had named a hound, he or she was yours when no longer needed for the hunt, in fact the dog would be dumped at your door.

The fine houses belonged to the rich and to doctors, and the estates—farms, as they were called—retained their old names. People knew one another, those they did not know they regarded with suspicion. They were white, Protestant, with an unstated tolerance for a few Catholics. In the houses the furniture was English and often antique, passed down through the family. It was horses and golf: you made your best friends in sport.

By the straight, two-lane blacktop road it was less than an

hour's drive to Washington and the downtown section where Vivian worked. Her job was more or less a formality, she was a receptionist in a title office, and on weekends she went home, to the races or thoroughbred sales or hunts through the countryside. The hunts were like clubs, to belong to the best one, the one she and her father were members of, you had to own at least fifty acres. The master of that hunt was a judge, John Stump, a figure out of Dickens, stout and choleric, with an incurable fondness for women that had once led him to attempt suicide upon being rejected by a woman he loved. He threw himself from a window in passion but landed in some bushes. He had been married three times, each time, it was observed, to a woman with bigger breasts. The divorces were because of his drinking, which befitted his image as a squire, but as master of the hunt he was resolute and demanded perfect etiquette, one time halting the field when they'd done something wrong and giving them a ferocious dressing down until someone spoke out,

"Look, I didn't get up at six o'clock to listen to a lecture."

"Dismount!" Stump cried. "Dismount at once and return to the stables!"

Later he apologized.

Judge Stump was a friend of Vivian's father, George Amussen, who had manners and was always polite but also particular regarding those he might call a friend. The judge was his lawyer and Anna Wayne, the judge's first wife, who was narrow-chested but a very fine rider, had for a time before her marriage gone with Amussen, and it was generally believed that she accepted the judge when she was convinced that Amussen would not marry her.

Judge Stump pursued women, but George Amussen did not—they pursued him. He was elegant and reserved and also much admired for having done well buying and selling property in Washington and in the country. Even-tempered and patient, he had seen, earlier than others, how Washington was changing and over the years had bought, sometimes in partnerships, apartment buildings in the northwest part of the city and an office building on Wisconsin Avenue. He was discreet about what he owned and refrained from talking about it. He drove an ordinary car and dressed casually, without ostentation, usually in a sport jacket and well-made pants, and a suit when it was called for.

He had fair hair into which the gray blended and an easy walk that seemed to embody strength and even a kind of principle, to stand for things as they should be. A gentleman and a figure of country clubs, he knew all the black waiters by name and they knew him. At Christmas every year he gave them a double tip.

Washington was a southern city, lethargic and not really that big. It had atrocious weather, damp and cold in the winter and in the summers fiercely hot, the heat of the Delta. It had its institutions apart from the government, the old, favored hotels including the Wardman, familiarly called the riding academy because of the many mistresses who were kept there; the Riggs Bank, which was the bank of choice; the established downtown department stores. Howard Breen, who was the owner of the insurance agency where George Amussen in principle worked, one day would inherit the many properties his father had amassed, including the finest apartment building in town, where the old man, in a fedora and with a spittoon near his foot, often sat in the lobby watching things with lizard eyes. Only the right sort of people were allowed as tenants and even they were treated with indifference. If, as was not often the case, he nodded slightly to one of them as they came or went, that was considered cordial. The apartments, however, were large with handsome fireplaces and high ceilings, and the employees, taking their cue from the owner, were mute to the point of insolence.

The war changed it all. The hordes of military and naval personnel, government employees, young women who were drawn to the city by the demand for secretaries—in two or three years the sleepy, provincial town was gone. In some respects it clung to its ways, but the old days were vanishing. Vivian had come of age during that time. Though she appeared at the club in shorts that were in her father's opinion a little too brief and wore high heels too soon, her notions were really all from the world she had been a girl in.

Bowman wrote to her and almost to his disbelief she wrote back. Her letters were friendly and open. She came to New York several times that spring and early summer, staying with Louise and even sharing the bed with her, laughing, in pajamas. She had not yet told her father about her boyfriend. The ones she had in Washington worked at State or in the trust department at Riggs and were in many ways replicas of their parents. She did not think of herself as a replica. She was daring, in fact, taking the train up to see a man she had met in a bar, whose background she did not know but who seemed to have depth and originality. They went to Luchow's, where the waiter said *guten Abend* and Bowman talked to him for a moment in German.

"I didn't know you spoke German."

"Well, until recently it wasn't a great thing to do," Bowman said.

He had taken German at Harvard, he explained, because it was the language of science.

"At the time I thought I wanted to be a scientist. I went back and forth between a number of things. I thought for a while I might teach. I still have a certain yearning for teaching. Then I decided to be a journalist, but I wasn't able to get a job as one. I heard about a job as a reader then. It was pure luck or maybe destiny. What do you think of the idea of destiny?"

"Hadn't thought about it," she said casually.

He liked talking to her and the occasional smile that made her forehead shine. She was wearing a sleeveless dress and the roundness of her small shoulders gleamed. Her little finger was curled and held apart as she ate a bite of bread. Gestures, facial expressions, way of dressing—these were the revealing things. He was imagining places where they might go together, where no one knew them and he would have her to himself for days on end, though he was uncertain of how it might happen.

"New York's a wonderful place, isn't it?" he said.

"Yes. I like coming here."

"How do you know Louise?"

"We were in boarding school, in the same class. The first thing she ever said to me was a dirty joke, well, not exactly dirty but, you know."

He told her about the time that the letters *ES* on the big sign above the Essex House had gone out and there it was, forty stories up, shining in the night. He went no further. He didn't want to seem coarse.

At the end of the evening at the front door he was prepared to say good night but she acted as if he were not there, unlocking the door and saying nothing. Louise was gone for the weekend to visit her parents. Vivian was nervous though she did not want to show it. He went upstairs with her.

"Would you like a cup of coffee?" she asked.

"Yes, that would be . . . No," he said, "not really."

They sat for a few moments in silence and then she simply leaned forward and kissed him. The kiss was light but ardent.

"Do you want to?" she asked.

She did not take everything off—shoes, stockings, and skirt, that was all. She was not prepared for more. They kissed and whispered. As she slid from her white panties, a white that seemed sacred, he barely breathed. The fineness of her, the blondish fleece. He could not believe they were doing this.

"I don't . . . have anything," he whispered.

There was no answer.

He was inexperienced but it was natural and overwhelming. Also too quick, he couldn't help it. He felt embarrassed. Her face was close to his.

"I'm sorry," he said. "I couldn't stop it."

She said nothing, she had almost no way to judge it.

She went into the bathroom and Bowman lay back in awe at what had happened and feeling intoxicated by a world that had suddenly opened wide to the greatest pleasure, pleasure beyond knowing. He knew of the joy that might lie ahead.

Vivian was thinking along less heady lines. There was the chance of her becoming pg though she had, in truth, only an inexact idea of how likely that was. At school there had been a lot of talk, but it was only talk and vague. Still, there were stories of girls who got that way the first time. It would be just her luck, she thought. Of course, it hadn't been entirely the first time.

"You make me think of a pony," he said lovingly.

"A pony? Why?"

"You're just beautiful. And free."

"I don't see how that's like a pony," she said. "Besides, ponies bite. Mine did."

She nestled against him and he tried to think along her lines. Whatever might happen, they had done it. He felt only exaltation.

They spent the night together when he came to Washington that month and drove to the country the next day to have lunch with her father. He had a four-hundred-acre farm called Gallops, mostly given over to grazing. The main house was fieldstone and sat on top of a rise. Vivian showed him around, the grounds and first floor, as if introducing him to it and, in a way, to her. The house was lightly furnished in a manner that was indifferent to style. Behind a couch in the living room Bowman noticed, as in seventeenth-century palaces, were some dried dog turds.

Lunch was served by a black maid towards whom Amussen behaved with complete familiarity. Her name was Mattie and the main course came in on a silver tray.

"Vivian says you work in publishing," Amussen said.

"Yes, sir. I'm an editor."

"I see."

"It's a small house," Bowman went on, "but with quite a good literary reputation."

Amussen, picking at something near his incisor with his little finger, said,

"What do you mean by literary?"

"Well, books of quality, essentially. Books that might have a long life. Of course, that's the top end. We publish other books, to make money or try to."

"Can we have some coffee, Mattie?" Amussen said to the maid. "Would you like some coffee, Mr. Bowman?"

"Thank you."

"Viv, you?"

"Yes, Daddy."

The brief conversation about publishing had been without resonance. It was of no more interest than if they had been talking about the weather. Bowman had noticed only popular titles in the bookcase in the living room, Books of the Month with jackets that looked pristine. There were a few others, dark and leather-bound, the kind that are handed down though no one reads them, in a mahogany secretary, behind glass.

As they drank coffee, Bowman made a last attempt to cast himself favorably as an editor, but Amussen turned the subject to the navy, Bowman had been in the navy, was that right? There was a neighbor down the road, Royce Cromwell, who had gone to Annapolis and been in the same class as Charlie McVay, the captain of the *Indianapolis*. Bowman hadn't run into him in the navy, by any chance?

"No, I don't think so. I was only a junior officer. Was he in the Pacific?"

"I don't know."

"Well, there was a big Atlantic fleet, too, for the convoys, the invasion, and all that. Hundreds of ships."

"I wouldn't know. You'd have to ask him."

Almost without effort he had made Bowman feel as if he were prying. The lunch had been one of those meals when the sound of a knife or fork on a plate or a glass being set down only marks the silence.

Outside, as they walked to the car, Bowman saw something moving slowly with undulant curves into the ivy bed along the driveway.

"There's a snake, I think."

"Where?"

"There. Just going into the ivy."

"Damn it," Vivian said, "that's just where the dogs like to sleep. Was it big?"

It had not been a small snake, it was thick as a hose.

"Pretty good-sized," Bowman said.

Vivian, looking around, found a rake and began furiously running the handle of it back and forth through the ivy. The snake was gone, however.

"What was it? Was it a rattler?"

"I don't know. It was big. Do they have rattlesnakes around here?"

"They sure do."

"You'd better come out of there."

She was not afraid. She ran the handle through the dark, shiny leaves a final time.

"Damned thing," she said.

She went to tell her father. Bowman stood looking at the thick ivy, watching for any movement. She had stepped right into it.

Driving back that day, Bowman felt they were leaving a place where not even his language was understood. He was about to say it, but Vivian commented,

"Don't mind Daddy," she said. "He's like that sometimes. It wasn't you."

"I don't think I made a very good impression."

"Oh, you should see him with Bryan, my sister's husband. Daddy calls him Whyan, why in hell did she pick him? Can't even ride, he says."

"You aren't making me feel much better. I can sail," he added. "Can your father sail?"

"He's sailed to the Bahamas."

She seemed ready to defend him, and Bowman felt he should not go further. She sat looking out of the window on her side, somewhat removed, but in her leather skirt, hair pulled back, face wide, with a thin gold chain looped around her neck, she was the image of desirability. She turned back towards him.

"It's like that," she commented. "You sort of have to go through the mud room first."

"Is your mother anything like that?"

"My mother? No."

"What's she like?"

"She's a drunk," Vivian said. "That's the reason they got divorced."

"Where does she live? In Middleburg?"

"No, she has an apartment in Washington near Dupont Circle. You'll meet her."

Her mother had been beautiful but you couldn't tell it now, Vivian added. She started in the morning with vodka and rarely got dressed until afternoon.

"Daddy really raised us. We're his two girls. He had to protect us."

They drove for a while in silence and near Centerville somewhere he glanced over and saw that she was asleep. Her head had fallen softly to the side and her lips were slightly parted. Sensual thoughts came to him. Her smooth-stockinged legs, for some reason he thought of them separately—their length and shape. He realized how deeply in love he was. She had it in her power to bestow immense happiness.

When they said good-bye at the station he felt that something definitive had passed between them. He possessed, despite the uncertainty, assurance, an assurance that would never fall away.

4. AS ONE

Freely, as they sat or ate or walked he shared with her his thoughts and ideas about life, history, and art. He told her everything. He knew she didn't think about these things, but she understood and could learn. He loved her for not only what she was but what she might be, the idea that she might be otherwise did not occur to him or did not matter. Why would it occur? When you love you see a future according to your dreams.

In Summit, where he wanted his mother to meet Vivian, to see and approve of her, he took her first to a diner across from City Hall that had been there for years. It had actually been a railroad car with windows all along the side facing the avenue. Inside, the floor was tile and the ceiling pale wood that curved down into the wall. A counter where customers sat—there were always one or two—ran the length of the place. It was more crowded in the morning; the railroad station, the Morris and Essex line that went to the city, was just down the street. The tracks were low and out of sight. At night the lights of the diner were the only lights along the street. You entered by a door opposite the counter and there was another door at one end.

It was here that Hemingway placed his story "The Killers," Bowman said.

"Right here, in this diner. The counter, everything. Do you know the story? It's marvelous. Fabulously written. If you never read another word of his, you'd know right away what a great writer he is. It's in the evening. Nobody's in the place, there are no customers, it's empty, and two men in tight black overcoats come in and sit down at the counter. They look at the menu and order, and one of them says to the counterman, This is some town, what's the name of this place? And the counterman, who's frightened of course, says, Summit. It's right there in the story, Summit, and when the food comes they eat with their gloves on. They're there to kill a Swede, they tell the counterman. They know the Swede always comes there. He's an ex-fighter named Ole Andreson who double-crossed the mob somehow. One of them takes a sawed-off shotgun from beneath his coat and goes into the kitchen to hide and wait."

"Did this actually happen?"

"No, no. He wrote it in Spain."

"It's just made up."

"You don't believe it's made up, reading it. That's what's so incredible, you absolutely believe it."

"And they kill him?"

"It's better than that. They don't kill him because he doesn't show up, but he knows they're after him, they'll come again. He's big, he was a boxer, but whatever he did, they're going to kill him. He just lies in bed in the rooming house, looking at the wall."

They began to read the menu.

"What are you going to have?" Vivian asked.

"I think I'll have eggs with Taylor ham."

"What's Taylor ham?" she said.

"It's a kind of ham they have around here. I've never really asked."

"All right, I'll have it, too."

He liked being with her. He liked having her with him. There were only a few other people in the diner, but how colorless they seemed compared to her. They were all aware of her presence. It was impossible not to be.

"I'd like to meet Hemingway," he said. "Go down to Cuba and meet him. Maybe we could go together."

"Well, I don't know," she said. "Maybe."

"You have to read him," he said.

Beatrice had been eager to meet her and was also struck by her looks, though in a different way, the freshness and naked, animal statement. How much one knows from the first! She had bought flowers and set the table in the dining room where they seldom ate, usually using a table in the kitchen, one end of which was against the wall. The kitchen with shelves but no cabinets was the real heart of the house together with a sitting room where they often sat in front of the fireplace talking and having a drink. Now there was this girl with somewhat stiff manners. She was from Virginia, and Beatrice asked what part, Middleburg?

"We really live nearer to Upperville," Vivian replied.

Upperville. It sounded rural and small. It *was*, in fact, small, there was one place to eat but no town water or sewage. Nothing had changed there for a hundred years and people there liked it that way whether they lived in an old house without heat or on a thousand acres. Upperville, in the county and beyond, was an exalted name, the emblem of a proud, parochial class of which Vivian was a member. There was no place to stay, you had to live there.

"It's beautiful country," Bowman said.

Beatrice said, "I'd love to see it. What does your family do there?"

"Farm," Vivian said. "Well, my father farms some but also he puts his fields up for grazing."

"It must be big."

"It's not terribly big, it's about four hundred acres."

"That's so interesting. Apart from farming, what is there to do?"

"Daddy always says there's lots to do. He means looking after the horses."

"Horses."

"Yes."

It was not that she was difficult to talk to, but you immediately felt the limits. Vivian had gone to junior college, probably at the suggestion of her father to keep her out of mischief. She had a certain confidence, based on the things she absolutely knew and which had proved to be enough. Like all mothers though, Beatrice hoped for a girl like herself, with whom she could speak easily and whose view of life could almost perfectly be combined with her own. Among her pupils, over the years, she could think of girls who were like that, good students with natural charm that you admired and were drawn to, but there were also others not so easily understood and whose fate you were not meant to know.

"Didn't Liz Bohannon come from Middleburg?" Beatrice

asked, bringing up a name, a horse and society figure of the '30s, always photographed with her husband aboard some ship sailing to Europe or in their box at Saratoga.

"Yes, she has a big place. She's a friend of my father's."

"She's still around?"

"Oh, very much around."

There were a lot of stories about her, Vivian said. When they first bought their place, Longtree, that was the name then, she used to ride in from the hunt and let the dogs come right into the house. They'd jump up on the table and eat everything. After she got divorced, she calmed down a bit.

"Oh, you must know her, then?"

"Oh, yes."

Vivian was eating somewhat carefully, not like a girl with a genuine appetite. The flowers, which Beatrice had moved to the side, were a lush backdrop for her, some young pagan goddess who had cast a spell over her son. Though it wasn't entirely a spell, Beatrice had no way to measure how much in need of love he was and what forms that took—meanwhile he was absolutely certain of one thing, that he would never meet someone like Vivian again. He saw himself tumbled with her among the bedclothes and fragrance of married life, the meals and holidays of it, the shared rooms, the glimpses of her half-dressed, her blondness, the pale hair where her legs met, the sexual riches that would be there forever.

When he told his mother he hoped to marry her, Beatrice, though afraid it would prove nothing, protested how unalike the two of them were, how little they had in common. They had a great deal in common, Bowman a little defiantly said. What they had in common was more vital than similar interests—it was wordless understanding and accord.

What Beatrice did not say, but what she deeply felt was that Vivian had no soul, but to say it would be unforgivable. She merely sat silent. After a moment, she said,

"I hope you won't rush into anything."

In her heart she feared, she knew the things you cannot see when you are too young. She hoped that with a little time the infatuation would pass. She could only press his head against her in love and understanding.

"I only want you to be happy, truly happy."

"I would be truly happy."

"I mean in your deepest heart."

"Yes, in my deepest."

It was love, the furnace into which everything is dropped.

In New York at a restaurant called El Faro where the prices were low, in back, beneath the darkened walls, Vivian said, "Louise would love this. She's mad about Spain."

"Has she been there?"

"No. She's never even been to Mexico. She was in Boston last weekend with her boyfriend."

"Who's that?"

"His name's Fred. They went to some hotel and never got out of bed the whole time."

"I didn't know she was like that."

"She was so sore she could hardly walk."

The place was full, there was a crowd at the bar. Beyond the single window, across the street were second and third floors with large, lighted rooms where a couple might live. Vivian was drinking a second glass of wine. The waiter was squeezing past tables with their order on a tray.

"What is this? Is this the paella?" she asked.

"Yes."

"What's in it?" she said.

"Sausage, rice, clams, everything."

She began to eat.

"It's good," she said.

The crowded tables and talk around them gave it an intimacy. He knew it was the time, he must say it somehow.

"I love it when you come up here."

"Me, too," she said automatically.

"Really?"

"Yes," she said and his heart began wildly.

"What would you think," he said, "about living here? I mean, we'd be married, of course."

She paused in her eating. He couldn't tell what her reaction was. Had he misstated something?

"There's so much noise in here," she said.

"Yes, it's noisy."

"Was that a proposal?"

"It was pitiful, wasn't it? Yes, it's a proposal. I love you," he said. "I need you. I'd do anything for you."

He'd said it, just as he meant to.

"Will you marry me?" he said.

"We'll have to get Daddy's permission," she said.

An immense happiness filled him.

"Of course. Is that really necessary?"

"Yes," she said.

She insisted that he ask her father for her hand although, as she said, he had already had considerably more.

*

The lunch was at George Amussen's club in Washington. Bowman had prepared himself carefully for it. He had gotten a haircut and wore a suit and shined shoes. Amussen was already seated when the steward showed Bowman in. Across a number of tables he could see his prospective father-in-law reading something, and he suddenly recalled the morning when he had gone to see Mr. Kindrigen, though that was long behind him. He was twenty-six now, more or less established, and ready to make the right impression on Vivian's impenetrable father, who, sitting alone, hair combed straight back, at his ease, looked at that moment like a figure from the war, even someone who had been on the other side, some commander or Luftwaffe pilot. It was noon and the tables were just filling up.

"Good morning," Bowman said as a greeting.

"Good morning. Nice to see you," Amussen replied. "I'm just looking at the menu here. Sit down. I see they have shad roe."

Bowman picked up the menu himself, and they each ordered a drink.

Amussen knew what the young man was there for, and in his mind he had laid out the salient points of his response. He was a methodical man of certain beliefs. One of the chief and unaddressed dangers society faced, he believed, was mongrelization, free interbreeding that could in the end have only dire results. He was a southerner, not from the Deep South but still from what might have been called Dixie, where the essential question was always, what is your background? His own was quite good. He had his great-grandmother's silver and some pieces of her furniture, cherrywood and walnut, and he had raised his two daughters with as much attention to their ability to ride and present themselves in company as anything else. He had gone to college, to the University of Virginia, but had dropped out for financial reasons in his junior year, something he never particularly regretted. He'd gone to the University of Virginia, he would say if asked. His father had managed warehouses and been well regarded, and Amussen was a respected name, perhaps with the exception of a cousin near Roanoke, Edwin Amussen, who owned a tobacco farm and had never married. His real wife was a colored girl, they said, and it was true that he had a girl, Anna, who'd been seventeen when she first came to the house to cook. She was dark-skinned, deep in color, plum-colored, he said, but fragrant with full, knowing lips. Two or three mornings a week she would come up the back stairs to the second-floor bedroom, a large room with a shaded porch, where he had gotten up earlier to wash and then lain in bed for half an hour in the coolness hearing her at work in the kitchen below. The curtains were drawn and it was only partly light. After entering the room she would slip off her cotton T-shirt and lie, as if to rest her upper body, on the bed, forearms folded beneath her head. On her naked back with its two strong halves he would then place five silver dollars in a familiar pattern, one at the nape of her neck, one a little way below that, and a third further down, past the small of her back. The last two were by her shoulders like the arms of a cross. Without haste he would raise her skirt, carefully, as if preparing to examine it, and on these mornings she had nothing on beneath. She had made herself ready, sometimes with a little shortening, and let him slowly, at the pace of a summer evening or long afternoon, begin, often hearing him discuss food, what he would like for dinner the next few days.

This went on for five years, until she was twenty-two and told him one morning, afterwards, that she was getting married. No need to change things on that account, he said blandly, but she said no. Once in a while, however, since she still possessed freedom of the house, she would appear in the morning unbidden.

"Trouble at home?" he asked.

"No. Jus' habit," she said, laying her upper body on the bed.

"You get six," he offered.

"No room for that extra."

"Here."

He put it in her hand, into her palm, which he loved.

No one knew of this, it existed by itself, like certain feverish visions of saints.

In 1928, at a dinner party in Washington, George Amussen had met Caroline Wain who was twenty with a slow manner of talking and a provocative smile. She had grown up in Detroit, her father was an architect. Four months after Amussen met her, they were married, and some six months after that, their first child, Beverly, was born. Vivian came a year and a half later.

Life in the country was pleasant for Caroline. She smoked and drank. Her laugh became hoarse and a small seductive roll of flesh slowly appeared above her girdle. She lay in bed with her daughters and sometimes read to them on rainy days. Amussen drove into Washington to work, occasionally coming back late or even spending the night, and his attention to Caroline, in a way that was important to her, dwindled. She brooded on this.

"George," she said one evening over a drink, "are you happy with me?"

She was not yet thirty but her face was a bit puffy beneath the eyes.

"What do you mean, darling?"

"Are you happy?"

"I'm happy enough."

"Do you still love me?" she persisted.

"Why are you asking that?"

"I just want to know."

"Yes," he said.

"Yes, you love me? Is that what you mean?"

"If you keep asking it, I don't know what I'll say."

"That means you don't."

"Is that what it means?"

There was a silence.

"Is it that there's someone else?" she finally said.

"If there was, it wouldn't amount to anything," he said.

"So, there is."

"I said, if there was. There isn't."

"You're sure of that? No, you're not, are you?"

"Why don't you listen to what I say?"

With that, she suddenly threw her drink in his face. He stood and brushed himself off, taking out a handkerchief to do it.

She threw a drink in his face at a party in Middleburg that fall and wept in the car on the way home from several others. She became known as a drinker, that was not so bad—drinking, even too much, was an aspect of character, like courage, in their society—but Amussen became tired of it and of her. Her angry moods were like a disease that couldn't be treated, much less cured. She had taken her pillow and was sleeping in the guest room. By the tenth year of their marriage they had separated and soon after, divorced. Caroline went to Reno for the divorce and left her two daughters, eight and ten years old, with her husband so as not to disrupt their schooling and routine. Although she retained custody of them, she did not exercise it strictly, and Amussen was content to let things continue this way, as they were.

Bowman met Caroline Amussen—she kept the name, which was worth something—in her apartment in Washington. She was wearing bedroom slippers but she had a somehow gallant air and was warm towards him. She liked him, she said, and later said it privately to her daughter. Bowman forgot the fact that girls, in time, became like their mothers. He felt that Vivian took after her father and would become her own woman.

The waiter came to take their order.

"How is the shad roe, Edward?" Amussen asked.

"Jus' fine, Mistuh Amussen."

"Do you have two orders of it?" he asked. "If you'd like to have it," he said to his guest.

Bowman assumed it was a southern dish.

"Do you do any fishing?" Amussen said. "Shad is bony, generally too bony to bother with. The roe is the best part."

"Yes, I'll have it. How do they make it?"

"In a pan with some bacon. They brown it. That's right, isn't it, Edward?"

It was at the end of lunch, when they were being served coffee, that Bowman said,

"You know, I'm in love with Vivian."

Amussen continued stirring his coffee as if he had not heard.

"And I think she's in love with me," Bowman went on. "We would like to get married."

Still Amussen showed no emotion. He was as calm as if he were alone.

"I've come to ask for your permission, sir," Bowman said.

The "sir" seemed a little courtly but he felt it was appropriate. Amussen was still occupied with stirring.

"Vivian's a nice girl," Amussen finally said. "She was raised in the country. I don't know how she'd take to city life. She's not one of those people."

He then looked up.

"How do you plan on providing for her?" he said.

"Well, as you know, I have a good job. I like my work, I have a career. I earn enough to support us at this point, and whatever I have is hers. I'll make sure she's comfortable."

"She's not a city girl," Amussen said again. "You know, from the time she was just a little thing, she's had her own horse."

"We haven't talked about that. I suppose we could always make room for a horse," Bowman said lightly.

Amussen seemed not to hear him.

"We love one another," Bowman said. "I'll do everything in my power to make her happy."

Amussen nodded slightly.

"I promise you that. We're hoping for your permission, then. Your blessing, sir."

There was a pause.

"I don't think I can give you that," Amussen said. "Not and be honest with you."

"I see."

"I don't think it would work. I think it would be a mistake."

"I see."

"But I won't stand in Vivian's way," her father said.

Bowman left feeling disappointed but defiant. It would be a kind of morganatic marriage then, politely tolerated. He was not sure what attitude to take about it, but when he told Vivian what her father had said, she was not disturbed.

"That's just Daddy," she said.

The minister was a tall man in his seventies with silvery hair who couldn't hear very well, having fallen from a horse. Age had taken the edge from his voice, which was silken but thin. At the prenuptial meeting he said he would ask them three questions, the ones he always asked couples. He wanted to know if they were in love. Next, did they want to be married in the church? And lastly, would the marriage last?

"We can definitely answer yes to the first two," Bowman replied.

"Ah," the minister said, "yes." He was absentminded and had forgotten the order of the questions. "I don't suppose it's so important to be in love," he admitted.

He hadn't shaved, Bowman noticed, there was a white stubble on his face, but he was more presentable at the wedding. Vivian's family was there, her mother, sister, brother-in-law, and some others Bowman had never met and also friends. There were fewer on the groom's side, but his Harvard roommate, Malcolm, and his wife, Anthea, were there, and Eddins with a white carnation in his buttonhole. It was a bright, cool morning, then afternoon, passing in an excitement that made it hard to remember. He was with his mother beforehand and could see her during the ceremony. He watched with a sense of victory as Amussen brought Vivian down the aisle. He put any misgivings aside, it was like a scene from a play. During the vows he saw only his bride, her face clear and shining, and in back of her Louise smiling, too, as he heard himself say, With this ring, I thee wed. I thee wed.

Eddins proved to be very popular or anyhow well-remembered at the reception, which was held at Vivian's house—her father had wanted it to be at the Red Fox, the old inn in Middleburg, but had been persuaded otherwise.

The bar was on a table covered with a white tablecloth and tended by two bartenders, reserved but polite, burnished somehow by inequality. In a bow tie and with the round face of good fellowship, Bowman's new brother-in-law, Bryan, came up to him.

"Welcome to the family," he said.

He had small, even teeth that made him seem friendly and worked in the government.

"Very nice wedding," he said. "We didn't have one. The pater offered us three thousand dollars—actually he offered it to Beverly—if we'd just go off and get married. He was probably hoping I'd run away with the money. He as much as told me so. Anyway, we eloped. Where are you from?"

"New Jersey," Bowman said. "Summit."

He was from the east, too, Bryan said.

"We lived in Mount Kisco. Guard Hill Road—they used to call it Banker's Row, every house belonged to a Morgan partner."

They had a four-car garage. Actually there were three cars and a chauffeur.

"Redell was his name. He was also the cook, very spooky kind of guy," Bryan said amiably. "He used to drive us to school. We had a Buick and a Hispano-Suiza, huge monster with a separate chauffeur's section and a speaking tube. Every day at breakfast, Redell would ask which car we wanted to take, the Buick or . . . The Hissy, the Hissy! we'd say. And then when we got away from the house, we would drive."

"You would drive?"

"My brother and I."

"How old were you?"

"I was twelve and Roddy was ten. We took turns. We made Redell do it. We threatened him. We said we'd claim he tried to molest us. Death rides, we called them."

"Where's Roddy now?"

"He's not here. He's out west. He works in construction in the West. He just likes it, the life."

Beverly joined them.

"We were talking about Roddy," Bryan explained.

"Poor Roddy. Bryan loves Roddy. Do you have brothers or sisters?" she asked Bowman.

"No, I'm the only one."

"Lucky you," she said.

She did not resemble Vivian. She was bigger and some- what ungainly with a receding chin and a reputation for being outspoken.

"So, what do we make of Mr. Bowman?" she asked her husband afterwards. She was eating some of the wedding cake with her hand cupped beneath to catch any pieces.

"He seems like a nice-enough guy."

"He's from Hah-vud."

"So?"

"I think Vivian made a mistake."

"What have you got against him?"

"I don't know. It's my intuition. I like his friend, though."

"Which one?"

"The one with the flower. He's nervous, look at him."

"What's he nervous about?"

"Us, probably."

Eddins was on his second drink but in Virginia he felt more or less at home. He had talked to an ex-colonel and to a not unattractive woman who had come with a judge. Also to Bryan, who mentioned the cars they used to have before the family lost their money and had to move to Bronxville, which was a real shame. Eddins had been watching a good-looking girl who was standing behind the judge and he finally walked her way.

"Do you come here often?" he asked as a try at wit.

"I'm sorry?"

Her name was Darrin, she was the daughter of a doctor. It turned out that she exercised horses.

"Horses need exercise? Don't they do that themselves?"

She regarded him somewhat scornfully.

Eddins tried to cover it up by talking.

"They said there might be thunderstorms today, but it looks like they're wrong. I like thunderstorms. There's a wonderful one in Thomas Hardy. Do you know Thomas Hardy?"

"No," she said briefly.

"He's English. An English writer. You can't top the English. Lord Byron, the poet. Incredible. The most famous man in Europe when he was still in his twenties. Mad, bad, and dangerous to know, I'm trying to model myself after him."

She failed to smile.

"Died of a fever at Missolonghi. They put his heart in an urn and his lungs in something else, I forget . . . supposed to end up in a church but they got lost. His body was sent back to England in a coffin filled with rum. Women came to the funeral, former mistresses . . ."

She was listening without expression.

"I have some English blood," he confessed, "but mostly Scottish."

"Is that right?"

"Wild, unbridled people. Wash their clothes in urine," he said.

"They what?"

"Anyway it smells that way."

He was making it up, he did that when he drank and to protect himself. She was so plainly not interested in what he was saying, too young to know what anything was about. He had imagined some kind of sophisticated, dissolute wedding, with a bridesmaid drunkenly going off with him, but there were no bridesmaids, there was only the maid of honor to whom he was not attracted. He wandered over to the groom.

"So, this will be your country estate, I take it."

"I don't think so," Bowman said.

"I met your father-in-law. Big landowner. Rich as a goat. Anyway you're a lucky man. Very lucky," he said, his eye on Vivian. "Still, I have this flower . . ." He took hold of his lapel. "I'm going to keep it in remembrance, press it in a book," he said looking down at it. "Would have to be a big book. I talked to your mother-in-law. Well turned out."

Caroline had been moving among the guests, a little heavier than she had been when last seen and her cheeks a little rounder. She was in an expensive black dress and managing to avoid being near her former husband.

Beatrice had said little. She had wept at the church. She had embraced Vivian and in return felt a dutiful response. It had all been like that, dutiful, restrained, with only smiles and polite talk.

She was bidding good-bye to her son. She had a chance to embrace him and to say with all her heart,

"Be good to one another. Love one another," she said.

Though she felt it was love cast into darkness. She had doubts that she would ever know her daughter-in-law. It seemed, on this bright day, that the greatest misfortune had come to pass. She had lost her son, not completely, but part of him was beyond her power to reclaim and now belonged to another, someone who hardly knew him. She thought of all that had gone before, the hopes and ambition, the years that had been filled, not just in retrospect, with such joy. She tried to be pleasant, to have them all like her and favor her son.

George Amussen she felt she knew, the self-possession and manners, the life that the house seemed to represent. He reminded her of her husband, whom she had long tried to banish from her thoughts but who remained in her life, distant and unassailable.

Vivian was happy. She was wearing a white wedding gown, she had yet to change, and though she was not yet used to the idea, she was a married woman. She'd married at home, with her father's blessing, more or less. It had happened, she had done it. Like Beverly she was married.

Bowman was happy or felt he was, she was his, a beautiful woman or girl. He saw life ahead in regular terms, with someone who would be beside him. In the presence of her family and friends he realized that he knew only one side of her, a side that attracted him but that was not her entire or essential self. Behind her as he looked was her unyielding father and not far away from him her sister and brother-in-law. They were all complete strangers. Across the room, smiling and alcoholic, was her mother, Caroline. Vivian caught his eye and perhaps his thoughts and smiled at him, it seemed understandingly. The unsettled feeling disappeared. Her smile was loving, sincere. We'll leave soon, it said. That night though, having driven to the Hay-Adams Hotel in Washington, wearied by the events of the day and unaccustomed to being a wedded couple, they simply went to sleep.

5. ON TENTH

There was a front room and glass doors to a bedroom with a bed by the window. The kitchen was narrow but long and the dishes often unwashed; Vivian was indifferent to housekeeping and her clothes and cosmetics could be found all over. Still, a glorious being emerged from her preparations, even when abbreviated. She had the gift of allure, even when her lips were bare and her hair uncombed, sometimes especially then.

The apartment was on Tenth Street, where old New York families had long lived and which was still quiet but close to everything, together with the neighboring streets a kind of residential island, ordinary and discreet. There were the photographs Vivian had brought, framed and two of them on the dresser, photographs of her jumping, leaning forward close to the horse's neck as they cleared, in a black rider's helmet, her face pure and fearless. She knew how to ride, that was in her face, to have the great beast moving easily beneath her, ears pricked back to hear and obey, the leather giving and cracking, the mastery of it. She and Beverly and Chrissy Wendt, the three of them coming from the horse show, getting out of the truck, a little dusty, in their riding pants, Vivian with her striking face, blond and yawning grandly as if she were alone and getting out of bed. Twelve and carelessly natural, mischievous even.

At the age of eight, her small feet wobbling in her mother's high heels and an imaginary cigarette in one hand, she appeared in the bedroom doorway. Her mother was at the dressing table and saw her in the mirror.

"Oh, darling," Caroline said noticing also the pearls, "you look beautiful. Come and give me a puff."

The joy of it. Vivian clattering in and holding her hand out near her mother's mouth. Caroline took a drag and exhaled an invisible plume.

"You're all dressed up. Are you getting ready to go to a party somewhere?"

"No," she said.

"You're not going out?"

"No, I think I'll just invite some boys over," Vivian said knowingly.

"Some boys? How many?"

"Oh, three or four."

"You're not going to favor just one?" Caroline said.

"Older boys. It depends."

The age of imitation when there are no dangers although it depended. In the past, girls might be married at twelve, queens-to-be knelt to be wed even younger, Poe's wife was a child of thirteen, Samuel Pepys' only fifteen, Machado the great poet of Spain fell madly in love with Leonor Izquierdo when she was thirteen, Lolita was twelve, and Dante's goddess Beatrice even younger. Vivian knew as little as any of them, she was a tomboy until she was almost fourteen. She loved make-believe with her mother. She loved and feared her father and with her sister quarreled constantly from the time they both could talk, so much so that Amussen had many times asked his wife to do something about it.

"Mommy!" Beverly cried out. "Do you know what she just called me?"

"What did she call you?"

Vivian was lingering and listening partway down the hall.

"She called me a horse's ass."

"Vivian, did you say that?" Caroline called to her. "Come here, did you say that?"

Vivian was resolute.

"No," she said.

"Liar!" Beverly cried.

"Did you or didn't you, Vivian?"

"I never said horse's."

It was not always fighting, but it might always come to that. When in time it became apparent that Vivian would be the one who was beautiful, their positions hardened and Beverly adopted her own raw-boned, caustic style. Vivian, in turn, became noticeably more feminine. Nevertheless they grew up doing everything together. They had ridden in the hunt from the time they were seven or eight. Vivian, though, was the favorite of the field master. Judge Stump, well-versed in such things, admired her form. In her well-fitted riding clothes he imagined her as a few years older with certain unfatherly thoughts though he was not her father, only a good friend. That might properly exclude one thing but not another. To George Amussen, the judge habitually and easily said "your beautiful daughter" in a way, he felt, that was fond and respectful, that could almost be a title. His fantasy of himself and Vivian, well, then, was not entirely far-fetched, his experience and her freshness unexpectedly but appropriately combined. This idea—it would be wrong to call it a plan—made him behave somewhat more stiffly towards her than he might have and seem even older and more inflexible than he was. He could feel it, but the more he tried the less he was able to do about it.

In Virginia that first fall, the weather for the races was rainy and cold. There was mud underfoot in the fields and the grass was matted flat where people had driven and walked. Spectators in bulky clothes lined the fences with children running about and dogs. Along the row of cars where people stood drinking in small groups came a stocky figure in an Australian army hat with one side pinned up, the brim dotted with water and a braided cord beneath his chin. It was the judge, who shook hands with Amussen, greeted Vivian courteously, and nodded and muttered something to Bowman. They stood in the rain talking, the judge talking only to Amussen while horses and riders, very small in the distance, galloped steadily across vast green slopes. The judge had not come to terms with Vivian's marriage. When lovely woman stoops to folly, he thought, but he stood where he could see her in the normal course of things and at one point caught her eye with what he felt was a fond look, water dripping from his brown hat.

By the time they got back to New York, Vivian had a fever and ached in every limb. It was the flu. Bowman filled a hot tub for her and carried her in a white robe to bed afterwards, watching her as she lay asleep with a damp, untroubled face. He slept on the couch that night so as not to disturb her and went to work but came home two or three times during the day to look after her. Her illness seemed to draw them closer, strangely affectionate hours as she lay, too weak to do anything, and he read to her and brought her tea. The two middle-aged men, neighbors, who lived together on the floor below stopped him on the stairs to ask about her. That night they brought her some soup, minestrone, they had made.

"How is she doing?" they asked solicitously at the door.

They could hear her coughing in the bedroom, Larry and Arthur, they were veterans of the musical theater, alcoholic and living under rent control. Vivian liked them, Noël and Cole, she called them, they had met in the chorus. The walls of their apartment were covered with framed theater programs and signed photographs of old performers. One of them was Gertrude Neisen. Gertrude, she was so fabulous! they cried. They had a piano they sometimes played and occasionally they could be heard singing. When Vivian began to recover they brought her a fluted glass vase with an arrangement of lilies and yellow roses from the flower shop on Eighteenth Street owned by an elegant man Arthur had once been involved with, Christos, who was friends with both of them. He, too, loved the theater and everything about it. Later he opened a restaurant.

The flowers lasted for almost two weeks. They were still there the evening of dinner at the Baums'. Bowman had never been to their house and Vivian hadn't met them. She was preparing for it, fastening her earrings with her face reflected in the hall mirror above the glamour of the flowers.

Baum's private life Bowman knew only by conjecture, it was European, he guessed, and secure. A doorman had been instructed to send them right up and as they walked down the short hallway a dog behind someone's door began barking. Baum himself showed them in. The first impression was of density. There was comfortable furniture and layered oriental rugs with books and pictures everywhere. It did not seem the house of a couple with a child but rather of people who had ample time for things. Diana rose from the couch where she had been sitting with another guest. She greeted Vivian first. She had very much wanted to meet her, she said. Baum made drinks from a tray filled with bottles on top of a low secretary. The other guest seemed very at home. Bowman at first took him to be a relative, but it turned out that he taught philosophy and was a friend of Diana's.

At dinner they talked about books and a manuscript by a Polish refugee named Aronsky who had somehow managed to survive the annihilation of the Warsaw ghetto and then of the city itself. In New York he had found his way into literary circles. He was said to be charming though unpredictable. How, the question was, had he gotten through? To this he answered he didn't know, it was luck. Nothing could be predicted, a thing as small as a fly could kill a mother of four. How was that? If she moved to brush it away, he said.

They'd been joined by another couple, a wine writer and his girlfriend, who was small with long fingers and hair that was thick and absolutely black. She was lively and wanted to talk, like a wind-up doll, a little doll that also did sex. Kitty was her name. But they were talking about Aronsky. His book, as yet unpublished, was called *The Savior*.

"I found it very disturbing," Diana said.

"There's something wrong with it," Baum agreed. "Most

novels, even the great ones, don't pretend to be true. You believe them, they even become part of your life, but not as literal truth. This book seems to violate that."

It was an account, almost official in its tone and lack of metaphor, of the life of Reinhard Heydrich, the long-headed, bony-nosed SS commander who had been second only to Himmler and one of the black-uniformed planners of the so-called Final Solution. As head of the police he was as powerful and feared as any man in the Third Reich. He was tall and blond with a violent temper and an inhuman capacity for work. His icy but handsome appearance was well-known, along with his sensual tastes. There was an episode when, coming home late at night after drinking, he had suddenly seen someone in wait in the darkened apartment, pulled his pistol and fired four shots that shattered the hall mirror in which it was he who had been reflected.

The truth of his past had been carefully hidden. In the town where he was born, the gravestones of his parents had mysteriously disappeared. His schoolmates were afraid to remember him, and his early records as a naval cadet had vanished, there was only the story that he'd been dismissed over trouble with a young girl. What was concealed, incredibly, was that Heydrich was a Jew, his identity known only to a small circle of influential Jews who relied upon him to both inform and protect them.

In the end, he betrays them. He betrays them both because he is perhaps not Jewish and because he ends up as they do, in death, all engulfing. He has been made governor of occupied Czechoslovakia and is ambushed in his touring car near Prague, an act ironically encouraged by unknowing

Jews in England, where the assassination was planned and organized.

The book was compelling in its authority and in details that were hard to believe had been invented. The floor of the hospital he had been taken to and the naked torso of Heydrich on the operating table as they tried to save him. Hitler had sent his own doctor. There was chilling authenticity. The Czech assassins who had been parachuted in escape but do not survive. They are trapped in the basement of a church and, surrounded by overwhelming German forces, take their own lives. The village of Lidice is selected for reprisal and all of its inhabitants, who had nothing to do with it, men, women, and children, are executed. There was no sound on earth, wrote Aronsky, like a German pistol being cocked.

Baum did not believe it, or if he did it was with reluctance. It was not that he had heard guns being cocked himself, which he had, but that he suspected the motive. He hadn't met Aronsky, but he was troubled in a deep way by the book.

"Its neatness," was all he managed to come up with.

"Heydrich *was* assassinated."

"I simply don't believe that he was Jewish. The book never makes it clear."

"One of Hitler's field marshals was partly Jewish."

"Which one?" Baum said.

"Von Manstein."

"Is that really a fact?"

"So it's been said. He's supposed to have admitted it in private."

"Perhaps. The thing is, I believe the book can confuse a lot of readers. And to what end? It can have a long existence even if it's eventually exposed as fiction. My feeling is that, especially on this subject, you have to respect the truth. Someone is doubtlessly going to publish it, but we're not going to," Baum said.

They went home in a taxi. Bowman was exhilarated.

"Did you like Diana?" he asked.

"She was nice."

"I thought very nice."

"Yes," Vivian said. "But the wine guy . . ."

"What about him?"

"I don't know if he understood we were married. He was making a pass at me."

"Are you sure?" Bowman said.

He had a feeling of satisfaction. His wife had been desired.

"He thought I had fabulous cheekbones. I looked like a Smith girl," she said.

"What did you say?"

"Bryn *Mawr*, I told him."

Bowman laughed.

"Why'd you say that?"

"It sounded better."

Dinner at the Baums'. It was admittance into their life, to some degree, into a world he admired.

He was thinking of many things but not really. He was listening to the small sounds in the bathroom and waiting. Finally, in familiar fashion, his wife came out, switching off the light as she did. She was in her nightgown, the one he liked with crossed straps in back. Almost as if unaware of him, she got into bed. He was filled with desire, as if they had met at a dance. He lay still for a moment in anticipation and then whispered to her. He put his hand on the swell of her hip. She was silent. He moved her nightgown up a little.

"Don't," she said.

"What is it? What's wrong?" he whispered.

It was impossible that she did not feel as he did. The warmth, the satisfaction, and now to complete it.

"What's wrong?" he said again.

"Nothing."

"Do you feel sick?"

She didn't reply. He waited, for too long it seemed, his blood trembling, everything going bitter. She turned and kissed him briefly, as if dismissing him. She was suddenly like a stranger. He knew he should try to understand it but felt only anger. It was unloving of him, but he could not help it. He lay there unwillingly and sleepless, the city itself, dark and glittering, seemed empty. The same couple, the same bed, yet now not the same.

It had snowed before Christmas but then turned cold. The sky was pale. The country lay silent, the fields dusted white with the hard furrows showing where they had been plowed. All was still. The foxes were in their dens, the deer bedded down. Route 50 from Washington, the road that had been originally laid out in almost a straight line by George Washington when he was a surveyor, was empty of traffic. On the back roads an early car with its headlights came along. First the trees, half-frosted, were lit, then the road itself, and finally the soft sound as the car passed.

They had Christmas at George Amussen's—Beverly and Bryan were not there, having gone to visit his parents—and the next day was to be dinner at Longtree, Longtree Farm, more than a thousand acres running almost to the Blue Ridge. Liz Bohannon had gotten Longtree in the divorce. The house, that had burned down and been rebuilt, was named Ha Ha.

Late in the afternoon they drove through the iron gates that were posted with a warning that only one car at a time could pass through. The long driveway led upward with evenly spaced trees on either side. At last the house appeared, a vast facade with many windows, every one of them lit as if the house were a huge toy. When Amussen knocked at the door there was a sudden barking of dogs.

"Rollo! Slipper!" a voice inside cried and then began cursing.

In a mauve, flowered gown that bared one plump shoulder and impatiently kicking at the dogs, Liz Bohannon opened the door. She had once been a goddess and was still beautiful. As Amussen kissed her, she said,

"Darling, I thought it was you." To Vivian and her new husband, she said, "I'm so glad you could come."

To Bowman she held out a surprisingly small hand that bore a large emerald ring.

"I was in the study, paying bills. Is it going to snow? It feels like it. How was your Christmas?" she asked Amussen.

She continued pushing away the importuning dogs, one small and white, the other a dalmatian.

"Ours was quiet," she went on. "You haven't been here before, have you?" she said to Bowman. "The house was built originally in 1838, but it's burned down twice, the last time in the middle of the night while I was sleeping."

She held Bowman's hand. He felt a kind of thrill.

"What shall I call you? Philip? Phil?"

She had beautiful features, now a little small for the face that for years had allowed her to say and do whatever she liked, that and the money. She was loved, derided, and known as the most dishonest horsewoman in the business, banned at Saratoga where she had once bought back two of her own horses at auction, which was strictly prohibited. Keeping Bowman's hand in hers, she led the way in as she talked, speaking to Amussen.

"I was paying bills. My God, this place costs a fortune to run. It costs more to run when I'm away than when I'm here, can you believe that? No one to watch. I've just about made up my mind to sell it."

"Sell it?" said Amussen.

"Move to Florida," she said. "Live with the Jews. Vivian, you look so beautiful."

They went into the study, where the walls were a dark green and covered with pictures of horses, paintings and photographs.

"This is my favorite room," she said. "Don't you like these pictures? That one there," she said pointing, "is Khartoum—I loved that horse—I wouldn't part with it for anything. When the house burned in 1944, I ran out in the middle of the night with nothing but my mink coat and that painting. That was all I had."

"Woody won't eat!" a voice called from another room.

"Who?"

"Woody."

A man with his hair combed in a careful wave came to the doorway. He was wearing a V-neck sweater and lizard shoes. He had a look of feigned concern on his face.

"Go tell Willa," Liz said.

"She's the one who told me."

"Travis, you don't know these people. This is my husband, Travis," Liz said. "I married someone from the backyard. Everybody knows you shouldn't, but you do it anyway, don't you, sweetheart?" she said lovingly.

"You mean I didn't come from a rich family?"

"That's for certain."

"Perfection pays off," he said with a practiced smile.

Travis Gates was a lieutenant colonel in the air force but

with something vaguely fraudulent about him. He'd been in China during the war and liked to use Chinese expressions, *Ding hao,* he would say. He was her third husband. The first, Ted Bohannon, had been rich, his family owned newspapers and copper mines. Liz had been twenty, careless and sure of herself, the marriage was the event of the year. They had already slept together at a friend's house in Georgetown and were wildly in love. They were invited and traveled everywhere, to California, Europe, the Far East. It was during the Depression and photographs of them in the papers, on shipboard or at the track, were an anodyne, a reminder of life as it had been and might be. They also went a number of times to Silver Hill to visit Laura, Liz's younger sister, who worked as a club singer, usually on a small stage in a white or beaded dress, and was also an alcoholic. She took the cure at Silver Hill every few years.

One night during the war, the three of them were stranded in New York when there was trouble with the car. The hotels were all full but because Ted knew the manager they were able to get a room at the Westbury. They had to sleep three in the bed. In the middle of the night Liz woke up to find her husband doing something with her sister, who had the nightgown up under her armpits. It was the tenth year of the marriage that had begun to be stale anyway, and that night marked the end.

Meanwhile the telephone was ringing.

"Shall I get that, Bun?" Travis said.

"Willa will get it. I don't want to talk to anyone."

She had picked up Slipper and was holding her cradled against her breasts as she showed Bowman the view from the window, the Blue Ridge Mountains far off with only one or two other houses in sight.

"It's starting to snow again," she commented. "Willa! Who was that?"

There was no response. She called again.

"Willa!"

"Yas."

"Who was that on the phone? What are you, going deaf?"

A lean black woman appeared in the doorway.

"I'm not going deaf," she stated. "That was Mrs. Pry."

"P. R. Y. ?"

"Pry."

"What did she say? Are they coming?"

"She say Mr. Pry afraid of coming out in this weather."

"Is Monroe back there in the kitchen? Tell him to bring out some ice. Come on," she said to Bowman and Vivian, "I'll show you some of the house."

In the kitchen she paused to try to coax words out of a mynah bird that was missing some tail feathers. It was in a big bamboo cage where it had made a kind of hammock for itself. Monroe was working at an unhurried pace. Liz took an all-weather coat from a hook.

"It's not that cold," she said. "I'll show you the stables."

Amussen was seated on a large upholstered couch in the living room, leafing through a copy of *National Geographic* and occasionally reading a caption. A young girl in jodhpurs and a sweater came in and sat carelessly down at the far end of the couch.

"Hello, Darrin," Amussen said.

She was named for an uncle but didn't like the name and preferred to be called Dare.

"Hi," she said.

"How are you feeling?"

She looked at him and almost smiled.

"Screwed out," she said, stretching her arms lazily.

"You always talk like that?"

"No," she said, "I do it for you. I know you like it. Did my father call?"

"I don't know. Anne Pry called."

"Mrs. Emmett Pry? Graywillow Farm? I went to school with her daughter, Sally."

"I guess you did."

"I rode all her horses and the grooms rode her."

"How's your momma?" Amussen said, changing the subject. "She's a sweet woman. Haven't seen her for ages."

"She's feeling better."

"That's good," Amussen said, putting down the magazine. "I see that you're feeling fine."

"Up every morning, no matter what."

"How old are you now, Darrin?"

"Why are you calling me Darrin?"

"All right. Dare. How old are you?"

"Eighteen," she said.

He rose and got a glass from a bar that was among the bookshelves. He continued looking for something.

"It's in the cabinet underneath," Dare said.

"How's your daddy?" Amussen asked as he found the bottle he was looking for.

"He's fine. Fix me one, too, will you?"

"I didn't know you drank."

"With some water," she said.

"Just branch water?"

"Yes."

He poured two drinks.

"Here you are."

"Peter Connors is here, too. You know him, don't you?"

"I don't know if I do."

"He's my boyfriend."

"Well, good."

"He follows me around. He wants to marry me. I can't think what he imagines that would be like."

"I guess you're old enough."

"My parents think so. I'll probably end up marrying some forty-year-old groom."

"You might. I don't think it would last long."

"No, but he'd always be grateful," she said.

Amussen made no comment.

"That's a nice sweater," he said.

The sweater was not snug, but still.

"Thank you," she said.

"What is it, silk? It looks like the things they used to have in that little shop over in Middleburg. You know, the one Peggy Court ran, what's the name?"

"Patio. You've probably bought a lot of things there."

"Me? No. But your sweater looks like Patio."

"It is. It was a gift."

"Oh, yes?"

"But I prefer Garfinkle's," she said.

"Well, you don't always get to choose where a gift comes from."

"I generally do," she said.

"Dare, now you behave."

They sat drinking. Amussen looked down at his glass but could feel her eyes on him.

"You know, my daughter Vivian is older than you are," he remarked.

"I know. And my father's going to call here, probably, and want me to be getting home."

"I guess you'll have to do that."

"I wish Peter's father would call him."

Amussen looked at her, the riding pants, her calm face.

"Where are you in school, now?" he said.

"I've quit school," she said.

He nodded a little, as if agreeing.

"You knew that."

"No, I didn't," he answered.

"Daddy's after me to go back, but I don't think so. It's a waste of time, don't you think?"

"I didn't get that much out of school, I guess. Want a refill?" he asked.

"Are you trying to get me drunk?"

"I wouldn't do that," Amussen said.

"Why not?"

Her boyfriend, Peter, who had red lips and crinkled blond hair came into the room just as she spoke, and smiled as a kind of admission of interrupting. He was a student at Lafayette and headed for law. He could sense that Dare was somehow annoyed. He knew little enough about her except for the difficulties she presented.

"Uh, I'm Peter Connors, sir," he said, introducing himself.

"Nice to meet you, Peter. I'm George Amussen."

"Yes, sir, I know."

He spoke to Dare.

"Hi," he said, and confidently sat down beside her. "It looks like it's snowing."

It was snowing, harder now, blowing along the fence rows, and the light was beginning to fade.

In the master bedroom with its oversized bed, medicines and jewelry on the night table, and clothes draped over the backs of chairs, Liz was talking to her brother, Eddie. The radio was playing and all the lights including the bathroom lights were on. Written in pencil on the wallpaper above the night table were various names with telephone numbers, first names for the most part, but also doctors and Clark Gable. Eddie lived in Florida, it was the first time she'd seen him since her marriage to Travis. He was her older brother, three years older, and had the handsome face of someone who had never done much. He had bought and sold cars.

"You're getting gray," she said.

"Thanks for the news."

"It looks good."

He glanced at her and didn't reply. She reached over and rumpled his hair affectionately. There was no response.

"Oh, you're still beautiful. You're as good-looking as when

you got all dressed up in your tuxedo for the DeVores' party, remember that? You were there on the steps smoking a cigarette and hiding it in case Daddy was looking. You were hot stuff. That big car."

"George Stuver in his daddy's LaSalle."

"I was so jealous."

"The Stuvers' LaSalle. I was with Lee Donaldson in the backseat that night."

"Whatever happened to her?"

"She had a hysterectomy."

"Oh, Christ. I hate doctors."

"You can't tell the difference from the outside. You have anything to drink up here?"

"No, I try not to have it around. I don't want it to become a problem."

"Speaking of that, where's the fly-boy? And how'd you get involved with him?"

"Sweetheart, don't start on that."

"He's a prize. Where'd you meet him?"

Eddie had liked Ted Bohannon, who he felt was his kind of man.

"We met in Buenos Aires," she said. "In the embassy. He was the attaché. It just happened that he came along. I was lonely, you know I don't like living alone. I was down there for three months."

"Buenos Aires."

"I got so sick of South America," she said. "Nothing is clean there, no matter where you go. They're so lazy, those people. It just burns me up to see the money we're throwing away down there. They have enough money of their own, my

God, they have money. You should see the ranches, they have a thousand people working for them. You have to see it with your own eyes. They told us that Perón made off with over sixty million. And then they ask us for money."

She was silent for a moment.

"The man I really wanted to marry was Aly Khan," she said, "but I never got close. I'd have been perfect for him, but he married that Hollywood cunt. Anyway, promise me something. Promise me you'll try and get to know Travis. Will you promise that?"

Outside the window the snow was pouring down in the early darkness. The room was comforting and secure. She was reminded of feelings of childhood, the excitement of snowstorms and the joy of Christmas and the holidays. She could see herself in the mirror in the bright room. She was like a movie star. She said so.

"Yeah, but a little older," Eddie said.

"Promise me about Travis," she ordered.

"Yeah, but there's something you could do for me."

He was a little short of money, it being Christmas and all. He needed something to tide him over.

"How much?"

"Tit for tat," he said pleasantly.

At dinner where they sat rather far apart at the big table the talk was about the storm that was raging and roads being closed. There was plenty of room for all of them to stay over, though, Liz said. She took it as a given that they would.

"There's plenty of bacon and plenty of eggs."

Eddie was talking to Travis.

"I've looked forward to meeting you," he said.

"Me, too."

"Where are you from?"

"California, originally," Travis said. "I grew up in California. But then the war, you know. The army. I was overseas for a long time, almost two years, flying the Hump."

"You flew the Hump? What was that like?"

"Rugged, rugged." He smiled like a poster. "Mountains five miles high and we were flying blind. I lost a lot of good friends."

Willa was serving. Monroe had been sent upstairs to make beds.

"Do you still fly?" Eddie asked.

"Oh, sure. I fly out of Andrews at the moment."

"I hear you have a nigger general in the air corps," Eddie said.

"It's the air force now," Travis said.

"I always heard it called the air corps."

"They changed it. It's the air force now."

"Does it really have a nigger general?"

"Darling, shut up," Liz said. "Just shut up."

Willa had gone back to the kitchen, closing the door behind her.

"It's hard enough keeping good help," Liz said.

"Willa? Willa knows me," Eddie said. "She knows I'm not talking about her."

"What branch were you in, Eddie?" Travis asked him.

"Me? I wasn't in a branch. The army wouldn't take me."

"Why was that?"

"Couldn't pass the physical."

"Ah."

"I rode in the Gold Cup, that's what I did," Eddie said.

Afterwards they went in to have coffee by the fire. Liz sat back on the couch with her bare arms along the top cushion and kicked off her shoes.

"Slipper me, darling," she said to Travis.

He stood up without a word and got them for her but stopped short of putting them on her feet. She bent with a slight groan to do it herself.

"You are the limit," she said to Eddie.

"What do you mean?"

"You're the limit."

Peter Connors, who had said very little during dinner, managed to speak briefly, alone, with Amussen. He was hesitant about it, he needed some advice. It was about Dare, he was in love with her but couldn't be sure of where he stood.

"You were talking to her this afternoon, I mean she got quiet when I came in. I wonder if it was about me. I know she looks up to you."

"We weren't talking about you. She's a spirited girl," Amussen said, "they can be hard to manage."

"How do you go about that?"

"I expect she'd let you know if she didn't want you around. I'd say, be patient."

"I don't want it to seem I don't have any backbone."

"Of course not."

In a way, that was the impression he was afraid he gave, at odds with his hopes and desires. And dreams. He didn't imagine anyone having dreams like his. She was in them,

they were about her. She was naked and sitting in an arm-
chair, one leg thrown carelessly over an arm. He is near her
in a cotton robe that has fallen open. She seems indifferent
but accepting, and he kneels and puts his lips to her. He lifts
her and holds her up by the waist, like a vessel, to his mouth.
He can see himself as they pass a dark silvery mirror, her legs
dangling, beginning to kick as he hardens his tongue. She is
leaning backward as in one smooth movement he sets her,
in the dream and to an extent in life, on his unholy hard-on
and as he does, comes in a flood.

After a while, except for Liz and Travis who were playing
cards, they had all gone to bed. The snow went on falling
though sometime in the early hours it stopped and stars
appeared in the black sky. Also it became even colder.

In the morning through windows that were half-covered with
frost the great white expanse of fields could be seen, not a
footprint on them, not a flaw. The whiteness reached into the
distance, into the sky. Two of the dogs had gotten outside and
were flying over the snow, throwing up a white trail like
comets as they ran.

One by one they all came down to breakfast in the dining
room. Liz and Dare were among the last. Bowman and Vivian
were just finishing. Amussen was still at the table.

"Good morning," he said.

"Good morning." Liz's voice was a little hoarse. "Look at
the snow," she said.

"It finally stopped. That was a real storm. Don't know if

the roads will be open. Good morning," he said to Dare as she took a seat.

"Morning." It was almost a whisper.

"Your daddy already called," Willa told her as she brought coffee.

They sat eating bacon and eggs. Travis joined them. Peter was the only one who didn't appear.

A terrible thing had happened during the night. After everyone had gone to bed and it was finally quiet, Peter, who had waited as long as he could, stepped out into the hall in his pants and undershirt, carefully closing the door behind him. The light was subdued. All was silent. Quietly he walked to Dare's room and put his face close to the doorjamb. He whispered her name.

"Dare."

He waited and whispered again, more intently.

"Dare!"

He was afraid she was asleep. He called again and then, overcoming his fear, knocked lightly.

"Dare."

He stood there, despite himself.

"I just want to talk to you," he was going say.

He knocked again. Just as he finished, his heart leapt as the door opened slightly and revealed George Amussen, who said in a low, authoritative voice,

"Go on to bed."

Liz all morning had been on the phone deciding whether or not to go to California. She wanted to go to Santa Anita and was asking about the weather there and if her horse would be running. Finally she decided.

"We're going."

"You're sure, Bun?"

"Yes."

Eddie watched it all without comment. Later he said,

"He won't be around for long. She'll marry someone else."

It would not be Aly Khan, who had been divorced and was planning to marry a French model when he was killed in a car crash. Liz read it in the paper. She had never really stopped thinking about being married to him. It was always a fond dream. They would be in Neuilly in the morning, watching the horses train, the early mist still in the trees. He'd be in Levi's and a jacket and they would walk back together to have breakfast at the house. She'd be the wife of a prince and converted to Islam. But Aly was dead, Ted had gone on to marry someone else, and her second husband had moved to New Jersey. Still she had lots of friends, some made one way, some another, and she rode.

Vivian had liked Christmas and being home. Liz, she could see, took to Philip, and even her father, who was in an amiable mood that morning, seemed to accept him more. They all said good-bye, Amussen said good-bye to Liz and then to Dare, whose boyfriend wasn't feeling well, rubbing a bit of egg from the side of her mouth as they talked briefly. He did it with his napkin in a fatherly way.

"Is Liz Bohannon really your father's cousin?" Bowman asked afterwards.

"They just call each other cousin, I don't know why," Vivian said.

The world was still white as they drove back to Washington, snow rushing across the road like smoke. Currently twenty two degrees in downtown Washington, the radio said. The highway was disappearing in bursts of wind. The fur was up around Vivian's face in the cold, the smooth miles passing soundlessly beneath. Good-bye to Virginia and the fields and strange feeling of isolation. He was taking Vivian home—in fact that was not what he was doing but it was what gave him the sensation of happiness.

7. THE PRIESTESS

Eddins had found a house in Piermont, a small factory town up the Hudson, quiet and parochial, even neglected, about thirty minutes from the city. The traffic going in was never heavy. Trucks were not allowed on the parkway, just cars usually with a single occupant. It was a plain white house with soiled asbestos shingles on a street that sloped down to the paper mill and the river. There was a downstairs room and kitchen and on the second floor two bedrooms and a bath with old fixtures. There was a narrow strip of exhausted lawn and a garden. The front step, just off the street, was made of two large, irregular stones laid flat. The street went steeply downhill, almost directly to the liquor store that was owned by the ex-mayor, who still knew everything that was going on in town.

He had recognized the house as soon as he saw it. It was a house like those he had grown up among, small southern houses, not those of doctors or lawyers or even of his father, who had a seed business. Eddins had loved his father, too old for the war but went in anyway, coming home on leave in 1943 in his khakis with crossed rifles on the collar, imperishable image. Men came home that way in the south, in uniform, it was a heritage. This was in Ovid, South Carolina —Oh-vid, as they pronounced it—oyster shell driveways and tin advertising signs, churches, whiskey bottles in brown paper sacks, and white-skinned girls with wavy hair who worked in stores and offices, you were born to marry one. It was in his blood, hard-imprinted there like the bottle caps and bits of foil trampled into the flat, fairground earth. There was also the gift of talk, the history of everything, told and retold, until you knew it all, the families and names. They sat on shaded porches in the afternoon or evening and talked in slow, intriguing voices of things that had happened and to whom. Time, in his memory, went at a different rate in those years, largely unmoving as you walked everywhere or if it was a good ways, sometimes drove. Just past town was the river, not wide, and flowing slowly, almost unnoticeably, but flowing, faint streaks of foam lying on it undisturbed, the water rusted and cold. On either bank as far as one could see, nothing: trees, river bank, a stray dog trotting on the road alongside. In the parts yard, half-fenced, the bodies of wrecked cars and, further along the road, one that had been driven one night straight into a tree, the hollowed doors hanging open, the engine gone.

He had come from that and it was now behind him, but it still existed, like the impression on a sheet of paper beneath the one you are writing on. He retained the deep things, a sense of family, respect, and also a kind of honor in the end. His mother's most valued possession had been an old dining table carved out of fiddleback mahogany that had been in her family since the 1700s. He also remembered the coast and the excitement of the road that led to it, though it was a long way away. They'd gone there when he was a boy, in the summer. The low sea islands, the great stretches of marsh grass, the beaches, and boats cocked as if to dry. The thing that appealed to him most about the house in Piermont was that it was like houses near the ocean. From it, he could look down at the vast river, wide and unmoving like slate, and at other times alive and dancing with light.

One night at a party he met a girl named Dena, tall, loose-limbed, with dark eyes and a space between her front teeth. She was from Texas and divorced, she told him, although that was not strictly true, from a man she described as a famed poet, Vernon Beseler, also from Texas—Eddins had never heard of him—who'd actually published poems, she said, and was friends with other poets. Intense but quick to laugh, she spoke with a drawl in a voice filled with life. She had a child, a little boy, who was staying at her parents' at the moment. His name was Leon, she said, and gave a little shrug, as if to say she hadn't chosen it. What is there about a woman who had fallen in love and gotten married and now stands before you in almost foolish friendliness, as a supplicant really, in high heels, alone and without a man? She was innocent, Eddins saw, in the real sense of the word. Also droll. She had a piece of scotch tape across her forehead when he came to pick her up the first time, she had put it there to prevent wrinkles and forgotten to take it off.

"What's that?" he said.

She reached up.

"Oh, my God," she said in embarrassment and confusion.

She told him about herself, stories of her life. She liked to sing, she said, she'd been in the choir. You weren't allowed to wear lipstick in school, but in the choir you could wear it and even some makeup. What happened to their faces? the townspeople used to ask.

She'd gone to Vassar.

"You went to Vassar? Where is Vassar?"

"It's in Poughkeepsie."

"What made you pick Vassar?" he said.

"Actually, I'm supposed to be smart. Not supposed to be," she said, "I actually am."

She loved Vassar, she said, it was like an English park, the old brick buildings, the tall trees. They used to live as if it belonged to them, they came to class in their pajamas. For dinner though, you had to wear white gloves and pearls. There was a girl named Beth Ann Rigsby. She wouldn't wear them, nobody could make her do anything. They wouldn't let her go to dinner. You must wear your white gloves and pearls, they told her. So she came down in her pearls and white gloves and nothing else. Eddins was enthralled. He gazed at her.

"Are you looking at my teeth?" she said.

"Your teeth? No."

"Are they too big? The dentist says I have a fabulous bite."

"You've got wonderful teeth. What were you like as a kid?" he said.

"Oh, I was a good kid. I got good marks in school. I had this thing, I was mad about Egypt. I told everyone I was an Egyptian, my mother was furious. I had a sign on my door that said You Are Entering Egypt. You want to hear some Egyptian words?"

"Sure."

"Alabaster," she said. "Oasis."

"Cairo," he said.

"I suppose. They had the first great queen of history and the most famous, Nefertiti. When you died, your heart was weighed against a feather symbolizing truth, and if you passed judgment you took up eternal existence."

She loved that he was listening to her.

"The pharaoh was a god," she said.

"Of course."

"When he died . . ."

"When God died?"

"It was just his way of leaving to join the other gods," she said as if consoling him.

In September they went to Piermont for the day and ate lunch in the little, faded garden. The sun was still warm. She was wearing blue shorts and high heels. Her legs were bare and her heels had chafed spots on them. They talked and laughed. She wanted to be liked. Later they came into the kitchen and drank some wine. Eddins was sitting sideways to the table. Without a word she knelt in front of him and began, a little awkwardly because she was nearsighted, to unfasten his clothing. The zipper of his pants melted, tooth by tooth. She was a little nervous, but it was almost as she had pictured it, the Apis bull. Smooth and just swelling his cock almost fell into her mouth and gaining confidence she began. It was the act of a believer. She had never done it before, not with her husband, not with anyone. This was what it was like, to do things you had never done before, only imagined. The light was soft, late in the day. *It just sort of flopped right out,* she later wrote in her diary. *He must of been thinking about it. It was ready.* It was just so natural. Once, with her son, Leon, when he was a year and a half old, she had tied a piece of white string around his genitals, not to mean anything, just to set them off, they were so perfect. She had wanted to confess that, to tell someone, and to do this was like confessing, like telling Neil. It was like a boot just slipped onto a full calf and she went on doing it, gaining assurance, her mouth making only a faint sound. She did it as well as she could, she wanted it not to end, but then it was too late for that. She could tell from the movement he was making and then the cries and the great unexpected, it seemed a huge amount— she nearly choked. For a moment she was proud of her nerve. He was still in her mouth. She did not move. After a long time, she sat back.

Eddins didn't speak or move. She was afraid to look at him, of having done the wrong thing. But she had wanted to. It had been because of her *ka*, the life force. Follow thy desire, they said, as long as thou shalt live, there is no coming back. She stood up and went to the sink to wash her face. There were brown rust stains under the faucets. She finished and walked into the living room and sat in a chair. Through the window, in the sunlight, she saw a white butterfly flying up and down in pure, ecstatic moves. After a few moments Eddins came and sat on the couch.

"Don't sit over there," he said quietly.

"All right. Then you didn't mind?"

"Mind?"

"In Egypt I would be your slave."

"Jesus, Dena."

He wanted to say something but couldn't decide what it would be.

"At the swimming meets . . ." she said.

"What swimming meets?"

"The swimming meets at school. The boys all wore these little, silky trunks and you could see some of them . . . were hard. They couldn't help it. It made me think of that."

"The little boys?"

"Not just them."

"I wish I were all of them and you were looking at me."

She knew he understood it all. She could feel the goddess in herself rising.

"No, I didn't mind," he said.

"I've never done it before."

"I believe you."

He realized she had misunderstood.

"I mean it was perfect, but I believe you."

"I felt you were the one. Was it really good?"

In response he kissed her, slowly, full on the lips.

She was afraid of saying something foolish. She looked down at her hands, then at him, then down again. She felt embarrassed but not that much.

"I should probably marry you," she said. She added, "I am married, though."

For more than a month before her son came to live with her again—he had been with his grandparents in Texas until she and Vernon supposedly worked things out—she and Eddins lived on Olympus. They lay head to foot, for him it was like lying with a beautiful column of marble, a column that could quench desire. Her mound was fragrant, warm with a kind of invisible sun. The bold, Assyrian parts of him were brushing her lips, stifling her moans. Afterwards they slept like thieves. The sun was bathing the side of the house, the cold air of fall seeped beneath the windows.

They came home late, she on his arm, long-legged and unsteady, head down as she walked, as if from drinking. In bed he lay spent, like a soldier at the end of leave, and she was riding him like a horse, her hair blinding her. He loved everything, her small navel, her loose dark hair, her feet with their long, naked toes in the morning. Her buttocks were glorious, it was like being in a bakery, and when she cried out it was like a dying woman, one that had crawled to a shrine.

"When you fuck me," she said, "I get the feeling that I'm going so far I'll go right through, I won't be able to come back. I feel like my head's going to give up, like I'm going crazy."

With Leon in the house they couldn't behave that way, but even going shopping with her, it was just the two of them then, Dena in a jacket and jeans leaning across the counter to see something, the worn blue fabric drawn across her seat tight as a glove.

At five, Leon was wearing glasses. He was not a boy who would be good at sports, but he had spirit. The resentment and hostility towards a strange man in his mother's bedroom and life he showed only briefly by being reserved. He knew instinctively who Eddins was and what he meant, but he liked him and was in need of a father. Also a friend.

"Look," he said by way of showing him his room, "here is where I keep books. This is my favorite book, this is about football. And in this book here, you can learn everything, you can learn about stars and what is the deepest hole in the sea, and about thunderstorms and how to stop them. This is my best book. And this!" he cried, "this is a story I wrote. All by myself, you can read it later. And this! This is about soldiers."

He picked up another.

"Do you know that where your belly button is you were attached when you were in your momma's . . . what is it again? Where women have hair down there . . . you know . . ."

Eddins hesitated, but Leon went on unconcerned.

"They tie a knot in it. They cut it off and it hurts. They tie a knot and stuff it inside you, really!"

He looked up through his glasses to see if he was believed.

He showed Eddins games in the yard, making up the rules as they went along.

"There!" he cried as he kicked the ball. "If it hits there, it's a goal! I have one point!"

"If it goes where?"

"There!" he cried, kicking it to another spot.

"Play fair."

"Oh, all right," Leon said but soon wanted to show Eddins something else.

Vernon Beseler was living another life near Tompkins Square with a woman poet named Marian. Only infrequently did he see his son. He was destined to be a father who would never disappear because of the way he did. One day he called and asked Dena to meet him, he was thinking of heading back to Texas and wanted to see her before he left.

"Do you want me to bring Leon?" she asked.

"How is Leon?"

"He's fine."

"No, don't bring him," Beseler said.

He asked her to meet him at the airport. Dena hardly

recognized him, he seemed gaunt and distracted. Despite herself she wanted to help him. He was the rebel and poet she had fallen in love with, and so much of her life, she felt, belonged to him.

"This woman you're living with, I don't think she's taking good care of you."

"She doesn't have to take care of me."

"Well, somebody should."

"What does that mean?"

"You don't look good," Dena told him.

He ignored it.

"Are you writing?" she asked.

That was the sacred thing. He had always been its apostle. Everything would be forgiven because of it.

"No," he said, "not at the moment. I may go and teach for a while."

"Where?"

"I'm not sure."

He was silent. Then he said, "To be born a mole, ever think of that?"

"A mole?"

"To be born blind, with no eyes, eyes that are sealed. Everything is darkness. Living under the earth in narrow, cold passages, afraid of snakes, rats, anything that might be there, able to see. Seeking a mate, there underground, beyond all light."

It was hard to look at him.

"No," she said. "I've never thought of it. I was born with eyes."

"Got to have mercy," he said.

He was trying to light a cigarette with what seemed intense focus, putting it between his lips, then striking a match and applying it with great concentration, shaking it out and depositing it in an ashtray. He took the cigarette from his mouth with trembling fingers.

"It's not from drinking," he said.

"It isn't?"

"I drink, but that's not it. I'm just a little bit past the red line. Marian doesn't drink. She's a moonbather. She likes to undress and sit in the rays."

"Where's she doing that?"

"She can do it anywhere," he said.

"Vernon, why don't we get a divorce?"

"Why would we get a divorce?"

"Because we're not really married anymore."

"We'll always be married," he said.

"I don't think so. I mean I don't think it makes sense."

"They'll be writing songs about us," he said. "I could write a couple. How's old Leon?"

"He's a wonderful boy."

"Yeah, I knew he would be."

"What about our divorce?"

"Yeah," Beseler said, smoking thoughtfully and saying nothing more.

Finally his flight was called.

"Well, I guess this is adios for a while," he said.

He kissed her on the cheek. That was the last time she saw him. She was from Texas, though, where they were loyal, and in some disdainful way she remained loyal to him, to the boy who'd been her husband, carried her off, and whose destiny was to be a famous poet, maybe a singer. He had played the guitar and sung in a low voice to her.

A lawyer in Austin, hired by his family, took care of the divorce through some associate in New York. She was given child support of four hundred dollars a month—she'd asked for nothing for herself—and Eddins, in effect, had a son.

Great publishers were not always great readers, and good readers seldom made good publishers, but Bowman was somewhere in between. Often, in the city late at night when the sound of traffic had vanished, Bowman sat reading. Vivian had gone to bed. The only light was a standing lamp by his chair, near his elbow was a drink. He liked to read with the silence and the golden color of the whiskey as his companions. He liked food, people, talk, but reading was an inexhaustible pleasure. What the joys of music were to others, words on a page were to him.

In the morning, Vivian asked what time he had come to bed.

"Twelve-thirty. About then."

"What were you reading?"

"I was reading about Ezra Pound in St. Elizabeths."

Vivian knew about St. Elizabeths. It was a synonym for lunacy in Washington.

"What's he there for?"

"Probably because they didn't know what else to do with him."

"I mean, what did he do?"

"You know who he is?"

"I know enough," she said.

"Well, he's a towering poet. He was an expatriate."

She didn't feel like asking what that was.

"He made some broadcasts for the fascists in Italy," Bowman explained. "They were addressed to America at the start of the war. He had obsessions about the evils of bank interest, Jews, the provincialism of America, and he talked about them in his broadcasts. He was at dinner in Rome one night and heard the news that the Japanese had just bombed Pearl Harbor, and he said, my God, I'm a ruined man."

"He doesn't sound that crazy," Vivian said.

"Exactly."

He wanted to go on talking about Ezra Pound and introduce the subject of the *Cantos,* perhaps reading one or two of the most brilliant of them to her, but Vivian's mind was elsewhere. He was not too curious about where that might be. He thought back instead to a lunch a few days before with one of his writers who had been to school only through the seventh grade though he didn't explain why. His mother had given him a library card and told him, go and read the books.

"The books. That's what she said. She'd wanted to be a teacher but she had these children. She was a disappointed woman. She said, you come from decent, hardworking people. Serious people."

Serious was a word that had haunted his life.

"She was trying to tell me something. Like all proud people, she didn't want to say it directly. If you didn't understand, that was too bad, but she wanted to pass this thing on. It was a heritage. We didn't have a heritage, but she believed in it."

His name was Keith Crowley. He was a slight man who looked to the side when he talked. Bowman liked him and liked his writing, but his novel didn't sell, two or three thousand copies was all. He wrote two more, one of which Bowman published, and then dropped from sight.

8. LONDON

He woke in darkness to a fierce rattling. It was rain, the drops hammering against the window. He'd been born in a storm, he was always happy in them. Vivian was curled beside him, deep in sleep, and he lay listening to the sheets of rain. They were leaving for London that evening, he and Baum, and it rained throughout the day, a wet mist streaming from the great wheels of trucks alongside as they drove to the airport, the windshield wipers of the taxi going. Bowman's expectations were anything but dampened. He was certain, he felt, to like England and the city he had dreamed of in college, the rich, imagined city with its legendary figures, its polished men and women out of Evelyn Waugh, the Virginias, the Catherines and Janes, narrow-minded, assured, only dimly aware of any life other than their own.

They sat beside one another on the plane, Baum calmly reading the newspaper as the engine noise swelled and they began to move, the takeoff with the plane trembling and the roar, water blurring the cabin windows. London, Bowman thought. It was early May.

In the morning there was England, green and unknown beneath broken clouds. They drove in from Heathrow in a cab making a sound like a sewing machine with the driver offering occasional comments in a language difficult to understand. Then there were the outskirts, drab and interminable, becoming at last streets at odd angles and buildings of Victorian brick. They turned onto a wide avenue, The Mall, with the dense green of a park alongside and black iron fence peeling past. At its end, far off, was a great pale arch. They were driving swiftly on the wrong side. Bowman was struck by the proud, outdated character of the city, its irregularity and singular names. The most important thing, its separation from the continent, was not yet known to him.

Though it was more than fifteen years after the war, the ghost of it was still present. England had won the war—there was hardly a family, high or low, that had not been part of it—through the early disasters when the country had been unprepared, the far-off sinking of warships that were thought to be indestructible, symbols and pride of a nation, the absolute catastrophe of the army sent to France in 1940 to fight beside the French and then find itself encircled and trapped on the Channel beaches in the hopeless disorder of men without equipment or supplies, everything abandoned in the retreat, and only by last-minute effort and German forbearance be brought home in every boat that could be found, large or small, exhausted, beaten. And still the task remained, the seemingly endless struggle, the unimaginable scale of it, the desert war, the determination to save Suez, the reeling war in the air, great walls collapsing in darkness, entire cities on fire, calamitous news from the Far East, casualty lists, the readying for invasion, the battles without end . . .

And England had won. Its enemies stumbled through ruins, went hungry. What was left of their cities smelled of death and sewage, the women sold themselves for cigarettes, but it was England, like a battered fighter somehow left standing, that had paid too much. A decade later there was still food rationing and it was difficult to travel, currency could not be taken out of the country. The bells that had tolled the hour of victory were long silent. The ways of before the war were unrecoverable. Putting out a cigarette after lunch, a publisher had said calmly, "England is finished."

They first stayed at the house of an editor and friend, Edina Dell, on one of the small enclaves that were called terraces, with a brick-walled garden and some trees outside the dining room, the bottommost room of the house. She was the daughter of a classics professor but seemed with her irregular teeth and offhanded manner to have come from a larger life, some great country house with paintings, worn furnishings, and known indiscretions. She had a daughter, Siri, the result of a ten-year marriage to a Sudanese. The daughter was a soft, seductive color, six or seven years old and filled with love for her mother, she often stood by her mother's leg with her arm around it. She was a gazelle, her eyes dark brown with the purest whites.

The man with whom Edina was involved was a large, elegant figure, Aleksei Paros, who came from a distinguished Greek family and was perhaps married—he was vague on the matter, it was more complicated than it seemed. He was an encyclopedia salesman at this stage, but even in his shirtsleeves, walking around the house looking for cigarettes, he gave the impression of someone for whom life would work out. He was tall and overweight and could charm men as well as women with little effort. Edina was drawn to men like him.

Her father had been this type and she had two illegitimate brothers.

Aleksei had been away, in Sicily, and had just come back by way of a London club the night before. He was known there, one of his habits was gambling. He liked to stroll about carrying his chips in one hand, stroking them unconsciously with his thumb. He had no system for gambling, he bet on instinct, some men seem to have a gift for it. Passing the chemin-de-fer table he might suddenly reach in and impulsively make a bet. It was a Mediterranean gesture, rich Egyptians did it. Except for his looks, Aleksei might have been one, a minor playboy or king.

He stood at the roulette table listening to the sound of the ivory ball as it circled, a long, decaying sound that ended in the fated clicking as it glanced off partitions between numbers and abruptly dropped into one. *Vingt-deux, pair et noir.* Twenty-two, the year he was born. Numbers sometimes repeated, but he did not have that feeling. There were some younger people at the table and a man in a worn suit keeping track of which numbers had come up on a card in his hand, then making a small bet on red or black. *Faites vos jeux,* the croupier was saying. A few more people arrived. Something invisible drew them to a particular table, something in the stale air. *Faites vos jeux.* A woman in an evening gown had pushed in, a younger woman, and people were standing sideways between the chairs. The baize cloth was thick with chips. As soon as someone bet, two more would follow. *Rien ne va plus,* the croupier was calling. The wheel was turning, now it was turning faster, and suddenly the ball shot out from an expert hand and began to circle fast in the opposite direction just beneath the rim, and at that moment, like someone jumping aboard as the ship pulled away, Aleksei placed fifty pounds on the six. The ball was making its beautiful circling sound one could listen to forever, a sound of immense possibilities, he stood to win eighteen hundred, and for five or six seconds that seemed much longer he waited calmly but intently, almost as if the guillotine blade were being raised, then the slowing and sinking of the orbit until the final instant when there was a steely hopping and the ball fell definitively into a number. It was not six. Like the practiced gambler he was, he showed no emotion or regret. He bet fifty pounds several times more and then moved to another table.

In the morning he sat in the garden with his coffee, the garden of reconciliation, as he called it. In his white shirt, at the round metal table he was like a wounded man on a hospital terrace. You could not be angry with him. He did not talk about the previous night but rather about Palermo, *palla-irma,* city with no signs.

"It's absolutely true," he said. "You can go anywhere and not a street is identified. Everything is in complete disrepair."

He was straightening a cigarette taken from a crushed pack. Everything he did was in a way the act of a survivor and at the same time of someone who would survive. He seemed to have played the game already somehow.

"Filthy with crime, I imagine," Edina said.

"Sicily? Yes, of course," Aleksei conceded. "There's some crime. But you don't see it. Kidnapping. Stealing women— that's why I didn't want to take you."

"For fear I'd be kidnapped?"

"Yes. We've already had our war over an abducted woman," he said.

"What can you do?" she said helplessly to Baum.

"We'll take a trip to America," Aleksei promised, "get a car and drive across the country, go to St. Louis, Chicago, see the Great Plains."

"Yes, of course," she said. "I've been counting on it."

She excused herself, in fact to do her yoga on the floor in her bedroom, to seek understanding, her arms and legs gently swimming in the quiet air, then later in the morning to read.

It was in London with its haughty shops on Jermyn and New Bond Street; the houses plaqued with the famous names of former occupants, Boswell, Browning, Mozart, Shelley, even Chaucer; the hidden luxury from imperial days with its guardians in the form of silver-trimmed doormen at the great hotels; the exclusive clubs; the bookshops, restaurants, and endless particular addresses on terraces, places, roads, courts, crescents, squares, avenues, rows, gardens, mansions, and mews; the many small, even shabby hotels with rooms without bath; the traffic; the secrets one would never know—in this London he formed his first idea of the geography of publishing, the network of people in various countries who knew one another, especially those who were interested in the same kind of books and possessed similar lists but, equally important, were friends, not intimate perhaps, but colleagues and rivals and through this and their common endeavors, friends.

They were, in the main, able and even superior men, some very principled, some less so. The most prominent or at least the most talked about British publisher was Bernard Wiberg, a stocky man in his late forties with an eighteenth-century face, not difficult to caricature, prominent nose and somewhat pointed chin together with arms that seemed a little short. He had been a German refugee and had come to England just before the war without a penny. In the first years he had shared a room, and his only extravagance was once a week having a coffee at the Dorchester surrounded by people having a meal that cost thirty shillings or more, one day he was determined to be among them.

He began by publishing books that were in the public domain, but doing them handsomely and marketing them with style. He had great success with racy memoirs of women who made their way up, preferably from a young age, man by man in Regency London, and he published, ignoring general outrage, some books about the holocaust but from the other side, including a best-seller called *Juliet of the Camps,* based on various myths about a beautiful Jewish girl who for a time saved herself by working in a concentration camp brothel where a German officer fell in love with her. It was both an insult to the countless victims and a lie to the survivors. Wiberg took a lofty tone.

"History is the clothes in the closet," he said. "Put them on and you will understand."

He was referring in a way to his own life and his family, all of whom had perished in the terrifying nightmare that had been Eastern Europe. He had put that behind him. His fingernails were polished and his clothes expensive. He was fond of music and the opera. He was quoted as saying that his publishing house was based on the arrangement of a symphony orchestra: the bass fiddles and drums were in back, the foundation, so to speak, of major works, tapering forward to flutes, oboes, and clarinets, which were books of lesser weight but which made people happy and sold by the carload. His greater interest lay in the drums—he wanted to have Nobel winners inscribe books to him, to have a beautiful house and give parties.

He possessed the house, actually an apartment of two entire floors that overlooked Regent's Park. It was luxurious, with high ceilings and walls enameled in deep, soothing colors and hung with drawings and pictures, one a large Bacon. The bookcases were filled with books, there was no noise from traffic or the street but instead patrician calm and a servant bringing tea.

Robert Baum and Wiberg had some innate understanding and over the years did a great deal of business together, each of them claiming the other had gotten the better of it.

Edina had a different view, not solely hers.

"There are wonderful German refugees named Jacob," she agreed, "excellent doctors, bankers, drama critics. He's not one of those. He came here and sought out the Achilles tendon, he took advantage of English Christian gentility. He did terrible things. The book about the Jewish girl who falls in love with the SS officer—you have to draw the line somewhere. And, of course, he climbed. He couldn't get into society but he always hired girls from the best families. He gave them money. Well, that's his real story. Robert knows my feelings."

In Cologne, Wiberg's counterpart, more or less, was Karl Maria Löhr, also a homely man, who had inherited the publishing house from his father, its founder, and who liked to sit on the floor of his office drinking whiskey and talking with writers. He had three secretaries, all of whom were or had been, at one time or another, available to him. One of them, Erna, often went with him on weekends, ostensibly to visit his mother who lived in Dortmund. Another, younger, was diligent and did not object to working late since she was unmarried. The night sometimes ended in a casual restaurant favored by artists and open late with a lot of talking and laughter, and then a drink in the paneled library of Löhr's house where Katja, the second secretary, kept extra clothes and even had her own bathroom. Silvia, the third one—she was actually in promotion, having changed jobs—had accompanied him to book fairs in Frankfurt and London and one especially memorable time to Bologna where they dined in a restaurant called Diana, on the leafy terrace to one side, and stayed at the Baglioni. There was often a long interval when he would not have slept with her and her relative newness and the travel excited him. She always came to bed holding her forearm beneath her breasts, which were a little heavy. Silvia was spirited and amusing things happened with her. Once in a waterfront bar in Hamburg a sailor asked her to dance. Karl Maria did not mind but then the sailor had wanted to give her twenty-five marks to go upstairs with him. She said no, and he made it fifty and followed her back to the bar, where he offered her a hundred marks. Karl Maria leaned forward and said, "*Hör zu. Sie ist meine frau*—she's my wife. I don't mind, but I think you may be getting too close to her price."

The sailor was drunk, but they managed to leave him and

go back to the hotel, where they had a last drink at the ornate, empty bar and laughed. Löhr could drink and drink.

The Swedish publisher was an urbane man who had brought Gide, Dreiser, and Anthony Powell to the house, as well as Proust and Genet. He published the Russians, Bunin and Babel, and later the great émigrés. He had been to Russia, it was a terrible place, he said, like a vast prison, a prison where all hope had to be abandoned, and yet the Russians themselves were the most wonderful people he had ever met.

"I like them more than I can say," he said. "They're not like we are. For some reason there's a depth and intimacy you find nowhere else. Perhaps it's the result of the endless tyrannies. Akhmatova, I would love to publish her but she's published by someone else. Her husband was executed by the Communists, her son spent years in a prison camp, she lived in a single room, under the surveillance of the secret police, always in fear of being arrested. Friends would visit her and, while talking of other things for the benefit of the eavesdropping police, she would hold up a piece of cigarette paper on which she had written the lines of a poem she had composed so they could read and memorize it, and when they nodded she would touch a match to the paper. When you go to their houses and sit down with them, in the kitchen usually, even if it's only drinking tea, they give you their souls."

Berggren himself did not possess that holy quality. He had the appearance almost of a banker, tall, reserved, with irregular teeth and blondish hair turned gray. He wore suits, often with a vest, and habitually took off his glasses to read. He had married three times, the first time to a woman with money and a house, an old house built a century before, with a tennis court and stone walks. She was conventional but very knowing and perhaps not wholly unaware when Berggren at a party managed to introduce her to his new mistress, to have her opinion, so to speak, since he trusted her judgment.

The mistress became his second wife—he regretted his divorce, he had loved his first wife, but life had turned a page. This second wife, Bibi, was stylish but also temperamental and demanding. The bills she ran up were always an unpleasant surprise, and she paid little attention to the cost of things like wine.

Berggren had been made for women. They were, for him, the chief reason for living or they represented it. He was not a man who was hard to live with, he was civilized and had manners though he could seem incommunicative at times. It was not a matter of being withdrawn, only that his thoughts were elsewhere. He generally avoided arguments although with Bibi it was not always possible. There was a hotel on Nackstromsgaten where he put up visiting writers, and he went there when things became too turbulent at home. The manager there knew him, and the desk clerk. The bargirl swirled cracked ice in a glass and then emptied it and poured in a Swiss wine, Sion, that he liked.

One afternoon he passed a shopwindow where a girl in her twenties in black fitted pants was arranging a dress dummy. She was aware of him standing there but she did not look at him. He stood there longer than he wished, he could not take his eyes from her. She, not the shopgirl but someone like her, became his third wife.

What the unseen part of their life was, who can say? Was she difficult or did she stand naked between his knees like the children of the patriarchs, her bare stomach, the swell of her hips? A certain unwanted coldness at his center kept him from real happiness, and though he married beautiful women, let us say possessed them, it was never complete and yet to live without them was unthinkable. The great hunger of the past was for food, there was never enough food and the majority of people were undernourished or starving, but the new hunger was for sex, there was the same specter of famine without it.

With Karen, Berggren did not feel young again but something better. Sex was more than a pleasure, at this age he felt joined to the myths. He had accidentally seen, a few years earlier, a wonderful thing, his mother dressing—her back was to him, she was seventy-two at the time, her buttocks were smooth and perfect, her waist firm. It was in his genes, then, he could perhaps go on and on, but one day he saw something else, perfectly innocent, Karen and a girlfriend she had known since school lying on the grass in their skimpy bathing suits tanning themselves, face down, side by side, talking to one another and occasionally the leg of one of them kicked idly up into the sun that was soothing their bare backs. He was sitting in his shirtsleeves on the stone terrace, reading a manuscript. He thought for a moment of going down to sit beside them, but he felt a certain awkwardness and the knowledge that whatever they were talking about, they would cease. He did not try to imagine what they were talking about, it was only their idle happiness in doing it while his own habits were less joyful and animated. He lit a cigarette and sat smoking calmly as he reread a few pages. They were standing up now and picking up their towels. On that day and other days he accepted the reality of what happened with women he loved, wives, principally, which was one of the things that led, despite his position and intelligence and the high regard in which he was held, to his suicide at the age of fifty-three, in the year that he and Karen parted.

9. AFTER THE BALL

Many of the guests had already arrived and others, with him, were on their way upstairs. The invitation had been off-handed, he was giving a costume party, Wiberg said, why don't you come? Together with Juno in a gold and white mask and a silver Viking in a helmet with great horns, Bowman climbed the wide stairs. The door to the grand apartment was open and within was a crowd of another world, a Crusader in a tunic with a large red cross; some savages dressed in green, with long straw wigs; a few people in evening clothes wearing black masks; and Helen of Troy in a lavender gown with crossed straps in the Grecian way over a very bare back. Bowman's costume, found at the last minute, was a hussar's frogged jacket, red and green, over his own pants. Wiberg, in the traditional British idea of the exotic, was dressed as a pasha. On the landing a six-piece orchestra was playing.

It was difficult to move in the crowd. They were not literary people, at least not from their conversation. There were people from the embassies and society, movie people, and people using the night to advantage, a woman sticking her tongue in a man's mouth and another—Bowman saw her only once—dressed as a carhop in very brief shorts, her legs shining in steel-colored hose, moving between several groups like a bee in clover. Wiberg talked to him only briefly.

Bowman knew no one. The music went on. Two angels stood near the orchestra, smoking cigarettes. At midnight, waiters in white jackets began serving supper, oysters and cold beef, sandwiches and pastries. There were figures in beautiful silks. An older woman with a nose as long as an index finger was eating greedily, and the man with her blew his nose in the linen napkin, a gentleman, then. There was also, but only if one knew, the upper-class harlot who'd been dropped from the guest list but had come despite that and as an act of insolence had fellated five of the male guests, one after another, in a bedroom.

Bowman, having run out of things to notice and places to stand, was looking at a collection of photographs in thick silver frames on a table, well-dressed couples or individuals standing in front of their houses or in gardens, some of them inscribed. A voice behind him said, "Bernard likes titles."

"Yes, I was just looking at them."

"He likes titles and people that have them."

It was a woman in a black silk pants-dress with a kind of pirate's bandanna and gold earrings to go with it. It was a halfhearted costume, it might easily have been her normal wear. She, too, had a long nose, but was beautiful. He was suddenly nervous and with the unmistakable feeling that he would say something foolish.

"Are you from the embassy?" she said.

"The embassy?"

"The American embassy."

"No, no. Nothing like that. I'm an editor."

"With Bernard?"

How did she know him? he wondered. But, of course, almost everyone there did.

"No, with an American house, Braden and Baum. You know," he confessed, "you're the first person I've talked to tonight."

A waiter was near them.

"Would you like a drink?" he asked.

"No, thank you. I've had too much to drink already," she said.

He could see that then, from her eyes and a certain hesitation in her movements.

"Are you here with someone?" he found himself asking.

"Yes. With my husband."

"Your husband."

"As he's called. What did you say your name was?"

Her name was Enid Armour.

"Mrs." he said. Mrs. Armour."

"You keep saying that."

"I don't mean to."

"It's all right. Are you staying in London long?"

"No."

"Another time," she said.

"I hope so."

She appeared to lose interest but pressed the edge of his hand as if in consolation as she moved away. He didn't see her again in the crowd although there were other lustrous figures. She might have left. He found out her husband's name from a list on a table near the door. At nearly three in the morning there were fantastic figures, a man dressed as an owl with shreds of cloth for feathers and a woman with a top hat and in black tights, sleeping or passed out on the couches. He went by them in his tunic like a lone figure surviving history.

His hotel was near Queen's Gate and the room was plain. He lay there wondering if she would remember him. The night, he realized, had been glamorous. It would soon be four o'clock and he was tired. He fell into a profound sleep that ended with the sun coming full through the window and filling the room. Across the street the buildings were blazing in the light.

E. G. Armour was listed. Wanting to call but uncertain, Bowman tried to summon his nerve. He was aware it was a foolhardy thing to do and decided yes and no half a dozen times while dressing. Would it be she who answered? Finally he picked up the phone. He could hear it ringing, where, he did not know. After several rings a man's voice said, hello.

"Mrs. Armour, please."

He was sure the man could hear his heart.

"Yes, who is this?"

"Philip Bowman."

The phone was put down and he heard her being called. His nervousness increased.

"Hallo," a cool voice said.

"Enid?"

"Yes?"

"Uh, this is Philip Bowman."

He began to explain who he was, where they had met.

"Yes, of course," she said though it sounded matter-of-fact.

He asked, because he would not have forgiven himself if he hadn't, if she could have lunch.

There was a pause.

"Today?" she said.

"Yes."

"Well, it would have to be on the late side. After one."

"Yes. Where should we meet?"

She suggested San Frediano on the Fulham Road, not far from where she lived. It was there that Bowman, who had been waiting, saw her enter and then move through the tables. She was wearing a gray pullover and a kind of suede jacket, an unapproachable woman who then saw him. He stood up a little clumsily.

She smiled.

"Hallo," she said.

"Hello."

It seemed his manhood had suddenly caught up with him, as if it had been waiting somewhere in the wings.

"I was afraid to call you," he said.

"Really?"

"It was a superhuman act."

"Why is that?"

He didn't answer.

"Did you finally speak to someone else last night?"

"Only you," he said.

"I don't believe it."

"It's true."

"You don't seem that withdrawn."

"I'm not. I just didn't find anyone I felt I could talk to."

"Yes, all those sultans and Cleopatras."

"It was a fantastic evening."

"I imagine it was," she said. "Tell me about yourself."

"I'm probably pretty much what you see. I'm thirty-four years old. And as you can probably tell, a bit in awe."

"You're married?" she asked casually.

"Yes."

"As am I."

"I know. I spoke to your husband, I think."

"Yes. He's on his way to Scotland. We're not on very good terms. I'm afraid I didn't quite understand the conditions of marriage."

"What are they?"

"That he would be looking for another woman constantly and I would be trying to prevent it. It's boring. Are you on good terms with your wife?"

"On a certain level."

"Which one is that?"

"I don't mean a particular level. I mean just down to a certain level."

"I don't think you ever really know anybody."

She was originally from Cape Town, it turned out, born on the steps of the hospital there which were as far as her mother got that night, she could never leave a party. But she was completely English; they moved to London when she was a little child. She was damaged though she did not appear to be. Her beauty was unwary. Her husband, in fact, had another woman, a woman who might come into some money, but he was not ready to get a divorce. Wiberg had anyway advised her to not get a divorce, she had no income and was better off as she was, he said. He meant by this nicely situated, from his point of view, to all appearances well-off and very decorative.

"How do you know Wiberg?"

"He's an amazing man," she said. "He knows everyone. He's been very nice to me."

"How?"

"Oh, in a number of ways. He lets me dress up like a pirate, for example."

"You mean last night."

"Um."

She smiled at him. He could not take his eyes from her, the way her mouth moved when she spoke, the slight, careless gesture of a hand, her scent. She was like another language, nothing like his own.

"Men must be after you in droves."

"Not in the way you'd like," she said. "Do you want to know what happened? The most frightening thing."

She'd been near Northampton and had an accident with the car. A bit shaken, she'd gone to this little hotel and ended up having dinner there and a glass of wine by the fire. She had taken a room and afterwards, at night, she heard two men talking in low voices outside the door as she got ready for bed. Then they tried to get into the room. She saw the door handle moving. Go away! she called. There was no telephone in the room, which they probably knew. They spoke through the door, they just wanted to talk to her, they said.

"Not tonight. I'm very tired," she said. "Tomorrow."

The door handle moved again, being tried. Just to talk, they assured her, they knew she would not be there tomorrow.

"Yes, yes. I'll be here," she promised.

After a while it was quiet. She listened at the door and

then, in great fear, opened it slightly, saw no one and took her things and fled. She drove off in the car with things banging and slept in it through the night near some houses under construction.

"Well, you have luck, don't you," he said. He took her hand, which was slender. "Let me look at it," he said. "This is your life line"—touching it with his finger. "According to this, you're going to be around for a long time, I'd say into your eighties."

"I can't say I'm looking forward to that."

"Well, you may change your mind. I see some children here, do you have children?"

"No, not yet."

"I see two or three. It breaks up a little there, it's hard to be certain."

He sat holding her hand which for a moment closed affectionately around his. She smiled.

"Would you do me a favor?" she said. "Come with me for a few minutes after lunch, would you? There's a shop just a few doors down that has a beautiful dress I've been looking at. If I tried it on, would you tell me yes or no?"

She tried on not one but two dresses in the small but stylish shop, coming out from behind the curtain and turning slightly from side to side. The white glint of a brassiere strap that she pushed underneath as an afterthought seemed a sign of purity. When she said good-bye, it was like a play ending. It was like the theater and coming out again to the streets. He saw his reflection in many windows as he passed and stopped to take measure of himself. He felt in possession of the city, not the Victorian city with its dark wood interiors and milky marble halls, the tall red buses that lurched by, endless windows and doors, but another city, visible yet unimagined.

She agreed to come to dinner, but she was late and after twenty minutes of feeling more and more conspicuous at the bar, he realized she would not appear. It was perhaps her husband or a change of mind but in any case it excluded him. He was aware of his insignificance, even triviality, and then suddenly it changed as she came in.

"Sorry to be late," she said. "Forgive me. Have you been waiting?"

"No, it's nothing."

The minutes of his unhappiness had instantly disappeared.

"I was on the telephone with my husband, having an argument as usual," she said.

"What were you arguing about?"

"Oh, money, everything."

She was wearing a suit and a black silk shirt. She looked as if difficulty of any kind was a remote thing. When they sat she was on a banquette against the wall and he was opposite, able to look at her all he liked and aware of the glamour she was bestowing on the two of them.

During dinner, he said,

"Have you ever fallen in love?"

"Fallen in love? Been in love, you mean. Yes, of course."

"I mean fallen. You never forget it."

"Funny you should say that."

She had fallen in love as a young girl, she said.

"How old were you?"

"Eighteen."

It had been the most extraordinary experience of her life. She'd had a spell cast over her, she said. It was in Siena, she was a student, part of a group of a dozen boys and girls and she was not really aware of the intensity of . . . There was a Ferris wheel and you went up and up and sometimes stayed there, and that night, high above everything, the boy beside her began saying the most thrilling, impossible things, whispering madly in her ear. And she fell in love. There had never been anything like that night, she said.

Never anything like it. Bowman felt disheartened. Why had she said that?

"You know how it is," she said, "how incredible."

It was the past she was talking about, but not only the past—he could not be sure. Her presence was fresh, unspoiled.

"Incredible, yes, I know."

She had hardly closed the door to her flat before he embraced and kissed her fervently, saying something she did not make out against her cheek.

"What?"

But he did not repeat it. He was opening the catch at the neck of her shirt, she did not stop his hands. In the bedroom she stepped from her skirt. She stood for a moment hugging herself and then slipped off the rest. The glory of her. England stood before him, naked in the darkness. She had been, in fact, lonely, she was ready to be loved. He was never more sure of his knowledge. He kissed her bare shoulders, then her hands and long fingers.

She lay beneath him. He was holding himself back but she showed he need not. They didn't speak, he was afraid to speak. He touched the tip of his cock to her and almost effortlessly it went in, the head only, the rest held back. He was in possession of his life. He gathered and went in slowly, sinking like a ship, a little cry escaping her, the cry of a hare, as it went to the hilt.

Afterwards they lay until she slid from beneath him.

"My God."

"What?"

"I'm drenched."

She reached for something on the night table and lit a cigarette.

"You smoke."

"Now and again."

His eyes were now accustomed to the darkness. He knelt on the bed to drink her in. It was no longer preliminary to anything. He was not exhausted. He watched her smoke. After a while they made love again. He pulled her over him by her wrists, like a torn sheet. At the last she began to give a slight cry, and again he came too soon but she collapsed. The sheet was wet and they moved to one side and slept, he lay beside her like a child, in full contentment. It was different than marriage, unsanctioned, but marriage had permitted it. Her husband was off in Scotland. The consent had been without a word.

In the morning she was still sleeping, her lips slightly parted, like a girl in summer with cropped blond hair and a bare neck. He wondered if he should wake her with a touch or caress, but she was awake, perhaps from his gaze, and straightened her legs beneath the sheet. He turned her onto her stomach as if she were a possession, as if they had agreed.

He sat in the tub in the bathroom, a chalky tub of a grand size found in beach resorts, as the water thundered in. His eye fell on a slight pair of white underclothes hung to dry on the towel rack. On the shelves and windowsill were jars and small bottles, her lotions and creams. He gazed at them, his mind adrift, as the warm water rose. He slid further down as it reached his shoulders, in a kind of nirvana not based on freedom from desires but on attainment. He was at the center of the city, of London, it would always be his.

She poured tea in a pale robe that came only to the knee, holding the top of it closed with one hand. It was still early. He was buttoning his shirt.

"I feel like Stanley Ketchel."

"Who is that?"

"He was a fighter. There was a famous newspaper story about him. Stanley Ketchel, the middleweight champion, was shot and killed yesterday morning by the husband of the woman he was cooking breakfast for."

"That's clever. Did you write that?"

"No, it's just a famous opening. I like openings, they can be important. Ours was. Not easily forgotten. I thought . . . I'm not sure what I thought but part of it was, impossible."

"I think that's been disproven."

"Yes."

They sat silent for a moment.

"The thing is, I have to leave tomorrow."

"Tomorrow," she said. "When will you be back?"

"I don't know. I can't be sure. It's presumably a question of work."

He added, "I hope you won't forget me."

"You can be sure."

Those were the words he pocketed and ran his fingers over many times, along with images of her that were as distinct as photographs. He wanted a photograph but prevented himself from asking for it. He would take one himself the next time and keep it between the pages of a book in the office with nothing written on it, no name or date. He could imagine someone accidentally coming across it and asking, who is this? He would without a word simply take it from their hand.

10. CORNERSVILLE

Caroline Amussen was living, as she had for years, on Dupont Circle in an apartment the furnishings of which, not particularly fashionable to begin with, hadn't changed in all the time she'd been there, the same long sofa, the same easy chairs and lamps, the same white enameled table in the kitchen where she sat smoking and drinking coffee in the mornings and, having finished the paper, listening to the radio and her favorite host, whose witticisms she repeated to her friends in a voice that had become slightly hoarse, a voice of experience and drink. Various women, divorced and married, were her friends including Eve Lambert, whom she'd known since they were little girls and who had married into the Lambert family and loads of money—she was still invited pretty regularly to the Lamberts' and occasionally went sailing with them although Brice Lambert, broad-faced and sporting, didn't often go sailing with his wife but with another party, it was said, a young reporter who wrote for the social column. The boat afforded absolute privacy and the rumor was that Brice had his girlfriend spend the day of sailing naked. So it was said. But how would anyone know? Caroline thought.

With her friends, she had lunch and often, in the afternoon or evening, played cards. She was still the best looking of them and except for Eve had made the best marriage, the

others had married, in her opinion, either lower-class or
uninteresting men, salesmen and assistant managers. Washington could be dull. At five every afternoon the thousands
of government offices would empty and the government
workers would go home having spent the whole day wasting
George Amussen's hard-earned money, as he always complained. The government should be abolished, he said, the
whole damned thing. We'd be better off without it.

Caroline's rent was paid by Amussen, no real burden for
him since his company managed the building and he could
take care of the rent by including it in other things, general
expenses. Her alimony was $350 a month and she received a
little extra from her father. It was not enough to give parties
with or gamble, but she did bet on the horses now and then
or dressed up in nice weather and went to Pimlico with
Susan McCann, who had almost married a Brazilian diplomat, should have, but there had been a disastrous weekend
in Rehoboth during which, she would afterwards confess to
Caroline, she had been too narrow-minded and he later began
seeing another woman, who had an antique shop in Georgetown.

Caroline, for her part, was not unhappy. She was optimis-
tic, there was still life to think about, both what had been and
what might be ahead. She had not given up the idea that she
might marry again and had been involved with several men
over the years, but none of them was right. She wanted a
man who, among other things, would make George Amussen
wonder if he'd made a mistake if they happened to cross paths
with him, which was bound to happen sooner or later,
although she was still angry and didn't care what he thought.

In her becalmed life she knew she was drinking too much, though a drink or two made you feel more like yourself and people were more lively and attractive when they drank.

"Anyway, you *feel* more attractive," Susan agreed.

"It's the same thing."

"Are you still seeing Milton Goldman?" Susan asked off-handedly.

"No," said Caroline.

"What happened?"

"Nothing actually happened."

"I thought you liked him."

"He's a very nice man," Caroline said.

Which he was and owned property on Connecticut Avenue a little further out, but she remembered very well the photograph of him as a child in what was almost a dress and with long curls along the side of his head like the men in black hats and coats that you sometimes saw in New York. It made her realize that she couldn't be married to him, not with the people she knew. She was thinking of Brice Lambert and also, though she was no longer part of it, of life in Virginia. But her own life went on, one week very much like another, one year following another, and you began to lose track.

Then one morning a bad thing happened. She woke unable to move her arm or her leg, and when she tried to use the phone her words had lost their shape. She couldn't make them sound right, they filled her mouth and came out deformed. She'd had a stroke, they told her at the hospital. It would be a long, slow process to recover. Ten days later she boarded a plane in a wheelchair and flew to her father's house near Cambridge, Maryland, on the Eastern Shore. Beverly had arranged it and taken her to the airport and settled her aboard, but having three children prevented her from doing more, and now Vivian would have to help.

The house was actually in Cornersville on a quiet road, a beautiful, half-derelict old brick house dating almost from Civil War days that Warren Wain, Caroline's father, had bought to restore and spend his retirement in, but the restoration had proved to be more than he could handle, even with the help of his son, Cook, Vivian's uncle. Warren Wain had been an architect in Cleveland, well regarded, and though some of his essential quality and good looks had come down to his daughter, less had come down to his son, who had also studied architecture but never gotten a license. For a long time he had worked in his father's office and his father in essence had supported him. He had few friends and had never married. He had gone with a divorced woman for four or five years and finally asked her to marry him. He did it by commenting that maybe they should get married.

"No, I don't think so," she said calmly.

"I thought you wanted to get married. Now I'm asking you."

"Is that what it was?"

"Yes."

"I don't think so," she said. "Anyway it wouldn't work out."

"It's worked so far."

"That's probably because we haven't been married."

"Just what in hell do you want?" he asked. "Do you know?"

She didn't answer.

The house was in sad disrepair. Bricks were piled at one

side of it and the walkway to the front door was only half-finished, part brick and the rest dirt. Inside there was unpainted drywall that had been put up to replace the old plaster. Panes in the small windows to the cellar were broken and Vivian could see a pile of empty bottles in there. They were Cook's, she found out. There were also, not yet known to her, many checks that had been made out to the liquor store in Cambridge and others to "Cash" on which Cook had signed his father's name. The old man knew about them but hadn't confronted his son. His arthritis was painful and now, with his daughter there invalided and unable to take care of herself, the tasks of daily life were almost more than he could handle. But he loved the country. They were near a large open field where you could see the weather, the sun rippling and sometimes the wind. On an inlet nearby he had seen a white goose that lived with the ducks there. Whenever a plane passed overhead, the goose looked up, watching and talking as he did. He watched it all across the sky.

Vivian was sleeping in the unfinished room that was intended to have been her grandfather's study. She stayed for two weeks the first time, cooking, taking her mother to doctor's appointments and once a week to the hairdresser to cheer her up. She was attentive and sympathetic to her mother but she was her father's child. Her father had taught her to ride and hunt and play tennis. She had taken to all that more than Beverly had, and in all likelihood loved her father more, too. He was a man who represented so many things, a little stubborn perhaps but beyond that all you could wish for.

Caroline, though she was unable now to do much more than mumble, rolled her eyes whenever Vivian mentioned

Cook. That was one of the clearer signs of what she was feeling. There was an inane smile on her face and a mouth full of struggling sounds, but her eyes had an expression of knowing, knowing and understanding. Tick, the black labrador that was Warren Wain's, lay peacefully at her feet, knocking the floor with his thick tail when someone would approach. Like the rest of the household he had seen better days. He moved a little stiffly and his muzzle had flecks of white but he had a good nature. Cook, not bothering to shave and wearing a shapeless sweater, took him for walks.

"How are they getting along?" Bowman asked when Vivian came back to New York.

"Cook is spending all the money and the house is a wreck," Vivian said.

"How's your mother?"

"Not very good. I don't think she's going to be able to stay there for long. They can't take care of her. You have to help her dress and other things, well, you know. I'll have to go back down there."

"Should she be in some kind of home?"

"I don't like the idea, but she'll probably have to be."

"Can Beverly help? She's a lot closer."

"Beverly is having some trouble herself."

"What is it? Her children? Bryan?"

Vivian shrugged.

"With the bottle," she said. "It runs in the family."

When she left for Maryland again, it was with the understanding that she might have to stay a few weeks longer, and when she arrived in Cornersville things seemed to be worse, for reasons that she soon understood. The bank account was overdrawn, and the old man had to do something. In his slippers and bathrobe at the breakfast table while Vivian was doing the dishes, he finally said,

"Cook, listen, I need to talk to you."

"Yes?"

"I have to say this, but have you been signing my name to anything?"

"Signing your name? No. What for? I signed it a couple of times," he said.

"Only a couple of times?"

"Twice. Two or three times is all." He was becoming uneasy. "When you were too busy on account of Caroline to do it."

"To do what?"

"Go to the bank," Cook said.

Wain sat quietly.

"You know, when I was in France, during the war . . ."

He could hardly remember the war, sitting in the unfinished house across from his failed son. He could hardly construct how he had gotten from there to here. Cook's face was bored and defensive.

"In the winter when it was cold," the old man said, "we'd pour a big circle of gasoline on the ground and light it and then jump in to warm ourselves before we flew. They said, what are you doing that for, aren't you afraid of getting burned? We'd probably be dead in an hour anyway, so what difference did it make?"

He'd been an observer in the flying corps and had some photographs of himself in uniform. He realized he'd gotten away from the point.

"I don't understand," Cook said.

"What don't you understand?"

"The point of it."

"The point is, I'll be dead and the bank account will be empty. There'll be nothing left. The house will fall down around you and you'll have Caroline to take care of, and that'll be the end."

"It was only a few checks. Just saving you some trouble."

"I wish you knew how to," Wain said.

The week after arriving, Vivian, sitting at her grandfather's dark desk against the wall in the unfinished study, wrote a letter. *Dear Philip,* it began.

She always wrote *Dearest Philip.* Was this an unintentional lapse or was it something more? Bowman felt a kind of fore-boding, a chill going through him as he read the strangely unfamiliar words. No one could possibly know what had happened in London. That was in another world, another completely. Nervously he read on. *Caro is about the same. It's very hard for her to talk and I feel like she gets tired of trying to make herself understood and she gives up, but you can tell things from her expression. It's mainly me who takes her out, me and grand-dad. Apart from that we watch tv or she sits in the kitchen with me a lot. Nothing much gets done on the house. Cook is really useless. He's in town doing what, I don't know, or back in the shed. But that's not why I'm writing.*

Bowman turned the page over. He was reading quickly, apprehensive.

I'm not sure how to put it or why it is, but for a while now

I've had the feeling that we've each been going our own way without a lot in common. I'm not talking about a particular thing (?)

Here, his eye skipped ahead. The question mark frightened him, he didn't know what it meant, but there was nothing. *I guess I can't blame you. And I don't blame myself. Probably it's always been this way, but in the beginning I didn't realize it. I really don't belong in your world and I don't think you belong in mine. I feel like probably I should be back where I fit in.*

The words unaccountably went through him like something fatal. It was a letter of parting. Two nights before she'd left they'd made love with a pillow doubled beneath her like an innocent naked child with a stomachache, and he felt her become engaged in a way that had never happened before, perhaps because of how they were going about it or perhaps they were entering another level of intimacy, but now he saw with a sudden and poignant regret that he'd been wrong, she had been responding to something else, something known to her alone.

Daddy would probably have a fit if he heard me saying this, but I don't want anything, any alimony. I don't want you supporting me for the rest of my life. We haven't been married for that long. If you could give me three thousand dollars to help me temporarily, that would be fine. Be honest, I'm not wrong, am I? We really weren't meant for each other. Maybe I'll find the right man, maybe you'll find the right woman, at least someone more suited to you.

Her daddy. Bowman had never had a strong masculine figure in his own life to teach him how to be a man, and he had been drawn to his father-in-law despite himself and the real distance between them. There was no connection—he had no idea what his father-in-law thought or would do. He remembered him sitting with almost criminal ease, buttering a piece of toast and drinking coffee at breakfast the morning after the big snowstorm in Virginia when they all slept over. He remembered it clearly afterwards.

The day after having written the letter, Vivian happened to see her uncle Cook coming along the side of the house pushing a wheelbarrow with something heaped in it, and then with a shock she saw a foreleg hanging over the rim. She hurried out as Cook set the wheelbarrow down by the front door.

"What happened? Is he hurt?" she asked anxiously.

"I found him out by the shed," Cook said.

The dog's eyes were closed. She took its paw.

"Is he dead?"

"I think so."

"You'd better call the vet. You'd better tell grand-dad," Vivian said.

Cook nodded.

"He was just lying there," he said.

Her grandfather came out to see. He was wearing an old straw hat, like a country lawyer. They could hear Caroline calling out something slurred. Wain stroked the dog's foot and then slowly, as if thinking of something else, began to gently smooth its fine black coat.

"Should we call Dr. Carter?" Vivian asked.

"No. No," Wain said. "No use calling him."

Tears were running down his face. He seemed ashamed of them. Dr. Carter was the bow-legged vet who couldn't see out of his left eye—he'd been hit on the head one time. He'd hold up a hand, "For instance, I can't see my hand," he would say.

Cook was standing silent and, to his father it seemed, emotionless. Wain was remembering what Cook had been like as a boy, mischievous but companionable, and what had gradually happened to him. He had a vision of what was to come, Cook, sullen and still handsome coming down the stairs to face foreclosure, naked legs first, wearing his gray paisley dressing gown, his silver hair uncombed. Tired and looking as if he had a headache, having spent it all.

"Well, what is it you want?" he would say.

Without any idea of what he would do, and Caroline slumped in her wheelchair, past trying to make herself understood.

11. INTERIM

It was bitter at first, being alone, being left. The pillow slip became dirty, he swept up himself. He felt angry but at the same time realized she had been right. They had been living a life of appearances and essentially she had had nothing to do, which included maintaining the apartment. The towels were usually damp, the bedding hastily pulled up, the windowsills had dirt on them. They had quarreled about it. Why didn't she clean up a little? he asked conversationally.

She disdained to answer.

"Vivian, why don't you spend a little time cleaning up the place?"

"It's not my ambition."

Her use of the word, whatever that meant, annoyed him.

"Your ambition. What do you mean, ambition?"

"It's not my aim in life," she said.

"I see. Just what is your aim in life?"

"I'm not saying," she said.

"And what is mine?"

"I don't know," she said dismissively.

He was enraged. He could have broken the table with one blow.

"Damn it! What do you mean you don't know?"

"I mean I don't know," she said.

It was useless trying to talk. He could barely bring himself to lie in bed beside her, the sense of alienation was so strong. It seemed she was radiating it. He was nearly shaking, he couldn't sleep. Finally he'd taken his pillow and gone to sleep on the couch.

Now there was no longer the presence, even unseen, of another or the awareness of someone else's moods or habits. The rooms were silent. There was only the framed photograph of her in the bedroom with its faintly Asiatic eyes, the slightly upturned nose and bowed upper lip. At night he sat reading, near his elbow a glass with ice and the amber of whiskey and its subtle aroma. Things she had said remained embedded in his memory, he knew they would not be soon covered over.

"I gave you your chance," she had told him.

She would say nothing more. His chance, was that what it had been?

"Vivian and I have split up."

"Ah," Eddins said. "Sorry to hear it. When did that happen?"

"A week ago."

"I'm really sorry. Is it permanent?"

"I think so."

"Ah, God. We looked at you as the gilded couple, polo, private income . . ."

"There was no private income. Her father is, among other things, very tight-fisted. I can't even recall if he gave us a wedding present."

"It's terrible. What are you going to do? Why don't you come up to Piermont and stay with us for a while? It's a working-class place but very nice. There're a couple of restaurants and some bars. There's a movie house in Nyack. From the kitchen table, well, in this case the dining table, you can look out at the river."

"You make it sound very appealing."

For a moment he was almost tempted, the casual and idyllic life, the old house uphill from town. He could imagine the rhythms, driving in in the brightness of morning and back out at night, sometimes late, the traffic having thinned, the clear night above the trees.

"I'll be all right," he said.

"You say that offhandedly but, remember, the door's really open to you. We'll even make a place in bed."

They sat silent for a few moments.

"I remember your wedding," Eddins said. "The drive through the beautiful country. The fine house. Whatever happened to the judge who liked full-chested women?"

"I haven't seen the judge for a while," Bowman said.

Vivian, however, happened to see the judge soon after her return, although "happened" is inexact. Judge Stump had heard the news and extended his sympathies. He invited her, not without some nervousness although he could always explain himself as being a family friend, almost an uncle, to lunch at the Red Fox. He was in a fine gray suit with his hair perfectly cut and groomed. After some polite but, as always with him, jagged conversation, he shared some news he thought she might be interested in. He was buying the Hollis house, the big one, not the nearby farmhouse, on Zulla Road.

He said this looking at the tablecloth, then glancing at Vivian.

"I hate that house," she said. "I'd hate to live in it."

"Ah," the wounded judge said.

"Has nothing to do with you," said Vivian. "It's just that I've never liked that house."

"Ah. I didn't know that."

She spoke her mind, he knew. To some extent, that suited him. She was the most desirable woman he had ever seen. They did not often have the chance to talk, really talk. Gathering his courage, the judge said,

"Well, there are other houses . . ."

For a moment she was uncertain of what he was saying.

"Judge . . ."

"John," he said.

"Are you . . . ?" she began with a smile.

He was not the sort of man to smile disarmingly. He did not smile when pronouncing a sentence or stating a fee, and he wanted, in this case, to clearly show how serious he was, but nevertheless he softened his expression slightly.

"I've already gone through one bad marriage," Vivian said.

The judge had gone through three, though he considered himself blameless.

"Why don't you think about Jean Clevinger?" Vivian suggested lightly not knowing that Mrs. Clevinger, rich and very lively, had almost from their first meeting rejected the judge out of hand.

"No, no," he protested, "Jean . . . we don't have anything in common. We don't share the really important, the deep things."

Vivian didn't want to hear or even guess what they were.

"I think you and I should just remain friendly," she said rather boldly.

The judge was far from discouraged by this. He felt satisfied, he had made progress. He could be patient for a bit, now that he had at least made it known. As they rose to leave, he more or less indicated the table and their lunch and suggested,

"Between us, hm? Between us."

Bowman told his mother the news. He hadn't wanted to face her disappointment or questions, but it was inevitable. He'd gone home for the weekend, he couldn't tell her on the phone.

"Vivian and I have separated," he said.

He felt a twinge of shame, despite himself, as if admitting a failure.

"Oh, my," Beatrice said.

"Actually, it was her idea."

"I see. Did she give a reason? What was wrong?"

"I really don't know the reason. We were just not right for one another."

"She'll come back," Beatrice prophesied.

"I don't think so."

There was a silence.

"Is that everything?" his mother asked.

"Everything? I don't know if it's everything. Do you mean, is there another man? No. Her mother had a stroke though I'm not sure that has much to do with it. A little, maybe."

"A stroke? She died?"

"No, she's in Maryland with her father. Vivian's helping take care of her."

"Well, I'm truly sorry," his mother said, referring to what, he didn't know.

She was not really sorry, she felt an unworthy joy.

"I hardly knew Vivian," she said with a tone of regret. "She never let me get close to her. Was it my fault, I wonder? Perhaps I should have tried harder."

"I don't know," he confessed.

He was taking it stoically, Beatrice thought, which might have meant indifference. It would be wonderful if that were the case.

"People deceive you," she said softly.

"Yes."

There were things she didn't know, of course, the letters with their red-and-blue-dashed envelope edges, letters from London, *I spend hours trying to stop thinking about you.* That particular, thrilling letter was still in his pocket. He kept it there so that he could take it out and read it again from time to time, on the street, if he liked, or at his desk.

"Why does mail from Europe take so long?" he asked an old agent at lunch. "The planes fly across in a matter of hours."

"It didn't take that long before the war," the agent said. "A letter took four days, maybe five. You took it down to the ship before it sailed and it was in London, delivered, five days later. With airplanes, we've only lost a day," he said.

The sun was finally shining in London, she wrote. She was really like a lizard, she longed to lie beside a pool with the sun on her or be a frog on a lily pad, not a big frog, just a slim green one able to swim well. She was a good swimmer, he knew—she had told him that.

She wrote lying in bed, having said no to invitations, *I miss you enormously.* To her, he wrote, *I think of you fourteen times a day. I think only, when can I have you again? There is that half hour of waking every morning when I lie silent, bathed in thoughts of you. I can feel your eyes opening, finding me.* He did not know her well enough to express the crude desire he really felt, he longed to but was not yet sure of himself. I love your body, he wanted to write, I'd like to take your clothes off quickly like unwrapping, tearing the paper from a marvelous gift. I'm thinking of you, day-dreaming, imagining. How beautiful you are. My utter darling.

In the end, he wrote these things. He was under the spell of her profile, her brilliant smile, her nakedness, and the wonderful clothes she wore in a privileged, distant world.

You have made me completely alive, she replied.

That summer he heard that Caroline had died, his mother-in-law, former. He had liked her, the inborn aplomb she had when drunk, which was often. Her voice slurred a little but she rode over it as if it were a fleck of tobacco on her tongue, as if she could pause and wipe it away with a finger. She had coughed and then fallen, first into silence and then to the floor, where Vivian had found her, but she was dead either then or by the time the ambulance came. Bowman sent a large order of flowers, lilies and yellow roses, which he remembered her liking, but he never had a response, not even a brief note from Vivian.

12. ESPAÑA

In October they went to Spain. She had been there before, not with her husband but before she was married, with friends. The English loved Spain. Like all northern peoples they loved southern France and Italy, lands of the sun.

The sky of Madrid was a vast, pale blue. Unlike other great cities, Madrid had no river, the grand avenues with their trees were its river, the Calle de Alcalá, Paseo del Prado. On various corners the police stood with their black hats and dark faces. The country was waiting. Franco, the aging dictator, the victor in the savage civil war that preserved a Catholic, conservative Spain, was still in power though preparing for immortality and death. Not far from the city a monumental tomb was being carved into a granite hillside, the Valley of the Fallen. Hundreds of men, prison laborers, were working to complete the sacred place where the great leader of the Falange would lie for eternity beneath a cross forty stories high, visited by tourists, priests, ambassadors, and until the last of them were gone, the brave men who had fought alongside him. Spain had bright skies but was shadowed. In a bookshop Bowman managed to persuade the cautious owner to sell him a copy of Lorca's *Romancero Gitano,* which was banned. He read some of it to Enid, who was unimpressed. The Prado was dark, as if it had been neglected or even abandoned, the masterpieces were hard to see. They ate at a restaurant that bullfighters favored, near the arena, also in others filled with noise and open late, and drank afterwards in the Ritz bar where the barman seemed to recognize Enid though she had never stayed there.

They went to Toledo for a day and then on to Seville, where summer lingered and the voice of the city, as the poet said, brought tears. They walked through walled alleyways, she in high heels, bare-shouldered, and sat in the silent darkness as deep chords of a guitar slowly began and the air itself stilled. Chord after ominous chord, the guitarist immobile and grave until a woman in a chair beside him, till then unseen, raised her arms and with a sound like gunshots began to clap her hands and then cry out in a wild voice a single word, *Dalé!* Over and over she cried, *Dalé, dalé!* urging on the guitar. Slowly at first she began to chant or intone—she was not singing, she was reciting what had always been known, reciting and repeating, the guitar like drums hypnotic and endless, it was the gypsy *siguiriya*, she sang as if surrendering her life, as if calling to death. She was from Utrera, she cried, the place Perrate was from, the place Bernarda and Fernanda . . .

Her hands were up near her face, clapping sharply and rhythmically, her voice was anguished, she was singing in blindness, her eyes closed, her bare arms, silver loops in her ears and long dark hair. The song was her song but it belonged to the Vega, the wide plain with its sun-dark workers and shimmering heat, she was pouring out life's despair, bitterness, crimes, her clapping fierce and relentless, a place called Utrera, the house in which it had happened, the lover left for dead, and a man in black pants and long hair suddenly came from the darkness, his steel-tipped heels exploding on the wood floor and his arms hung above his head. The woman was singing with even greater intensity amid the relentless chords, the savage, tight beat of the heels, the silver, the black, the man's lean body bent like an S, the dogs trotting in darkness near the houses, the water running, the sound of the trees.

They sat afterwards in a bar open to the narrow street, barely speaking.

"What did you think?" he said.

She replied only, "My God."

Afterwards in the room he began to kiss her wildly, her lips, her neck. He slipped the dress straps from her shoulders. You could never have anyone like this. His old, fettered life was behind him, it had been transformed as if by some revelation. They made love as if it were a violent crime, he was holding her by the waist, half woman, half vase, adding weight to the act. She was crying in agony, like a dog near death. They collapsed as if stricken.

He woke as the light was hitting the frail lace curtains. The bath restored him. She was still sleeping, not even breathing, it seemed. He looked at her in wonder. As he stood there, her hand came slowly out from the sheets and touched against him, then pushed the towel aside and closed gently around his cock. She lay gazing without a word. It had begun to swell. A small, transparent drop fell to her skin and she raised her wrist and licked it.

"I married the wrong man," she said.

She lay face down and he knelt between her legs for what seemed a long time, then began to arrange them a little, unhurriedly, like setting up a tripod. In the early light she was without a flaw, her beautiful back, her hips' roundness. She felt him slowly enter, she reached beneath, it was there, becoming part of her. The slow, profound rhythm began, hardly varying but as time passed somehow more and more intense. Outside, the street was completely silent, in adjoining rooms people were asleep. She began to cry out. He was trying to slow himself, to prevent it and make it go on, but she was trembling like a tree about to fall, her cries were leaking beneath the door.

They woke after nine with the sun full on one wall. She came back from the bathroom and got in bed again.

"Enid."

"Yes?"

"Can I ask you something practical?"

"What do you mean?"

"I haven't been using anything," he said.

"Well, if anything should happen . . . if anything should happen, I'd say it was his."

"When men are having affairs, do they still sleep with their wives?"

"I would think, yes, but not in this case. He hasn't as much as touched me for a year. More than a year. I suppose you can tell."

"That's disappointing. I thought it was me."

"It is you."

Outside, the sun was pouring down. In the great cathedral the remains of Columbus in an elaborate coffin were held aloft by statues of the four kings, of Aragon, Castile, León, and Navarre, and in the treasury there was still gold and silver that had come from the New World.

Seville was the city of Don Juan, Andalusia, the city of love.

Its poet was García Lorca, dark hair, dark brows, and a pointed face like a woman's. He was homosexual and an angel of the re-awakening of Spain in the 1920s and '30s, books and plays filled with a pure, fatal music, and poems rich in colors with fierce emotion and despairing love. He was born in a wealthy family, but his sympathies and love were for the poor, the men and women who worked all their lives in the burning fields. He grew to scorn the church that did little for them, a playwright and friend of the gypsies whose first love was music and who played the piano in his room upstairs in the house just outside town. His color was green and also silver, the color of water at night and of the immense fertile plains that it irrigated and made rich.

The fame of the poet, when it appears, is like no other, and this happened to Lorca. He was killed in 1936, at the very start of the civil war, arrested and executed by right-wing countrymen and buried in an unmarked grave he was made to dig for himself. His offense was everything he had written and stood for. The destruction of the finest is natural, it confirms them. And for death, as Lorca said, there is no consolation, which is one of the beauties of life.

Among the greatest of the poems was the dirge for the death of his friend, a bullfighter who had retired but then returned to the ring as an homage and tribute to his brother-in-law, the great Joselito. In a tight, embroidered suit, perhaps a bit too tight, he was performing in a provincial ring when a cry rose from the crowd. The sharp, curved horn of the bull had ripped like a knife through the fitted pants and the white flesh beneath.

Two days after being gored, *lily flowers around the green*

groin, Ignacio Sánchez Mejias died in a hospital in Madrid where he had insisted on being taken. In deep liturgical sounds like the tolling of bells, the famous lament begins. *A las cinco de la tarde,* at five in the afternoon. The heat is still staggering. The doomed man, still in a ripped suit, is lying in the small infirmary.

At five in the afternoon.

The lines repeat themselves and roll on. A boy is bringing a white sheet, at five in the afternoon. The bed is a coffin on wheels, at five in the afternoon. From far off the gangrene is coming, at five in the afternoon. His wounds are burning like suns, at five in the afternoon, and the crowd is breaking the windows.

You lived, said Lorca, by dying and being remembered. Mejias' death, in 1934, was like an apprenticeship for his own, prefigured but not yet known. The fierce storm that would tear the country apart was already gathering. The boy with the white sheet was coming, the bucket of quicklime was ready, and the smoothed-over dirt of the bull ring was already in shadows.

He read the *Lament for Ignacio Sánchez Mejias* aloud for the first time to a roomful of gypsies during Holy Week and slept that night in the huge white bed of a gypsy dancer, *the solitary rose of your breath on my cheek.*

They ate, that day, in a restaurant over a bar, with narrow stairs up which the waiters had to come with their trays. It was open to the air, there were no walls, only a roof of canvas. They were seated to one side, but to be with her was to be seen by everyone. The river, flowing slowly, was beneath them.

"What are *almejas?*"

"Where do you see that?"

"Here," he said. *"Almejas a la Casera."*

"No idea."

They ordered fried whitings, little fish, and potatoes. Even through the canvas there was the warmth of the sun. All the tables were filled, one with a party of Germans who were laughing.

"That's the Guadalquivir," Bowman said, pointing down.

"The river."

"I like names. You have a very nice name."

"The notorious Mrs. Armour."

"I also like putting my hands on you."

"Yes, I know."

"You do?"

"Mm."

They went on to Granada. The sunbaked country floated past the window of the train, through his own reflection. There were hills, valleys, thousands upon thousands of olive trees. Enid was sleeping. Perhaps from a dream or something unknown there was a faint, childlike snore, once only. She had never seemed more serene.

In the distance, on a small hill near a village, was a white house surrounded by trees, a house he might live in with her, the bedroom above the silent garden, cool and green, doors to the balcony that overlooked it, mornings of love with the sun slanted across the floor. She would bathe with the door left open and at night they would drive to a city—he had no idea which one, one not far, they were all magical—and then back later in the deep, starry night.

At the same time, he was unsure of her, you would have to be, especially when she had been silent or withdrawn. He felt he was the object of her thoughts then, or worse, not even a part of them. She sometimes glanced at him briefly as if judging. He knew not to show fear but she sometimes made him uneasy with her composure. There were times when she left to go on an errand, to the pharmacy or the consulate—she never bothered to explain why she'd gone to the consulate—and he suddenly felt with a certainty that in fact she was really leaving, that he would go back to the hotel and her bags would be gone, the clerk at the desk would know nothing. He would run in the street looking for her, the blondness of her hair in the crowd.

The truth is, with some women you are never sure. They had traveled for ten days and he felt he knew her, in the room he knew her, at least most of the time, and also sitting at the chestnut-colored bar of the hotel, but you could not know someone else all of the time, their thoughts, about which it was useless to ask. She did not so much as acknowledge the existence of the handsome bartender, so intent was she on whatever she was thinking at the time. The bartender was used to being admired and stood almost disconsolately waiting a few steps away. She hated the thought of going back to London, Enid then said.

"Me, too," Bowman said.

She was silent.

"Your husband," he continued.

"Oh, partly my husband. Well, more than partly. I don't want to leave here. Why don't you move to London?"

He hadn't expected it.

"Move to London," he said. "Are you going to get a divorce?"

"I'd love to. I can't at the moment."

"Why is that?"

"Oh, there are two or three reasons. Money is one of them. He won't give me any money."

"Couldn't you get it in court?"

"It's exhausting to think of. The battle. The courts."

"But you'd be free."

"Free and alone."

"You wouldn't be alone."

"Is that a promise?" she said.

They didn't return to London together. He took the plane to New York from Madrid. As it happened, there was no one in the seat next to him and he sat looking out the window for a while and then sitting back with a feeling of relaxation and deep happiness. Spain was falling away beneath them. She had taken him there. He would remember for a long time. The high, wide steps of the great hotel, the Alfonso XIII, up which, as ascending to an altar, bankers and Nationalist generals had walked. The dirt paths in the Retiro, the ranks of white statues.

On the flyleaf of the book of Lorca poems he carefully wrote the names of the hotels, the Reina Victoria, Dauro, del Cardenal, Simón. They had slept in a bed with four pillows, lost in the whiteness of them. The word for naked in Spanish was *desnudo*. It was the same in any language, she remarked.

He ordered a drink. The announcements were finished and there was only the low, steady sound of the engines. He saw himself sitting there as if from the outside somehow, but he was also thinking about himself. He could see himself, all of himself, from his hand holding the glass right down to his feet. How lucky he was. He could see the leg of another passenger, a man in first class, a gray-suited leg. He felt superior to the man, whoever he was, to everyone. You smell like soap, she had said. He'd had a bath. You washed all the man-smell away. It'll come back, he'd said. The suited leg made him think of New York, of the office. He thought of Gretchen with her stigma and how it somehow made her more desirable. He thought of the girl in Virginia that Christmas, Dare, who breathed a sexuality, she would be yours in a minute if you were the one . . . if you were the one. It had happened and he was, in Spain with a woman who had given him the feeling of utter supremacy. He had crossed some line. Her blond hair, her lean style. He saw himself now to be another kind of man, the kind he had hoped, fully a man, used to the wonder. Enid smoked cigarettes, she did it only now and again, and breathed out the rich fragrance slowly. The light in the Ritz made her beautiful. The sound of her high heels. There is no other, there will never be another.

Later in the fall he came back to the office after lunch. It was growing colder, the crowds in the street had wind-freshened faces. The sky was without color and the windows of buildings, as happened at ever earlier hours, were alight. The office seemed unusually quiet, had everyone gone out? It was eerily still. They were not gone, but they were listening to the news. A frightening thing had happened. The president had been shot in Dallas.

13. EDEN

In the small white house in Piermont, together with his wife and Leon, Eddins was living the life of a philosopher king. The house was still plainly furnished, two old wicker chairs with cushions were near the couch and there was a worn oriental rug. There were books, bamboo night tables in the bedroom, and a sense of harmony. They wanted for nothing. In the kitchen, which was also the dining room, was the table on which they ate and where Eddins often liked to sit reading with a cigarette burning in an amber holder and a feeling of the house around him, on his shoulders, as it were, his wife and Leon upstairs and sleeping and he, like Atlas, supporting it all.

Around the town they dressed casually, Eddins, as he said, in house-painter style, the locale seemed to call for it. He wore an overcoat, a scarf and suit jacket, sweatpants, and a fedora although he dressed up when he went into the city. He drove, usually alone, and always with a feeling of exhilaration when, crossing the George Washington Bridge, he saw the great skyline in the distance. At night, driving more freely and amid less traffic the farther he got from the city, he arrived home still humming a little with the energy of Manhattan.

For a long time they remained one of the new couples one always envies, a couple free of habit and familiarity, of history even, and at parties as they stood talking to people she would, unseen, hold his thumb. At night they would lie in bed listening to the stairs creak and watching television, hardly bothering to tell Leon to turn out his light. Night with the great river silent. Night with bits of rain. The entire house creaked in winter, and in the summer it felt like Bombay. Because of Leon, they could no longer sit, like William Blake and his wife, naked in the garden, but on the headboard of the bed she had printed a small sign that said *Umda,* a kind of Egyptian king or chief, and he wore only the bottoms of his pajamas.

In town and in the neighboring village, Grand View, they had made friends. At Sbordone's one night they met a somewhat doleful-looking painter named Stanley Palm who looked like Dante in the painting of him seeing Beatrice for the first time and lived in a cinderblock house on the river with a small studio to the side of it. He was separated from his wife, Marian. They had been married for twelve years and had a nine-year-old daughter named Erica. Erica Palm, Eddins thought to himself. He liked the sound of it. Erica and Leon. It was unusual but very modern, the parents of both of them had been divorced or at least had come undone. In Palm's case it was because his wife had gotten discouraged and given up on him: he was going nowhere. He had no gallery in New York, no reputation. He taught three days a week in the art department at City College, the rest of the time he worked in his studio on paintings that were sometimes all one color.

Palm didn't have much luck with women though he hadn't abandoned hope. Especially at bars he had no luck. In the city he stopped for a drink and to a woman who seemed to be by herself, ventured,

"Come alone?"

He could be sized up in a glance.

"No. My friend is getting me a drink," she said.

Palm saw no one and finally asked,

"Where are you from?"

"I'm from the moon," she said coolly.

"Ah. I'm from Saturn."

"You look it."

He'd been separated for more than a year. It was hard to understand things, he confessed to Eddins. There were painters doing very well who were not any better than he was. There were people for whom everything seemed easy. On impulse one night he called Marian.

"Hi, babe,"

"Stanley?"

"Yeah," he said somewhat threateningly, "it's Stanley."

"I didn't recognize your voice for a minute. You sound funny."

"Do I?"

"Have you been drinking?"

"No, I'm fine. What are you doing?" he asked more casually.

"What do you mean?"

"Why don't you come over here?"

"Come over there?"

He decided to go ahead with it, in the spirit of the times.

"I feel like fucking you," he said rather quickly.

"Oh, gosh," she said.

"No, I mean it."

She changed the subject, he'd clearly been drinking or listening to something.

"What have you been doing with yourself?" she asked.

"Nothing. I've been thinking about us. Why don't you be nice about it?"

"I have been nice."

"I'm feeling really lonely."

"It's not loneliness."

"What would you call it?"

"I can't come over."

"Why not? Why not be a good-hearted woman?"

"I have been. Lots of times."

"That's not helping me now," he said.

"You'll get over it."

She talked to him a while longer. At the end she asked if he felt any better.

"No," he said.

Then one day at the Village Hall, where he'd gone with some announcements of a show he was part of, there was a dark-haired girl in a tight sweater who seemed friendly. Her name was Judy, she was younger but they talked for a while and she was impressed that he was a painter. She had never met a painter before, she said. She gave him a ride back towards Piermont and along the way, as if in a trance, he reached over and slipped a hand inside her leather jacket, like a rock star, as she drove. She said nothing and became his girlfriend. Soon he told her about an idea he had which was to open a restaurant, the kind that was in New York that painters and musicians went to. It would be Italian and he had a name for it, Sironi's, after a painter he admired.

"Sironi's."

"Yeah."

Judy was enthusiastic. She would help with everything, she said, and be a partner. Palm saw a dream coming true, the kind of dream that seldom dies. Sironi's would be in town somewhere, although there was also a possible location up on 9W. Judy was in favor of town, she didn't like the idea of being away from everything, particularly late at night.

"Why do you want to be up there?" she said.

"Well, there's an old place for rent there right next to a curve. Marian didn't like the idea, either."

"What does Marian have to do with it?" Judy said.

Stanley had known they were not going to get along and had even been uneasy about Judy spending nights with him. He had her park a little down the road.

"What's wrong? You afraid someone will see me?"

"It's not that. It's Erica," he said.

"Doesn't Marian know you have a girlfriend? And what business is it of hers, anyway?"

"Marian doesn't have anything to do with it, and it doesn't matter what she thinks. I don't give a damn what she thinks."

"Yes, you do," Judy said.

Stanley was bothered by this. He did talk to his wife a lot, she sometimes called when Judy was there. It was plain who he was talking to. But he was an artist, he felt he should not be constrained by bourgeois mentality or behavior. He asked Marian to write a letter saying that he was free to see anyone he liked and to make love to anyone he liked though she declined to say in any place he liked and in any way he liked.

Judy read the letter and began to cry.

"What is it?"

"Oh, God!"

"What?"

"You have to get her permission!"

The colored sketches Stanley had made of the front and also the bar area of Sironi's notwithstanding, an unrelated event stopped everything. The mayor, who had been in office for years, a man with a family and many relatives in town, had been having an affair with a cashier who worked at the Tappan Zee Bank, and they were sexually engaged one night in his car when a diligent policeman shined a light in the window. The cashier claimed rape but then regained her poise, and the mayor sought to explain it to the policeman, who, unfortunately, was the chief of police. The mayor's attempts to keep him from entering it on the blotter were of no avail, and the result was a state of hostility that divided the town into two camps with the mayor's wife on the police side, and a state of administrative paralysis. Sironi's permits were indefinitely stalled.

In the city one day Eddins had lunch at the Century Club, in the distinguished surroundings of portraits and books, with a successful literary agent named Charles Delovet, who was well-dressed and walked with a slight limp said to be from a ski accident. One of his shoes had a thick heel though it was not obvious. Delovet was a man of style and attractive to women. He had some major clients, Noël Coward, it was rumored, and also a yacht in Westport on which he gave parties in the summer. In his office he had a ceramic ashtray from the *Folies Bergère* with a dancer's long legs in relief and, imprinted around the rim: *Plaire aux femmes, ça coûte cher*—women are expensive. He'd been an editor at one time and he liked writers, loved them, in fact. He rarely met a writer he didn't like or who didn't have some quality he liked. But there were a few. He hated plagiarists.

"Penelope Gilliatt. Kosinski," he said, "what a phony."

When he was an editor, he remarked, he bought books. As an agent, he was selling them. It was much easier than deciding whether or not to buy something, and the best part was that once you sold a book, your responsibilities were over. The publisher took on all that, and if the book did well, so did you. If it didn't, there were always more manuscripts out there. You also had the opportunity, he said, to see a writer grow and advance, there was a relationship.

One of Delovet's innovations had been to advertise that any and all submissions would be read. He charged a fee. A group of readers were kept busy reading and then writing rejections. *Not quite strong enough in the narrative sense . . . With more character delineation this might find a publisher . . . We were genuinely excited reading parts of this . . . Not quite our cup of tea . . . Fuck your cup of tea!* one furious writer had written back.

Another idea had been to auction books rather than submit them, as was customary, to one publisher at a time and wait for a response. The publishers at first refused to participate but then slowly broke ranks and were willing to bid against one another if the book was promising enough or the author had a big-enough name.

At lunch that day, the conversation was amiable and expansive. It was the whiff of money that came off Delovet, the double-breasted suit and silk tie that looked as if it had never seen a knot before. Eddins found himself attracted.

"Tell me, Neil, what are you making? What salary?"

Ah! thought Eddins. He added a couple of thousand to the figure and gave it unhesitatingly. Delovet made a gesture almost of dispensing with it, at least as a consideration. Not what it could be, he indicated.

"Should I consider this a job offer?" Eddins asked.

"Absolutely," Delovet said.

There and then they settled on a new salary.

Robert Baum knew that editors were always liable to accept a better salary or higher position. He relied on the reputation of the firm to make up some of the difference. He knew Delovet from experience and also rumors that some of the writers he represented never received royalties they had earned, especially foreign royalties that were hard to trace. He described Delovet succinctly,

"He's a crook."

Eddins got a haircut and bought a new trenchcoat for the fall at the British American House. He foresaw a life that suited him. At first, he was occupied largely in picking up loose ends, working with clients of lesser importance, including a couple of southern writers, one of whom had started out as a preacher in Missouri and had, Eddins felt, a natural gift.

It was all done by mail. Eddins typed or had the secretary

do it, letters to them telling them where a story had been rejected with perhaps an encouraging word from an editor. They might try *Harper's* now, or *The Atlantic,* he would say. He tried to give consolation. He was fond of writers, certain types of them, alcoholics particularly and men who had the same idiom as himself. The ex-preacher had written a story that could make you cry about a raw-boned wife on a farm and a blind sow, but nobody seemed to want it. Flannery O'Connor had used up all the possibilities for southern stories, the writer said bitterly.

Eddins had sympathy for them. He could almost hear their drawling voices. They had RFD addresses. The one who was not the ex-preacher lived far out in the country with his aging father. Eddins felt that he was disappointing them. You ought to do what was expected of you, that was the code. If at the age of five you were expected to go out in the fields and work, you did it and likely were the better for it. If you were called on to serve your country, you went and didn't make much of it afterwards, like his father or the men before him who, after the surrender, walked hundreds of miles home to try and pick up their lives again.

It got to the point where one day he suggested to Delovet that they might advance some money to the two writers as publishers sometimes did, even putting them on a monthly stipend, but the idea wasn't even acknowledged. The yacht in Westport was without an engine, it turned out, but Eddins didn't know this until much later. Meanwhile he was learning the details and more of being an agent. Dena came into the city to look around, as she said, and have dinner, and once or twice the three of them stayed for the weekend at a slightly run-down, big hotel near the bottom of Fifth Avenue.

New Year's Eve was celebrated in Piermont, at Sbordone's with Stanley and his girlfriend. The waitress had bad legs and was so tired by the end of the evening that she sat down with them. On New Year's morning, which was silent and bright, Eddins woke early in the comfort of his own bed. Dena was soft in sleep, her face seemed as peaceful and pure as he had ever seen it. He felt ragged but fresh, filled with desire. Moving the covers down a bit, he stroked her into half-awakedness, his hand in the small of her back and venturing further. He felt her confirming touch. They could hear their son downstairs and were careful to make no sound as they welcomed the new dawn. Afterwards they lay half-asleep again in each other's arms. The New Year. 1969.

14. MORAVIN

An old writer, William Swangren, still respected for an early book or two, had submitted a novel they were going to have to turn down, a kind of American *Death in Venice*, done elegantly enough but past its time, and Bowman, to break the news, had invited the old man to lunch. He couldn't come to lunch, Swangren explained, it would be more convenient if they met at his apartment. A little put off by the grandness, Bowman nevertheless agreed.

The building, of white, institutional brick, lost among others off Second Avenue, was not what he expected. There was a small lobby and an elevator operated by an ununiformed doorman. Swangren, in a checked shirt and bow tie, came to the door. It was a small, even cramped apartment with a view only of other buildings across from it. The furnishings were of no particular style, there was a couch that could be converted into a bed, bookcases, a bedroom with the door closed—Swangren had a companion named Harold he had long lived with—and near the kitchen a large framed print, it was ice blue, of a naked youth, his sex lolling between his legs. On the drinks table beneath it, Swangren prepared iced tea for them, talking as he did, a handsome figure still with his hair a faded white—the fate of blonds—and tobacco stain at the corners of his mouth. His talk was anecdote and gossip, as if he had known you forever—he had known everyone, Somerset Maugham, John Marquand, Greta Garbo. He'd lived for years in Europe, France mainly, and knew the Rothschilds.

They sat and talked freely and with pleasure. Swangren clearly liked company. He talked about scandals in the American Academy, questionable members, and the quarrels of poets. Also homosexuality in the ancient world, the intercrural pleasures of the Greeks, and his own experiences with gonorrhea. It took eighteen months to cure with a French doctor putting a tube up him every day and painting the lesions with Argyrol.

They talked and drank tea. Bowman waited for the right time to bring up the matter of the novel, but Swangren was talking about the night Thornton Wilder had invited him to dinner in his hotel room.

"Somewhat frightened by my famous homosexuality," Swangren said. "There was a bottle of bourbon and a bucket of ice in front of each of us, we were supposed to be discussing Proust, but I have no memory of what was said. I only remember that we drank too much, and that I was so excited and exhausted that I had to say I was going home to bed. Wilder stayed up until dawn, going from bar to bar, talking to anyone he could. He was very shy, but in a strange city he did it to find out what interested ordinary people. He had little family. He had a brother. His sister was in a madhouse."

Swangren had been born on a farm in eastern Ohio and had a farmer's broad hands. In the Alleghenies, he said, they often had coal beneath their land, and after working all day, the farmers would go down to mine a little coal. As they dug underground they would leave staggered columns of coal, pillars, to support the roof, and when the vein finally ran out, they would retreat, mining the pillars as they went. Pulling pillars, they called it.

That was what he was doing at this stage, he said. Pulling pillars.

In the end, Bowman liked him so much that he changed his mind about the book. They took it. Unfortunately, it sold few copies.

Everything, during this time, was overshadowed by the war in Vietnam. The passions of the many against the war, especially the youth, were inflamed. There were the endless lists of the dead, the visible brutality, the many promises of victory that were never kept until the war seemed like some dissolute son who cannot ever be trusted or change but must always be taken in.

At the same time, as if in some way meant to heal, came a wave of new art, like a sudden, unexpected tide flooding in. Part of it was painting, but there were also the European films with their freshness and candor. They seemed to offer a humanity that was otherwise at risk. Bowman had refused to march in uniform in a big demonstration against the war because of a confused sense of honor, but he was adamantly opposed to the war, what thinking person would not be?

His life, meanwhile, was like a diplomat's. He had status, respect, and limited means. His work was with individuals, some greatly gifted, some also unforgettable, Auden in his carpet slippers arriving early and drinking five or six martinis and then a bottle of Bordeaux, his wrinkled face wreathed in cigarette smoke; Marisa Nello, more a mistress to poets than a poet herself coming up the stairs reciting Baudelaire in atrocious French. It was a life superior to its tasks, with a view of history, architecture, and human behavior, including incandescent afternoons in Spain, the shutters closed, a blade of sun burning into the darkness.

He had moved to an apartment on Sixty-Fifth Street, not far from the vine-covered mansion where he had waited to talk to Kindrigen long ago. He had a cleaning woman who came three times a week and also shopped for him, the list was on a small blackboard in the kitchen together with special things she might do. He had his dinner in the apartment only occasionally, she sometimes prepared it and left it in the oven. Usually he was out for dinner, either at a restaurant or private party. He might be at the movies or the theater. He sometimes went to the theater on impulse without a ticket. In a suit and tie he stood outside with a sign printed on a shirt cardboard that read Needed, single ticket, and rarely failed to get one. At the opera he liked *Aida* and *Turandot* best, sitting in the darkness of white faces, given over completely to the great arias and a feeling of certainty in the world.

Sometimes there were publishing parties, the young women who longed to make a life of it in their black dresses and glowing faces, girls who lived in small apartments with clothes piled near the bed and the photos from the summer curling.

He loved his work. The life was unhurried but defined. In the summer the week was shortened, everyone left at noon on Friday and in some cases did not come back until noon

on Monday having gone to houses in Connecticut or Wainscott, old houses that, had you been lucky, you could have
bought ten years earlier for a song. He particularly admired
a house that belonged to another editor, Aaron Asher, a farmhouse almost hidden by trees. There were other houses that
always brought images of an orderly life, kitchens with plain
sideboards, old windows, the comforts of marriage in their
common form, which at times surpassed everything—breakfast
in the morning, conversations, late hours, and nothing that
suggested excess or decay.

In life you need friends and a good place to live. He had
friends, both in and out of publishing. He knew people and
was known by them. Malcolm Pearson, his former roommate, came to the city with his wife, Anthea, and often their
daughter to go to the museums or visit a gallery whose owner
he knew. Malcolm had become older. He disapproved of
things, he walked with a cane. Am I becoming old, Bowman
wondered? It was something he rarely thought about. He had
never been particularly young, or to put it another way, he
had been young for a long time and now was at his true age,
old enough for civilized comforts and not too old for the
primal ones.

He was turned to for advice, even for solace. A woman
editor that he liked, a woman with a knowing face who had
the ability to sense meaning in an instant, had been having
problems with her son. At thirty, he was mentally precarious
and had never been able to find himself. At one point he had
turned to God and become devout. He had gone on a pilgrim-
age to Jerusalem and read the Bible all day. His passion, he
confessed to his mother, "was for the absolute." It frightened

her, of course. As sometimes with tormented souls, he was very kind and gentle. His father had rejected him.

There was only so much, in fact little, that Bowman could do other than listen and try to comfort her. Therapists had already failed. Still, somehow he was a help.

He was regarded as a man who had not yet started a family but was in the perfect position to do so. He seemed young for his age, forty-five. He had no gray in his hair. He seemed on good terms with life. He was regarded also as the somewhat mysterious figure who had the power to perform an almost magical transformation, to turn one into an author. He could bestow that, it was thought. She loved to read, the blond woman seated next to him confessed. It was at a dinner party for twelve in a large apartment filled with art, a grand piano, and two main rooms that seemed to serve one another, one with comfortable chairs for drinks and the other with a large dinner table, a buffet, a couch in one corner, and windows that looked out over the park.

She loved to read, she said, but the only thing was she never remembered what she'd read—*Dona Flor and Her Two Husbands,* that was the only title she could think of just then.

"Yes," Bowman said.

He had just taken another bite when,

"What kind of books do you publish?" she asked.

"Fiction and nonfiction," he said simply.

She looked at him for a moment in wonder, as if he had said a marvelous thing.

"Tell me your name again."

"Philip Bowman."

She was silent. Then she said,

"That's my husband," indicating a man across the table.

He was a lawyer, Bowman had already been told.

"Do you want to hear a story?" she asked. "We were staying at a friend's house on Cape Cod and this guy, an architect, was there. Very nice guy. He was supposed to have a date, but she never showed up. He'd just been divorced. He'd been married to an actress and it only lasted a year. It was very painful for him. Are you married?" she asked casually.

"No," Bowman said. "I'm divorced."

"That's too bad," she said. "We've been married for twelve years, my husband and I. We met in Florida—I'm from Florida—I was just floating around after school, working in an antique shop, hanging pictures, and he saw me and fell in love. He saw this blond WASP—you know, men have this thing in their minds—and that was really it."

Beyond her and past the hostess, Bowman could see the doorway to the brightly lit kitchen.

"What are you looking at?"

"A mouse just ran across the floor there," Bowman said.

"A mouse? You must have really good eyes. Was it big?"

"No, just a little mouse."

"Anyway, do you want to hear the rest of the story?"

"Where were we?"

"The architect . . ."

"The divorced architect."

"Yes. Well finally the woman, his date, showed up. She was in a tight-fitting dress. She was all wrong for him. I mean, she made a big entrance. I used to dress like that. I know. The thing is," she suddenly said, "I fell madly in love with this guy. He was divorced, he was so vulnerable. After dinner

I fell asleep on the couch and I looked up later and there he was. We talked for a while. He was so handsome. He was a Catholic. I had fantasies, you know? I would have given anything to have him, but it was impossible at the time."

She was drinking wine. She had lost what might have been called her poise. She said, "You probably don't understand, maybe I haven't told it right. He was two years younger than me, but we had a real rapport. Can I tell you something? There hasn't been a day gone by that I haven't thought about him. You probably hear stories like this all the time."

"No, not really."

"I mean, it's just fantasy. We have two children, two really nice children," she said. "We met in Florida—that was in 1957—and now we're here. Do you know what I mean? It all went by in such a rush. My husband is a good father. He's been good to me. That night, though. I can't explain it."

She paused.

"He kissed me when he left," she said.

She looked into Bowman's eyes and then looked away.

Near the end of the evening she found him near the door and, without saying anything, put her arms around him.

"Do you like me?" she asked.

"Yes," he said to console her.

"If somebody writes that story," she said, "it's all right with me."

Enid had never asked if he liked her. He had been mad for her. In England they had driven north, into Norfolk, green and flat with large houses and dismal towns, horse country, to see a dog. In Newmarket, four or five stable boys in shirt-sleeves were standing on a corner, one of them languidly pissing against a wall. He brandished his cock at them, at her, as they passed.

"Very nice," said Bowman. "English lads, then?"

"Unmistakably," Enid said.

A few miles past town they came to the house they had been looking for, a low, stuccoed house at the end of a drive. A man in a gray sweater with cheeks that were almost meat-colored came to the door.

"Mr. Davies?" Enid asked.

"Yes."

He'd been expecting them.

"You'll want to have a look at him, I suppose," he said.

He led the way around the corner of the house to a large wire enclosure in back, and as they approached, dogs began barking. More joined in.

"Take no notice," Davies said. "It's good for them to see people."

They walked along the fence until, nearly at the end, "There he is."

A young greyhound lying in a corner of the kennel rose slowly and with a slow dignity came to the wire. He was very much the dog of kings, white with a gray saddle and gray like a helmet around the head. Rulers of the East were buried with their greyhounds. Enid put her fingers through the mesh to touch his ear.

"He's very beautiful."

"Just short of five months old," Davies said.

"Hello," she said to the dog.

She'd been given the dog by a friend. Its name was Moravin, and the sire was a dog with a decent record named Jacky Boy. Davies was a trainer. He'd been around dogs all his life. His father, he told them later, had been a builder and always wanted to own a racehorse but settled for dogs. They ate less. Davies had had some success, but you never knew, they could also betray you. Some were promising but never came to much. They were bred to run, but not all of them ran well. Some were fast out of the box, some good at distances, there were wide runners that liked to go to the outside and others that liked to run on the rail.

"They're all different," he said.

He was cautious in his expectations, but he had some hopes for this dog, who, even at a young age, was very intent on the rag doll and pursued it wildly, catching it in his long white rows of teeth. Later, he timed out well and had no trouble running in practice with two other dogs.

In his first race finally, everything went wrong. Right at the start he was bumped by another dog and never got free of the pack. He was caught at the back of it the whole way. It was a disappointment, the trainer said on the phone.

"It doesn't seem fair," Enid said.

"It may not have been, but there's no such thing as fair in a race. It's only a first race. He'll just need his confidence again."

He was run with a couple of other dogs a few times. He showed some speed and then, in his next race, he came in fourth. It was out of London, Enid hadn't been there.

In his third race, at Romford, he was in box number two at odds of twenty to one. Something on the rail shot past. The doors flew open and out they came. He was in front most of the way, and they were so closely bunched at the finish you could not tell, but as it turned out he won by a head. "Hats off to the graders!" they cried and played a fanfare, it had been so close—hats off not to the judges but to the men who'd determined the odds. In the papers that week were the first plaudits, *Running well* and *Don't rule him out.*

He won twice more. It began to have meaning. *Won three of the last five*, they wrote and, more impressively, *Speed to burn. Won by four lengths.*

Bowman flew over for it when he was to run at White City, the great London track that drew people from the theater district and had some glamour. He felt heady that evening with Enid. They were a racing couple.

En route they stopped for a drink. It was somewhere near a hospital, a sign over the bar offered fifteen percent off to medical staff and to patients with thirty or more stitches. At the track there was a huge crowd with people moving through it, talking and drinking. The night was dark, there were clouds and a feeling of rain. Moravin was posted at three to one. Davies had already rubbed the dog down with an embrocation of his own, shoulders, body, all the way to the powerful hindquarters as if preparing for a Channel swim, and then up and down each leg. He then stretched the legs, the dog had ceased resisting this and lay quietly as it was done.

He was running in the fifth race. By then it had begun to rain lightly as the dogs were being led out. There were two white dogs, Moravin and a dog named Cobb's Lad. The crowd was becoming quiet.

"I've never been so nervous," Enid whispered. "I feel as if I were about to run myself."

For some reason, Bowman noticed, the odds had dropped to three to two. The business of getting the dogs into the boxes had begun. Suddenly from out of darkness, the mechanical hare went by and the boxes sprang open. They were off and running close together as they rounded the first turn and came around on the far side. The rain was falling harder. It was slanting across the lights in silver sheets. You could barely distinguish one dog from another, but a white dog was close to the lead. The pack was flying, low and streaming through the rain. How one of them could pull away from the rest was hard to imagine. As they went around the final turn, the head and shoulders of a white dog could be seen, and like that they crossed the finish. It was Moravin.

The rain was still heavy as, beneath an umbrella, he was being walked by Davies to cool down. Bowman borrowed one from a woman standing next to them and took Enid to the winner's stand as Moravin was being led onto it, stepping with a daintiness, the gray markings along the side of his head making him look like an outlaw in a mask. His tongue was trembling in his open mouth as the trainer held him raised up in victory, in his arms like a lamb. Enid's dog.

They had a drink together afterwards, it was likely that Davies had had one already. His face was filled with pleasure.

"Fine dog," he said several times. "You had money down on him, missus, I hope."

"Yes, a hundred pounds."

"They dropped the odds on him. The bookmakers were betting their own money to lower the odds. They feared him. They feared him."

He was staying outside the city with a friend, he said. He was more talkative than he'd been. With elation, he confided, "Shows promise, don't he?"

They left him at the pub and went to dinner with some people on Dean Street, among them an older woman with a marvelous face like a prune and a voice, as it turned out, that was a little hoarse. Bowman was drawn to her. She said something in Italian that he didn't quite hear, but she declined to repeat it. She'd been married to an Italian, she said.

"He was shot after the war."

"Shot?"

"In reprisal," she said. "He knew it would happen. There was a lot of that. His sister, my sister-in-law, who only died a year ago, had the distinction of having spat in Winston Churchill's face in the Piazza San Marco. They were Fascists, I couldn't help that. My husband was charming in every other way. It was all quite a while ago, you're not old enough."

"No, I am."

"You're what? Thirty-five?"

"I'm forty-five."

"I remember the French Colonial Exposition, 1932 or '33," she said. "The Senegalese troops in their blue uniforms, red hats and bare feet. It was a different world, quite different. What has your life been like?"

"Mine?"

"What are the things that have mattered?"

"Well," he said, "if I really examine it, the things that have most influenced my life, I would have to say the navy and the war."

"Men have that, don't they?"

He was not sure he had told the truth. His mind had just drifted back to it involuntarily. And among his dreams it had been the one that most consistently recurred.

Two weeks later, preparing for the Derby, Moravin ran at Wimbledon and fell on the turn, without cause, it seemed. He had a carpal fracture, not serious, but lying in a cast he seemed shamed, as if knowing what had been expected of him. Enid stroked his shoulders, the smooth gray and white of his coat. His small ears were laid back. His gaze was elsewhere.

The bone, though, was slow to heal. It was a drawn-out affair. She went to see him when it had finally healed, but there was something that had not come back. Whatever it was was invisible. He stood elegant and lean, almost entirely like the others, but he never ran again.

"I'm absolutely heartbroken," she said.

When he was asked about it later, Davies said,

"Yes, he could have run in the Derby, but he had this fall. It's always something like that. If there's ever anyone you really fucking hate, buy him a greyhound."

Enid had come to the airport with him, something she never did. As they stood waiting he'd felt an uneasiness. It was not in anything she said, only in the silence. It was slipping away and he could not stop it. They were not going to marry. She was already married and under some strange obligation to her husband—Bowman had never discovered just what it was. She had said that she couldn't live in New

York, her life was in London. He was only a facet of it there, but he longed to remain that.

"Maybe I can get back next month," he had said.

"That would be lovely."

They said good-bye in the main area. She gave a little wave of her fingers as he left.

He felt an emptiness as he boarded the plane, and even before they took off, an intense sadness. As if he were leaving it for the last time, he watched as England slowly passed behind them. Suddenly he missed her terribly. He should have somehow fallen to his knees.

In the carpeted hallway of the Plaza one winter evening, Bowman came face to face with a somewhat shapeless woman in a blue dress. It was Beverly, his ex-sister-in-law, with a chin that had almost completely vanished.

"Well, if it isn't Mr. New York," she said.

Bryan was beside her. Bowman shook his hand.

"What are you two doing in New York?"

"I'm going to the powder room," Beverly responded. "I'll meet you in the bar, wherever it is," she said to Bryan.

Bryan was unruffled.

"Don't pay any attention to her," he said when she had left. "We came up to see a couple of shows. Bev wanted to have a drink in the famous Oak Room bar."

"It's straight ahead. You look good."

"You do, too."

There was not much to talk about.

"How is everything?" Bowman said. "How's Vivian? We're not in touch."

"She's fine. Not much changed."

"Remarried? I guess I would have heard."

"No, she hasn't remarried, but you know who has? George."

"George? Remarried? To who?"

"A woman who lives down there. Peggy Algood. I don't think you know her."

"What's she like?"

"Oh, you know. She's about ten years younger than he is. She's easy to get along with. She was married a couple of times before. She's supposed to have sent a postcard to her mother when she was on her second honeymoon: *Algood no good, too.* Maybe that's just a story. I like her."

"Ah, Bryan, it's nice to see you. It's too bad our lives . . . diverged. How is Liz Bohannon? Is she still around?"

"She's still around. I don't think she still rides. We don't get invited there. Beverly said some things one time."

Of Bryan, it might be said that he was candid about his wife and uncomplaining. He treated her offhandedly, as he might treat bad weather.

"What show are you seeing?" Bowman asked.

"*Pal Joey.*"

"Yeah, that's good. It would be great to see you again sometime."

"For me, too."

15. THE COTTAGE

On a hot day in June, Bowman drove north from New York, generally following the Hudson for more than four hours to Chatham, a place once sacred for a love goddess, the poet Edna Millay, a siren of the 1920s, to spend two days working on a manuscript with a favorite writer, a square-faced man in his fifties with blue eyes and thinning hair who in his youth had dropped out of Dartmouth and gone to sea for three years. Kenneth Wells was his name. He and his wife—she was his third wife, he didn't particularly look like a man who'd been married a number of times, he was homely, his eyesight was bad; she had been married to his neighbor and one day the two of them had simply gone off to Mexico together and not come back—lived in a house that Bowman liked and that always stayed in his mind as a model. It was a plain wooden house not far from the road and resembled a farm building or stables. You entered through the kitchen or into it. There was a bedroom on one side and the living room on the other. The main bedroom was upstairs. The interior doors, for some reason, were slightly wider than usual with glass in the upper half of some. It was like a small family hotel, a hotel in the West.

It had been a long day. The summer had come early. Sun struck the trees of the countryside with dazzling power. In towns along the way, girls with tanned limbs strolled idly past stores that looked closed. Housewives drove with kerchiefs on their heads and their men in hard yellow hats stood near signs warning Construction Ahead. The landscape was beautiful but passive. The emptiness of things rose like the sound of a choir making the sky bluer and more vast.

It was the period when, in Paris, the lengthy and futile negotiations to end the war in Vietnam were continuing for month after unsuccessful month. America was in endless and violent upheaval, the entire nation torn apart by the war, but Wells seemed curiously uninvolved. He was more interested in baseball, from other passions he lived apart. He was an avid reader, so was his wife. Their bookshelves were divided into his and hers, their books were kept apart. On an old, marble-topped buffet were stacks of books, many of them new. Nearby on the wall a postcard of the Piazza Maggiore in Bologna was pinned, along with a photograph of a girl in a bikini, and another of a dish of pasta clipped from some magazine.

"T T T," Wells said.

"T T T?"

"Tits, towers, and tortellini."

He grinned and showed the spaces between his teeth that were like walrus tusks pointing in several directions. There was also a black-and-white photograph of German women weeping with emotion at a Nazi parade and upstairs, though no one ever saw it, a framed photo of a woman's naked legs and lower body tumbled across a bed. He wrote sophisticated crime novels, the investigator in which was an overweight woman in her fifties named Gwen Godding who had been married four times, the second and longest time to a California highway patrolman. She'd been widowed twice and had an eye towards marrying again. She was engaging and intelligent and described by Wells as having makeup like a disguise or put on by an undertaker. His research was meticulous, and he could work like a farmer, in fact his muscled jaws made him look like one. He wore wire-rimmed glasses, sometimes two pairs at a time, but to examine something closely pushed them up onto his forehead. His books sold very well, and the first of them had been bought for the movies as the vehicle for a quite mature star.

Wells liked to write, to sit at his desk reading and then begin to type. Only rarely did he talk about his time at sea, the working life, as he called it, staggering home in the morning, shirttail out, with a six-pack of beer and a case of the clap. He remembered being in Samoa in some hotel where the sign said Limited Room Service, Due to Great Distance from the Kitchen.

"You can't say that about this place," he said.

They were sitting in the kitchen.

"What made you decide to live up here?" Bowman asked.

"I wanted to get away from the water," Wells said. "When we left Mexico—I got tired of Mexico, huge mosquitoes, *animales,* they called them—we lived in St. Croix, in Frederiksted. We had an old Danish sea captain's house down by the water with wooden shutters, hibiscus, palm trees. Have you been to Frederiksted? The town is almost all black. Nobody seems to work. The bank had a For Rent sign on it, but you could see stunning black women in white evening dresses coming from the hotel at night out onto the street. The library was right across from where we lived. You could see the tall schoolgirls in there sprawled by the desks, their arms dangling over the chairs, boys whispering to them all day long. You could understand what slavery was about. The books—no one read any books—the only books taken out were those on pregnancy."

His wife, Michele—Mitch, he called her—was a calm woman in her forties, unhurried and attentive to him, tolerant. She knew his views and his character. Although there was little evidence of discord between them, there must have been some, but from the pair of them Bowman felt a strong pull towards connubial life, joined life, somewhere in the country, the early morning, misty fields, the snake in the garden, tortoise in the woods. Against that was the city with its myriad attractions, art, carnality, the amplification of desires. It was like a tremendous opera with an infinite cast and tumultuous as well as solitary scenes.

He felt the absence, not necessarily of marriage, but of a tangible center in life around which things could form and find a place. He realized what had brought it to mind, this house, Wells', and the description of the captain's house in Frederiksted. He imagined a house of his own, though only vaguely. For some reason he saw it in the fall. It was raining, rain was a blur on the windows and he had lit a fire against the chill.

He took the time to look.

"I'm interested in a small house with an exceptional room or two," he told the agent.

She was a tart woman who was a member of the board of the golf club nearby.

"I don't know what you mean by exceptional room," she said.

"Well, why don't we begin by looking at something? Show me one or two of your favorites."

"What is the price range you're interested in?"

"Let's say from two thousand dollars up," Bowman said to annoy her.

"I don't have anything in that range," she said. "Also, I really have a business to run."

"I know you do. Tell me, what can I buy a two-bedroom house for?"

"It depends entirely on the house and the location. I would say, between sixty and two hundred thousand dollars, south of the highway."

"I don't want a house in the trees, the woods. I'd like a house that's well-situated and open to the light," he said.

It was hard to tell if she was sensitive to what he was saying or not. She showed him nothing of interest although at the end of an astrigent hour and a half, passing through some open fields bounded by trees, she slowed down near a driveway and said,

"This is more expensive, but I thought I'd show it to you."

She was in fact showing her authority. They drove down a long straight road, not overly maintained, in the shadow of foliage overhead. It was almost sepulchral. The green was intense. Then it unexpectedly opened to a dark wooden house on a slight rise, a sort of Adirondack house built to the mountain gods, in the open but surrounded by a tall canopy of trees like a layer of clouds. It was a house named Crossways and had been designed by Stanford White, another of whose great houses, Flying Point, on the ocean, had burned.

They went up wide wooden steps and into a serene interior with comfortable furnishings and devoid of haphazard light. The floors were polished but not shining. The windows were large and clear. The house was cruciform in shape with each arm looking down its own alley of trees to the fields. It had passed through the hands of several owners and its price was in millions.

When they were in the car again, Bowman said,

"That was worth it."

But he did not go to that agent again.

He didn't like women who looked down on you for whatever reason. Within limits, he liked the opposite. You rarely found all the qualities you sought. It was not something he spent time thinking about. He'd had various love affairs. As he became older, the women became older, too, and less inclined to foolish or carefree acts. But the city was teeming, the feminist movement had changed it. He was usually in a suit. He always wore one to work. On the escalator at Grand Central, a girl with a nice face, composed and brown, said to him,

"Hello. Are you going where?"

"I'm sorry?"

"I was asking if you are going to near here," she said.

"I'm going to Forty-First Street," Bowman said.

"Ah. Do you have an office?"

He couldn't quite tell what she wanted.

"Why do you ask?"

"Oh, I just thought we could exchange numbers and you could call."

"For what?" he said.

"Business," she said simply.

Her raincoat, he noticed, was not entirely clean.

"What kind of business?"

"You can say."

She looked at him openly. She had an outsider's dignity, a West African dignity, and also a touch of weariness.

"What's your name?" he asked.

"My name? Eunice."

He felt in his pocket for bills. He took one out and put it in her hand, a ten.

"No," she said, "you don't have to."

"Take it, Eunice. It's a down payment."

"No."

"I have to go," he said and walked away.

For the twenty-fifth anniversary of the publishing house, Baum gave a party in a French restaurant. There was a large crowd, almost all of them people Bowman knew. On the far side of the room he caught sight of Gretchen, who had long since become an editor herself, at a paperback house. She was married and a mother. He made his way across to her to say hello.

"It's so nice to see you," he said.

She still had the quality that had allowed her to ignore the terrible blemishes although these were now gone. On her smooth forehead and cheeks were only some faint etched scars, barely noticeable.

"How have you been?" he asked.

"Very well," she said. "And you?"

"The same. You look wonderful. It's been a long time. What is it, six years?"

"More," she said.

"It doesn't seem it. We miss you. Neil left, I guess you know that. He went to work for Delovet. He went over to the enemy."

"I know."

"You were a great distraction to him," Bowman said. "You had a boyfriend, though."

"I didn't have a boyfriend," she said.

"I thought you did."

"I was married."

"I didn't know that."

"Just briefly," she said.

"You seemed so innocent."

"I was innocent."

She was still innocent. Also, he hadn't noticed it before, slightly shy.

"I miss Neil," he said. "I don't see him very often these days."

"He sent me some poems," she said. "Back then, I mean."

"I didn't know that. He was smitten. There were some poems he didn't send you."

"Really?"

"Oh, nothing terrible."

"I wasn't sure if you liked me," she said.

"Me? I'm surprised to hear you say that. I liked you very much."

"Neil wasn't the one I was interested in," she said.

In the same undramatic way, she went on, "You were the one. I didn't have the nerve though."

He felt inept.

"I was married."

"It didn't matter," she said.

"You shouldn't be telling me now. I don't know, it's too disorienting."

"Since I'm confessing it," she said, "I might as well say nothing has changed."

It was said quite simply.

"Why don't you call me? I'd love to see you," she said.

She was looking directly at him. He didn't know what to say. Just then her husband, who had been getting drinks at the bar, came back. The three of them talked together for a few minutes. Bowman had the feeling that they all knew. That evening he didn't talk to her again.

He saw her now, of course, in a different way. He was tempted to call her but felt it would not be right, from a moral viewpoint and something besides. They were not the people they had been. He admired her, however, the marred girl she had been, the poised woman she now was. She was the age when she could still be naked. He could be gone from the office for several hours in the afternoon, almost any afternoon, and so could she. It was not indiscretion, it was what was due her.

You're a fool, he told himself. He saw himself in the mirror in the morning. His hair was thinner now but his face, it seemed, was the same. He had come to the point where he was certain of his abilities, how to make writers want to be published by him, among others. He knew that some of the best writers began as journalists and sometimes ended as journalists when the passion faded. He knew also that he had the ability to turn people against him. That came with the rest of it. He could talk about books and writers and literature blooming in one country and then another, not through one great writer but always through a group of them, almost as though you had to have enough wood for a real fire, one or two big sticks were not enough. He went on about Russian writing, talking too much about Gogol, perhaps, and about the French and English. They had their great periods, Paris, London. Now it was undoubtedly New York.

"Would the genius mind telling us his name?" a man across the table asked.

He was involved, though not that closely, with certain poets, not as their editor, if editor was the correct word, since poems were essentially inviolable. Poetry was largely left to McCann, who had been hired more or less to replace Eddins. He was an easterner who walked with a cane. He'd had polio, both he and his roommate at Groton, the two of them had helped the stricken football captain from chapel and had come down with it. At the time, in the 1930s, there was an epidemic every fall—parents lived in terror of it. McCann was married to an English journalist who wrote for the *Guardian* and was often away on assignment.

Poetry books sold few copies. Publishing them was a

charitable act, Baum used to say, mainly to arouse McCann, although the books were an important ornament to the reputation of the house. Since few people read poetry after college, the struggle for prominence among poets was all the more fierce and the award of one of the important prizes or a secure academic position was often the result of intense self-promotion, flattery, and mutual agreements. There were perhaps poets in parochial cities living drab lives like Cavafy's, but those Bowman knew were quite social and even urbane, well accustomed to the current in which they were swimming, brushing against one another as they went, a Yale Younger Poets to one, a Bollingen to the next, a Pulitzer.

He was never able to find a house to buy. He rented one instead on a narrow road just past Bridgehampton that ended with a yellow Dead End sign at the beach. The only close neighbor was a man about his own age named Wille, who was friendly enough and parked his car on the grass near his kitchen door.

Bowman came out on weekends beginning in late spring. There was an active life that began about then. He knew people and was invited to dinners. He bought several cases of good wine to be able to bring a couple of bottles to the hostess. The house was always unlocked. He liked to come on the train which had a bar car and seats that could be reserved. Sometimes he drove, not leaving the city after one in the afternoon in order to avoid the heaviest traffic or waiting until nine or ten o'clock when the road was emptier.

It was knocked together and temporary compared to the

rest of his life, but it was carefree and gave him the chance to know the area better and to make it more his own. When the right house finally appeared, he would be confident in buying it. He parked his car on the sandy lawn as Wille did and felt very much at home.

16. SUMMIT

Beatrice had been having difficulties. In appearance she was practically unchanged, she looked just as she had for years, but she had become forgetful. She couldn't remember her own telephone number at times or the names of certain people she knew very well. She knew their name and it would come to her afterwards, but it was embarrassing not to be able to say it.

"I must be losing my mind," she said. "Who was that, again?"

"Mr. DePetris."

"Of course. What's wrong with me?"

Nothing, really. She was past seventy and in every respect in good health. Her son came to visit every other week. Only rarely did she go into the city anymore, she had everything she needed there in Summit, she said. She'd gone to New York many, many times, to see shows, to shop, but not in a long while.

"It's been years," she said.

"No, it hasn't," Bowman said. "We went to the museum, don't you remember?"

"Yes, of course," she corrected herself.

It was true. She remembered it then. She'd forgotten.

Then she began having a little trouble with her balance.

There were always flowers in the house, often yellow jonquils, and she dressed nicely, but walking through the dining room one afternoon, unexpectedly she fell. It felt as if the floor had shifted beneath her feet, she said. She hit her arm against the edge of the dining room table and opened a long gash. She went to the emergency room and as a matter of routine saw her regular doctor afterwards. He noticed that she was unblinking and that there was a slight, rhythmic tremor in her hand, signs of Parkinson's disease.

She didn't know why her hand shook, she told her sister. "It shakes a little, but if I move it, it doesn't. Do you see?"

"Hold your hand out," Dorothy said. "You're right, there's nothing."

But later in the kitchen Beatrice dropped a glass.

"Yes, I'm fine," she said, "but here I am, can't even hold a glass."

"It's nothing," Dorothy said. "Don't move. I'll sweep it up."

"No, Dorothy, let me. I'll do it. It's the second one I've broken this week."

She continued to have problems with her balance, she was no longer confident about it, and also she became a little stooped. Age doesn't arrive slowly, it comes in a rush. One day nothing has changed, a week later, everything has. A week may be too long a time, it can happen overnight. You are the same and still the same and suddenly one morning two distinct lines, ineradicable, have appeared at the corners of your mouth.

In the end, however, it was not Parkinson's, although for a long time the doctor believed it was. Beatrice had fallen twice more and was fumbling with the tasks of daily living. Finally, Dorothy came to live with her. The Fiori had been sold when Frank had been diagnosed with a brain tumor and had gone mad. He had also gone off with one of the waitresses. Dorothy described it as madness.

"But he had a tumor?"

"Oh, yes."

Bowman saw his uncle as having had a premonition and wanting to open his long-folded wings, such as they were, a last time—he'd been in a hospital in Atlantic City and had left with a woman named Francile.

"Have you heard from him?" Bowman asked.

"No," Dorothy said. "But, you know, he's crazy."

In fact, they did not hear from him again.

As time went on, Beatrice began, almost casually it seemed, to have hallucinations or pretend to. Especially in the evening she would see people who weren't there and talk to them.

"Who're you talking to?" Dorothy asked.

"Mr. Caruso," Beatrice said.

"Where is he?"

"There. Isn't that Mr. Caruso?"

"I don't see anyone. There's no one there, Beatrice."

"That was him. He wouldn't talk to me," she explained.

Caruso owned the wine and liquor store, or had. Dorothy was certain he'd retired.

Beatrice also knew, although at first she did not say it, that she was not in her own house. Although she had lived in it for nearly fifty years, she was certain she had been taken someplace else. There began to be times when she didn't recognize Dorothy or even her son. It turned out finally that she had something that resembled Parkinson's and was often taken for it, a less well-known condition called Lewy body disease, the bodies being microscopic proteins that attacked nerve cells in the brain, some of the same cells affected in Parkinson's. The diagnosis had taken a long time because the symptoms of the two diseases were similar. Hallucinations, however, were a distinction.

The exact cause of Lewy body was not known. The symptoms gradually worsened. The end was inevitable.

Beatrice was so often herself that it seemed the episodes were a lapse and might gradually disappear, but it turned out the opposite. Her essential person, however, was intact.

"Dorothy," she said one day, "do you remember when we lived at Irondequoit Bay? The old trunks that were in the attic, what was in them, I forget?"

"Oh, my God, Beatrice, I don't know. A lot of stuff, clothes, old photographs."

"What became of all that?"

"I don't know."

"I wonder. I have some keys to trunks, but I don't know which ones."

"There are none."

"Where are they?" Beatrice asked.

She had a recurring dream or perhaps thought about the trunks. She was sure there had been trunks. She could see them. Then she was not sure. They could have been something she imagined. It was her memory that she had the keys to but could not make fit. Nor could she make Dorothy see who had somehow come into the house. And there were the concerns of daily life. Where was the medicine that she was supposed to take?

"Two times a day?" she asked again.

"Yes, two."

"It's hard to remember," Beatrice complained.

Bowman came by train, looking out at the haze of the Jersey meadows, marshes really. He had a deep memory of these meadows, they seemed a part of his blood like the lone gray silhouette of the Empire State Building on the horizon, floating as in a dream. He knew the route, beginning with the desolate rivers and inlets dark with the years. Like some ancient industrial skeleton, the Pulaski Skyway rose in the distance and looped across the waters. Nearer, in a rush, blank factories of brick with broken windows went past. Then there was Newark, the grim, lost city of Philip Roth, and churches with trees growing from the base of neglected spires. Endless quiet streets of houses, asylums, schools, all of an emptiness it seemed, intermixed with bland suburban happiness and wholesome names, Maplewood, Brick Church. The great, smooth golf courses with immaculate greens. He was of it, from it, and as he rode, unconnected to it.

On the corner stood the diner where he had taken Vivian the first time. It was not even the diner that Hemingway wrote about, he now knew. That was in another place called Summit, near Chicago, but there had been other misconceptions at the time. He had been wrong about a number of things. He remembered, but only as a collection of certain incidents that were like photographs, what Vivian had been like. He didn't remember her voice and only with wonder—

partly with wonder—what had persuaded him that she was the girl he should marry.

He had walked to school on Morris Avenue, Summit High School, a very good school, so well regarded that Ivy League colleges would accept without question any student the principal recommended. Before the war, that did not seem extraordinary, it was simply the way of things. In those days, Japan existed only in newsreels and cheap goods marked *Made in Japan*. No one, no ordinary person dreamed that this curious, distant country out of Gilbert and Sullivan was as dangerous as an open razor and had the discipline and daring to do the unthinkable, cross in strength and absolute secrecy the most northern Pacific to attack at dawn on a quiet morning the unsuspecting American fleet in Pearl Harbor, an almost fatal blow. Pearl Harbor, no one even knew where Pearl Harbor was, they had only a vague idea. When the grave news was broadcast in America interrupting the quiet Sunday afternoon, it was accompanied with no details and almost made no sense. The Japanese. Attacking. The complete unexpectedness.

He had been a schoolboy. His mother was in her thirties. He barely remembered his father. It was a somewhat shameful thing to have divorced parents. He knew only one other boy like himself, a strange boy named Edwin Semmler with a large head, extremely shy and an outstanding student—he was called The Brain. Everyone in the class or almost everyone had gone to the senior prom and the parties at the hotel, almost everyone but not Semmler. No one expected him to. No one knew much about him, he averted his head when walking past people. Bowman had several times tried to talk to him without much success. As it turned out, he was killed in the war. He was in the infantry, it was hard to imagine. Kenneth Keogh hadn't been killed, but it was almost as bad. He'd also been in the infantry, as a sergeant, and had come through the war unharmed. During the Occupation, in barracks, he'd been hit in the spine by a bullet accidentally fired by someone cleaning a rifle and he was paralyzed from the waist down. In a wheelchair he took the train to work in New York every day, Bowman had seen him several times, the same Kenneth Keogh but with legs of rags.

On Essex Road in a white house above a steep lawn lived the most unimaginable girl in town, Jackie Ettinger, who was a year or two older and too glorious to know. She hadn't stayed, she'd gone away to school in Connecticut and become a model. She was eighteen when he was sixteen. Another world. She'd been taken to the Brook, a supper club—he had never been inside it. Later she had gotten married. Even now, were he to meet her, even with all he now was, he would have been at a loss for words. She had been a figure in his imagination for a long time. When he had been in midshipman's school, he had thought of her and even later when he was living in the little room without a bath off Central Park West, a shabby room, and first heard that she was married. He was the boy left behind in some poem he had read that was in the form of a letter written by a girl who had gone off into society. Her father had become rich, and now, back from a dance she was writing a letter at midnight to a boy she once knew and had kept track of and who still had her heart.

What had become of all of them? They had gone into business. Several were lawyers. Richter was a surgeon. He wondered about his favorite teacher, Mr. Boose, younger than the other teachers, earnest and made fun of behind his back, Boozie, they called him. He would be retired by now if he had stayed at the school. He had written to Bowman several times during the war.

There was an afternoon when his mother did not recognize him. She asked him who he was.

"I'm Philip. Your son."

She looked at him and then looked away.

"You're not Philip," she said, as if refusing to become involved in a game.

"Mother, I really am."

"No. I'd like to see my son," she said to Dorothy.

The incident, although unreal, was very disturbing. It seemed to cut the tie between them, as if she were renouncing him. He would not let her do it.

"I'm not Philip," he said, "but I'm your good friend."

She seemed to accept it. Her confusion was his, he realized, his to understand. She was becoming strange, unknowing, and she plainly felt alone. He thought of Vivian and her loyalty to her mother, whom he had liked. That had been a touching thing. He thought of his own mother and how he had loved her, what she had been like on the many mornings, the meals they had had together, that she had prepared for him. He knew they must take care of her and not leave her now.

But in November, Beatrice slipped and fell in the bathtub breaking her wrist and hip. Dorothy hadn't been able to lift her out of the tub, they had to call an ambulance. The fall had been frightening. Beatrice was in pain and knew what had happened. She bore the routine of the hospital with some confusion but without complaint. The nurses were patient with her.

Bowman came immediately. The hospital had whispering hallways and closed doors to many of the rooms. He found his mother weakened and quiet. She was afraid that she might not leave the hospital.

"Of course, you'll leave," he assured her. "I talked to the doctor. You'll be fine."

"Yes," she said.

They sat silent for a while.

"I'm having a lot of trouble," she said. "I can't seem to do things, I don't know why. When you die," she said, "what do you think happens to you?"

"You're not going to die."

"I know, but what do you think happens?"

"Something glorious."

"Oh, Philip. Only you would say something like that. Do you know what I think?"

"What?"

"I think that whatever you believe will happen is what happens."

He recognized the truth in it.

"Yes, I think you're right. What do you believe will happen?"

"Oh, I'd like to think that I'll be in some beautiful place."

"Like what?"

She hesitated.

"Like Rochester," she said and laughed.

Her attention span was shorter after she left the hospital and she was in reality only part of the time. She was also more fearful. Dorothy could only with difficulty take care of her at home, and it would inevitably become worse.

To Bowman, the idea of a nursing home was repellent, it meant he was abandoning her. The home was a place for the aged no one would care for any longer. Nothing was left for them as they lay waiting or shuffling along the corridors or were wheeled, head lolling, from place to place. They might live like this for years. Beatrice might be tired, she might be depressed, but she was not like them. She had grown old, but not to become that. It was worse than dying. As she had said, what happened was what you believed would happen. You were yourself until the end, until the very last moment. In the nursing home, what you believed was left behind.

17. CHRISTINE

In London, Bernard Wiberg looked more and more like a lord, which many in knowing circles said he soon might be. He was resplendent in his dark, bespoke suits, and his self-regard, while great, was no greater than his success. For books meant to be taken seriously he was the favored and hoped-for publisher, and for books written to make money, he had an unerring eye. If he bought a book, it was always at an advantageous price, no matter how high that might be. Books he paid little for managed to gain a following, and books that he was obliged to pay a great deal for always earned out. It didn't matter what things cost, it was what they were worth.

He was soon to be married, so it was said, to a former ballerina who was often in photographs in glamorous magazines, at parties or dinners. She was a woman who seemed to live a superior life, and as Lady Wiberg she could expect this to continue. At the opera or ballet, Wiberg was a figure of style, in white tie when the occasion called for it, and his household retained its elegance. He'd dined with the Duke and Duchess of Windsor in France, tremendous protocol, everyone had to be there before the royal couple entered. He was encouraged by Catarina, the ex-dancer, to give occasional after-theater suppers, *soirées*, she liked to call them, the dining table laid with plates of cold beef, pâté, and pastries, and wine with well-known labels. Intimately and just between them she called him her *cochon*. In his bathrobe or white braces he could be Falstaff or Figaro with her and she had an irresistible laugh.

Enid remained his friend, more so when his fiancée was in Bolzano visiting her family or was involved with a production somewhere, no longer as a performer, but she was developing a reputation as a consultant, even as a choreographer. Enid had become involved in films, first as an assistant to a producer, making reservations for him at restaurants and on airplanes and being present at dinners. She spent some time on location of a film being shot, learning about continuity and what a script girl did. The crew were friendly, but she was a stylish-looking outsider, also in the evening when they gathered and drank. At a pause in the conversation, the American director, in front of everyone, asked her offhandedly, "So, tell me, Enid, do you fuck?"

"I'd be a fool if I didn't," she coolly answered and in a way that seemed to exclude him.

He did not pursue it further. Her reply was often repeated.

Bowman had been in London for the Book Fair, and his homeward flight had been delayed. He landed in New York at nine in the evening. It was half an hour before he had his bags and went out to get a cab. There was a crowd, he had to share a cab with someone also going to the West Side, a woman with three or four pieces of luggage. She moved her legs to give him more room. She was sitting back in what might have been a coat with the sleeves lying as if open. They rode in silence. Bowman was prepared to keep to himself without looking at her again. In the city, strange women were not always as they appeared. There were women with grievances, disturbed women, women avidly seeking men.

As they came to the expressway, she said,

"Where are you coming from?"

It was the way she said it. She almost seemed to know him.

"London," he said, looking at her more closely for the first time. "And you?"

"From Athens."

"That's a long flight," he commented.

"They're all long. I don't like to fly. I'm always afraid the plane is going to crash."

"I don't think you have to be afraid of crashing. It's quick. It's all over in a second."

"It's what happens before that, when you know you're about to crash."

"I suppose so, but how would you prefer to die?"

"Some other way," she said.

In the light from oncoming cars he could see her dark hair and lipstick that made him take her for Greek. The expressway paralleled Manhattan, which was like a long necklace of light across the river. At the far end was the financial district and then, from midtown on up, the countless tall buildings, the great boxes of light. It was like a dream, trying to imagine it all, the windows and entire floors that never went dark, the world you wanted to be in.

"Do you live in Athens?" he asked.

"No," she said easily, "I was taking my daughter to visit her father."

"I've never been to Greece."

"That's a pity. It's a marvelous country. When you go, go to the islands."

"Any one in particular?"

"There are so many," she said.

"Yes."

"There are places that time seems never to have touched, absolutely unspoiled."

They looked at one another without speaking. He did not know what she might be seeing. She had clear, smooth features.

"The people have something you don't find here," she said. "They have a joy of life."

"That's nonsense," he said.

She ignored it.

"Were you in London on business?"

"Yes, business. The London Book Fair."

"Are you a publisher?"

"Not really. I'm an editor. A publisher has different responsibilities."

"What sort of books do you edit?"

"Mainly novels," he said.

"The friend I'm staying with was in a novel. She's rather proud of it. Eve was her name in the book. That's not her name."

"Which book is that?"

"You know, I forget the title. I only read the parts about her. She knew the author. So, tell me your name," she said after a pause.

Her own name was Christine, Christine Vassilaros. She

was not Greek, she was married to a Greek man, a business-man, from whom she had separated. Her friend, Kennedy, the one who'd been written about, was also separated and living in a rent-controlled apartment that was a grand relic of life before the two World Wars and the time between them. I'm not giving up the apartment, she had said. It was like an apartment in Havana, bygone and only sparsely furnished, on Eighty-Fifth Street.

They arrived at Bowman's street first. He handed her something more than half the fare.

"It was very nice of you to share the cab," he said. "Can I call you sometime?" he straightforwardly asked.

She wrote down a telephone number on the back of an airline stub.

"Here," she said.

And she pressed it in his hand.

As the cab left, he had an exalted feeling. The taillights going down the street, bearing her away. It had been like theater, a glorious first act. The doorman greeted him.

"Good evening, sir."

"Yes, good evening."

I've met the most wonderful woman, he wanted to say. He had met her by chance. He thought about it excitedly while going upstairs, and then in the apartment. She was married, she had said, but that was understandable—at a certain point in life, it seemed everyone was. At a certain point also you began to feel that you knew everyone, there was no one new, and you were going to spend the rest of your life among familiar people, women especially. It was not that she had been friendly, it was that but more. He felt like trying the telephone number, but that was foolish. She wouldn't have even arrived at her street yet. He was already impatient. He must somehow not seem it.

When she came to lunch a day later, he knew it was all in vain. She was younger than he thought, but he could not be sure. They sat facing one another. She had the neck of a woman of twenty, and her face had only the faintest lines from expressions, from her smile. There was almost a physical thrill to her. He didn't want to succumb to it, but he was unable to prevent it, her bare neck and arms. She was certainly aware of it. Don't become intoxicated, she seemed to say. He could look at her so closely. Her gleaming dark hair. Her upper lip was arched. She held her fork with a kind of languor as if ready to discard it, but she ate with generous mouthfuls as she talked, not diverted from the food. Her other hand was raised and half-closed, as if drying her nails. Long, disdainful fingers. It turned out she had lived in New York, on Waverly Place, she and her husband, for a number of years.

"Six," she said. She had worked as a broker.

He was looking at her. You wanted to watch her.

"It was beautiful," she said. "That's a nice part of the city."

"You know New York then," he said feeling jealous.

"Very well."

She didn't say much more or much about her husband. His business was in Athens, that was all. They'd been living in Europe.

"In Athens?"

"But we're separated."

"Are you still on good terms?"

"Well . . ."

"Intimate terms?" he found himself asking.

She smiled.

"Hardly," she said.

He felt he could say anything to her, tell her anything. There was a kind of complicity, even if nascent, between them.

"How old is your daughter?" he asked.

She was fifteen. He was astonished to hear that.

"Fifteen! You don't look as if you could have a fifteen-year-old daughter," he said and added casually, "how old are you?"

She made a slight, disapproving expression.

"Thirty-two?"

"I was born during the war," she said. "Not at the beginning of it," she added.

He was aware of his own age, but she didn't bother to ask it. Her daughter's name was Anet.

"How is that spelled?" he said.

It was a beautiful name.

"She's a marvelous girl. I'm mad about her," she said.

"Well, your daughter . . ."

"It's not just that. Do you have children?"

"No," he said.

He almost felt he'd fallen short in her eyes. He was visibly older, he was single, he had no family.

"But that's a very nice name," he repeated. "Some names are like magic. Unforgettable."

"That's true."

"Vronsky," he said as an example.

"Not a very good name for a girl."

"No, of course not. Unforgettable, but not good."

"I'd almost have another child just to name it. If you were to have a child, what would you name it?" she asked.

"That's something I've never really thought about. If it was a boy . . ."

"Yes," she said. "A boy."

"If it was a boy, Agamemnon."

"Ah. Yes," she said. "Of course. Achilles is a good name, too. Agamemnon sounds a little more like a horse."

"He'd be a wonderful boy," Bowman argued.

"I'm sure he'd be. With that name he'd have to be. And what would you name a girl? I'm almost afraid to ask."

"A girl? Quisqueya," he said.

"I see you're a traditionalist. What was that name, again?"

"Quisqueya."

"It must be some figure in history or a novel."

"It's a Peruvian name."

"Peruvian? Really?"

"No, I made that up," he confessed.

"Anyway, it goes very well with Bowman."

"Quisqueya Bowman," he said. "Well, let's just keep it in mind."

"And her sister, Vronsky."

"Yes."

All right, become intoxicated. It was always from the first word, the first look, the first embrace, the first fatal dance. It was there waiting. Christine, I know you, he thought. She was smiling at him.

He had to tell someone afterwards, he had to say it, it was simply bursting from him. He said it to the doorman,

"I've met the most wonderful woman!"

"Oh, yeah? Good for you, Phil."

He'd never called him by his first name before although they sometimes chatted. His name was Victor.

You'll meet her, Bowman felt like saying but realized how man-about-town it sounded, and also he did not know if it would happen. He might have regretted saying anything, but he hadn't been able to help it. The apartment looked bright, welcoming. It was her presence, her initial presence, in his life.

They went to a dinner party given by a husband and wife who published art books, a branch of publishing all to itself, art books and also large-format books on architecture and even more particular subjects, hotels of the Amazon, things like that. Jorge and Felice Arceneaux, it was she who had the money. There were eight at the table, including a young French journalist and a biographer who was writing a life of Apollinaire, the poet who'd been badly wounded in the First War. Christine was perfect. Her looks, of course. They were certainly very conscious of her, and she was graceful and did not say much. She didn't know any of them and didn't force herself on them. The biographer, who had been working on the book for years, once had the chance to actually meet Apollinaire's old mistress, not the one who threw herself out of a window when Apollinaire died but another one, who was Russian, Apollinaire had written about her in a poem.

"I was thrilled to be able to meet her. I mentioned the poem, of course. She was old by then. Do you know what she said? She said, *Oui, je mourrai en beauté,* I'll be beautiful until

I die, I'll die beautiful—you can't translate it exactly. When I die, I'll still be beautiful, something like that."

From this they began talking about dying and then heaven.

"I don't like the idea of heaven," the hostess said. "For one thing, the people who would be going there. There's no such thing as heaven, anyway."

"Are you certain?" someone said.

"Certain enough. And if I'm wrong, well, you might as well sin on earth—there's not going to be any of that in heaven."

"Are you married?" the biographer asked Bowman and Christine.

"No. Not quite," Bowman said to finish more interest on the biographer's part.

He had not been thinking of marriage but of everything that might lead up to it. He had been thinking ceaselessly of Christine. He knew he would have to do something ordinary, asking her up to the apartment for a drink or a nightcap, the word seemed old-fashioned and even preposterous. He was certain she liked him, but at the same time he was nervous about putting it to the test. He hated the idea of being awkward. At the same time he knew it to be unimportant, that once they were past that, anything awkward would be forgotten. But it didn't matter what he knew, or else he'd forgotten all he knew. The journalist was telling the story of a notorious murder—it wasn't clear where it had happened—that was solved because of traces of semen, he pronounced it semean, found on a cigarette. He managed to repeat the word several times. No one bothered to correct him.

As they left the table, Christine said in a low voice, "Semean?"

"It must be the French pronunciation," Bowman said.

"*Seminé*," she suggested.

"It's the title of a song."

"Um. I'll try some," she remarked as if they were talking about an odd menu item. She added, "Do you happen to have any?"

Was she still kidding? She was not looking at him.

"Yes," he said. "Lots."

"I thought you might say that."

For a few moments in the cab they rode quietly, as if they were going to the theater. Then he kissed her, fully, on the mouth. The taste was fresh. He smelled her perfume. He held her hand as they rode up in the elevator.

"Would you like something to drink?" he asked.

"Not really."

"I'm going to have a little something."

He poured some bourbon. He felt she was watching him. He drank it rather quickly. He began to kiss her again, holding her by the arms.

In the bedroom, he removed her shoes. Then, in only the light from the other room, they undressed on opposite sides of the bed.

"Lots, you said."

"Yes."

She went into the bathroom. She came out and he said, "No, stand there for a moment."

He tried to look slowly at her but couldn't. It was the first time, it was always blinding.

"Come here," he said.

She lay beside him for a few minutes, the first minutes, as a swimmer lies in the sun. He could see her nakedness, almost all of it, in the near dark. They made love simply, straightforwardly—she saw the ceiling, he the sheets, like schoolchildren. There was no sound but the float of traffic distant and below. There was not even that. The silence was everywhere and he came like a drinking horse. He lay for a long time on top of her, dreaming, exhausted. She had not made love for more than a year, and she lay dreaming, too, and then asleep.

They woke to the fresh light of the world. She was exactly as she had been the night before though her mouth was pale now and her eyes plain. They made love again, he was like a boy of eighteen, invincibly hard. The apartment was beautiful in a way it had never been, the light in it, her presence. They had not been too hasty in going to bed together, nor had they waited too long. These were merely the days of initiation, he knew. So much was still to come.

They drank orange juice and made coffee. He had to go to work.

"Can we have dinner this evening?"

"No, I'm sorry, I can't this evening . . . darling—it's too early to call you darling, isn't it?" she said.

"I don't think so."

"Well, this once."

"Go ahead."

"Darling," she said.

18. AS I DO NOW

Tim Wille was a furniture designer, a little nervous and wild-eyed. When he talked to you he looked elsewhere, often at the wall. He no longer drank. He had been arrested while driving with a blood alcohol level that was .17 above the maximum limit. He'd spent the night in jail and thousands of dollars in lawyer's fees over the following year. It was the best thing that ever happened to him—he gave up drinking, he said. He still had the look of it, though, along the edges.

Someone was singing at his house, it was hard to make out what. It was a party. The sound drifted over in a loose, romantic way. She liked Bowman's house, Christine said. Although she had lived in New York, she had never been out here.

"It's like the cane fields or something."

They could hear the sea, the continuous, low sound of waves that lay beneath the wind.

He took her to a restaurant on the highway, a farmhouse set back from the road and run by a Greek family, a mother and two sons who were both in their fifties. The older one, George, was in the kitchen. Steve, who was less taciturn, handled the front, and the mother was cashier and ran the bar. The restaurant was known for steak, grilled over coals, and various Greek dishes like moussaka. When Steve came to the table, Christine said to him in Greek,

"So, what do you have to eat?"

He looked at her and nodded slightly.

"What do you like?" he said in Greek.

"*Skorthalia,*" she said. "Toasted *kesari*. Lamb and rice. *Metrio* afterwards."

He responded with a smile. She was wearing a silk, apricot-colored shirt. Her teeth were white as calling cards. Later, the older brother came to the door of the kitchen to look.

"I'm very impressed," Bowman said. "How long did it take you to learn Greek?"

"How long did it take me? One marriage," she said.

The restaurant was crowded, almost every table was filled. A dwarf girl came in with her mother. She was barely four feet tall and had a stunted leg. She was wearing a kind of sweatshirt and her fingernails were painted blue. It was painful to see her twisting walk, but her face was serene.

"It's like Greece," Christine said. "Everyone comes, the whole town."

There was a rather heavy woman, heavy but confident and definitely attractive in a flowered dress at a table near the door. Her name was Grace Clark. She was with another woman and a man, Gin Lane from the look of them. She had murdered her husband, Bowman said.

"Really?"

"I don't know if she murdered him, but he was shot five times. She was in the city at the time, she claimed. She'd gone in to see the dentist but had gotten the day wrong. The police couldn't shake her story. Her husband was a closet homosexual, he used to bring Puerto Rican boys to the house when she was gone. Very few people knew. She must have known. She had three witnesses to the fact that she didn't kill him, she said. She was one, her husband was one, and God was the third."

"She could prove she was in the city?"

"I don't think so. That's the point. No one was ever charged. The case has never been solved."

They were drinking a second bottle of retsina.

"She was married two or three times before. I mean, what does it take to shoot your husband five times and claim you were away when it happened? I've met her, she's actually an interesting woman."

"I've never known a murderer, at least I don't think I have. I do know some thieves."

He was intensely aware of being there with her, the pleasure of it. He could see himself sitting across from her, the two of them. That was part of the pleasure.

The ocean that night could be heard from some way off. The sound of the waves was even and unending. They went to look. It was after eleven and the beach was completely empty, not even a light in any of the houses near it. The water was black, rising and then with a roar showing its teeth. They stood watching. He was a little drunk. Christine was hugging herself.

"Do you want to go for a swim?" he asked half-seriously.

"No. Not me."

He felt a sudden desire, a wild recklessness, the image of the sea in Tahiti with the fervent sailors diving from their ships, the sea off Oahu or the California coast with a storm beginning to blow. Leander had swum the Hellespont.

"It would be wonderful," he said. "Let's go in."

"Are you crazy?"

He was elated, also boasting. He had gone swimming at night though not in the breakers. The big waves were rhythmically swelling, peaking, and then crashing down. He stooped to take off his shoes.

"You're not really going in?"

"Just for a minute."

He was taking off his shirt and pants. She stood in disbelief.

"I'll just see how cold it is."

He was aware of the unreality of it, the bravado, but he was standing in his shorts, at night, at the sea's edge. Turning back had become impossible.

"Philip," she said. "Don't."

"It's all right. I'll be all right."

"No!"

The first rush of water around his ankles was not as cold as he'd expected. As he moved forward, a surge swept in and the water rose up to his waist. Suddenly there was a wave rising before him and he dove into it, the steep black water, and came up in the face of another one about to break. He dove again, coming up this time farther out. The outer line of waves was rising here. It was deeper. The bottom was gone, his feet could no longer touch it. He fought against panic. He was rising and falling in the swells, the waves thundering. He tried to sense their rhythm. A swell lifted him and he looked towards shore. He couldn't see her. The waves were coming in sets of five or six, he couldn't tell. He had to wait until it was calmer, which he was afraid it would not be. Swimming he tried to control his breath. Suddenly his heart jumped. Something was there in the darkness! It was a swimmer's head. Christine.

"What are you doing?" he cried.

He was frightened at seeing her. He was having enough difficulty himself.

"Can you touch bottom here?" she said.

"No," he said. "Do you know how to get back?"

"No."

"Stay with me! Watch out! Here's one! Dive!"

They came up together. Her face looked white, fearful.

"When you're lifted up, when it's about to break, swim with it hard, stretch out, like a knife."

They were rising steeply.

"Now!" he called.

They began swimming together but it broke past them. Then came another. They were too late, it collapsed beneath them. They both disappeared in the surf but came up in time to dive beneath a breaking wave. They were closer in.

"Now!" he cried again. "Go!"

She tried to run in the waist-high water but was pulled back and fell in the rush of a wave. She managed to get back on her feet and stumbled out. He followed her.

"Oh, my God," she said.

She stood with her arms around herself, shaking.

"That was something," he said.

"Yes." It was hard for her to speak.

A surge of water came in around their feet. He took her in his arms. He could feel her chest heaving as she breathed. He admired her immensely.

"What made you do it?"

"I don't know. Love madness."

"You've never done it before?"

"Not in water like that."

They went back to the house shaken but exultant. She sat with a robe pulled up around her.

"Are you cold?"

"A little."

"Do you want something to drink?"

"No."

"Are you sure?"

"Yes. I'm getting warmer."

"I couldn't believe it when I saw you out there. Weren't you afraid?"

"Yes."

"Why did you do it?"

"I don't know," she said. "I had to."

He lay in bed while she showered. He had bought two extra pillows and was lying amid them as he waited. The feeling beforehand was like no other. He heard the shower being turned off and finally she came out, her hair hastily dried, and taking off the robe, slipped into bed beside him. No one was ever more desired. He pulled her to him to be able to hold her more fully. Her hand was between his legs.

"Oh, my," she whispered.

"That's right."

He felt like a god. They were only beginning.

*

He woke in the early light. It was strangely quiet, the waves had stopped breaking. A long vein of green lay in the sea. On the window was a pale moth waiting for morning.

"Christine," he said softly in her ear. "Don't wake up. Can you do it while you're sleeping?"

Afterward, they lay as if dismembered. One leg, clad in a white pajama, was up among the pillows near her head. She stroked the bare foot. The sheets, which had been of an incredible softness, were kicked out of place. Far down the beach, unseen, an American flag flew from a single tall pole like a signal of decency and goodness.

"This is the way you fall in love," he said.

"Is this the way you did?"

"Oh, God no."

He was silent then.

"I was stricken," he said. "I was blinded by it. I didn't know anything. Of course, neither did she. That was a long time ago. Then we got divorced. We were simply different kinds of people. She had the courage to say it. She wrote me a letter."

"It was that easy?"

"Oh, not at the time. Things are never that easy at the time."

"I know," she said. "I married for sex."

"I hoped that was what I was marrying for."

"Women are very weak."

"That's funny. I haven't found that to be so."

"They're weak. A bracelet, a trinket, a ring."

"I notice you're still wearing one."

"It's sentimental," she said. "I can't wait to take it off."

"Let me," he said but did not move.

"You certainly deserve to."

He didn't want to say anything further but to let that remain like a last chord. Then he said,

"I was very impressed when you were speaking Greek. He was impressed, too."

"I don't really know that much."

"You seemed to have no problem."

"My problem is that I need to find a place to live. I need to earn money, and I need a place to live."

"I'll help you."

"Do you mean that?"

"Absolutely. A woman like you can have anything she wants."

"A woman like me," she said.

Yes, like her. The thought of traveling with her, the two of them together in Greece—he ignored the fact of her husband there—the Greece she had told him about. He imagined it, Salonica, Kythira, the women in black, the white boats that linked the islands. He'd never been there. He'd read *The Colossus of Maroussi,* wild and exaggerated, he'd read Homer, he'd seen *Antigone* and *Medea* and listened to the fabulous voice of Nana Mouskouri filled with life. Not all at once but somehow together he thought of Aleksei Paros who had more or less disappeared, Maria Callas, the shipping magnates, the white wine that tasted of pine sap, the Aegean, white teeth and dark hair. It was all a brilliant dream, Greece was in one's blood, they wailed at the grave there, they washed the bodies of the dead. But it was not death that drew him, it was the opposite. With Christine it would be unimaginably rich, living in the sunlight, on the water, on terraces hidden by vines, in the bare rooms of hotels. She would shake it flat and read some of the Greek newspaper to him, perhaps she would, he imagined her able to do anything. He wanted the Greek words for morning, night, thank you, love. He wanted some dirty Greek words so he could whisper them. Nude, he remembered, was the same in every language but probably not in Greek. He loved her nude, he loved thinking of it. He was for the moment emptied of desire but not in the broader sense.

Outside, the day was made up of various silences. The hours had come to a stop. She was quiet, thinking of something, perhaps of nothing. She could not possibly know her allure. He was lying with a smooth-limbed woman who had been stolen from her husband. She was now his, they were in life together. He was thrilled by it. It fit his character, the daring lover, something he knew he was not.

The train that Dena and her son, Leon, were taking to Texas to see her parents went to Dallas and they lived near Austin but would come with their car. Dena wanted to see the country, and Leon was excited by the idea. In the dark lower level of Penn Station where the trains arrived and left, overlapping voices announcing departures filled the air, godlike and final. Eddins stopped to ask a porter for directions to the right car, and they came to it a few moments later and the three of them carried the luggage down the corridor to their compartment where Eddins helped them stow it and stayed talking to them. There hadn't been time to take them to lunch as he'd intended. Leon was becoming nervous, the train was about to leave, he said. He was as tall as Dena, taller.

Eddins looked at his watch.

"There's still three or four minutes," he said.

"Your watch may not be right."

"Tell them I'm really sorry I couldn't come," he said to Dena. "Next time, all right?"

"Take care of yourself," she said.

He hugged each of them.

"Have a good trip."

Out on the platform he stood by the window, waiting. Perhaps he heard it, but in the compartment there was a kind of low sound and electric trembling just as, exactly on time, the train began to move. He waved and they waved back. He blew a kiss and walked along beside them for five or ten feet until he began to fall behind as the train picked up speed. Face pressed to the glass, Dena waved good-bye. It was three forty-five in the afternoon. They would be in Chicago in the morning and from there take the Texas Eagle to Dallas. It was their first trip to Texas on a train. They had always flown there.

They were in darkness at first, beneath the streets, but then broke out into daylight, deep in a series of concrete cuts that took them to the Hudson, the train smooth and swaying slightly as the speed increased. They could hear the low, familiar sound of the whistle far ahead. As if exhilarated by it, they continued to go faster,

They went along the river. On the opposite side were dark granite cliffs covered in green. It was a bluish day with the clouds shaped like smoke. The stations, all strangely vacant late in the day, sped by, Hastings, Dobbs Ferry. Soon after, in the distance was their own town, Piermont, almost completely hidden in trees.

"There it is," Dena said. "That's Piermont."

"I'm trying to see our house."

"I think I see it."

"Where?"

They tried to pick it out but there was too much foliage that hid even their street, and moments later they were passing beneath the shadowy steel of the bridge at Tappan Zee.

For a long while they followed the idling river. They went by Ossining and the great prison there, Sing Sing, that she pointed out. Leon had heard of it but never seen it. It was where they had executions, he knew.

As the tracks drifted inland, away from the river, there were marshes and trees. Peekskill, a station flashing past. Then, with the sun still high above the hills, there came the steep, silent walls of West Point, part of the cliffs it seemed. They went by the empty ruins of an old castle on a small island. Then two kids pressing themselves against a rock embankment as the train sliced the air from their chests. The river narrowed and became blue. Geese were flying along it, powerful, free, almost skimming the surface. A radiant light was spilling through the clouds and at the heart of it, the sun. From far off came the sharp sound of the train's whistle.

Leon was by the window and Dena looked past him as the country unrolled and the day began to pass into evening. She wished that Neil had decided to come. It was so beautiful. He would have some ice brought and they would have a drink. She could hear the tinkle of ice in the glasses. Perhaps they would go to Chicago another time and see the city, almost as great as New York, people said. Somehow the river had begun to go beneath them and disappear as they slowly entered Albany with its somber state buildings and ancient streets. There were the solitary spires of churches, reassuring, silhouetted in the last light.

Sometime after seven, they walked forward to the dining car for dinner.

"This is going to be great," Dena said.

She began to sing happily, nothing could be finer than to be in Carolina, even though the Limited went up along Lake Erie and the Texas Eagle went nowhere near the Carolinas.

The train was lurching. They almost lost their balance. She was right, the dining car was like the stage in a theater, brightly lit, with waiters in white jackets moving smoothly past the tables as the train jerked and swayed beneath their feet.

"This is like shooting the rapids," Leon called.

The head waiter showed them to a table by themselves. The menu listed broiled sirloin steak and oven fries. Past the wide, black window yellow lights that looked like lanterns floated along in the rural dark, then sudden, surprising clusters of red lights or a single white one going by like a comet. They ordered a glass of wine.

The porter had made up their berths while they were at dinner, fresh white sheets and taut blanket. Leon took the upper bunk and at about nine-thirty he climbed up into it. He took off his shoes and put them in a kind of hammock that hung along the side, then his shirt and pants, slipping out of them while lying down. The train meanwhile had stopped and didn't move for what seemed a long time.

"Why are we stopped?" he called. "Where are we?"

"We're in Syracuse," Dena told him. "We're still in New York. Way up."

They could hear voices, people who were coming aboard late and some of them passing along the corridor.

"Where will we be in the morning?" he asked.

"I don't know. We'll see."

Finally the train began to move again. The country went past like a somber painting, trees in the darkness lit by the windows of the train. Lone, sleeping houses, black and silent. The lights of a town with vacant streets. Dena felt a strange happiness in the quiet of the compartment.

After a while, she said,

"Are you asleep?"

There was no answer. She saw the window becoming flecked with rain and slowly fell asleep herself, opening her eyes again as they began to join a wide expanse of other tracks curving in on theirs. It was Buffalo. Afterwards they crossed a river and traveled along Lake Erie passing forlorn stations, not a soul.

Sometime around one in the morning, its cause unknown, an electrical fire broke out at the end of the car, and the corridor filled with smoke. Dena woke from the acrid smell. Something was coming under the door of the compartment. She was half-asleep but got up quickly to see what it was. Smoke was coming in along the doorjamb, and when she opened the door it poured in on her. She closed it, coughing and crying out to Leon. No one had pulled the emergency brake or spread the alarm. The train had not slowed. A porter in the next car finally noticed. They jammed the doors open but could not get in because of the smoke. By the time the train was stopped and windows broken open, seven passengers, those in compartments closest to the fire, were dead, asphyxiated. They included Dena and Leon, her son.

19. RAIN

The ways divide. In the house above the river to which a room had been added, a small room with a window at one end and of a size that almost invited one in to sit and open a book or gaze out into the little garden, untended but nevertheless intimate because of the sculpture in it, a piece of natural sculpture that had been part of a tree that was cut down and sawed into two-foot logs, one of them, thick and upright, happening to have the shape of a woman's body from waist to where the legs began, a kind of primitive altarpiece, neo-African, rounded, dark, immune to weather—in this house where Eddins, his wife, and son had lived in happiness, free from all danger, where the neighbors were good people, the streets were quiet, the police, finally past the bitter feud with the mayor, were friendly and knew you by name, here, among the trees and village calm, like something fallen from the sky, a great engine detached from an airliner high above and unseen and unheard hurtling down, death had struck, destruction, plunging into life like a sharpened stake.

The ways part. Eddins' life was now broken in two. The pieces were not equal. All that was happening and that could happen in the future was somehow lighter, inconsequential. Life had an emptiness, like a morning after. He kept rejecting the accident. He could hardly remember the funeral except that it was unbearable. They were buried in the cemetery in Upper Grandview, above the road, in graves that were side by side. Dena's mother and father had come. Neil was hardly able to face them. He couldn't rid himself of a feeling of guilt. He was a southerner, he had been raised to honor women and give them protection, to defend them. It was a duty. If he had been on the train, somehow this wouldn't have happened. He had failed them, like the philosophy professor in Valley Cottage whose house had been broken into and he and his aging wife assaulted. He was never the same afterward. It was not so much the injuries and continuing fear, it was the shame he felt. He hadn't been able to protect his wife.

Eddins appeared in many ways unchanged, his usual though slightly more casual self. He had a flower in his buttonhole, a boutonniere, he talked to people, joked, but there were things you could not see. He had failed them. He was stained.

For a while he continued to live in the house, but he disliked coming back to it in the evening, to the emptiness and what seemed the knowledge of the world that he was there alone. He rented a small apartment in the city, below Gramercy Park, where in the evening he watched the news and had a drink, sometimes a second or third, and decided not to cook dinner, simple as it was. He was not depressed, but he was living with the feeling of injustice. There were times when he almost broke into tears over his loneliness and what he had lost. He saw them now for what they were and had been, the great days of love. She had asked for and had demanded so little. She had given her love so completely, her great smile, her teeth, her lighthearted foolishness. I love you so much—who could say that with the overwhelming truth of countless acts of love behind it? He hadn't done all he should have, he should have given more. I would give it now, he thought, and he said it aloud, I would so much give it! Ah, Jesus, he said, and rose to fill his drink. Don't become a drunk, he thought. Don't become an object of pity.

Bowman had the other. Without a wife or girlfriend he had seemed settled into a single life, of habit, not uncomfortably, appearing in a dark-blue suit at restaurants and readings, at ease in the visible world, familiar.

It turned out to be other than that.

He was not fully living with Christine, she had resisted it until her life, she explained, was on a more even keel. She continued to spend the night with him in the apartment two or three times a week. She would meet him at the end of the day, sometimes with a bunch of flowers or a fashion magazine, the European edition with its suggestion of the glamour of life there.

They were not married, but they had the pleasures of guiltless love. It was impossible to have enough of her. What Chekhov had meant was that lovemaking that took place once a year had a staggering power, the power of a great, religious experience, and more often than that it was merely something like nourishment, but if that were the price, Bowman was only too willing to pay it.

In the morning there were pieces of her clothing lying about, her shoes, which he particularly liked, near a chair. She was in the narrow kitchen making coffee. They could live in harmony, he knew from the way she talked and behaved, from their intimacy. He had fallen in love before, deeply in love, but it had always been with an other, someone not like himself. With Christine there was the feeling of always having known her. If she could rid herself of her husband, they would marry.

His thoughts were of this as he walked across Central Park, green and immense, with its boundary of tall buildings shining in the morning light. For all of her assurance and poise, Christine was seeking stability. She had confessed it, and it was something he could provide along with much more. He was noticing the youthfulness of various people he passed. He was in the middle of life and just beginning.

On the weekend it rained. They stayed in. They lay on the bed in the quiet of the afternoon, the rain like mist on the window. She was watching something on television, an old movie, Italian, as it happened, and he was reading Verga, Sicilian. A woman in a low-cut dress sat polishing her nails while two men talked. It was in black and white, white shirts, Italian faces, dark hair. The subtitles were partly washed out, Christine was hardly reading them. As Bowman read, her hand slipped inside his robe and held his cock, almost distractedly, although as it swelled her thumb began to move softly along it. The sound had been muted. He could hear himself as he swallowed. He could see from the corner of his eye Christine's soft cheek. She was contentedly watching the film. His cock was hard, smooth as a scar. By the shore of a lake a woman in a black slip was struggling with a man. She suddenly broke free and ran but then for some reason gave up and awaited her fate. In the close-up her face was resigned but filled with scorn.

He had stopped reading, the words made no sense. The movie went on. The woman was about to be killed. He would never forget her tear-streaked face or bare arms rising to embrace her murderer. He was feeling excruciating pleasure. The movie went on and on. Occasionally Christine's hand would gently tighten as if to remind him. Finally the credits were shown.

He was free to do anything. It had never been this way, not with Vivian, certainly not with Vivian, not with Enid. She was naked from the waist down and he had her turn to her stomach and picked up his book and resumed reading, one proprietary hand resting on her buttock. She lay unmoving, her face turned away. They were not equals, not now. All his life, then, had been in preparation. In a while they began. The city lay silent. He rubbed his cock slowly along her raised cunt as if bathing its length. Finally he seated it. There was a long lovemaking in which his mind went blank. They neither saw nor heard the rain.

Afterwards they were like victims, face up, unable to move.

"It's like nothing else in the world. I simply can't imagine anything on earth more . . . extreme," he said.

"Heroin," Christine murmured.

"Have you ever had heroin?"

"Four times as pleasurable as sex. Pleasure that can't be compared with anything else. Believe me."

"So you've taken it."

"No, but I know."

"I don't want to be thought of as just a nice man."

"You're not a nice man. You're a real man. You know you are," she said. "That night in the taxi, I already knew."

Everything he had wanted to be, she was offering him. She had been given to him as a blessing, a proof of God. He had never really been paid. He had never been paid in the one true coin. She had held him casually in her hand, he had known what she was thinking. They might have lain like that and talked for days or been silent. The afternoon had been unforgettable.

"Why are we always so tired?" he asked. "It can't be that much effort."

"Yes, it can," she said.

Eddins recovered slowly. He had finally accepted what had happened, but he was crippled by it. He was less committed to life and more passive. Unlike his former self, he could sit quietly listening. He sat listening to two women next to him in the theater before the curtain went up talking enthusiastically about a movie they had seen, what had happened in it and how it was so like life. They were in their forties, probably, and no different from women he might be more interested in if he knew them, but he had no interest in knowing them. Or, for that matter, the couple two rows in front of him, the woman. He had been struck by her beautiful, full hair and the fur collar on her coat. Her head was almost leaning against the man's, and from time to time she would turn slightly to say something to him. She had Slavic cheekbones and a long nose that came down straight from her forehead, a Roman nose, a sign of authority. He could look at a woman's face, he thought, and almost recite her character. Delovet's girlfriend who was an actress or former actress, a little on the short side to be one in either case, Eddins marked at first sight as a drinker and probably nasty if not made love to. Delovet was finding it difficult to detach himself from her. He was bored by her, impatient, but at the same time he liked to show her off. Her name was Diane Ostrow, she was called Dee Dee. Eddins had never come across anyone who'd seen her on the stage. She had black hair and a voracious laugh. Also just enough shrewdness to keep from slipping any further down. She could be persuaded without much effort to name several stars she had slept with. She liked it when they stood on their head naked for her.

"A number of them did it?"

"Two," she said casually. "So, what kind of things do you like to do?" she asked Eddins.

"Wrestle," he said.

"Really?"

"I wrestled for the university," he said. "I was a terror."

"Which university?"

"All of them," he said.

One day in a taxi heading south on Park, he saw a woman on the corner in expensive shoes and her coat tied at the waist with a cloth belt, a woman with the assumption of her class in every detail. She doubtless lived along the avenue and perhaps had ordinary concerns or cares, but the image of her impressed him with its poise or even, in its way, gallantry.

He began to pay some attention to his clothes and appearance. He bought some soft cotton shirts and a blue silk scarf. When the weather was good he walked to work.

It was around this time that he met a divorced woman named Irene Keating in the New York Public Library. It was after a lecture and people were standing along the hallway drinking wine. She was by herself, not completely comfortable but wearing a nice-looking dress. She lived in New Jersey, a few minutes away, she said.

"More than a few minutes," he said.

"Do you live in the city?"

"I have a house in Piermont," he said.

"Piermont?"

"At the foot of the Ngong Hills."

"The what?"

"Not well-known," he remarked.

She was not literary but he liked her face that showed a pleasant nature.

"I thought the lecture—what did you think of it?—I thought it was a little boring," he said.

"I'm so glad you said that. I was falling asleep."

"Not a bad feeling. At certain times, that is. Do you come in often?"

"Well, yes and no. I usually come in hopes of meeting someone interesting."

"You'd do better in most bars."

"Why aren't you in one, then?" she said.

He took her to dinner a few days later and ended up telling her stories about Delovet, his yacht without a motor in Westport, and his former Romanian girlfriend, of whom he liked to say, "I could have her deported," about Robert Boyd, the ex-preacher that Eddins had never met but liked so much.

Boyd's father had died, and he was living alone in the country, in desperate need as always.

"You'd like him. His letters have such dignity."

She listened rapt. She asked if he would come to dinner at her house.

"I'll cook something good," she said.

He agreed to come that Friday. Then, on the train there in the evening crowd he found himself regretting it. They were all going home to their families. Their life was familiar to them.

She met him at the station and they drove to her house five or six blocks away. It was an attached house with brick steps and an iron railing. Inside, however, it was less forbidding. She wanted to hang up his coat, but he said, no, just leave it on the chair. She poured champagne and had him come into the kitchen, where she had put on an apron over her dress and continued cooking as they talked. She seemed younger and excited.

"Is the champagne any good?" she asked. "I just go by the price."

"Very good."

"I'm glad you could come," she said.

"Have you lived here long?"

"Taste this," she said, holding a spoonful of what looked like consommé out to him.

It was delicious.

"I made it myself. From scratch."

The table was set for two. She lit the candles and after they had sat down seemed to relax a little. The light in the room had a soft hue, perhaps it was colored by the champagne. She filled their glasses again. Suddenly she stood up—she had forgotten to take off her apron, which she stripped away, mussing her hair. She sat down and then stood again, leaning deliberately across the table to kiss him. They had never kissed before. The consommé was in front of them; she raised her glass slightly.

"To the night of nights," she said.

They ate roast squab, the birds succulent and brown on their beds of buttered rice. He didn't remember how it proceeded from there. The bed was wide, and she seemed nervous as a cat. She tried to get away from him as much as she drew him towards her, she hadn't made up her mind or she kept changing it. She kicked and turned away, he felt he was trying to catch her. Afterwards she apologized and said it was the first time she had made love in three years, since her divorce, but she loved it. She kissed his hands as if he were a priest.

In the morning she had no makeup. For some reason—the purity of her bare features—she looked like a Swede. She talked about her marriage. Her ex-husband had been a businessman, a sales manager. In the daylight the house seemed drab. There were no bookshelves. The magical dining room, he noticed, had some kind of striped wallpaper. It had been there when they moved in, she said.

20. THE HOUSE ON THE POND

It was all still asleep, untouched by the wand. Along the road there were farmhouses, some with their land, and one, old and white, that was a boardinghouse. You could rent a room by the week or for the season and look out at the flat, unbroken fields and walk meditatively or ride a crippled bicycle to the beach about a mile away. Further along was a cemetery that the road split around like a wrecked ship and still further a drab, unpainted house beneath the trees that was rented to young people who sometimes had parties outside at the end of the day and into the evening, cars parked around haphazardly and pitchers of cheap wine.

In earlier years the painters had all come because it was cheap and because of the light, clear, transcendent light that seemed to come for miles in the long afternoon. Life was casual. There were large houses behind the hedges and others on flag lots, some from the earliest days. The flood of discovery had not yet swept in. Simple cottages, some belonging to the farmers, stood on the dunes.

The country suited Christine, she said this herself. It was beautiful and open. The light was such as you had never seen, the air and the wind from the sea. She avoided going back to the city and Bowman came on the long weekends. Her feeling of happiness greeted him. Her glorious smile. At the roadside stand with its flatbeds of produce, fresh corn, tomatoes, straw-berries right from the field, they recognized her. Normally hardened to customers, when she stood at the counter with her arms filled, they relented and smiled.

She had decided to renew her broker's license, and she went to see Evelyn Hinds, whose name she'd seen on For Sale signs. Mrs. Hinds' office was in her house just off New Town Lane, white with a white picket fence and a neatly lettered sign.

Evelyn Hinds was a dumpling of a woman with bright eyes that took things in immediately and a ready laugh. She was at ease with people. Her first husband had crashed at sea—it was thought he crashed, no one ever saw him again—but she'd been married two times after that and was on good terms with both her former husbands. Christine came to see her in dark slacks and a short linen jacket.

"Chris, can I call you that?" Mrs. Hinds said. "How old are you, do you mind my asking?"

"Thirty-four," Christine said.

"Thirty-four. Really? You don't look it."

"Well, it's worse than that. I sometimes claim to be a bit younger."

"And you live out here?"

"Yes, I'm living here now. I have a sixteen-year-old daughter. I was a broker in the city for seven years."

It was not quite that long but Mrs. Hinds didn't question it.

"Who were you with?" she said.

"A small firm in the village, Walter Bruno."

"Did you do sales or rentals?"

"I did mostly sales."

"I love to put customers together with houses."

"I like that, too."

"It's like marrying them off. Are you married?"

"No, I'm separated," Christine said. "I'm not looking for a husband."

"Thank goodness."

"What do you mean?"

"No one else would have a chance," Mrs. Hinds said.

She liked Christine and took her on.

It was a small agency, just four of them. She told Bowman she was going to like it.

"I've seen her name," he said. "What's she like?"

"Very straightforward, but there's one other important thing. Now that I'm doing it again," she said, "I'll find you a house."

Anet, who had come home from school, was waiting at the station with her mother, and Bowman met her for the first time when he got off the train. She had a fresh, young face and hung behind Christine a bit. Car doors were slamming and families calling out to one another.

"These have been the most beautiful days," Christine told him as they walked to the car. "They say it's going to be like this all through the weekend."

"When did you get here?" he asked Anet.

He wanted it to be easy between them.

"When did I get here?" she turned to Christine.

"On Wednesday."

"It's great to have you here," he said.

They worked their way out of the traffic around the station

and went along in the early evening, the headlights bright and flowing ahead like an invitation to a wondrous night.

"Where should we go?" he said to Christine. "Did you make dinner?"

"I have some things at home," she said.

"Should we go to Billy's? Let's go there. Have you been to any of these places yet?" he asked Anet somewhat foolishly.

"No," she said.

"I'd rather go to that first place, the two brothers," Christine said.

"You're right. That's a better idea."

As they went up the steps and then in, Bowman felt a full-bodied happiness, the two women and the aura they gave. Anet talked during the meal but only to her mother. Bowman enjoyed it, however. It seemed comfortable. They drove home through a deep, luxurious blue, past houses with their reassuring lights.

Anet was not shy but she kept her distance from him. She belonged to her mother and, certainly, to her father. She was loyal to them both. It was hard to win her acceptance. He also sensed her unhappiness that he was her mother's lover, a word he never used—there was a jealousy born in the blood. She expressed it by excluding him although they sometimes sat together, the three of them, in a natural way listening to music or watching TV. He noticed the womanly gestures that were like her mother's. He was always, despite himself, aware of her presence in the house, sometimes terrifically aware. His thoughts went back to Jackie Ettinger, the girl long ago in Summit, the almost mythic girl. He never knew Jackie. It seemed he would not know Anet either.

When he was away from her—during the week—he was able to think about it more calmly, the figure he wanted to be, the longtime consort—that was not the word—the man her mother loved, probably not in any way more sexually than Anet's father although that was clearly not so, given the intensity of Bowman's feelings, an emotional intensity that was almost constantly present.

On a Sunday morning when the heat of the day had not yet begun but the light was dazzling all along the beach, the surf in a line almost violent in its brightness, they sat near the dunes with sections of the paper, reading in contemplation, feeling the sun. The water was cold, there were only a few other people. It was like Mexico, he felt, though he had never been there. The simplicity. It was June and summer had arrived. People were there but not yet the crowds. It was a kind of exile. They were reading what had happened in the world. When the sun was above their shoulders they would go home for lunch.

The Murphys in Antibes must have had such a life. They'd had a house, themselves, further east. Gerald Murphy liked to swim and swam for a mile in the ocean every day. Bowman had mentioned this but to no one's interest. Other people, three or four of them, were swimming he noticed. He got up and went down to the water. He was surprised to find it warmer than he expected. It came in around his ankles almost temptingly. He went in up to his knees.

He came back to where they were lying near the weathered palings.

"The water's warm," he said.

"You always say that."

"It's quite warm."

"Brrr," Anet said.

"Come in and see."

"Anet, you go."

"I'm afraid of the waves."

"Those are no waves, those are just swells. Come on, I'll go in, too. Philip almost drowned me last summer."

"How?"

"In some real waves. They're not that big today. Come on, let's go in."

The water was chilly at first. Anet stood in it unwilling but Christine went in and she followed, reluctantly walking deeper. The bottom was smooth. They passed the low line of waves and into the water beyond, where the swells lifted them gently. They swam without speaking, just their heads above the water, rising and falling. The sky seemed to smooth all feelings. Twice in the weeks past Anet had remarked to him after some jot of advice, "You're not my father," and he had felt the sting, but now she smiled at him, not in warmth but satisfaction.

"Well?" he said to her.

"I love it," she replied.

They came out as a trio, out of breath and smiling. Anet walked ahead of them, lithe and striding, running her fingers through her hair to straighten it out. She sat down close to Christine, their knees almost touching, and leaned against her in happiness.

She had made some friends, among them a girl named Sophie, who was self-possessed and had wavy blond hair. She was the daughter of a psychiatrist. On a rainy day they had sat, the four of them, playing hearts. Sophie had taken off an earring and was examining it as the play went around the table. When it came to her she sloughed a low spade.

"You made a mistake," Bowman commented helpfully.

"Did I?" she said. She was practicing for life.

She didn't bother to pick up the badly played card, but then almost patiently took it back and played another. Christine admired her aplomb and the dark-red lipstick she used, until the night Anet went to the movies with her and didn't come back until after midnight. Christine had waited concerned, watching television. She finally heard the door close in the kitchen.

"Anet?" she called.

"Yes."

"Where've you been? It's the middle of the night."

"I'm sorry. I should have called."

"Where've you been? The movie let out hours ago."

"We didn't go to the movie," Anet said.

Bowman felt he should not be listening. He went into the kitchen but could still hear them.

"You said you were going to the movies."

"Yes, I know."

"What *did* you do?"

"We walked."

"You walked? Where?"

"Just on the street."

Christine's waiting had made her nerves jagged, and there was something resistant in Anet's voice.

"Have you had anything to drink?"

"Why do you ask that?"

"Never mind why I ask. Have you?"

There was silence.

"Have you been smoking? Grass?"

"I had a glass of wine."

"Where were you drinking? It's against the law."

"It's not against the law in Europe."

"This isn't Europe. Where were you? Who were you with?"

"We were with some friends of Sophie's."

"Boys."

"Yes."

She was speaking in a lower voice.

"Well, who are they? What are their names?"

"Brad."

"Brad who?"

"I don't know his other name."

"Who was the other boy?"

"I don't know," Anet said.

"You don't know their names."

"Sophie does," Anet said.

Her voice had begun to waver.

"Why are you crying?"

"I don't know."

"What are you crying about?" Christine repeated.

"I don't know!"

"Yes, you do."

"I don't!"

"Anet!" Christine called.

She had left the room. After a few moments Christine came into the kitchen.

"I could hear it all," Bowman said.

Christine was clearly disturbed.

"It's my worst nightmare," she said.

"She seemed very forthcoming. It didn't sound like anything much."

"Why is she doing this?"

"She's not really doing anything. They do meet boys."

"How do you know?"

"What does that mean, how do I know?"

"You don't have a daughter."

"No," he said.

The front door slammed. Christine closed her eyes and put her forefingers over them to soothe them.

"Do you know I'm afraid I'm going to hear a car start. Darling, please. Would you go out and make her come in? I'm just too keyed up to."

Bowman said nothing, but after a few moments he went outside in the darkness. Finally he made her out past the end of the driveway. She had heard him coming but didn't turn. He had no confidence in what he was doing.

"Anet," he said. "Can I talk to you for a minute?"

He waited.

"I don't really have much say in this," he said, "but I think it probably amounts to less than it seems."

She seemed not to be listening.

"Perhaps you could just give her a call next time, say everything's fine, you'll be a little late. Could you do that?"

She wouldn't reply. She was watching something white moving along the dark tops of the far-off trees. It went along and then seemed to turn somehow and disappear. Almost immediately it came back higher.

"It's a heron," he said.

As they watched, it went towards the solid black trees and then up through an opening in the topmost branches, into the night sky.

"That was a heron?" she said.

"You could see its neck."

"I didn't think they flew at night."

"I guess they do."

"Heron gone," she said.

He glanced at her to see if she'd intended the pun but couldn't tell. His fear of her had lessened and, saying nothing further, he followed her back towards the house.

On an afternoon that fall, Christine called him. Her voice was filled with excitement.

"Philip?"

"Yes. What is it?"

"The most wonderful thing. I found the house."

"What house?"

"I found a perfect house, the one you've been looking for. I knew it the minute I saw it. It's an old house, not terribly big, but it has four bedrooms, and it's on a pond, part of a pond. There's an old couple who've owned it for thirty years. They haven't listed it, but they're interested in selling."

"How did you find it?"

"Evelyn knew about it. She knows everything that's going on."

"How much is it?"

"Only a hundred and twenty thousand."

"Is that all? I'll take it," he said airily.

"No, but let me show it to you this weekend. You have to see it."

The pond could not be seen from the road. It was down below. There was a long dirt driveway that appeared to end between two ancient trees. It was a clear October morning. As they drove up, suddenly there was the house. He would never forget the first sight of it, the feeling of familiarity he immediately had though he'd had no idea of what to expect. It was a beautiful old house, like a farmhouse but in isolation near the pond. They entered through the kitchen door across a narrow porch. The kitchen itself was a large square room with open shelves and a pantry in what had been a closet. The main bedroom was downstairs. There were three small bedrooms above. The stairway banister, he noticed, was plain unfinished pine worn smooth by hands. The floorboards were wide and the windows also.

"You're right," he said. "It's a nice house."

"It's wonderful, isn't it?" she said.

"Yes, it's really something special."

The walls and ceiling were in good condition. There were no leak stains or cracks. Two of the small bedrooms he thought could be combined.

The view from upstairs was of two good-sized houses across the water, half-hidden in trees.

"Does it have heat?" he said.

"Yes. There's a half basement with a furnace."

They walked outside and down to the pond where, not far out, the dim outline of a sunken rowboat could be seen.

"There's how much land, did you say?"

"There's all this. The property goes to the road. It's a little over an acre."

"One twenty," he said.

"That's all. That's a very good price."

"Well, I think I'll have to buy it."

"I'm so happy! I knew you'd want it."

"It's going to be very nice living here. We could even get married."

"Yes, we could."

"Is that an acceptance?"

"I would have to get a divorce."

"Why don't we get married and get the divorce later?"

"And we could live in jail," she said.

"That would be all right."

He bought the house, including some furnishings, for $120,000. He bought it in both their names, a country house that was ideal, big enough to have a guest or two occasionally, perfectly located, a house unto itself.

The bank in Bridgehampton took a generous view of his assets and gave him a mortgage of $65,000. He had some difficulties coming up with the difference. He sold most of the stocks he owned and borrowed $8,000 on a line of credit.

They closed the first week in December and moved in that very day carrying two upholstered chairs bought from an antiques—really, used furniture—dealer in Southampton. They were very happy. That night they lit a fire and made some supper. They drank a bottle of wine and while listening to music, part of another. A dreamed-of night, their first in the house. In bed she slipped the nightgown over her head and let it fall to the floor. She lay in his arms, it was like a wedding night. He took her arm and pressed his lips to the inside of her elbow in a long fervent kiss.

Soon after came Christmas. Anet had gone to Athens to be with her father. The house as yet had little furniture, only a sofa, some chairs, two tables, and a bed. The windows had neither shades nor curtains, and it would have been stark to be there for the holidays, even with a tree. In the city, the streets were alive. It was Christmas in New York, crowds hurrying home in the early darkness, captains of the Salvation Army ringing their bells, St. Patrick's, the brilliant theater of the great store windows, mansions of plenty, the prosperous-looking people. They were playing "Good King Wenceslas," bartenders were wearing reindeer antlers—Christmas of the Western world, as in Berlin before the war, the deep green forests of Slovakia, Paris, Dickens' London.

There was a party at Baum's. Bowman hadn't been in the apartment for a long time. As he came in with Christine and a man in a white jacket took their coats, he thought back to having been there the first time with Vivian in her confident young naïveté.

"Philip, it's so good to see you," Diana greeted him.

"This is Christine Vassilaros," he said.

"Hello," Diana said taking Christine's hand in hers. "Please come in."

The room was crowded. Diana was paying special attention to Christine, no doubt having heard about her. Christine had a daughter, she learned, and asked,

"How old is she?"

"She's sixteen."

"She must be a beauty," Diana said with sincerity. "Our son, Julian, is in law school at Michigan. He refused to go to Harvard. It was elitist. I felt like killing him."

"Do you want a cigar?" Baum asked Bowman.

"No, thanks."

"These are really fine. They're Cuban. Take one, smoke it later. I've started smoking cigars. One a day. I like to sit and smoke one after dinner. A cigar should touch your lips exactly twenty-two times, anyway that's what someone told me. Otherwise, as Cheever said, hick. Actually, he was talking about how to hold a cigar properly. I forget how that was."

"My one regret," Diana said to Christine, "is that we didn't have more children. I wish we had three or four."

"Four is a lot."

"The happiest days of my life were when Julian was a little boy. Nothing really compares with that. You're fortunate," she told Christine, "you can still have children. That's the whole point of it, it really is. Now we're free, more or less. We go to Italy. It's beautiful, but then I think of the love of a little boy."

"I love Italy," Baum said. "The people. You know, I call my Italian colleague and his secretary answers the phone— his assistant, I should say. Roberto! It's wonderful to talk to you! You should be in Rome, it's such a beautiful day, the sun is shining, you should be here! There's nobody like them."

"Why do you call her his assistant?" Diana asked.

"His secretary, then."

"They're not all like that. She's a bit of a songbird. Eduardo is nothing like that. You talk to him and he says, hello, I feel terrible, the world is a mess. He's the publisher."

Other guests were coming in. Diana left to greet them. Baum stayed to talk on with Christine, he liked her looks. After the party, he asked his wife,

"What did you think of Philip's new girlfriend?"

"Is she new?"

"Well, not exactly new but certainly not old."

"No, she's quite a bit younger."

"It's made him a bit younger."

"Yes, that's the general belief," Diana said.

That spring Beatrice Bowman died. She had been weak and disoriented for a long time. She thought her son was someone else, and his visits had long periods of silence when she seemed to at least be aware of his company while he sat near her and read. To the world she knew, to the few friends who had by then drifted away, to everyone except himself and Dorothy, it was no longer important that she live. What had been her life, the people she knew and the deep pool of memory and knowing, had vanished or dried up and fallen apart. Or so it seemed when she could think about it. She would not have wanted to go on, but she had not been able to prevent it. Outwardly she was still handsome if baffled, and the lines in her face were gentle. She had many times said a final good-bye.

In contrast to her normal agitation, she died calmly. She simply did not wake one morning. Perhaps she had known something the night before, some not quite familiar sadness, a lessening of strength. Except for not breathing, one sleep was indistinguishable from the other.

She left no instructions. Bowman agreed with Dorothy that she should be cremated, and together they went to the funeral home to arrange for it. They asked for the casket to be open, they both wanted to see her for a last time. In the silent room, there his mother lay. They had done her hair and put some light cosmetic on her lips and cheek. He bent and kissed her brow. It seemed indecent. Some quality in her that he knew, not merely life, had been erased.

She had never told him all she knew, nor could he remember all the days of childhood and things they had done together. She had given him his character, a part of it, the rest had formed itself somehow. He thought, with a kind of desperation, of things he would like to talk to her about or talk about once more. She had been a young woman in New York, newly married, and in the blazing summer morning had been blessed with a son.

His stepmother, as it happened, died the same spring. He had never met her or either of the preceding ones. Someone sent him a clipping from a Houston paper. Vanessa Storrs Bowman was her name, she was seventy-three, a social figure. Examining the photo he read on until with a stab of something—it was not grief—he saw that his father had died two years earlier. He felt a strange jolt of time, as if he had been living a partly fraudulent life, and though in all the years he had never seen or heard from his father, some essential connection was now gone. Vanessa Storrs Bowman had two brothers and her father had been president of an oil company. The impression was of money, even wealth. He thought of his mother and the distant rich relative, cousin perhaps, whose mansion just off Fifth Avenue he remembered having been pointed out to him. Did he remember this or was it a dream, three or four dark granite stories, a green roof, and iron and glass doors? Perhaps it did not really exist. He had always expected to pass by it some day but never did.

21. AZUL

The year he had the house, the spring of that year and the summer were the happiest time of his life although some of the earlier times he had forgotten. There hadn't been the money to do much except buy a little furniture for the upstairs, but in the bareness, the simplicity, was ample room for happiness. There were the seasons, the trees, the grass that was a little too long sloping down to the water, the sun a mirror on the windows of the houses across from them.

Summer mornings, the light of the world pouring in and the silence. It was a barefoot life, the cool of the night on the floorboards, the green trees if you stepped outside, the first faint cries of the birds. He arrived in a suit and didn't put it on again until he went back to the city. The house couldn't be locked—the catch on the kitchen door was misaligned. The sills were cracked by the weather and peeling, he'd scraped and filled some of them but hadn't gotten around to the painting. Buying the house had meant a cash payment of more than fifty-five thousand dollars. He had managed to scrape it together. He had never been much concerned about money. He earned thirty-four thousand a year, and that didn't include lunches and often dinners that were on the expense account. His apartment was rent-controlled, and he was paying less than half of what the rent should really be. Going to Europe twice a year was at no expense to himself, and occasionally that was true of other places, Chicago, Los Angeles. In almost every way his life was comfortable.

Beatrice had left nothing, the long illness had used up everything she had. He expected to be his aunt Dorothy's heir, but he had no idea of what that might amount to. Dorothy lived in a small apartment with the piano that Frank had liked to sit at in the afternoon and play the light, tinkling music she loved. She lived on a little income she had and Social Security. Every summer for a couple of weeks she visited Katrina Loes, a childhood friend who had a house in the Thousand Islands. She had never asked for anything—her needs were modest. If you ever need anything . . . Bowman had said. The answer was always, she didn't.

When Anet came back from school that summer, she had changed, although she was still loving towards her mother and even-tempered. She had felt the pull of common life, of others, a particular person perhaps, though she seemed not to have a boyfriend. She was conscious of being attractive. She was trying it out, not on Bowman. She was used to Bowman and called him Phil. She was not much in evidence through the summer, she was off with her friends, playing tennis or at one of their pools or endlessly, it seemed, talking.

One hot afternoon, she was up in her room and they suddenly heard a terrifying scream. Christine ran to the stairs.

"What is it? Anet!" she cried.

Anet had rolled over on a wasp. The sting had awakened her. She was in pain and weeping. It had been so sharp and unexpected. Christine was trying to comfort her. Bowman came with a washcloth soaked in cold water.

"You'll be all right," he promised. "Hold this on it. Where did it go?"

"Where did what go?"

"The bee."

"I don't know," Anet said, sobbing.

"When they sting you, they lose their stinger. It tears loose. It has barbs on it. Don't try and pull it out."

It had not been a bee though no one knew. Anet had been sleeping in shorts that were now half-pulled down.

"You'll be all right," he said.

"It hurts."

She was breathing in hitched, uneven breaths.

"Do you see it?" she asked.

As if they were campers, she pulled the waistband still lower, turning her head to look down at herself as she did. She was perfect except for a small area of redness.

"It doesn't look bad," Bowman said with some understatement. "Now let's see the other one," he joked.

"The other one is fine," she said coolly.

But he felt comfortable with her, treating her like a child, even his own child, and perhaps she felt it as well.

Early one evening he sat outside smoking a cigarette and looking at the smooth surface of the pond that was absolutely still and across to the other houses where lights were already on and a car was slowly making its way, half-hidden by trees, to one of them. The sky was clear and a deepening blue. To the west he could see a bank of clouds filled with occasional blooms of light. There was no sound, it was too far off. Only the darkness of the clouds being eerily lit. Finally there came a first faint rumbling.

Christine came out on the porch.

"I thought I heard thunder."

"Yes. Look over there."

She sat down beside him.

"I didn't know you smoked," she said.

"Just once in a while," he said. "I only smoke Gauloises, like the French movie stars, but you can't get them here. This is just an ordinary cigarette."

"Oh, look at that," she said.

In the sky there had been a jagged line of intense white that went to the ground. After what seemed a long interval came a soft, muttering thunder.

"There's going to be a storm."

"I love storms. I can hear it."

"If you count the time you can tell how far away it is," he said.

"How do you do that?"

"It's about one mile for every five or six seconds between the lightning and the sound."

She waited until there was another flash of lightning and began to count.

"What was that, about twelve seconds?"

"Just about."

The thunder had been indistinct, it was hard to tell. There was now a clear bank of dark clouds, and the thunder became more threatening, like the roar of an enormous beast. The storm was coming closer, it seemed to be coming with greater speed. The sky was dark and lit by erratic flashes and voltage. A wind had risen. It smelled of rain.

"Are we going to stay out here?" she said.

"Just for a couple of minutes."

The great storm cloud, the front edge of it, was already moving over them. It was almost black and of immense size, like the side of a mountain. It seemed to cover the world. Lightning struck about half a mile away with a tremendous crackling and almost immediately it struck closer with an ear-splitting crash.

"We'd better go in."

"Come with me," she pleaded.

"I'm coming."

They were barely inside when there was another great flash of lightning. The thunder seemed overhead. From where she had been let out on the road, Anet came running towards the house and in by the kitchen door. She was frightened.

"You should have stayed in the car!"

It had become night. It was almost completely dark. They sat together in the living room and amid the thunder heard the first distinct sound of rain. Soon it was a torrent. It poured down. Suddenly the lights went out.

"Oh, my God."

"Are we all right here?" Anet cried.

There was a loud, violent crack and the room went bright as lightning struck just outside. In that instant he could see the two of them, their arms around one another and their faces white.

"No, no, it's all right," he said.

"Can it come inside?" Anet cried.

"No. It can't."

From time to time as the rain fell he saw them in flashes that were less intense. Then almost abruptly the rain lessened. The thunder was further away. The earth seemed calmed. Finally Christine said,

"Is it over?"

"I think so."

"How long do you suppose the lights are going to be out?" Christine said.

"We have some candles."

"Where?"

"They're in one of the kitchen drawers," he said. "I'll get them."

He found and lit one. In its faint light they sat shaken.

"I was afraid it was going to hit the house," Anet said. "What if it had hit the house?"

"Do you mean, would the house catch fire? Probably. You weren't frightened, were you?" he said.

"Yes."

"Well, it's all over. I was born during a big thunderstorm." She was still unnerved.

"Maybe you're used to them," she said.

The thunder had become soft and distant.

"Is this the only candle?" Christine said.

"There's just the stub of another one."

Outside it was now evening. After a while he went upstairs to see if the houses across the pond had any lights.

"No," he said coming down. "There'll be lights in town.

Let's go in and get something to eat, and we'll find out what's going on."

At the Century he had a late lunch with Eddins in the library. They sat at a table near the window looking down, more or less, at the street. Eddins was wearing a blazer and a yellow silk tie. He and a partner were buying the agency—Delovet was retiring, he said. They'd agreed on a price and on which books Delovet would continue to receive a portion of the commissions.

"I think most of the clients will stay with us," he said. "No plans to change the name."

"No, that's going to go down in infamy."

"Well, there is that, but we'd rather it just go smoothly."

"Why is he retiring?"

"You know, I'm not sure. To devote himself more to pleasure, not that he hasn't always. He's gotten away with a lot."

"What happened to the actress?"

"Dee Dee?"

Delovet had finally broken up with her. She had become a drunk. The last time Eddins saw her, she had fallen down some stairs at a party. You poor, drunk woman, Delovet told her. She was long gone. Delovet was taking his harem to France.

"Travel still seems to have its allure," Eddins said. "Too many people though, too many tour buses. There's no parking anywhere. I recall when I was a boy, there were 130 million people in the country, I remember the figure, we learned it in class. There was a thing called recitation, perhaps that was something else. The world was smaller: there was home, there was the Nawth, and there was California—no one had ever been to California. Vincent," he said, beckoning to a waiter, "could you put this in the freezer for a few minutes? It's a little warm."

The room had emptied out. They were not in a hurry. Eddins had a book on the best-seller list and a sizeable advance for another.

"Dena wanted to travel," he said. "She always longed to see the Leaning Tower. She wanted to have dinner on the Nile looking out at the pyramids. She should have married a more successful man, some tycoon. I should have been more of a success. She was an absolutely wonderful woman. I can't tell you. As a man, I feel it would not be right. You've traveled, you're lucky. I remember the English woman. What became of her?"

"She's in London," Bowman said. "In Hampstead, actually."

"Ah, you see, I don't even know where that is. Hampstead. Probably some place with great lawns and women strolling in long gowns. You know, I never saw her—you told me about her, but I never had the chance to see her with my own eyes. Superb woman, I'm sure. You're still handsome, you swine. Was she tall? I don't remember. I prefer tall women. Irene isn't very tall. I'm afraid she's not going to become tall. That would be a lot to ask. Should we have another bottle of this warm wine? No, I'm afraid that would be too much. Why don't we have something at the bar instead?"

They had often stood at the bar as new members when Eddins was wonderfully sociable. He was still sociable and even better dressed. He tightened his silk tie slightly as they went down to the bar.

"Now, Christine," he said. "How is Christine?"

"What do you mean, how is she?"

"Nothing, just in the ordinary conversational way. I haven't seen her. She's living in the country? You have her quartered out there?"

"Stabled."

"You villain. Have you ever thought of settling down."

"There's nobody more settled than I am."

"Getting married," Eddins explained.

"There's nothing I'd like to do more."

"I remember your last wedding, your first wedding, that is. Whatever happened to that sultry girl who was having an affair with your rich father-in-law?"

"He died, you know."

"He died? It was that intense?"

"No, no, that had nothing to do with it. He was married again, happily married. That was quite a while ago. It seems like centuries. People still had family silver."

"I'd like to think that particular girl never got any older. Whatever happened to her? What do you suppose she's up to these days?"

"You know, I don't have any idea. Vivian might know."

"Vivian was quite good-looking, too."

"Yes, she was."

"Women have that quality. They're going to let them be members here, what's your position on that? Probably not the good-looking ones, just the ones you avoid at parties. We're in the middle of the woman thing. They want equality, in work, marriage, everywhere. They don't want to be desired unless they feel like it."

"Outrageous."

"The thing is, they want a life like ours. We both can't have a life like ours. So, the old fellow died, eh? Your father-in-law."

"He died, and my father died."

"Sorry to hear that. Mine did, too. He died just this last spring. It was sudden, I couldn't get there beforehand. I come from a small town and a respectable family. We knew the doctor, we knew the president of the bank. If you called the doctor, even at some god-awful hour, he'd come to the house. He knew you. He knew your whole family. He'd held you up by the feet when you were two minutes old and whacked you to get the first wail of life out of you. Decency, that was a word you lived by. Loyalty. I'm loyal to all that, boyhood, the Old South. You have to have loyalty to things. If you don't have loyalty, you're alone on earth. I have a wonderful photograph of my father in his infantry uniform, he's smoking a cigarette. I don't know where it was taken. Photography is a tremendous thing. In this photograph he's still alive."

He paused as if to reflect or turn the page.

"I'm selling this book to the movies," he said. "Handsome sum of money, but what jackals they are. Unworthy. They have too much money, limitless. I had a writer named Boyd, an ex-preacher, he could write, he had the gift. I couldn't sell his stories. It's a shame. He wrote a story I'll never forget about a blind pig, it would break your heart. His ambition was to sell a story or two to *Harper's*. Not very much to ask, other people managed to do it, other writers who for some reason or other they preferred."

They shook hands on the street. It was past two and a beautiful afternoon. The light seemed unusually clear. He walked up Madison then. There was no neighborhood quite like it—the galleries on the side streets with fragments of statues, the bourgeois apartment buildings on the corners, monuments really, not of impressive height, eight or ten stories with wide windows. The traffic was not heavy, the green of the park only a block away. On the sidewalk the few tables of a small restaurant were empty now. Women were shopping. An old man was walking a dog.

There was a bookshop further up that he liked. The owner was a slight man in his fifties who was always dressed in a suit and came, it was said, from a well-to-do family in which he was the errant son. From childhood he had always loved books and wanted to be a writer, later copying out pages of Flaubert and Dickens by hand. He'd imagined himself in a light-filled room in Paris working in solitude and had eventually gone to Paris but was only lonely there and unable to write.

The bookshop was in his image. There was only a small display window, and the shop was narrow in front, squeezed by an adjoining stairway to the apartments above, but it widened in back to the size of a room that was filled from top to bottom with shelves of books any of which Edward Heiman could put his hand on without hesitation, as if he had originally placed it there himself. His recommendations could be relied on. His customers were largely known to him, if not by face, then by name, although people unfamiliar to him also came in and lingered. He had grown up a block or two away on Park Avenue where he still lived, and it was to the disappointment of the family that he'd become a bookseller. Best-sellers were displayed on a pedestal in front though sharing the space with lesser-known books.

He did much of his business by telephone. Customers would call and order books they had heard of, and they would be delivered that day to the apartment, sometimes including a title or two of his choosing that could be returned. His idea of what was worthwhile was not without its own cachet, worthy books that had eluded the critics—all but the most perceptive—and when opened had a seductive power of information or intellect or style. Women particularly liked his advice and found him sympathetic although his manners made him seem almost shy. He had a fondness for women who wore masculine clothes, he had once remarked to Bowman—Japanese women especially. He liked women writers, even those whose reputation was based on second-rate or even political work. Men had had all the advantage for centuries, he felt, and now women were having their turn. The excesses were to be expected.

"*Clarissa,*" he said in his quiet voice. "That's a terrifying book. It deserves response. We don't sell many copies of *Clarissa,* of coursc, but that doesn't mean much. Whitman gave away more copies of *Leaves of Grass* than he sold, which I could do with any number of books here. We're not selling much John Marquand or Louis Bromfield either, but that's a different matter."

He was married although his wife never came around. Someone described her as very attractive. Not in the physical sense. It was her entire person.

A woman as unique, then, as her husband with something

like his tastes or perhaps with tastes of her own. He lived in the world of books. She was not that interested in books, she preferred clothes and certain friendships. There were too many books altogether—you might read one once in a while . . . Edward Heiman was perhaps like Liebling or Lampedusa in his own Sicily. Their wives were off somewhere.

Bowman continued walking. It was a part of the city he liked, a comfortable, well-off part where eccentricities could be paid for. The white brick building where the old writer, Swangren, had lived was only a few blocks away, and Gavril Aronsky's chaotic apartment was nearby. *The Savior* had been a notorious book, half a million copies sold at least. Baum had never uttered a word of regret for not having published it. Aronsky had written four or five more books, but his reputation had gradually become thinner and thinner. As he aged, he had become thinner also until he finally looked like a starving bird. When someone mentioned *The Savior,* Baum had remarked merely,

"Yes, I know the book."

In Clarke's a soft feeling of reminiscence came over him. The bar was almost empty at that hour of the afternoon. The crowds had gone back to their offices. There were a few drinkers down near the front window where the sunlight prevented you from seeing them clearly. He was remembering Vivian and her friend, Louise. Also George Amussen and his lasting disapproval. His two daughters had shared his love of horses and had each married the wrong man. The thing about Vivian was that she was—Bowman hadn't really understood it at the time—so ineradicably part of it, the drinking, the big houses, and cars with mud-crusted boots and bags of dog food lying in back, the self-approval and money. All of it had seemed inessential, even amusing.

He ordered a beer. He felt himself floating in time. He could see himself in the mirror behind the bar, shadowed and silvery, as he had seen himself years before when he had just come to the city, young and ambitious with the dream of finding his place there and all that implied. He studied himself in the mirror. He was midway or a little past that depending on where you began counting. His real life had begun at eighteen, the life he now stood at the summit of.

22. SAPORE DI MARE

Christine was in the city less often, but she and Bowman were like a married couple who were together on the weekends. Her life was really in the country, which seemed somehow right for her. She had friends, many of them his friends, and she was good company. She had made almost four thousand dollars commission on the house. She offered to help with the mortgage by making the payments for a while since she was really living there.

Sometime around Thanksgiving she went to look at a house that was under construction in Wainscott and met the contractor who was inside cutting some floorboards. He stopped and turned off the saw. He asked if he could show her the house. He was building it to sell it, and when he did would probably build or remodel another. He'd have to see how it went. They walked around. She was in heels and had to be careful going up the unfinished stairs. Houses always looked wonderful before the walls went up. He had an easy, persuasive way of talking and asked if she could have lunch with him sometime to talk about the business of selling the house. It was casual—he didn't say more than that.

His name was Ken Rochet. They had lunch in a restaurant across from the harbor where it was a little noisy, but they were able to talk. He'd come from the site. There was even a bit of sawdust on his hands. He was wearing a blue polo shirt. He seemed at home in the world. He worked, read, cooked, and lived with women, though none of that was known to her. She was drawn to him as she'd once been drawn to her husband, irresistibly, without consent. There was something in her that turned towards such men. It was beyond anything she might explain. It was the blue shirt faded from countless washings that seduced her. He knew more about real estate than it had seemed, but still she was able to advise him. He watched her go to the ladies' room and then come back. She was wearing a print dress. She looked to him like a glorious feathered bird and he a fox.

He had a hardness she liked. He was husky and played second base on the local softball team. At his favorite bars and restaurants the hostesses knew him. She didn't want to meet him in places where her car might be noticed, and they went instead to a restaurant never very crowded and sat drinking and talking at the bar with their cars parked near each other amid the trees. Evening fell and on into the dark. Her chin was in the palm of her hand and her slender fingers outstretched. He told her about his brother with whom he had been in a terrible accident. His brother had been in the passenger seat. He was brain-dead on arrival at the hospital—this was in Providence—but they kept him on life support for three days. His wife finally agreed that it was hopeless, but she wanted to keep him breathing until they could take some semen from him—they had no children and she wanted a child.

"What finally happened?"

"I'll tell you sometime," he said.

"Tell me now."

"They used mine. She did."

"So you're a father."

"I guess technically," he said.

"It's not so technical."

That first night, as it happened, Christine's car wouldn't start when she was leaving. It was Bowman's old car—he'd had it for more than ten years.

"What are you driving a Volvo for, anyway?" Rochet asked her.

"It's not my car," she said.

"Whose is it?"

"That's another story. Don't ask me now."

"It's an old married couple's car," he said.

"Well, it started before. Do you know anything about cars?"

"I'm afraid I do," he said.

It wasn't much—the lead on the battery terminal was loose. He carefully scraped it clean with a penknife and worked it down.

"Try it now."

It started, and she followed him driving out.

His house had a small porch and, like hers, was always unlocked. It was really a small summer house with two rooms upstairs and down. He had only a half bottle of wine, and she drank it with him feeling nineteen again.

"Take off your shoes, if you like," he suggested.

He reached down and untied his. They sat barefoot, drinking in the dark. He kissed her throat, and she let him take off her blouse. They made love on the couch. The next time she came they went upstairs. It was supposed to be just for a look, but she turned to him at the top and slowly took off her earrings. He was on her like a beast. It was his house they went to but not always. He came walking up the driveway having prudently parked on the road. She was waiting. He followed her into the house. Who owns it? he asked her. It had a nice dry feeling. The walls needed painting. She got out of bed with a terrible thirst after hours of lovemaking.

Bowman knew nothing and never suspected. He saw himself as Eros and Christine as his. He lived in the pleasure of possessing her, unbelievable as it was, the simplicity and justice of it. As if he were part now of the secret world of the senses, he saw what he had not seen before. Walking to work he passed a florist's and caught a glimpse of, in back among the dense greens, a girl bent forward at the waist and another figure, a man stepping in behind her. The girl changed her stance slightly. Was he really seeing this, Bowman thought, in the morning as the ordinary world went past? An older woman, about to walk by him, paused to look, too, as just in that moment it changed. The girl was merely bending over to arrange some flowers, and the man was beside, not behind her. It might have been an omen or part of one, but he was not open to omens.

The first that he learned was word being forwarded to him in Chicago, where he was attending the booksellers convention. A suit had been filed against him. It was seeking sole ownership of the house. He immediately called Christine and left a message. It was early evening, but she didn't call back. He couldn't reach her until the next day.

"Darling, what is all this?" he asked.

Her voice seemed cool.

"I can't talk about it just now," she said.

"What do you mean?"

"I'm just not able to."

"I don't understand, Christine. You have to explain. What's going on?"

He was experiencing a sudden, frightening confusion.

"What is it?" he said. "What's the matter?"

She was silent.

"Christine!"

"Yes."

"Tell me. What's happened?"

"It's about the house," she said as if giving in.

"Yes, I know. What about it?"

"I can't talk. I have to go."

"For God's sake!" he cried.

He had the sense of being reduced to nothing, a sickening sense of not knowing. When, back in New York, he had the full details, he insisted on meeting and talking, but she would not. But I love you, I loved you, he was thinking. And she was unperturbed. She was cold. How did it happen, that something no longer mattered, that it had been judged inessential? He wanted to take her by the arms and shake her back to life.

Her claim was that the house was hers and that it had been bought in both their names only because she was unable to qualify for a mortgage. She was suing for breach of an oral contract and for sole title to the house. Bowman's lawyer was a man in Southampton, a former alcoholic with silvery hair. He had handled cases like this—she had almost no chance of prevailing.

"The Statute of Frauds," he explained, "dating all the way back requires a written contract for transfer of ownership. That's your defense. We'll cite the lack of writing. There was nothing written, correct?"

"Absolutely nothing."

"She's living in the house now?"

"Yes."

"Does she have a lease?"

"No. She's . . . we live together."

"You have a current relationship."

"It's not current."

Bowman saw her again for the first time at the trial. She avoided looking at him. Her lawyer argued that she was the equitable owner of the house and that the outward appearance of the sale had in fact been a transaction designed for her benefit.

The jury, which had only been listening idly, seemed attentive when she rose to testify. She was tastefully dressed. She described her long search and how at last she had found a small house that she and her daughter could live in, and the express oral agreement with Bowman that the house would be hers. She was living in the house and paying the mortgage. Bowman felt an inexpressible contempt at her lies. He indicated it in a look he exchanged with his lawyer, who seemed unconcerned.

In the end, however, it became her word against his, and the jury decided in her favor. She was awarded title. The house was gone. Only afterwards did he learn that there was another man.

He felt himself stupid for not knowing, a fool, but there was something that was worse, the jealousy. It was agonizing to think of her with someone else, of someone else having her, her presence, the availability of her. Suddenly everything had fallen away. He had felt himself above other people, knowing more than they did, even pitying them. He was not related to other people—his life was another kind of life. He had invented it. He had dreamt himself up, running heedless into the surf at night as if he were a poet or beach boy in California, as if he were a madman, but there were the very real mornings, the world still asleep and she asleep beside him. He could stroke her arm, he could wake her if he liked. He felt sick with the memory of it. He was sick with all the memories. They had done things together that would make her look back one day and see that he was the one who truly mattered. That was a sentimental idea, the stuff of a woman's novel. She would never look back. He knew that. He amounted to a few brief pages. Not even. He hated her, but what could he do?

"This may sound crazy," he would say, "but I still want her. I can't help it. I've never thought about killing anyone, but in that courtroom I could have killed her. She knew all along what she was doing, I never would have believed it."

He was humiliated. It was a wound that would not heal. He could not stop examining it. He tried to think of what he had done wrong. He shouldn't have agreed to her living in the country—she would have never met the other man. He shouldn't have been so trusting with her. He shouldn't have been such a slave to the pleasure she gave, though that would have been impossible, and she had cared nothing for him. He knew there would not be another. It would be better never to have met her, but what sense did that make? It had been the luckiest day of his life.

23. IN VINO

Eddins and Irene lived in the house in Piermont for several years after they were married, but she was unhappy in the house where there had been a drawer still filled with his former wife's things that she finally made him get rid of. They moved back to the city, to an ordinary apartment in the Twenties near Gramercy Park decorated with her furniture from New Jersey. When Bowman went there for dinner she had dressed carefully but was wearing no makeup. Eddins brought him in.

"You remember Philip, darling."

"Yes, of course," she said a bit impatiently. "It's nice to see you."

The apartment was somehow a little gloomy. Their dog, a black Scottie, didn't bother to sniff at him. They sat having a drink in the living room. Irene—it must have been unknowingly—asked Bowman about his house. It was near the ocean, wasn't it?

"I don't have that house now," he said. "That was a while ago."

"Oh, I see. I was going to say my ex-brother-in-law had a house down near the shore."

"Yes, I like the ocean."

"He liked to sail," she said. "He had a boat. I remember

it. I often went out on it, a number of times. The marina where he kept it was filled with boats. All kinds of them."

She went on about her brother-in-law, Vince.

"Phil didn't know him, darling."

"Neither did you," she said. "No need to say anything bad about him."

He poured her a little more wine.

"All right," she said. "Just a little. That's enough."

"Oh, it's not very much. Let me at least fill your glass."

"Not if you want dinner," she said.

"It won't hurt dinner."

Irene said nothing.

"My daddy liked to drink," Eddins said. "He used to say he was more interesting when he drank. My mother used to say, interesting to who?"

"Yes," Irene said.

She went into the kitchen, leaving them to drink. Eddins was good company, rarely in a bad mood. When Irene came back in, she said that dinner would soon be ready if they were.

"Yes, we're ready, darling. At home, you know, we used to call it supper. Dinner was midday or sometimes a little later."

"Dinner or supper," she said.

"No, it's just a small distinction. Another distinction might be that you drink at supper."

"We always called it dinner."

"The Italians," he said, "don't call it dinner."

"No?"

"They call it *cena*."

"That's not what we call it," she said. "The main thing is, would you like to have it?"

"Yes, what are we having for dinner?"

"You're calling it dinner now."

"Only to please you. I'm actually calling it a draw."

He smiled at her, as if in understanding. They went into the dining room where there was a table and four chairs and two rounded corner cabinets with plates displayed on their shelves. Irene brought in the soup. Eddins remarked,

"I read somewhere that in navy messes—I think this was on a carrier—they served sherry in the soup. Is that true? What savoir faire."

"We didn't have any sherry," Bowman said.

"Do you ever think back to all that?"

"Oh, occasionally. It's hard not to."

"You were in the navy?" Irene said.

"Oh, long ago. During the war."

"Darling, I thought you knew that," Eddins said.

"No, how would I know that? My brother-in-law, the one who sails, was in the navy."

"Vince," Eddins said.

"What other brother-in-law do I have?"

"It's just that he hasn't come up for a while."

Irene did not reply.

"Phil was also at Harvard," Eddins said.

"Oh, come on, Neil," Bowman said.

"He wrote the Hasty Pudding show."

"No, no," Bowman objected. "I didn't write any pudding show."

"I felt sure you had. That's a disappointment. Have you ever heard of a writer named Edmund Berger?"

"I don't think so. Did he write it?"

"He came in to see me. He's written a couple of books, and he's writing one now about the Kennedy assassination. Is anyone still interested in that, do you think?"

"Then why is he writing it?" Irene said.

"He has the real story. Kennedy was assassinated by three Cuban sharpshooters, one on the grassy knoll and two in the book depository. All witnesses agree on that. Cubans, I said? How do you know that? They have their names, he said. It was the CIA. How did Jack Ruby know when Oswald was going to be taken out of his cell? Jack Ruby! Who was he?"

"I don't know. A police informant," Bowman said.

"Perhaps, this fellow Berger says."

"Why are we talking about this?" Irene said.

"Let's assume for the moment that it's as Berger says, and it wasn't Oswald. Oswald repeatedly said he hadn't shot Kennedy. Of course he'd deny it, but then why was it that the police interrogated him for six hours but there were no notes taken? That's because the CIA destroyed them."

"I think that all this has been pretty much gone over," Bowman commented.

"Yes, but not all put together. The Reverend King."

"What about the Reverend King?"

"There's more there than meets the eye. Who shot him?" Eddins said—he was enjoying it. "They convicted someone, but who knows? The other day a shoeshine man on Lexington asked me if I really believed that the police weren't behind it."

"Why talk about this?" Irene said.

"I don't know, but they seem to shoot all these people, Robert Kennedy, Huey Long."

"Huey Long?"

"These are momentous acts. The dark curtain falls. All of life changes. When Huey Long was shot, I remember a shudder went through the entire south. Not a family that didn't go to bed that night in fear. I remember that. The whole of the south."

"Oh, Neil," Irene cried.

"What, darling? Enough of that? I'm sorry."

"All you do is talk, talk, talk."

He pursed his lips slightly as if in consideration.

"You shrew," he said.

She left the table. There was silence for a while. Eddins said,

"I'm going to have to walk the dog. Care to come with me?"

He was quiet in the elevator going down. On the street they didn't walk far. They went into Farrell's, a bar two blocks away, and stood having a drink near the door. The bartender knew Eddins.

"You know what I always imagined? Remember the *Thin Man* movies? I imagined sitting at the bar with my wife—not this kind of bar, something a little more on the swell side, there's one further east—sitting and talking, nothing special, just about one thing or another, about someone who's come in or where we might go later, the passing scene. She's wearing nice clothes, a pretty dress. That's another thing, isn't it, how they dress. I like to dress up a little. Anyway we're talking, kind of a pleasant hour. She has to go to the ladies' room, and while she's gone the bartender notices her empty glass and asks me if my wife would like another. Yes, I say. She comes back and doesn't even notice it's a new drink, just picks it up and takes a sip, anything happen while I was gone?"

Neil was good company still. He had a certain dying flair. He could look at his life as a story—the real part was something he'd left behind, much of it in his boyhood and with Dena. Of Irene, he would say,

"We each have our territory."

Farrell's was dark and the television was on. The bar ran back the length of the room. They stood there, each with a foot on the rail. The dog sat quietly, looking at nothing.

"How old is he?" Bowman said.

"Ramsey? Eight. He's actually Irene's dog, but he likes me. When she walks him she drags him along. She won't wait. He likes to take his time. If she's getting ready to take him out, he just lies there. She has to call him. With me, he jumps up and goes right to the door. She doesn't like that, but it's not up to her. She just isn't the one he likes. Anyway he's not that young."

He was inclined to say neither was he, but he felt as if he'd already said enough. He had to take Ramsey on his walk. He and Bowman said good night. Ramsey was hard to see in the darkness. He was square, more or less, and absolutely black. They liked him at the Chinese laundry. Lambsey, they called him. The week before, Eddins had gone up to Piermont to visit Dena's grave, hers and Leon's. The cemetery seemed empty, the long silence of it. He stood at the grave. She had been his wife, and he had seen them off on the train. He hadn't brought flowers. He left and drove to the florist and came back with some. There was no need to pray for anything. He put flowers on each grave and laid the remaining ones on others around. He read the names on some of them, but there were none he recognized. He thought of some things that were just known to himself and Dena. He began to cry.

On the street in Piermont he happened to run into the old waitress from Sbordone's. She was walking along with something in a brown paper bag in one hand, a narrow bag. Eddins stopped her.

"Veronica?" he said.

"Yes."

"How've you been?"

"I'm sorry?"

"You remember me, don't you? I used to come to Sbordone's, my wife and I. Do you remember?"

"Yes, now I do."

"She died. I finally moved away."

"I'm sorry to hear that, but I remember."

"Too bad the bar's not open. I'd buy you a drink."

"Well, I stopped drinking except at funerals."

She touched the paper bag.

"This is just to have around in case somebody dies suddenly."

"You know, you haven't changed," he said. "Do you mind my asking, are you married?"

"No," she said. "I used to wish I was."

"The same with me," he said.

There was also Joanna, the fat girl, enormously fat with a wonderful personality who was a teller at the bank. She was good-natured, forthcoming, with a beautiful voice, but unmarried. No one would think of marrying her. She could speak French. She'd spent a year and a half in Quebec, studying. She impulsively joined a choir there the first week and he, this man, was in it. His name was Georges. He was older and had a girlfriend, but before long he dropped the girlfriend and took up with Joanna. She came back to the States, but he was a teacher and a Canadian, he couldn't leave. He would come to New York on the weekend, two or three times a month. It went on for nine years. She was terribly happy and knew it would end, but she wanted it to last as long as it could and didn't say anything. In the tenth year they got married. Someone told Eddins she was going to have a child.

24. MRS. ARMOUR

She came into the restaurant alone and stood for a time at the bar continually searching for something in her bag. At last she found it, a cigarette. She put it between her lips. The slowness of her acts was somehow frightening. No one watched openly. To a man sitting there she said,

"Pardon. May I have a light?"

She waited with some poise until he produced one and then walked forward to be seated. The restaurant was full but the headwaiter was able to put her at a small table near the front. There she ordered a bottle of wine. While waiting she carefully tapped the ash from her cigarette onto her plate.

The restaurant was called Carcassonne. It also could be called fashionable, the name was on the window in discreet gold lettering. It was across from the large wholesale meat market, somewhat like the old restaurant in Paris across from Les Halles, but the market was closed at that hour and the square was empty and quiet.

She ordered dinner but was not attentive to it, eating only a little of the food and allowing the rest to be taken away. She drank all the wine, however, spilling some of the last glass, hardly noticing.

"Waiter," she said, "I'd like another bottle of wine."

He went off and after a while came back.

"I'm sorry, madam," he said. "I can't give you another bottle."

"What?"

"I'm very sorry," he said. "I can't."

She said,

"What do you mean, you can't? Where's the headwaiter?"

"Madam," he began.

"I want the headwaiter," she said.

She was oblivious to everyone. She turned and looked around for him as if alone in the room.

The headwaiter came. He was in a dinner jacket.

"I've ordered a bottle of wine," she told him. "I would like a bottle of wine."

She was an upper-class woman unjustly tried.

"I'm sorry, madam. I think the waiter has told you. We can't give you another bottle."

She seemed at a loss as to what to do.

"Let me have a glass of wine, then," she said.

He didn't answer.

"One glass."

He walked off to occupy himself at his stand. She turned in her chair.

"Excuse me," she said to the people behind her. "Do you know a place near here called Hartley's?"

"Yes. It's just a few steps."

"Thank you. I'll have the bill," she announced to the waiter. She looked at it when it was brought.

"This can't be the bill," she said.

"This is the bill, madam."

She was searching in her bag. She couldn't find something.

"I've lost a hundred pounds!" she said.

The headwaiter had come.

"Just while I've been here!"

"Can you pay the bill, madam?" he said.

"I've lost a hundred pounds," she insisted and began looking around her feet.

"Are you certain?"

"Quite certain," she said clearly.

"You have to settle this bill, madam," he said.

"But I've lost the money," she said. "Haven't you heard me?"

"I'm afraid you have to pay this."

He knew there was no lost money. She shouldn't have been given a table. That was completely wrong. She was rummaging in her bag again.

"Ah," the waiter said standing up.

He had found two folded fifty-pound notes under her chair.

"Now may I have a bottle of wine?" she said.

"Yes, madam," the headwaiter said. "But you cannot open it here."

"Then what good is it?" she asked.

"You cannot open it here," he said.

When the waiter came back with the bottle, she refused to take it.

"I don't want it," she decided. "Do you have some paper to put it in?"

"I'm sorry, madam."

"Well, I can't walk in the street with it."

She stood looking at him. Then she handed him money, but he didn't take it. The waiter did. She stuffed the remaining bills into her bag carelessly. They brought her the wrapped bottle, and she asked the man at the next table which way was it to Hartley's?

"To the left," he said.

"The left."

"Yes."

She said good night to the headwaiter. He nodded.

"Good night."

Outside she turned to the right and a minute or so later passed by the window going in the other direction. She was seen in Hartley's sitting, composed, smoking a cigarette. The wine was in a cooler beside the table.

Wiberg was now Sir Bernard Wiberg though he looked like an Arab king—a thousand camels would be tethered at his grave. He'd been to Stockholm twice for the awarding of the Nobel Prize and had the distinction of having published the winners. He had, in fact, been a factor in their winning. He'd made sure their names were often mentioned, not too often and not too boldly for it was possible to upset the flow of opinion especially as it had to make its way through the panel of Swedish judges, but Wiberg could help make a writer distinguished—he had an instinct for these matters just as he did for publicity and promotion. Certain books could attract attention, certain writers at a particular time. Even excellence, he knew, had to be presold.

Unlike other rich men he did not ask himself if he was truly that much better than a down-at-the-heels man he passed on the street. He had perhaps a deeply buried fear of losing all his money, but it was nothing like the fear a woman has. He smoked Cohiba cigars and sometimes got a box of them to Baum in New York. He watched his weight. His wife was there to remind him not to eat a number of things he was fondest of. She would sometimes say, when he pleaded, oh, all right, but just a very small piece. At a large dinner, catching sight of him about to eat something forbidden, she would merely wag her finger discreetly. She was in charge of all domestic matters. Any of her husband's desires, he communicated through her. The house in the country was something she had encouraged him to buy although he didn't care for the country. She wanted a small house near Deauville, but he didn't like France. He liked Claridge's, being among his equals, talking to young women from time to time. He liked sitting in the study across from the Bacon, which, as it happened, his wife disliked.

It was done by a disturbed person, she said.

"He's not as disturbed as you think," Wiberg said. "Quite the opposite. I think of him as being essentially free, if you can call someone who is a slave to his desires free."

"What are the desires?"

"Drink. Sadistic lovers. It's not only the desires. The colors are so gorgeous. The black, the flesh color, the purple. You can almost hear some frightening music or silence."

"I especially don't like the teeth."

They had been to a show of Bacon portraits.

"Or the way he turns faces into awful custards," she said.

Catarina was still very handsome although she had not performed in some years. Her figure was good, she still possessed a waist, and her throat was smooth. She looked much younger than she was. She still called him her *cochon* and he was interesting to her except when talking at length about himself. His taste for Bacon was inexplicable. He also owned a Corot, many prints, and a painting by Braque.

Wiberg had never met Bacon, he had only read about him, the disorderly life, the years in Morocco with young men quite cheap. In Bacon there was a sheen of awful sanctimony. There was love and disgust of the flesh and staggering dissolution. There was all that had happened in the world during one's life. Bacon also had the gift of language. He had gotten it in Irish kitchens and drawing rooms and in the stables where, as a boy, he'd been had by the grooms. His eloquence came from his father's coldness and disapproval and the great freedom of finding his own life in Berlin with its vices and Paris, of course. He belonged to the netherworld with its bitchy language, gossip, and betrayals. He had never concealed himself or tried to conform to any idea of artist, which allowed him to become a greater one. His lovers had drunk or drugged themselves to death, and amid the rubbish of it all, the taste for fine clothes and disdain of what others were tied to, his idleness and obsessions had spattered the walls and set him free. He never painted over on a canvas. It was always once and for all.

There was a superb biography waiting to be written, Wiberg felt, but only after Bacon died. Bacon had been born in 1909, eleven years before Wiberg. It would be a matter of luck.

*

As it happened, Enid Armour knew Bacon. She mentioned it one night at a dinner and Wiberg was immediately interested. She had met him at least twice in the club in Soho he always went to. Henrietta Moraes had introduced her. What was he like? Wiberg asked.

"He was friendly. We got along quite well. I was in hopes he might like to do a portrait of me and make me famous. I know you have that painting of his."

"I should have bought more," Wiberg confessed.

She was not looking well these days, he thought. She looked a little worn. He saw her only on occasion now, always socially, but still it was a surprise that she'd met Francis Bacon even though she was in that sort of crowd. She was still by herself as far as he knew. She had several times in the past suggested that he might find some position for her— she could do publicity perhaps, but he knew it would be the wrong thing to employ her. Catarina would know of it, and he didn't want to defend having hired her. Her glamour, anyway, seemed a little fatigued. There were women who were always interesting even after the waning of their attractiveness, however, and he had always liked Enid's frankness. She was not self-pitying.

"I'm afraid I've passed the peak. You can only rely, I mean really rely, on your looks for so long," she said dejectedly.

"We all have the same problem," he said.

Was he joking?

"You'll always be handsome," she said.

"Less and less, I'm afraid."

"As long as you have your money," she said.

She'd been in a scene in some restaurant, he'd heard.

"Yes," she admitted wearily.

"Who were you with?"

"No one."

"No one?"

"I was just having dinner by myself."

She had become less careful with herself, she knew. She had drunk far too much that evening and spent a lot of money. She didn't care to remember it. She had gone on to some place where there was a woman sitting with her dog on the banquette. She'd reached over to stroke it.

"What a lovely dog. What's its name?"

She didn't remember what the woman had said.

"I had a magnificent dog," she said. "He was a racing dog. A champion, the most beautiful dog. Have you ever seen them run? They literally fly. The most beautiful thing, really, and so gentle, that's what's amazing. So really gentle and brave." She knew she was becoming maudlin. "You can't help but love them. It was at a time when I had no cares."

25. IL CANTINORI

Bowman was a friend of the Baums' though he and Robert Baum were never strong personal friends. Aside from occasional parties they rarely saw one another in the evening, but they were having dinner one night at a restaurant that was one of Baum's favorites, Il Cantinori, in the large room that was like someone's own dining room but filled with white tablecloths and flowers and on a quiet street. The service was good—Baum was well known there, of course—and the food excellent. He and Diana had just been to Italy. It was always difficult, she said, to come home. She adored Italy. Apart from everything else, it was one of the few places where one's hopes for the future could be restored. Beautiful, unspoiled fields and hills. Great houses that families had lived in for five hundred years. It was deeply consoling. Also the general sweetness of the people. She had wanted to go to the post office and asked for directions from a man standing outside a shop. He was explaining it to her when a passerby stopped to say that was not the best way and described another. The men began arguing back and forth until finally the passerby said, *Signora, per piacere, viene,* and began leading her down a series of small streets and across a square to an imposing building, like a national bank, where she could buy some stamps.

"Where else in the world would they do that?" she said.

Over the years, Diana had become an influential figure and a woman of principled opinion, often feared. She was a serious person. Fashionable and chic were for her words of criticism, even contempt. What she wanted was your politics and your opinions, if any, about books. She went to movies because she enjoyed them, but she did not take them seriously. The theater was a different matter. She was not beautiful—she never had been and it was no longer of importance—but she had an enviable face, even to the slight darkness beneath her eyes, and a well-defined position.

She was fiercely loyal and expected loyalty in return. A journalist she knew who was a friend had written a long piece on Robert Baum, interviewed in his office and over several lunches. Baum could be jaunty. His house, on its own and together with one or two others, represented at least half of American literature. There was really no one above him. He had changed little over the years although he was wearing more expensive clothes and sometimes a felt hat. He could be charming and casually say, oh, fuck them or him as readily as any agent. He took care of his writers but was not, in private, always reverent about them. The article had quoted him referring to "major writers" and "major frauds." Also "major, major writers." Diana had found it embarrassing. At a reception she bumped into the journalist, who asked, "You're not angry with me?"

"No, just indifferent," Diana said.

She was never evasive. She had a slight New York accent, but she was not New York as only people from elsewhere can be, she was the genuine article. When she liked or championed a writer it was a crown for them although not one without weight. But she respected and defended them. To a young woman who had been telling stories of a brief affair with Saul Bellow to editors all over town, she had said coldly,

"Look, that simply isn't done. You have to *earn* the right to betray an important writer."

Diana had grown up, in the years before the war, on a diet of politics and current events in an apartment at the outer limit of respectability, far up on Central Park West. Her father had a small textile importing business and like everyone else had to struggle during the Depression, but the family sat down together every evening for supper and talked about what was happening in the city and the world as well as what was happening at school. From the time she was eight years old she read the *Times* every day, the four of them did, including the editorial page. No other newspaper was allowed in the house. In high school she read the *Daily News* on the subway with a feeling of sin.

She revered her father, whose name was Jacob Lindner. She liked his hair, his smell, his solid legs. The vision of him in the morning in her parents' small bedroom in his undershirt as he finished getting dressed was one of the prime images of her childhood. She loved his kindness and strength. In the end, with a longtime friend, he invested far more than he should have in some property in Jersey City and they could not keep up the mortgage. The bank foreclosed, and they were wiped out. He said nothing except to his wife, but they all knew. We'll be all right, he told them, somehow.

Years after, on the subway, a disturbing thing happened

to her. She was sitting across from a bag lady, a poor old woman with all her possessions in a plastic bag.

"Hello, Diana," the woman said quietly.

"What?"

She looked at the woman.

"How is Robert?" the woman asked. "Are you still writing?"

She hadn't written since college. She must have misheard, but suddenly she recognized who it was, a classmate, a girl she had known named Jean Brand who had been in college with her and had gotten married just afterwards. She had been good-looking. Now there were gaps where her perfect teeth had been. Diana opened her bag and took all her money out of her purse. She pressed it into her friend's hand.

"Here. Take this," she managed to say.

The woman reluctantly took the money.

"Thank you," she said quietly. Then, "I'm all right."

Diana thought of her father. No one had helped him. He never recovered from the loss. We'll be all right, he would say.

She told Robert the story, but no one else. Merely telling it upset her. She had met Robert when she was eighteen. He was attracted to her but she was too young—he took her to be fifteen at the most. He was already a man. He had been in the war. When they got married, Diana had almost no sexual experience. She'd never known another man. I doubt that my mother ever knew another man, she said, and what did she miss? I don't think anything.

She was completely satisfied by marriage, by the intimacies that really could not be found elsewhere. She knew that views on that had changed, that young women were now much freer, especially before marriage and that second and even third marriages were common and often happier, but all of that was outside her own life. She and her husband were inseparable. It was deeper even than marriage, but, oh, she had loved her father. She had been formed by his standards and ideals.

There was an idea that Baum had perhaps been involved with a woman in the office, and that Diana had known of it—she certainly would have known—but whatever she and her husband said concerning it, no one knew. The woman, who had gone on to another job as a publicist, was a tall, unmarried Catholic woman named Ann Hennessy, long-limbed, with a somewhat reserved personality. She was unmarried at thirty-eight and had some sort of past. Baum liked her sense of humor. He had often gone on long lunches with her. They might be seen together but never appeared to be hiding anything. She had gone to Frankfurt twice.

Bowman liked Diana very much although he was always a bit cautious with her. He liked her, he was certain, more than she liked him or more than she showed, but that night at the restaurant she was unusually open, as if they were often together.

"I'd like to live in Italy," she mused aloud.

"Who wouldn't, darling," Baum said.

"One thing I always think of, in Italy they didn't round up the Jews. Mussolini wouldn't allow it, say what you like about him." The Germans did that.

"No, that came later," Baum said. "Mussolini was happy to let Ezra Pound broadcast though. He thought that was OK."

"Oh, Ezra Pound," Diana said. "Ezra Pound was crazy. Who listened to Ezra Pound?"

"Probably not a lot of people. I think it was shortwave, anyway, but it was the idea of it."

"I don't think they should have given him that prize, the Bollingen. They did it as soon as they could. It was too soon for that. You don't honor someone who's thrown sewage on top of you and stirred up ignorance and hatred."

Baum had fought in the war, but he knew and had even published men who'd avoided it, who'd managed to get deferments or some way fail the physical, but that was only craven. It was different than aiding the enemy, different than finally going back to Italy, landing in Naples and giving the Fascist salute.

"I was against it," he said.

"Yes, but you didn't say anything. Don't you agree with me?" she said to Bowman.

"I think I was against it at the time."

"At the time? That was when it was crucial."

They were interrupted by a well-dressed man in a dark suit who had come to the table and said,

"Hello, Bobby." And to Diana, "Hi, ya, Toots."

He looked prosperous and athletic. His well-shaved cheeks almost gleamed. He was a friend and an early backer named Donald Beckerman.

"I don't want to interrupt your dinner," he said. "I wanted Monique to meet you. Sweetheart," he said to the woman with him, "this is Bob and Diana Baum. He's a big-shot publisher. This is my wife, Monique."

She was dark-haired with a wide mouth and the look of someone smart and unmanageable.

"Sit down for a minute, won't you?" Baum said to them.

"So, how are things going?" Beckerman said when they sat. "Any new best-sellers?"

He was one of three brothers who had gone into business together, investments, and made a lot of money. The middle brother had died.

"I'm Don," he said to Bowman reaching out his hand.

The waiter had come to the table.

"Will you be having dinner, sir?" he asked.

"No, we're at a table back there. We're just sitting here for a few minutes.

"Bobby and I were in prep school together," Beckerman said. "We were the only two Jews in the class. In the whole school, I think."

He had a winning smile.

"Ever go to one of the reunions?" he asked Baum. "I went about seven or eight years ago. You want to know something? Nothing has changed. It was terrible to see them all again. I only stayed the one evening."

"You didn't see DeCamp?"

It was a classmate who was a rebel that Baum liked.

"No, I didn't see him. He wasn't there. I don't know what ever happened to him. Did you ever hear?"

While they were talking, his wife said to Bowman,

"Have you known Donnal a long time?"

"No, not long."

"Ah, I see."

She was Beckerman's second wife. They'd been married

for a little more than two years. They lived in his large, corner apartment in an expensive building near the armory. Monique had made it very comfortable. She had put a lot of his former wife's furniture out on the street and gotten rid of all the dishes.

"I threw them away," she said.

"It was a lot of dishes," Beckerman commented. "We kept a kosher house."

"I'm not kosher," Monique said.

She was from Algeria. Her family were French colonists, *pieds-noirs,* and when the trouble started they left and came back to France. She became a journalist. It was for a right-wing Catholic paper, but she had nothing to do with the politics, she only wrote book and theater reviews and sometimes interviewed writers. She met Beckerman through some friends.

As he sat there, Bowman was more and more conscious of not being one of them, of being an outsider. They were a people, they somehow recognized and understood one another, even as strangers. They carried it in their blood, a thing you could not know. They had written the Bible with all that had sprung from it, Christianity, the first saints, yet there was something about them that drew hatred and made them reviled, their ancient rituals perhaps, their knowledge of money, their respect for justice—they were always in need of it. The unimaginable killing in Europe had gone through them like a scythe—God abandoned them—but in America they were never harmed. He envied them. It was not their looks that marked them anymore. They were confident, clean-featured.

Baum was not religious and did not believe in a God who

killed or let live according to an unknowable design unconnected to whether you were decent, devout, or useless to the world. Goodness had no meaning to God, although there had to be good. The world was chaos without it. He lived as he lived because of that and seldom thought of it. In his deepest feelings, however, he accepted that he was one of his people and the God they believed in would always be his as well.

"Do you go to France?" Monique asked.

"Not very often," Bowman said.

She had a rather coarse complexion, he observed, and was not beautiful, but she was the one you would pick out. She might be an ex-girlfriend of Sartre's, he thought idly, though he had no idea what any of them were like. Sartre was short and ugly and made very frank arrangements that he could imagine her understanding.

He decided to say,

"Do you miss living in France?"

"Yes, of course."

"What things do you miss?"

"Life here is easier," she said, "but in the summer we go to France."

"Where do you go?"

"We go to Saint-Jean-de-Luz."

"That sounds very nice. Do you have a house there?"

"Near there," she said. "You should come."

It was no longer women of an Eastern European swarm, the toiling mothers and wives. It was now women who were glamorous and smart as in nineteenth-century Vienna, a breed of women, New York was known for them. No one called them Jewesses anymore. The word evoked rabbinates and pious, backward villages along the Pale. They were stylish, ambitious, at the center of things. Their allure. He had never gone with one. Their lives had warmth and no scorn of pleasure or material things. He might have married one and become part of that world, slowly being accepted into it like a convert. He might have lived among them in that particular family density that had been formed by the ages, been a familiar presence at seder tables, birthday gatherings, funerals, wearing a hat and throwing a handful of earth into the grave. He felt some regret at not having done it, of not having had the chance. On the other hand, he could not really imagine it. He would never have belonged.

26. NOTHING IS CHANCE

A train had just left and in the crowd slowly making its way up the stairs he was almost certain he saw her, not looking his way. His heart jumped.

"Anet!" he called.

She saw him and stopped, people passing around her.

"Hi," she said. "Hello."

They moved to one side.

"How have you been?" he asked.

"I've been fine."

"Let's go to the top of the stairs."

He had been going down to catch the train. If he had been a minute earlier he would have been standing on the platform and getting on as she got off, almost certainly at another door, and he would never have seen her.

"How have you been?" he said again. "Are you in school? It's been a while."

"No, I'm still in school, but I'm taking a break. I'm taking a year off."

She was wearing no lipstick. There was the piercing squeal of another train coming in and the groan of the cars.

"So, what are you going to be doing?"

"This is so unbelievable. Actually, I'm looking for a job."

"Really. What kind of job?"

She laughed a little in saying it,

"In fact, I was looking for a job in publishing."

"Publishing? That's a surprise. How did that come about?"

"I'm a Lit major," she said, making a little face of disbelief.

She was so unaffected that the pleasure from seeing her welled up.

"Well, it's lucky we bumped into each other, isn't it? Look, I'm having a little thing tomorrow for a friend in British publishing, Edina Dell, but some other people will be there. It's just drinks. Why don't you come?"

"Tomorrow?" she said.

"Yes, at about five-thirty. At the apartment. Do you remember where I live? I'll write it down. Here." He wrote it on a card.

They went up to the street together to say good-bye. They stood for a few moments on the corner. He was unaware of the buildings around them, the traffic, the tawdry signs of the shops. She was going east. He watched her walk away, younger and somehow better than others in the crowd. He had always liked her.

He doubted she would come. She must have known about the trial and its consequences and thought of him as the enemy. As it happened, he was wrong.

She arrived a little late. She came into the room almost unnoticed to find people drinking and talking and also at least one person her own age, Edina's daughter, Siri, slender and half-black with great bushy hair. Edina was wearing a long, gauzy dress of violet and rose. She took Anet's hand and said, "Who is this stunning girl?"

"This is Anet Vassilaros," Bowman said.

"You're Greek."

"No. My father is," Anet said.

"The great love of my life was a Greek man," Edina said. "I used to fly to Athens to see him. He had a fabulous family apartment there. I could never get him to come back with me. Do you work in publishing? No, you're still in school."

"No, I'm actually looking for a publishing job."

"I shouldn't think you'd have to look long."

Bowman introduced her to several others. This is Anet Vassilaros, he said. There were two other women about Edina's age, women who worked and whose names she didn't get. There was a tall English agent, Tony something. Bowman had bought flowers and arranged them around.

She talked to Siri, who had a soft voice and was in school in London somewhere.

"Is she an adopted daughter?" Anet asked Bowman when she had a chance.

"No, she's her real daughter. She has a Sudanese father."

"She's really beautiful."

Tony had left, saying good-bye to her. By seven-thirty, most of the others were going. Anet got ready to leave.

"No, don't go yet," Bowman said to her. "We haven't had a moment to really talk. Sit down. I'm just going to turn the TV on. There's a piece about a writer of mine at the end of the news."

It would be a few minutes. He turned off the sound and as they sat there, inevitably thought of her mother. He remembered the images shifting silently on the screen like jumps in reality, the face of the actress as she pleaded and then threw open her coat, defiant and submitting.

"You know, I never had the chance to tell you that I'm sorry about what happened," Anet said. "I mean about my mother and the house. I don't really know all the details."

"They're not worth going into."

"You don't hate her?"

"No, no," he said easily.

He was sitting with her daughter now, to whom he had always been careful not to show too much attention or false affection. He was able now to think freely about her.

"Who is that?" she asked.

It was a painting on the jacket of a book on Picasso that was on the coffee table, a disjointed portrait of eyes and a mouth out of place.

"Marie-Thérèse Walter," he said.

"Who is Marie-Thérèse Walter?"

"She's a famous model of Picasso's. He met her when she was seventeen. He saw her outside a Metro station and gave her his card. He began to paint her and fell in love with her. They had a child. Picasso was much older than she was— I'm leaving out a lot of it—but when he died she committed suicide."

"How old was she then?"

"Oh, she must have been in her sixties. I think she was born in about 1910. Picasso was 1881. I just read that again the other day."

"Do you know what Sophie called you? Do you remember Sophie? She called you the professor."

"Did she? Where is Sophie?"

"She's at Duke."

"You know what I have to say to Sophie?"

"What?"

"Oh, well, I don't really have anything to say to her. Listen, do you want to do something?" he said. "Stay here a minute."

He went into the kitchen. She could hear the refrigerator door open and after a few moments close. He came back with something in his hand, a small, folded piece of white paper. He put it on the table and began to unfold it. It was a packet with silver foil inside. She watched him open the foil and there was a lump of something dark, like wet tobacco.

"What is it?"

"It's hash."

There was the moment like the one at a dance when before taking your partner's hand for the first time, you know without touching whether he or she can dance or be any good.

"Where did you get it?" she asked calmly.

"From Tony. The tall English fellow. He gave it to me. It's Moroccan. Shall we try it? You use this little white pipe."

He started carefully pushing some of the brown lump into the bowl of the pipe.

"Do you do this a lot?"

"No," he said. "Never."

"Don't pack it too tight. You should have said you smoked it all the time."

"You'd have seen right through me," he said.

He lit a match and held it close to the bowl, sucking on the stem. Nothing happened. He lit another match and after a few tries drew in a little smoke. He inhaled it and coughed, handing the pipe to her. She drew on it and passed it back to him. They took turns without talking. In a few minutes they were high. He felt a gorgeous well-being and sense of ascent.

He had occasionally smoked grass, not very often, sometimes at dinner parties, sometimes in the library afterwards with the hostess and one or another of the guests. He remembered a dizzying night in a divorcée's apartment when he'd asked where the bathroom was, and she took him through a number of rooms into hers, her bathroom, and turned on the light and he was in a palace of mirrors, bottles, and creams, brightly lit. There were overlapped towels on the floor.

"Should I leave you alone?" she had said.

"Just for a minute," he managed to say.

"Are you sure?"

And once he'd been given a couple of joints by a handsome Romanian he happened to meet. He smoked one of them with Eddins in the office, and they were laughing helplessly when Gretchen came in. They thought she had gone home.

"What are you guys doing?" she said. "I know what you're doing."

Bowman tried to keep from laughing.

"What is it?" she asked.

"Nothing," he said and broke out laughing again.

"You two are really stoned," she said.

This was different. He felt things shimmering, shifting. He looked at her as she drew on the pipe, her brows, the line of her jaw. He was able to observe her closely. She had shut her eyes.

"Are you wearing perfume?" he said.

"Perfume?" she said vaguely.

"You are."

"No."

He took the pipe. The hash was almost gone. He drew in and looked to see if there was a glow. He touched the ash. It was cold. They sat for a while in silence.

"How are you?" he said.

She didn't answer. The TV was playing without sound.

She smiled and tried to but couldn't express something.

"We should go out," she said.

"It's too late. Too late. The museums will be closed. I don't know if you want to do that anyway."

"Let's go out," she said and stood up.

He tried to focus on the idea.

"We can't. I'm too high."

"Nobody will know," she said.

"All right. If you say so."

He composed himself. He knew he was incapable of going anywhere.

On the street there were few people. They went a little way down the block. He was too loose.

"No, I don't want to walk," he said. "Let's take a cab."

It seemed almost immediately that one stopped. As they got in, the driver said,

"Where to?"

"Anet."

"Yes."

"Where do you live? You want to go home? Oh," he said to the driver, "just drive around."

"Where do you want to go?" the driver said.

"Drive down, no, go across Fifty-Ninth to Park, no, don't do that. Go to the West Side Highway and go uptown. Then I'll tell you."

They sat back as they drove. It was now dark and they were going along the river. On the far side was an almost continuous line of buildings, houses and apartments lit like hives, some of them very big, bigger than he seemed to remember. He was going to explain it, how there used to be nothing across there, but it was of no interest. Light shone on the surface of the river. He remembered the ride with Christine, the night he first met her. Cars went past them. The necklace of the George Washington Bridge hung like a strand of jewels.

"Where are we going?" she said. "We've been driving and driving."

He told the driver to turn around.

"You're right, that's enough of this," he said to her. "Are you hungry?"

"Yes."

After a while he said,

"Driver, get off at Ninety-Sixth Street, will you? Go over to Second Avenue. We'll go to a place I know," he said to her.

They finally stopped at Elio's. He managed to pay the cab driver, counting the money out twice. Inside there was a crowd. The bartender said hello. The tables in front that were the best were all filled. An editor he knew saw him and wanted to talk. The owner, whom he knew very well, told them they would have to wait fifteen or twenty minutes for a table. He said they would eat at the bar. This is Anet Vassilaros, he said.

The bar was equally busy. The bartender, Alberto—he knew him— spread a large white napkin on the bar in front of each of them and put down knives and forks and a folded napkin.

"Something to drink?" he asked.

"Anet, do you want anything? No," he decided. "I don't think so."

He ordered a glass of red wine, however, and she drank some of it. Conversations were going on all around them. The backs of people. He was nothing like her father, she was thinking, he was in a different world. They sat side by side. People were edging past. The bartender was taking orders for drinks from the waiters, making them, and ringing up checks. He came towards them holding two dishes of food. The owner came while they were eating and apologized for not having been able to seat them.

"No, this was better," Bowman said. "Did I introduce you?"

"Yes. Anet."

The editor stopped by them on his way out. Bowman didn't bother to introduce him.

"You haven't introduced us," the editor said.

"I thought you knew one another," Bowman said.

"No, we don't."

"I can't do it right now," Bowman said.

The owner came back and sat on a stool beside them. Things were becoming a little quieter. It had been a busy night—she hadn't had time to eat dinner herself. People leaving paused to say good night.

"Let me buy you an after-dinner drink," she said. "Do you like rum? We got in some really good rum. Let me get you some. Alberto, where's that bottle of the good rum?"

The rum was strong but extremely smooth. Anet didn't drink any and the three of them sat talking for a while. More people came in, and the owner left them. They went back to the apartment. They had left the party, and Anet curled up on the couch. He gently removed her shoes. He felt colonial for some reason, as if in Kenya or Martinique, the heat of the rum. She was asleep. He felt completely assured. He gathered up her legs, put an arm beneath her, and carried her into the bedroom. She hadn't protested but as he laid her on the bed he felt she was not asleep. Nevertheless, he went out of the room for a few moments. He looked at the couch where she had been lying. It was all happening, it seemed, by itself. He went back into the bedroom and quietly, after taking off his own shoes, lay down beside her. Before he could consider anything else she half-turned and rolled against him, like a child. He put his arm around her and began slowly caressing her back, slipping his hand beneath her blouse. The feel of her bare skin was glorious. He wanted to touch her every-where. Their heads were close as they lay there, and after a while they began to kiss.

From then it became more intense and also uncertain. He had pulled up her skirt rather than trying to remove it. Her legs were incredibly youthful. She was wearing panties and he began slipping them off, but she resisted. He caressed her. She was responsive, but when he tried once again she pressed her legs together.

"No," she said. "Please."

She moved from side to side and pushed his hand away, but he was insistent. Finally, not without relief, she gave in. She became his partner in it, more or less, and at length felt him climax, not realizing it at the time. They lay quietly together.

"You all right?"

"Yes."

"You sure?"

"Yes."

After a few moments,

"Where's the bathroom?" she asked.

When she came back she had taken off her skirt. She got in bed again.

"You're a great thing," he said.

"I probably disappointed you."

"No," he said, "far from it. You didn't disappoint me. You wouldn't know how to."

"Why is that?"

"You just wouldn't," he said and after a pause, "I have to go away later this week."

It was a sudden inspiration. It came about simply.

"I have to go to Paris," he said.

"Nice."

"For three or four days. Have you ever been there?"

"When I was a little girl we went."

"Do you want to come?"

"To Paris? Oh, I can't."

"Why is that? You're not doing anything except looking for a job."

"I'm supposed to go out to my mother's this weekend."

"Just say you can't. Say that you have an interview."

"An interview," she said.

"Say that you'll come the following week."

Lying this close he could feel her complicity.

"Call her tomorrow and it won't be at the last minute. You've done things like this before."

"Not really. I wouldn't want her to find out."

"She won't."

Going home the next morning she wanted to shower and change clothes. She thought of what she had done, fucked her mother's former boyfriend, Philip. She hadn't intended to—she hadn't seen him in almost four years—but somehow it had happened. It had been a surprise. She felt an illicit pleasure and entirely grown up.

27. FORGIVENESS

They landed in the early morning and from the moment they got off the plane even the air itself seemed different, perhaps it was her imagination. They had only cabin baggage and there was no wait, the customs men lazily waved them through. In the big arrival hall while he changed some money, Anet noticed almost with surprise that all the newspapers were in French. They went out the door and found a taxi.

Paris, the legendary Paris, they were driving towards it at eight in the morning on a highway that became more and more filled with traffic as they drove. They didn't bother to talk. They sat back in the seat as they had done the first night. His suit was slightly creased, his collar open at the neck. He sat looking out of the window like an actor after a performance. She was a little worn from the flight as well though excited. Occasionally they exchanged a word or two.

After a while the outlying houses of the *banlieues* began to appear, first separate and apart and then becoming groups and solid blocks with shops of some kind and bars. In long lines of cars they inched into the city and then sped along the streets. They went to a hotel on rue Monsieur le Prince down from the Odéon. The restaurant where he had once seen Jean Cocteau on his very first trip to Paris was up at the *place*. In the other direction was the boulevard with all that was going on.

Their room was on an upper floor and looked down on a large, enclosed space that was actually a school playground. Past the roofs at the far end were other roofs and chimneys and the myriad small streets, some of which he knew. They stood at the floor-length window, which had an ironwork railing outside.

"Seem familiar to you?"

"Oh, no. I was only five years old when I was here."

"Are you tired? Are you hungry?"

"I am a little hungry."

"Go ahead and get ready. I'll take you to a wonderful place for breakfast."

In a big brasserie on boulevard Montparnasse, half-empty in the morning, they had orange juice, croissants, fresh butter, jam, and the bread that is found only in France, along with coffee. From there they went walking to Saint-Sulpice and down the small streets, Sabot, Dragon, where the shops were just opening like flowers, to the famous Deux Magots though she had never heard of it. It was a beautiful day. They sat and had coffee and went on along narrow sidewalks with slender iron bollards, brushing shoulders with students and older women, down to the river to look at Notre Dame. He had shown her only a part of what he knew.

That night they went to dinner at Bofinger, a kind of palace, always crowded, the great cupola over the main room blazing with noise and light and colossal vases of flowers. There was not an empty table. People sat in twos, threes, fives, talking and eating. It was an astounding sight.

"I'm going to order the big *fruits de mer*," he told her. "Do you like oysters?"

"Yes. Maybe," she said.

They came on a large round tray heaped with crushed ice on which rows of gleaming oysters lay, along with shrimp, mussels, and small black shellfish like snails. The lemon halves were covered with gauze. There was butter and thin, dark bread. The wine he ordered was a Montrachet.

She tried an oyster.

"You have to eat two or three to get the idea."

He showed her. A little squeeze of lemon on them first.

She liked the second one better. He was ahead of her, he had eaten four or five. A woman with dark-blond hair at the next table leaned towards them.

"Pardon me, what is this, what you are eating?" she said.

Bowman had to show it to her on the menu. She said something to the man who was with her, then turned back.

"I'm going to have it," she said to them.

Later the same woman talked to them again. She was more familiar.

"Do you live in Paris?" she asked.

"We're just on a trip here."

"Yes, that's the same," the woman said.

She had dark lipstick. She was from Düsseldorf, she said.

"Are you working?" she asked Anet.

"Sorry?"

"Do you work?"

"No."

"I work in a hotel. I'm the manager."

"What are you doing here?"

"We're just in Paris," she explained, "for a visit. If you

come sometime to Düsseldorf, you must stay at my hotel. Both of you," she said.

"It's a good hotel?" Bowman said.

"Very good. What is that wine you're drinking?" she said. She called the waiter.

"Bring another bottle for them," she said. "Put it on my bill."

She gave them her card a little later. It was clearly meant for Anet.

After she and her companion left, they drank the second bottle. There were still people waiting for tables. The overall sound of talk and dining never diminished.

In the taxi they caressed each other's hand. The city was brilliant and vast. The shops were lit along the avenues as they passed. In the room he took her in his arms. He whispered to her and kissed her. He let his hands move down her back. She was twenty. He had known her when she was even younger, a young girl, at her birthday party, running with her girlfriends along the edge of the pond in the sunlight in their tops and underpants, kicking at the water, splashing each other and calling out, fucker-sucker! He'd been surprised at the language. He lifted her onto the bed.

This time it was in all fullness. His palms on either side of her were pressed flat against the sheet, and he held himself half-raised on his arms. He heard her make a sound like a woman, but that was not the end. He paused for a moment and began again. It went on for a long time. She became exhausted.

"I can't," she pleaded.

In the morning the room filled with light. He got up and

closed the curtains, but there was a gap where the sun slipped through and lay across the bed. He pushed the covers away, and the strip of sunlight lay across the top of her legs. The pubic hair shone. She was unknowing but after a minute or two, feeling the air perhaps or her nakedness, she turned over. He bent and kissed the small of her back. She was not quite awake. He parted her legs and knelt between them. He had never been more confident or sure. This time he went in easily. The morning with its stillness. He stayed unmoving, waiting, imagining unhurriedly everything that was to follow. He was making it known to her. Barely a movement, as if it were forbidden. At long last he began, slowly at first with infinite patience that gradually gave way. His head was bowed as if in thought. The end was still far off. Far, far. The band of sunlight had moved towards the foot of the bed. He thought he might outlast it, but then slowly he could feel it mounting. His hand was on her body to steady it, his knees holding down her legs. The faint cries of children in the playground. Sweet Jesus!

Afterwards she had a bath. The water was good and hot. She put up her hair and got in, first her legs and then slowly the rest of her. She was in Paris with him, in a hotel. It was all outrageous, she thought. She was amazed at how it had come about. It was also perfectly natural, she didn't know why. She was washing away the traces of travel, lovemaking, everything, and becoming fresh for the day. He could hear the pleasant sounds of it as he lay in the bed. He was in the person of his former self, in London, Spain, lying quietly, full, so to speak, with what had been accomplished.

"I love this hotel," she said when she came out.

*

The Paris he showed her was a Paris of vistas and streets, the view across the Tuileries, coming into place des Vosges, rue Jacob, and rue des Francs-Bourgeois, the great avenues with their luxurious shops—the price of heaven—the Paris of ordinary pleasures and the Paris of insolence, the Paris that takes for granted one knows something or that one knows nothing at all. The Paris he showed her was a city of sensual memories, glittering in the dark.

Days of Paris. They omitted the museums and the student quarter, boulevard Saint-Michel, and the hurrying crowds, but he took her to see, in the dedicated mansion on rue de Thorigny, the pictures and etchings—many of them grotesque but others supreme—that Picasso had done of Marie-Thérèse Walter during their long love affair in the 1920s and '30s. Some of them were painted in a single inspired afternoon or only days apart. She had been naive and docile when he met her, and he taught her to make love on his terms. He liked to paint her pensive or asleep, and his etchings of her are more beautiful than any incarnation, worthy of worship. In their presence, things assume their true importance, of how life can be lived.

Although he made her iconic, she was not at all interested in art or the circles he belonged to, and Picasso eventually chose another woman.

She remembered going to have a drink with a man Philip particularly liked, a publisher, Christian something, a big, white-haired man with manicured hands. It was in the bar of a hotel not far from his office where he went every afternoon after work and sat in one of the leather armchairs and drank and talked. She had an impression of someone solid and sweet-smelling from soap and cologne. He filled the chair. He was like a large, sacred animal, a fatted bull, barely able to turn in his stall but handsome. He was cordial to them, talking about Gide, Malraux, and others whose names she didn't recognize.

"Are you a writer, *mademoiselle*?" he asked her.

"No," she said.

"You have to watch out for this fellow," he said gesturing towards Philip. "You know that."

"I know," she said.

He was making the assumption that everyone made and that embarrassed her a little, although sometimes not. On the street it didn't embarrass her or in restaurants, but in shops.

On the way back to the hotel they stopped and she wrote some postcards on the terrace of a restaurant that had a glass partition along the sidewalk.

"So, who are you writing to?"

She was writing to her roommate—you don't know her—and to Sophie.

"Ah, Sophie again."

"She's great. You'd like her."

"Are you writing one to your mother?"

"Are you kidding? She thinks I'm having an interview." She paused and looking at the card she was writing said, "You know, you really should tell me. Are you mad at her? Have you forgiven her yet?"

"I'm in the process of it," he said.

He was smoking a cigarette as they sat there, a French

cigarette. It seemed fatter than an ordinary one. He put it, a little inexpertly, she thought, to his lips and took a light drag and as some of the bluish smoke slid up over his face, exhaled.

"Does the smoke bother you?"

"No, it has a nice smell."

"You've never smoked, have you?"

"No, unless you count smoking a little dope."

"It used to be that women weren't allowed to smoke."

"What do you mean, weren't allowed?"

"They were allowed, but it was considered unseemly. No woman would smoke in public."

"When was this? In the middle ages?"

"No, before the war."

"Which war?"

"The world war. The first one."

"I don't believe you."

"It's true."

"That's incredible," she said. "Let me try a puff."

She took the cigarette, drew a little on it, and coughed. She handed it back.

"Here."

"Strong, isn't it?" he said.

"Much too strong."

They were going to Flo for dinner.

"Flow?" she said. "What's that?"

It was down a darkened alley that was unlikely to have anything like a restaurant. At last they came to it.

"Oh," she said seeing the sign, "so that's it. Flo."

"The *w* is silent," he said.

They had a booth that was too near the kitchen, but it was

a good dinner. At the end of it they saw a fight. There was a great crash of dishes and a woman in a black coat was shouting and hitting the manager. He was trying to push her out the door. Finally he succeeded and she stood in the street cursing as a waiter brought her handbag out to her. She shouted something more at the manager, who bowed slightly. Good night, madame, he said to her. *A demain,* he said.

Where Flo was, Anet had no idea. It was somewhere in Paris. She didn't speak French, and her outline of the city was of certain avenues without beginning or end, certain Metro stops and signs—Taittinger, La Coupole—and streets that had caught her eye. All of it would never arrange itself, especially at night and when drinking. They were driving back to the hotel, the shops fleeing past lit as always. They seemed familiar somehow.

"Where are we?" she said.

"I can't read the signs. I think we're on boulevard Sebastopol."

"Where's that?"

"It's a big boulevard. Goes right into Saint-Michel."

She could never have done this, she thought. She would never have done it by herself. It was still amazing and so easy. She'd remember it for a long time. She probably could go on with him if she liked for a few months. She'd had boyfriends, two anyway, but it had been different. They were just very young. Did you get the condoms—they were free at the dispensary, but sometimes they ran out of them. They wanted a fistful of them, but then it was usually over quickly. She saw something familiar and tried to think of where they were. They were crossing the Seine. They turned down another street. Above the buildings the top of the Eiffel Tower, brilliantly lit, was floating in the dark.

In the room she lay down in her clothes and let him undress her. He caressed her for a long time and she made plain she was his. He was tracing the cut with his tongue. He turned her over and put his hands on her shoulders and then slowly down along her body as if it were the neck of a goose. When at last he entered her it was as if he were speaking. He was thinking of Christine. Forgiveness. He wanted it to last a long time. When he felt himself going too far he slowed and began again. He could hear her saying something into the bedding. He was holding her by the waist. Ah, ah, ah. The walls were falling away. The city was collapsing like stars.

"Ah, God," he said after. "Anet."

She lay in his arms.

"You are something."

The late hour. The absolute completion. He had been lucky, he thought. In a day or two more, probably, she would begin to be tired of opera like this. She would suddenly recognize how old he was, how much she missed her friends. But it would stay in her life. It would stay in her mother's. He smoothed her hair. She relaxed in sleep.

She slept until nine. The room was quiet. He'd gone down to look at the newspaper, and she turned over and slept a while longer. When she came out of the bathroom she saw a piece of paper lying on his side of the bed. She picked it up and as she read it her heart seemed to scatter. She quickly put on some clothes to go down to the desk. The elevator was in use. She couldn't wait and ran down the stairs.

"Have you seen Monsieur Bowman?" she asked the clerk.

"Ah yes. He left."

"He left for where?"

"I don't know. He called a taxi."

"When was that?"

"An hour ago. More."

She hardly knew what to do. She couldn't believe it. She had missed something. She went back to the room and sat on the bed with a sickening feeling. Now that she looked she saw that his things were gone. She looked in the bathroom. It was the same. She was suddenly frightened. She was by herself. She had no money. She picked up the note again and read it. *I'm leaving. I can't bother now to explain. It was very nice.* It was signed with an initial, *P.* This time she broke into tears. She fell back on the bed and lay there.

He had gone to a rental agency and gotten a car, a larger one than he wanted but it was all they had, and it was a long drive. He made his way out of the city by the Porte d'Orléans and drove south towards Chartres and towns further on where he had never been. It was sunny and clear. He had a vague idea of going all the way to Biarritz with its two great beaches like wings on either side and the ocean breaking in long white lines. There was little traffic. He had gotten up early and quietly gathered his things. She was sleeping, an arm beneath the pillow, a bare leg showing. The freshness of her, even afterwards. He had forgiven her mother. Come and get your daughter, he thought. At the door he paused and looked at her a last time. He paid the hotel bill while waiting for the taxi. He didn't try to imagine what she would do.

28. TIVOLI

Of the people he had started with, at about the same time, Glenda Wallace had done well. A senior editor, she was strong-minded and direct though she'd been less so when she was younger, and along the way she had developed a sharp, bitter laugh. She had never married. She had an ailing father she had looked after for years. After he died she bought a house in Tivoli, a town on the Hudson past Poughkeepsie. She'd had no connection with the town, only that she saw it and it appealed to her, the small business section, the undisturbed feeling, and the road going down to the river with the old houses.

As an editor she'd had little to do with fiction and seldom read any. She published books on politics and history and also biographies and was widely respected. She had become shorter over the years and Bowman one day noticed for the first time that she was bowlegged. He admired her, and it was because of the fact she was there and made it seem less remote that he rented a weekend house in Tivoli himself the next year.

Driving to Tivoli, north along the Saw Mill River, was pleasant. It was mostly woodland with very little business clutter, but it also felt strange. Wainscott and the towns around it had almost been home, and he had decided to go elsewhere not out of fear of seeing Christine or her daughter, but simply to eliminate the possibility of it and to put it all behind him. He didn't want to be reminded of what had happened. At the same time he didn't mind reflecting on part of it, the part in Paris.

The house belonged to a professor in the economics department at Bard who had gotten a fellowship in Europe and would be gone with his family for a year. Academic life had its stringencies. It was a decent-looking house, but aside from the fireplace there was not much in the living room, a sofa, some chairs, and a small table. The dishes in the kitchen were plastic and there was a miscellaneous collection of glasses, but the kitchen door opened onto a little garden with hedges and a wooden gate to the street.

The house and its meager comforts made publishing seem a rich life, though not as rich as it had been. It had changed greatly from the days when there were only eight of them in the entire firm and writers sometimes spent the night on a couch at the end of the hallway after drinking in various bars until two or three in the morning. There were always dinners and late hours. Drinking in Cologne with Karl Maria Löhr, who never tired and after a while never made sense but who somehow bound writers to him by ordeal. Nights in the German darkness, driving around in the icy fog. You couldn't remember where you had been or what had been said, but that didn't matter. There was a kind of intimacy. Afterwards you spoke as friends. He had thought at times of becoming a publisher himself. He probably had the temperament, but he would not have enjoyed the business part. That could be the province of someone who did, a congenial, perfect partner, but he had never encountered him, not at what would have been the right time.

The power of the novel in the nation's culture had weakened. It had happened gradually. It was something everyone recognized and ignored. All went on exactly as before, that was the beauty of it. The glory had faded but fresh faces kept appearing, wanting to be part of it, to be in publishing which had retained a suggestion of elegance like a pair of beautiful, bone-shined shoes owned by a bankrupt man. Those who had been in it for some years, he and Glenda and the others, were like nails driven long ago into a tree that then grew around them. They were part of it by now, embedded.

To make the house more comfortable he rearranged the furniture, moved the table and brought a leather chair from the city. He put some books, a bottle of whiskey, and some nice glasses on the table. He also brought up a pair of framed Edward Weston photographs, one of them of Charis, Weston's legendary model and companion. He unfastened and stored in a closet the sets of little slatted shutters that were inside the windows and instead hung some white muslin curtains that admitted more light.

In the mornings he had a soft-boiled egg. He put the egg in a pan of cold water and when the water came to a boil it was done. Carefully tapping around it with a knife, he removed the top, put in a bit of butter and some salt and ate the soft white and warm, runny yolk with a spoon. Afterwards for an hour or so he read the newspaper he'd brought up with him before sitting down with a manuscript. His life seemed simpler and in this bare house almost penitent. The next week he brought up a Navajo rug that had been in the closet and felt a little more at home.

Among the first people he met in Tivoli were a professor, Russell Cutler, and his wife, Claire, an avid woman with a slight lisp. "Between ourselves," she would say, slightly thickening it. Cutler had written scholarly books but was now working on a detective novel, not without difficulty. His wife read every page and crossed out things she disapproved of or considered sexist. She was long-necked with long hands and the sari slipping from her shoulder the night Bowman came to dinner. There was a large dining table covered with a dark green, patterned cloth, and she had written out the menu and gone to the trouble of having two different wines and two fruit tarts for dessert. Her friend Katherine, with a striking feline face, had been invited, too, and busied herself helping the hostess. At the table she seemed not so much unwilling to speak as attentive—almost as if waiting for a tidbit—to anything Bowman might say.

"You're an editor, Claire says," she ventured finally.

"Yes."

"A book editor?"

"Yes, I edit books."

"That must be a wonderful life."

"Yes and no. What do you do?"

"Oh, I'm just a secretary here, at Bard. But I love New York. I go to New York every chance I get."

She had landed at Bard somehow. She had come to New York, which was what she had always wanted to do, after a divorce but hadn't been able to find a job she liked. She stayed with a friend, a French woman who was a painter and had said to her, if you come to New York, you must stay with me, but when Katherine moved in, said she would have to charge her some rent.

"Yes, of course," Katherine had said.

It was what she said to everything. In Houston they had come to take away the furniture. Yes. Of course. She had an aristocratic disposition, she dismissed misfortune. She was a model secretary, nicely dressed, helpful, and efficient. It was her looks and the possibilities they suggested. She loved gossip. She liked to mimic. She remembered everything. Though she seemed to be a woman whose main interests were clothes and parties, her real passion was books. She loved books—no one ever loved them more. She read two or three a week. She would come home from a bookshop with a bag of them and start reading one while taking off her shoes. She would still be reading when Deborah, the girl she shared a house with, came home late after orchestra practice. Her own life she treated as a tragicomedy, but writing she treated seriously. The dream she concealed was to become a writer, but she avoided ever saying anything about that.

The next morning in Germantown in the little grocery Bowman saw her standing in one of the narrow aisles. He almost didn't recognize her. She looked younger. He said hello.

"That was a nice evening at the Cutlers'," he said. "Did you enjoy it?"

"Oh, yes. You were amazing."

"Was I? I didn't realize that. What are you shopping for?"

"I don't know. I didn't even make a list," she apologized. "Such a beautiful day, isn't it?"

"It feels like summer."

"I don't really have much planned. Are you doing anything? Let's have lunch."

"Oh, yes!" she cried. "Where shall we go?"

There were only a couple of choices, and in the end they went to Red Hook, to the diner. Only a few people were there. They sat in a booth. She drew in her cheeks as she read the menu, a kind of sophisticated pose.

"What are you doing?" he asked.

"Pardon?"

At the same time he sensed that she was more at ease.

"I'm going to have the corned beef hash," he said. "How do you happen to know the Cutlers?"

"Oh, Claire. I met her at a lecture. Three professors were explaining the poems of Wallace Stevens. I asked her afterwards if she understood any of it. Between ourselves, she said, hardly a word."

"Yes, between ourselves. What about her husband?"

"Russell? He knows nothing about anything. He likes to make his own wine."

"Is that what we were drinking?"

"Oh, no. His wine is undrinkable. You spit it out."

"Where are you from, Katherine?"

"Oh, a town in Oklahoma you've never heard of. Hugo."

"You grew up there?"

"Well, yes," she said, "but I left the day I graduated from high school and went to the city, and I had a little accident."

"What was that?"

"I got married. I was eighteen and I just married the first man I met. He was good-looking but he turned out to be a drug addict, a horrible drug addict. I didn't realize it, of course, being eighteen, but that's what happened. He lost all his money. He had loads of money from his father. We lived in a huge house and had to move out of it. We had four in help plus the gardener, who slept in the garage."

It sounded as if she were making it up, at least parts of it, but he decided to believe it.

"Oh, my, they were trouble," she said. "The maid's boyfriend was a big Mexican who drove his pickup to the back door and they would load it with meat from the freezer. I was afraid of him. Whenever I came back and saw the truck I would turn around and drive off for at least half an hour. I didn't want to catch them. It was terrible. The only one I liked was the housekeeper, who ran off to Florida and called one day from a shopping center to say they were down to eight dollars and her daughter had entered the Miss Florida contest. If I would just send them some money she promised to pay it back."

She was aware of her good looks as she performed, which is what it was. She paused.

"Are you married?" she asked casually.

"Oh, a long time ago. We've been divorced for years."

"What happened?"

"Nothing happened, really. I mean, that's from my point of view. She probably had some grievances."

"What did she do?" Katherine asked.

"Do you mean work? She didn't work. She didn't read, that was one thing."

"Don't you just wonder at people like that? What was her name?"

"Her name was Vivian."

"Vivian!"

"Vivian Amussen. Very good-looking."

She felt a little stab of unhappiness, even jealousy. It was just automatic.

"Amussen," she said wittily, "Like the river."

"No. Two s's."

She felt he was losing interest.

"Do you have lots to do?"

"Today, do you mean? I have some work I should do."

"I have a million things to do."

"I shouldn't be keeping you," he said.

"Oh, you're not keeping me. I'm just afraid that I'm boring you."

"You're not boring me, not a bit."

"So, are you going to the Susan Sontag talk?"

"When is that?"

"It's at the college. It's tonight."

"I hadn't thought about it. Are you going?"

"Yes."

"Maybe I'll see you there."

She was already thinking of what to wear. She decided on a certain summery frock.

"What did you think of the food?" she asked as he was paying the check. "Here, let me pay for mine."

She found her wallet but he put his hand over it and the bills she was clutching.

"No, no," he said. "It's my lunch. Publishers always pay for lunch."

She had a good feeling as they stood there, as if she could

hug herself. She felt he liked her as a woman. That was unmistakable. She felt she was perhaps a companion for him
although at the end he had seemed rather abrupt—it was
probably a matter of not really knowing him.

The day had been warm. It was still light outside as people
walked in and tried to find empty seats. The hall was completely filled. Like a lone bird rising from the flock a hand
waved from the middle of the audience. She had saved him
a seat. Susan Sontag, when she came onto the stage on a wave
of applause, was a dramatic figure in black and white—black
trousers, black raven hair with a great shock of white running
through it and a bold, sharp face. She spoke for half an hour
about film. There were many students taking notes. Katherine sat attentive, her chin held slightly forward as she listened.
At the end as they left she asked him as if in confidence,

"What did you think?"

"I wondered what all those girls were writing down."

"Everything she said."

"I hope not."

Just outside they encountered Claire, who was smiling
with joy.

"Wasn't that marvelous!" she cried.

"It was quite a performance," Bowman agreed. He felt like
a drink, he said.

"Shall I come with you?" Claire asked congenially.

"Sure," he said.

They went in two cars—Claire rode with Katherine—to
the Madalin Hotel, which was in the center of Tivoli and had

a good bar. Bowman arrived after they did. He had parked in front of his house just two blocks away.

It was a weekend night and there was a crowd. Claire continued talking about Susan Sontag. What did they really think of her—she meant what did Bowman think.

"She's a figure from the Old Testament," he said.

"She's such a powerful person. You just feel it."

"All powerful women cause anxiety," he said.

"Do you really think so?"

"It's not a question of what you think. It's what anybody thinks."

"You do?"

"Men do," he said.

She was a little dismayed. It sounded chauvinistic.

"I thought she said some very interesting things about film."

"Film," he said.

"Being the supreme art of the century."

"Yes, I heard that. I suppose it's true. It sounded a little extreme."

"But haven't you been really transported by certain movies? You always remember them."

He was listening and he now heard clearly what it was, a slight *th* on the *s* as if the tip of her tongue didn't get out of the way quickly enough. She had said "transthported."

"Didn't you find it amazing when she said that if Wagner were born today he'd be a film director?"

"Amazing is not the word. I wonder why she picked Wagner. She skipped too many of them. She skipped Mozart."

"Yes, I suppose," Claire agreed.

"Dancing is more important than movies," he said.

"Do you mean ballet?"

"No, just dancing. If you know how to dance you can be happy."

"I realize you're joking now."

"No."

They went on talking and drinking. Katherine was annoyed that Claire had come with them and that she wouldn't stop talking. Oh, Claire! she said several times or ignored her. The noise in the bar was deafening.

Claire took up a different tack.

"What things are you interested in?" she asked Bowman.

"What am I interested in?"

"Yes."

"Why do you ask that?"

"I don't know."

"I'm interested in architecture. Painting."

"I mean in a personal way."

"What do you mean, personal?"

"What about women?"

There was a moment's pause and he began laughing.

"What's funny?"

"Yes," he said. "I'm interested in women." ·

"I was just asking. Kathy should get married, don't you think?" she remarked.

"Are those two things connected?"

"Oh, God, Claire, what are you talking about?" Katherine said.

"You're such a desirable woman," Claire said. "No, really," she said to Bowman, "don't you think so?"

"You're embarrassing her."

He was becoming annoyed. This was a relentless woman, he thought, and also without much humor. He wondered what bound the two of them together. Some hidden understanding women always have.

"You do agree, don't you? She is desirable."

He looked at Katherine.

"Yes, I'd say so."

When Claire went to the ladies' room, Katherine apologized,

"I'm deeply sorry for this. She's crazy. Can you forgive me?"

"You haven't done anything wrong."

"She's not used to drinking. All they have is that terrible wine. I'm really sorry."

"It's all right. Really."

"Anyway I just wanted to say . . ."

Claire was coming back.

"Hello, again," she said.

"Stop being a fool," Katherine hissed.

"What?"

"Are you ready to go?"

"What's going on? I haven't finished my drink."

"I've finished mine."

"I see that."

"I have to be going anyway," Bowman said.

"So soon?" said Claire.

Katherine said nothing. She had an expression of acceptance.

"Good night," Bowman told them.

He made his way out through the people in the bar. There was a crowd waiting to get into the restaurant across the street and others who'd come out of it were lingering. It was warm. Music was playing somewhere. Two girls sat on a large rock that was embedded in the sidewalk, smoking and talking. There were a lot of cars.

He was in his pajamas an hour later when someone knocked on the door.

"Yes? Who is it?"

They knocked lightly again.

He opened the door and Katherine was standing there. She had stayed at the bar, he saw.

"I had to come and apologize," she said. "I was so embarrassed. I woke you, didn't I?"

"No, I was awake," he said.

He was regarding her cooly, she felt.

"I only wanted to make sure you knew I didn't put her up to that."

"I didn't think that."

"I just wanted to tell you tonight."

"Can you get home all right?"

"Yes."

"Are you sure?"

"Yes."

It had been a mistake, she realized. She was not sure what to say. She moved her fingers in a foolish little good-bye and walked quickly to the gate.

The town would have been dull without her and her longing to live a somehow different life. She was tired of the former one. The encounters in it had not been happy although she retained her high spirits for the most part. She had a brief affair with a visiting anthropologist who came to teach for a week and met her the first day. She said nothing about it to Bowman, to whom she was faithful in a deeper way, and also it had just been Monday to Friday. She already regretted it. When Bowman came to pick her up one evening he happened to notice a book the anthropologist had written and given to her. It had a vulgar inscription that he mused over while she was finishing dressing, but he had closed the book and he said nothing about it when she appeared.

She came to the city as often as she could and stayed with Nadine, her French friend, and listened to stories of Nadine's misfortunes in love. Robert Motherwell had wanted her to be his mistress, but she insisted it had to be marriage and so nothing happened. She had a husband at the time but was getting divorced.

"That was the mistake of my life, *de tout ma vie*," she said with her slight accent. "If I had done it, would I be any worse off than now? And I would at least have the memories of love, the *souvenirs*. This way I don't have a husband or the memories."

She was fifty-two but acted younger.

"I was so innocent as a young woman," she said. "You would not believe it. I was nineteen when I got married. I knew nothing in those days, absolutely nothing."

When her husband was not prepared to make love, she said, she couldn't understand why.

"As a young girl I imagined it was hard all the time." She laughed at her own naïveté. "But there was one thing I learned that's the most important thing."

"Yes!" Katherine said. "What is it?"

"Do you really want to know?"

"Yes. Tell me."

"Never give men your best," Nadine said. "They come to expect it."

"Yes, that's exactly my mistake."

"You can never relax," Nadine said. "Of course, sometimes you can't help it, but it's never a good thing."

All of this, Katherine told to Bowman as they ate oysters and drank. She confided in him. She loved talking to him.

"Have you ever wanted to write?" she said.

"No. As an editor you have to do the opposite. You have to open yourself to the writing of others. It's not the same thing. I can write. Originally I wanted to be a journalist. I can write flap copy but not anything with real luster. To do that you have to be able to shut out the writing of others."

"Do you have favorite writers?"

"What do you mean?"

"That you've worked with."

After a moment he said,

"Yes."

"Who?"

"Well, the writer I value the most lives in France. She's lived there for years. I see her only very occasionally, but it's always such a pleasure. As they like to say, she's the real thing."

"She must be wonderful," Katherine managed to say.

"Yes. Dedicated and wonderful."

"Who is it?"

"Raymonde Garris."

Katherine knew the name. She was crushed by it. It seemed the name of an indescribably fascinating woman. It would be marvelous to know her, to know any of them. Then one night at dinner there was Harold Brodkey, who had written the long story about orgasms. Harold Brodkey! She could hardly wait to tell Claire.

Or tell about going to the Frick.

She was wearing a pair of new red shoes that were too tight for her. She had to take them off in the ladies' room to rest.

"Did you like it?" he asked as they were preparing to leave.

"Yes. It was absolutely beautiful," she said. "And you can learn so many things."

"What do you mean?"

"I don't know. You can learn what to wear when you have your portrait painted. You can learn how to hold a dog."

He looked at her disapprovingly.

"You know I don't know anything about art," she said. "I only know what you tell me."

She was not being ironic. She liked male authority, especially his.

"Nadine is going to be very impressed that we went to the Frick. She imagines me as only going to bars and sitting with my skirt pulled up."

Together they stepped out into the early evening. She was holding his arm. The sky was a deep, rain blue, almost no light remaining but the clouds were still lustrous. Windows were lit in every building on the avenue and across the end of the park.

Later in the fall she met him on a Friday evening in the bar of the Algonquin, where he liked to go. It was a small room, more like a club, behind the front desk and often crowded at that hour. It was as if there was a great party being held in the hotel, spilling from the elevators and rooms and the bar was a kind of refuge from it, calmer though filled. There were many men in suits and ties. She had just read Marguerite Duras, *The Lover,* for the first time and was going on about it.

"Oh, God, didn't that image of the girl just kill you? On the ferry in a sepia-colored silk dress. It was her, Marguerite Dura."

"Duras," Bowman said.

"Duras? Is that how you say it?"

"Yes."

"I thought you didn't pronounce the final *s* in French," she said plaintively.

He could not help being touched by her.

"Bowman?" he heard someone behind them call. "Is that you?"

It was followed by a cackle.

"For God's sake," Bowman exclaimed.

"Excuse me, sir, aren't you Phil Bowman?"

Lanky, grinning, older, with a pot belly, it was Kimmel. Bowman felt an inexplicable warmth rise within him.

"See, I told you," Kimmel said to the blond woman with him.

"What are you doing here?" Bowman said.

Cackling again, with his elbows loose, Kimmel doubled over laughing.

"Kimmel, what the hell are you doing here?" Bowman said again. "I can't believe it."

"Who is this?" Kimmel said, ignoring him. "Is this your daughter? Your father and I were shipmates." He turned to the blond woman. "Donna, I want you to meet an old pal, Phil Bowman, and his daughter—I'm sorry, I didn't get your name," he said smiling with charm.

"Katherine. I'm not his daughter."

"I didn't think so," Kimmel said.

"My name's Donna," the woman said, introducing herself. She had an appealing face and seemed a bit too big for her legs.

"What are you doing in New York? Where are you living?" Bowman asked.

"We're on a little business trip," Kimmel said. "We're living in Ft. Lauderdale. We were in Tampa, but we moved."

"My ex-husband is in Tampa," Donna said.

"Tell them who you were married to," Kimmel said.

"Oh, they don't want to hear about that."

"Yes, they do. She was married to a count."

"I was twenty-eight, you know?" she said to Katherine. "I'd never been married, and I met this tall guy in Boca Raton who had a Porsche. He was German and had tons of money. We sort of started up and I thought, why not? My father practically disowned me. I was over there trying to kill them, he said, and here you're going to marry one. It turned out after we were married that he didn't have any money—his mother did. She only spoke German to me. I tried to learn German, you know, but it was hopeless. He was a nice guy, but it lasted about two years."

"And then you two met?" Bowman said.

"No, not right away."

"Donna was very close to the governor for a while," Kimmel said.

"Hey," she said.

"Whatever happened to Vicky?" Bowman asked.

"Vicky?"

"In San Diego."

"You know, I saw her after that," Kimmel said. "I could see it wouldn't work. She was too bourgeois for me."

"Bourgeois?"

"And her father was a killer."

He turned to Katherine,

"Your dad, I don't know if he's told you about his swash-buckling days in the Pacific during the war. We were getting ready to invade Okinawa. Everybody was writing farewell letters except the mail was cut off. Everybody was desperate. The exec said, Mr. Bowman! The ship is depending on you. Bring back the mail! That was it. Like the message to Garcia."

"The message to who?" Donna said.

Kimmel cackled,

"Ask him."

Then he became serious,

"Tell me, Phil, what are you doing these days?"

"I'm an editor."

"I figured you'd end up commanding the fleet. You know, you haven't changed a bit. Except for your appearance," he said.

"Is it true," Donna said, "that this one here was blown right off the ship?"

"Three of them," Kimmel said. "It set a record."

"You weren't exactly blown off," Bowman said.

"The whole damn ship was exploding."

"Well, we managed to get it to port. Brownell and I."

"Brownell!" Kimmel cried.

He looked at his watch.

"Hey, we're going to have to get going. We have tickets to a show."

"What are you seeing?" Katherine said.

"What are we seeing?" he asked Donna.

"*Evita.*"

"That's it. It was great seeing you."

They shook hands and near the door Kimmel waved one arm loosely in good-bye. Bye bye, waved Donna.

Like that, they were gone. All of it had come back so swiftly. The past seemed there at his feet, the neglected past. He felt oddly freshened.

"Who was that?" said Katherine.

"That was the Camel," Bowman said.

He couldn't help smiling.

"The camel?"

"That was Bruce Kimmel. He was my cabinmate on the ship. The crew all called him the Camel. He walked like one."

"You were in the navy," she said. "I didn't know that. During the war."

"Yes, both of us."

"What was it like?"

"That's hard to explain. I actually thought of staying in the navy."

"I loved listening to you and the Camel. Did you know him a long time?"

"Quite a long time. Then he jumped overboard in the middle of the ocean during a big attack. That was the last time I saw him."

"Until tonight? That's so incredible."

Nadine was looking forward to finally meeting Bowman. Katherine was coming into town to go to a party with him a few days before Christmas, she hoped it would be more than a party. The course of things seemed right for it. He was not seeing anyone else, she knew, and Christmas was like Mardi Gras, at parties anything might happen. The parties at Christmas were not like other parties, they were gayer and more warmhearted.

Snow was forecast for the day she was coming, which made it even more perfect. Perhaps she wouldn't be able to get back to Nadine's afterwards. She might be wearing his bathrobe in the morning and they would look out together on a city all covered with white.

With snow on the way everyone was let off work early. She hurried to her house. The snow had already begun falling. She never imagined that it would interfere. Deborah came in to report it was already two or three inches deep on the roads, the bus that was to leave at four was already delayed. An hour later Katherine had to call and say she was not going to be able to get to the city.

"Oh, God," she cried, "this is so terrible."

"It's just a party," Bowman said not knowing all that was intended. "It's not that important."

"Yes, it is," she moaned.

She was heartbroken. Nothing could console her.

That evening in New York it was snowing heavily, the beginning of a huge storm. Guests were late to the party and some had decided not to come, but many were there. Coats and women's boots were piled in the bedroom. A piano was playing. Bus service was suspended, someone was saying. The room was filled with people laughing and talking. Platters of food were being put out on a long counter that was open to the kitchen. A whole ham glazed a rich brown stood with slivers being cut off and eaten. On the television, two announcers, a man and a woman, were following the progress of the storm but could not be heard over the noise. There was a strange sense of unreality with the snow falling more and more heavily outside. It was almost impossible to see across the street. There were only the blurred lights of apartments in the shifting white shrouds.

Bowman stood by the window. He was under the spell of other Christmases. He was remembering the winter during the war, at sea, far from home and on the ship Armed Forces

Radio playing carols, "Silent Night," and everyone thinking back. With its deep nostalgia and hopeless longing it had been the most romantic Christmas of his life.

Someone was standing just behind him watching in silence, also. It was Ann Hennessy, who had been Baum's assistant and was now working in publicity.

"Snow at Christmas," Bowman remarked.

"That was a wonderful thing, wasn't it?"

"When you were a child, you mean."

"No, always."

They were laughing in the kitchen. An English actor was just arriving in a fur-collared coat after his last performance. The host had come to greet him and to say good-bye to guests who were afraid of not being able to get home.

"I think I'm going to go myself, before it gets worse," Bowman decided.

"Yes, I think so, too," she said.

"How are you going? I'll see if I can find a cab. I'll drop you off."

"No, that's all right," she said. "I'll take the subway."

"Oh, I don't think you should take the subway tonight."

"I always take it."

"There could be delays."

"I get off just a block away from my door," she said as if to reassure him.

She went to say good night to the host and his wife. Bowman saw her get her coat. She drew a colored silk scarf from one of the sleeves and wound it expertly around her neck. She put on a knit hat and tucked her hair into it. He saw her turn up her collar as she went into the hall. He stood at the window to see her figure appear in the street, but she apparently stayed close to the building, making her way alone.

She was, in fact, not solitary. She had, for some years, been involved with a doctor who had given up his practice. He was brilliant—she would never have been attracted to an unintelligent man—but unstable, with wide changes of mood. He went into rages but then pleadingly begged her forgiveness. It had exhausted her emotionally. She was a Catholic girl from Queens, a bright student, shy in her youth but with the poise of someone who goes their own way indifferent to opinion. It was the strain of her relationship with the doctor that had made her give up her job as Baum's assistant. She didn't explain the reasons. She merely said it had turned out to be more than she felt capable of doing and Baum knew her well enough to accept it and the obvious fact that she had a somewhat troubling life of her own.

Bowman knew none of this. He merely felt some strange connection to her, probably because of the sentimentality of the occasion or a grace in her he had not seen before. It was better not to have seen her home or even to see her leaving the building. The snow was coming down, some people were calling to him.

30. A WEDDING

In the summer of 1984, on a Sunday afternoon, Anet married Evan Anders, the son of a New York lawyer and his Venezuelan wife. Four years older than Anet, with the dark hair and brilliant smile of his mother, he had a degree in mathematics but had decided to fulfill a long-held ambition and become a writer. He was working meanwhile as a bartender, and it was during this adventurous period in his life that he and Anet decided to get married. They had been going together for more than a year.

The wedding was in Brooklyn in the garden of some friends. Anet was not religious and in any case not Greek Orthodox but as a gesture towards her father a few details of a Greek ceremony were included. They were going to wear the little crowns that Greek couples wore, and the wedding rings would be on the finger of the right hand rather than the left. There were fifteen or sixteen guests not including the parents of the bride and groom, the best man who was the groom's younger brother, Tommy, and Sophie, who was maid of honor. The others were young couples and a few young women who had come singly. It was a very warm afternoon. A table with pitchers of iced tea and lemonade had been set up to one side. There would be drinks afterward at the reception. Several of the women were fanning themselves as they waited.

William Anders and Flore, his wife, liked Anet very much. She was a little reserved, he felt, but perhaps it was only towards him. He was a lawyer of the utmost probity. He was not a man of rash actions. He was the trustee of large estates and had clients that he had represented for years and were his friends, but with his son's girlfriend something had passed between them from the first all-telling look. He might have chosen her himself and perhaps it was this she sensed and was wary, but at the wedding that day it seemed to him that she returned his look without caution.

Several of the guests had already seated themselves in the rows of chairs, including Christine and her husband. She was wearing a hat with a wide brim that shaded her face and a print dress with a pattern that looked like blue leaves. Everyone noticed her. In the wedding party photograph she appeared to be a woman of thirty standing with one foot forward of the other like a model. In fact she was forty-two and not yet entirely prepared to let youth have the stage.

Some taped music was playing, a string quartet. Anet was usually bored by string quartets but had felt that one was right for the occasion and anyway in the house she could barely hear it. Tommy had caught a glimpse of her in one of the rooms as he came through the house into the garden. She was standing in her white wedding gown and they were pinning it in places. She was too involved to notice or smile at him, too nervous, but proud to be marrying in front of her parents, especially her mother with whom she had been on bad terms for quite a while although by now that had been largely forgotten, that is to say, no longer talked about.

It was Christine who had met her on her arrival back at Kennedy. In the taxi they had sat in tense silence. Christine was seething. It was not that she thought her daughter was innocent although in a way she did, but she had never imagined anything as sordid as Anet sleeping with her former boyfriend. Finally she said,

"So, tell me what happened. I know what happened, but I want you to tell me."

"I don't want to right now," Anet said in a subdued voice.

"Whose idea was it to go to Paris? Was that your idea?"

Anet didn't answer.

"How long had it been going on before that?" Christine demanded.

"Nothing had been going on."

"Nothing? Do you expect me to believe that?"

"Yes."

"So, how did it happen that he left you? What caused it?"

"I don't know."

"You don't know. Well, I know."

Anet was silent.

"He wanted to show you were a little slut. He didn't have to try very hard. You know, he's thirty years older than you are. What did he do, tell you he loved you?"

"No."

"No. Does anyone else know about this?"

Anet shook her head. She began to cry.

"You are stupid," Christine said. "You're a stupid little girl."

*

That was six years before, and now her father came in to ask if she was ready. He was giving her in marriage, he was bringing her into the garden on his arm. As they stood together the music of the quartet stopped and was replaced by the familiar opening chords of the wedding march. All heads turned as Anet, almost magical in white, walked with her father from the house. She had a look of calm and even pleasure on her face although she felt her lower lip quivering. She lowered her head for a moment to gain control of it. Her husband-to-be was smiling as she came towards him, Sophie was smiling, nearly everyone was.

During the ceremony when it came to the crowns that seemed woven of cloth with tails of ribbon, the minister said,

"O Lord, crown them with glory and honor."

They put them on and then exchanged them and did the same with the rings, three times, from bride to groom and groom to bride to symbolize the weaving together of their lives as everyone watched in rapt silence. At the end they drank together, husband and wife, from a single cup of wine. There was applause and congratulations and embraces before the party made its way indoors where champagne and a buffet were waiting.

31. WITHOUT END

He had asked her, more or less on impulse, if she would like to come to dinner with Kenneth Wells and his wife, neither of whom she had met, who were down for a few days to talk about the book he was writing and to break the boredom of the country. It seemed the right occasion.

"Have you met them?" Bowman said. "I think you'll like them."

He had not been able to conceal that he had been for a while attracted to Ann, he was not sure how greatly. But he did not want a romance, an episode. Their work was too closely related for that. He felt it would be crude. On the other hand, there she was, he now saw, in her heels and quiet manner permitting him to think about her.

She arrived at the restaurant that night wearing black pants and a white, ruffled shirt and Wells stood up like an obedient schoolboy when she joined them.

"I love your books," she told him.

Michele Wells was drinking a glass of wine. Wells had ordered a bourbon old fashioned.

"What's that?" Ann asked.

He described it briefly.

"My father used to drink them," he explained.

"I'll try one."

"Do you drink them?" he asked with some pleasure.

"No, this will be the first time."

"I haven't heard that for a while," Wells said. "Actually when he died my father was drinking scotch. He'd had a heart attack and one evening he asked for a drink. He wanted a scotch with a little water and he asked the nurse if she would have one with him. They sipped their drinks and talked a little and when he'd finished my father said to her, how about one for the road? She poured it and he was drinking it, and he died."

Wells was stimulated by the presence of another woman. His combed-back gray hair and glasses made him look Germanic. There was nothing much to do in Chatham in the evening except watch television.

They'd been watching *Brideshead Revisited*, Michele said. "The actor who plays Sebastian is wonderful."

Wells made a vulgar remark.

"I thought this was going to be a clean in body, clean in mind night," she said.

"Ah, yes. I remember," he admitted.

In fact she liked obscene talk, in private, especially if it had some literary or historical flavor. He sometimes referred to her pussy as the French Concession and went on from there. He had fallen in love with his wife before he ever saw her, he said. He saw a pair of legs beneath some sheets being hung up next door to dry.

"You never know what they're drawn to," Michele said. "The next thing, we were off to Mexico."

When the waiter brought the menus, Wells took off his glasses in order to examine his more closely. Later he asked a number of questions about the dishes and how they were prepared, unwilling to be hurried. There was something about his homeliness and manner that allowed him to do this.

"What's everyone want, red or white?" Bowman asked.

It was decided red.

"What's your best red?"

"The Amarone," the waiter said.

"We'll have a bottle of that."

"Very good wine," Wells said. "It comes from the Veneto, probably the most civilized part of Italy. Venice was the great city of the world for centuries. When London was filthy and sprawling, Venice was a queen. Shakespeare laid four of his plays there, *Othello, The Merchant, Romeo and Juliet* . . ."

"*Romeo and Juliet*," Ann said. "Isn't that in Verona?"

"Well, that's nearby," Wells said.

When the food came, he turned his entire attention to what was on his plate. He ate like a favored priest and he responded while chewing.

"I've never been to Venice," Ann said.

"You haven't?"

"No, I just never have."

"The time to go there is January. No crowds. Also, bring a flashlight to see the paintings. They're all in churches without real lighting. You can put in a coin and get some light, but it only lasts about fifteen seconds. You have to have your own light. Also, don't stay on the Giudecca. It's too far from everything. If you go there, tell me, and I'll tell you what to see. The cemetery is the best thing, Diaghilev's grave."

Ann seemed fascinated by every word.

"Diaghilev's grave is not the best thing," Bowman said.

"Well, it's close to it. I'll play a game with you, best thing in Paris, best thing in Rome, best thing in Amsterdam. The winner gets a prize."

"What's the prize?"

The prize would be Ann Hennessy, Wells thought to himself but was far from being drunk enough to say it.

It was a very congenial dinner. The Amarone was substantial and they ordered another bottle. Ann's face shone. She was a catalyst for the evening. Bowman hadn't noticed the gracefulness of her hands before. He saw that she certainly had been Baum's mistress though she had the quality of resisting suspicion. He could tell by looking at her that she had been. Later he saw that he was wrong when they all stood on the dark street bidding an extended good-bye and she had her hands clasped together in front of her like a young girl and something—the animation—had gone out of her. He flagged a cab and she got in ahead of him without a word.

"I enjoyed the evening," he said as they drove.

She said nothing.

"You were wonderful tonight," he said.

"Was I?"

"Yes."

After a while she began looking in her handbag for her keys.

Her apartment was on Jane Street. The building had no doorman, just two sets of locked glass doors.

"Would you like to come up?" she said unexpectedly.

"Yes," he said. "For a few minutes."

She lived on the third floor, and they walked up. The

elevator was out of service. She turned on the lights as they came into the apartment and took off her coat.

"Would you like something to drink?" she said. "I don't have much here. There's a little scotch, I think."

"All right. I'll have just a little."

She found the bottle and a glass but didn't get one for herself. She poured him a drink and sat down almost at the other end of the couch. She was a little drunk, he then saw, but she had regained some simple glamour in the pants and ruffled shirt. She sat looking at him. She wanted to talk. There were some things she wanted to say, but she did not. She sat silent. Bowman felt uncomfortable, and for want of anything to do moved close to her on the couch and calmly kissed her. She seemed to consider it.

"I should go home," he said.

"No, don't," she said. "You can . . . ," she didn't finish it. "Don't go."

She reached down and slipped off her shoes. Her instinct was to not embrace him. She would not have felt comfortable doing it. She stood and went unhurriedly into the bedroom. He felt she was going to lie down and pass out. After a few minutes he went to the bedroom door.

"Will you lie in bed with me?" she said.

On the platform at Hunters Point, where he caught the early train on most Fridays in the spring and fall, he walked back to where the rear cars would be when the train arrived. It was quarter to four and few other people were there yet. There was an old man in a linen suit with a handkerchief in his breast pocket and a blue shirt and tie reading the folded page of something with a magnifying glass, a widower who lived alone or perhaps a man who had never married, but what man at that age had never married? He'd be getting off at Southampton as he had probably done for many years. Walking off into the evening dark.

The train had pulled in. Passengers were clattering down the stairs from the street. Bowman got aboard and took a seat by the window. It was consoling, going into the country. The weekend lay ahead. The conductors in their hard blue caps were checking their watches. Finally, with a slight jolt, the train began to move.

For a while he read and then closed the book. The commercial suburbs and warehouses were left behind. At crossings there was evening traffic, lines of waiting cars with their headlights on. The boulevards were jammed. Houses, trees, unknown places flowing past, embankments, mysterious ponds. He had passed through it many times. He knew nothing about it.

He had left Tivoli the year before—the professor had come back from Europe—it had only been an interlude in any case. He promised to see Katherine in New York, but his life was separating from hers. He rented a house not far from the one he had first rented in Wainscott. His former life, he felt, was being returned to him. Ann Hennessy came for a weekend. There was a certain awkwardness, but it vanished over dinner.

"I have a bottle of Amarone at the house," he mentioned.

"Yes, I noticed it."

"You did? What else did you notice?"

"Very little. I was too excited."

"Well, the Amarone will calm you."

"Hardly."

But it led to the subject of Venice.

"I'd love to go there," she said.

"There's a wonderful guidebook on Venice—I think it's out of print—by a man named Hugh Honour. An historian. It's one of the best guidebooks I've ever read. I may have a copy. He has a companion named John Fleming. They're known as the Honour and the Glory. They're English, of course.

"I dislike the word 'gay,'" he said. "They're too eminent to be called gay. Perhaps in private they call themselves gay. The Roman emperors weren't gay. They swam naked in pools with young boys trained for pleasure, but it seems strange to call them gay. Depraved, pleasure-addicted, pederast, but not gay. It destroys the dignity of perversion."

"I hadn't thought of Roman emperors."

"Well, Cavafy then. It doesn't seem right to call him gay. Or John Maynard Keynes. It's too colloquial. Cavafy was a deviate. I think he uses the word himself. Gay doesn't seem right. But there are certain gay practices. You're familiar with them?" he said offhandedly.

"I suppose so," she said. "I'm not sure."

"I don't mean to suggest anything," he said.

"That's all right."

Though she waited, he did not continue.

It was the first of many weekends. They became a kind of informal couple. It was not in evidence at work where they preferred not to show it, but in the evenings and in the country. There they had leisure and no encumbrances. She slept in a simple white gown that he gently pushed upward from her hips, where it remained halfway or she pulled it over her head and off. Her bare skin was cool. Her arm was placed alongside her, her hand open. He laid himself in her narrow palm.

In June the water was still too cold for swimming. If after a minute he had the courage to dive in, in a split second he regretted it. But the days were beautiful and long. The beaches were still empty. Sometimes the sun, because of clouds, lay on only a section of the water, turning it almost to white while the rest remained deep blue or gray.

By July the ocean was warmer. They went to swim early in the day. In the parking lot a white van with its side cut away sold coffee and fried-egg sandwiches and later, cold drinks. A few kids were already lounging around and walking barefoot on the asphalt. The beach was uncrowded at that hour and stretched out of sight in both directions. Ann's bathing suit was a dark red. Her arms and legs had lost the city paleness.

The temperature of the water was perfect. They swam together for fifteen or twenty minutes and then came out to lie in the sun. There was little wind, the day was going to be hot. They lay with their heads not far apart. Once, she opened her eyes for a moment, saw him, and closed them again. Finally both of them sat up. The sun felt heavy on their shoulders. More people had come, some with umbrellas and chairs.

"Do you want to go in again?" Bowman said, standing.

"All right," she said.

They walked straight in, and when it was to the waist he dove, arms stretched out and his head tucked between them. The water was a dusty green, pure and silky with a gentle swell. This time they didn't swim together but went different ways. He swam towards the east, slowly falling into a steady rhythm of it. The sea was passing around him, beside him, beneath him in a way that belonged to him alone. There were a few other swimmers, their solitary heads showing further in. He felt he could go a great distance, he was filled with strength. With his head down he could see the bottom, smooth and rippled. He went a long way and at last turned and started back. Though he was tiring he felt he could not swim enough, stay long enough, in this ocean, on this day. Finally he came out, spent but elated. Not far from him a group of children, ten or twelve years old, were running into the water in a long, uneven file, girl with girl, boy following boy, their faces and cries filled with joy. He began walking towards Ann, who had come out earlier and was sitting in her sleek red bathing suit, he'd been able to pick her out from a distance.

With a feeling of triumph—he could not explain it—he stood drying himself before her. It was nearly eleven. The sun had terrific weight, it was like an anvil. They walked up together to where the car was parked off the road. Her legs seemed to have tanned even more as she sat in the seat beside him. The cheekbones of her face were burned. As for himself, he was completely happy. He wanted nothing more. Her presence was miraculous. She was the woman in her thirties in stories and plays who for some reason, circumstances, luck, had never found a man. Desirable, life-giving, she had slipped through the net, the fruit that had fallen to the ground. She had never spoken about their future. She had never mentioned, except in enthusiasm, the word "love." Standing before her that day though, having come out of the sea he had nearly said it, knelt beside her and said it, the love he had for her. He had nearly said, will you marry me? That was the moment, he knew.

He was unsure of himself and of her. He was too old to marry. He didn't want some late, sentimental compromise. He had known too much for that. He'd been married once, wholeheartedly, and been mistaken. He had fallen wildly in love with a woman in London, and it had somehow faded away. As if by fate one night in the most romantic encounter of his life he had met a woman and been betrayed. He believed in love—all his life he had—but now it was likely to be too late. Perhaps they could go on as they were forever, like the lives in art. *Anna*, as he'd begun to call her, *Anna, please come. Sit here beside me.*

Wells had married again sure of even less. He had seen a woman's legs and talked to her in the neighboring yard. They had run off together and his wife had formed her life around his. Perhaps it was a question of that, arranging a life. Perhaps they would travel. He had always meant to go to Brazil, to the place where Elizabeth Bishop had lived with her Brazilian companion, Lolta Soares, and to the two rivers, one blue and the other brown, that came together and she had written about. He had always wanted to go back to the Pacific, where the only daring part of his life lay, and travel across it, its vastness, passing the great forgotten names, Ulithi, Majuro, Palau, perhaps visiting a few graves, Robert Louis Stevenson's or Gauguin's, ten days by boat from Tahiti. Sail as far as Japan. They would plan trips together and stay in small hotels.

She had gone to visit her parents. It was October, he was alone. The clouds that night were a dark blue, a blue such as one seldom sees covering a hidden moon, and he thought, as he often did, of nights at sea or waiting to sail.

He was content to be alone. He'd made himself some dinner and sat afterwards reading with a glass at his elbow, just as he had sat in the little living room on Tenth Street, Vivian gone to bed and he sitting reading. Time was limitless, mornings, nights, all of life ahead.

He often thought about death but usually in pity for an animal or fish or seeing the dying grass in the fall or the monarch butterflies clinging to milkweed and feeding for the great funeral flight. Were they aware of it somehow, the strength it would take, the heroic strength? He thought about death, but he had never been able to imagine it, the unbeing while all else still existed. The idea of passing from this world to another, the next, was too fantastic to believe. Or that the soul would rise in a way unknown to join the infinite kingdom of God. There you would meet again all those you had once known as well as those you had never known, the countless dead in numbers forever increasing but never as great as the infinite. The only ones missing would be those who believed there was nothing afterwards, as his mother had said. There would be no such thing as time—time passed in an hour, like the time from the moment one fell asleep. There would be only joy.

Whatever you believed would happen was what happened, Beatrice said. She would go to some beautiful place. Rochester, she'd said, as a joke. He had always seen it as the dark river and the long lines of those waiting for the boatman, waiting in resignation and the patience that eternity required, stripped of all but a single, last possession, a ring, a photograph, or letter that represented everything dearest and forever left behind that they somehow hoped, it being so small, they would be able to take with them. He had such a letter, from Enid. *The days I spent with you were the greatest days of my life . . .*

What if there should be no river but only the endless lines of unknown people, people absolutely without hope, as there had been in the war? He would be made to join them, to wait forever. He wondered then, as he often did, how much of life remained for him. He was certain of only one thing, whatever was to come was the same for everyone who had ever lived. He would be going where they all had gone and—it was difficult to believe—all he had known would go with him, the war, Mr. Kindrigen and the butler pouring coffee, London those first days, the lunch with Christine, her gorgeous body like a separate entity, names, houses, the sea, all he had known and things he had never known but were there nevertheless, things of his time, all the years, the great liners with their invincible glamour readying to sail, the band playing as they were backed away, the green water widening, the *Matsonia* leaving Honolulu, the *Bremen* departing, the

Aquitania, Île de France, and the small boats streaming, following behind. The first voice he ever knew, his mother's, was beyond memory, but he could recall the bliss of being close to her as a child. He could remember his first schoolmates, the names of everyone, the classrooms, the teachers, the details of his own room at home—the life beyond reckoning, the life that had been opened to him and that he had owned.

He had been weeding in the garden that afternoon and looked down to see, beneath his tennis shorts, a pair of legs that seemed to belong to an older man. He mustn't, he realized, be going around the house in shorts like this when Ann was there, probably not even in the cotton kimono that barely came to the knee or in an undershirt. He had to be careful about such things. He always came out and went back in a suit. He'd come in the one from Tripler & Co., a midnight blue with a thin pinstripe.

It was the suit he wore to his aunt's funeral in Summit. He went with Ann—he had asked her to come with him. The funeral was at ten in the morning. It was brief, and they left soon after. They had come on the early train. Crossing the marshlands in the first bluish light, New York in the distance looked like a foreign city, someplace where you could live and be happy. On the way he told her about his aunt, Dorothy, his mother's sister, and his wonderful uncle, Frank. He described their restaurant, Fiori, with its red plush and couples who dropped in for dinner on their way home from work and others coming in later, not expecting to be seen. It had been years since it existed, but it seemed very real to him that morning, as if they could drive there for dinner and sit with a drink listening to *Rigoletto,* and the waitress would bring them steaks, slightly charred with a small pat of butter melting on top. He wanted to take her there for the first time.

His mind moved elsewhere, to the great funerary city with its palazzos and quiet canals, the lions that were its feared insignia.

"You know," he said, "I've been thinking about Venice. I'm not sure Wells was right about the best time to go there. January is so damned cold. I have a feeling it would be better to go before then. So what, if there're some crowds. I can ask him about hotels."

"Do you mean it?"

"Yes. Let's go in November. We'll have a great time."

COMET

A STORY BY JAMES SALTER

COMET

Philip married Adele on a day in June. It was cloudy and the wind was blowing. Later the sun came out. It had been a while since Adele had married and she wore white: white pumps with low heels, a long white skirt that clung to her hips, a filmy blouse with a white bra underneath, and around her neck a string of freshwater pearls. They were married in her house, the one she'd gotten in the divorce. All her friends were there. She believed strongly in friendship. The room was crowded.

"I, Adele," she said in a clear voice, "give myself to you, Phil, completely as your wife . . ." Behind her as best man, somewhat oblivious, her young son was standing, and pinned to her panties as something borrowed was a small silver disc, actually a St. Christopher's medal her father had worn in the war; she had several times rolled down the waistband of her skirt to show it to people. Near the door, under the impression that she was part of a garden tour, was an old woman who held a little dog by the handle of a cane hooked through his collar.

At the reception Adele smiled with happiness, drank too much, laughed, and scratched her bare arms with long show-girl nails. Her new husband admired her. He could have licked her palms like a calf does salt. She was still young enough to be good-looking, the final blaze of it, though she was too old for children, at least if she had anything to say about it. Summer was coming. Out of the afternoon haze she would appear, in her black bathing suit, limbs all tan, the brilliant sun behind her. She was the strong figure walking up the smooth sand from the sea, her legs, her wet swimmer's hair, the grace of her, all careless and unhurried.

They settled into life together, hers mostly. It was her furniture and her books, though they were largely unread. She liked to tell stories about DeLereo, her first husband—Frank, his name was—the heir to a garbage-hauling empire. She called him Delerium, but the stories were not unaffectionate. Loyalty—it came from her childhood as well as the years of marriage, eight exhausting years, as she said—was her code. The terms of marriage had been simple, she admitted. Her job was to be dressed, have dinner ready, and be fucked once a day. One time in Florida with another couple they chartered a boat to go bonefishing off Bimini.

"We'll have a good dinner," DeLereo had said happily, "get on board and turn in. When we get up we'll have passed the Gulf Stream."

It began that way but ended differently. The sea was very rough. They never did cross the Gulf Stream—the captain was from Long Island and got lost. DeLereo paid him fifty dollars to turn over the wheel and go below.

"Do you know anything about boats?" the captain asked.

"More than you do," DeLereo told him.

He was under an ultimatum from Adele, who was lying, deathly pale, in their cabin. "Get us into port somewhere or get ready to sleep by yourself," she'd said.

Philip Ardet had heard the story and many others often. He was mannerly and elegant, his head held back a bit as he talked, as though you were a menu. He and Adele had met on the golf course when she was learning to play. It was a wet day and the course was nearly empty. Adele and a friend were teeing off when a balding figure carrying a cloth bag with a few clubs in it asked if he could join them. Adele hit a passable drive. Her friend bounced his across the road and teed up another, which he topped. Phil, rather shyly, took out an old three wood and hit one two hundred yards straight down the fairway.

That was his persona, capable and calm. He'd gone to Princeton and been in the navy. He looked like someone who'd been in the navy, Adele said—his legs were strong. The first time she went out with him, he remarked it was a funny thing, some people liked him, some didn't.

"The ones that do, I tend to lose interest in."

She wasn't sure just what that meant but she liked his appearance, which was a bit worn, especially around the eyes. It made her feel he was a real man, though perhaps not the man he had been. Also he was smart, as she explained it, more or less the way professors were.

To be liked by her was worthwhile but to be liked by him seemed somehow of even greater value. There was something about him that discounted the world. He appeared in a way to care nothing for himself, to be above that.

He didn't make much money, as it turned out. He wrote for a business weekly. She earned nearly that much selling houses. She had begun to put on a little weight. This was a few years after they were married. She was still beautiful—

her face was—but she had adopted a more comfortable outline. She would get into bed with a drink, the way she had done when she was twenty-five. Phil, a sport jacket over his pajamas, sat reading. Sometimes he walked that way on their lawn in the morning. She sipped her drink and watched him.

"You know something?"

"What?"

"I've had good sex since I was fifteen," she said.

He looked up.

"I didn't start quite that young," he confessed.

"Maybe you should have."

"Good advice. Little late though."

"Do you remember when we first got started?"

"I remember."

"We could hardly stop," she said. "You remember?"

"It averages out."

"Oh, great," she said.

After he'd gone to sleep she watched a movie. The stars grew old, too, and had problems with love. It was different, though—they had already reaped huge rewards. She watched, thinking. She thought of what she had been, what she had had. She could have been a star.

What did Phil know—he was sleeping.

Autumn came. One evening they were at the Morrisseys'—Morrissey was a tall lawyer, the executor of many estates and trustee of others. Reading wills had been his true education, a look into the human heart, he said.

At the dinner table was a man from Chicago who'd made

a fortune in computers, a nitwit it soon became apparent, who during the meal gave a toast,

"To the end of privacy and the life of dignity," he said.

He was with a dampened woman who had recently found out that her husband had been having an affair with a black woman in Cleveland, an affair that had somehow been going on for seven years. There may even have been a child.

"You can see why coming here is like a breath of fresh air for me," she said.

The women were sympathetic. They knew what she had to do—she had to rethink completely the past seven years.

"That's right," her companion agreed.

"What is there to be rethought?" Phil wanted to know.

He was answered with impatience. The deception, they said, the deception—she had been deceived all that time. Adele meanwhile was pouring more wine for herself. Her napkin covered the place where she had already spilled a glass of it.

"But that time was spent in happiness, wasn't it?" Phil asked guilelessly. "That's been lived. It can't be changed. It can't be just turned into unhappiness."

"That woman stole my husband. She stole everything he had vowed."

"Forgive me," Phil said softly. "That happens every day."

There was an outcry as if from a chorus, heads thrust forward like the hissing, sacred geese. Only Adele sat silent.

"Every day," he repeated, his voice drowned out, the voice of reason or at least of fact.

"I'd never steal anyone's man," Adele said then. "Never." Her face had a tone of weariness when she drank, a weariness that knew the answer to everything. "And I'd never break a vow."

"I don't think you would," Phil said.

"I'd never fall for a twenty-year-old, either."

She was talking about the tutor, the girl who had come that time, youth burning through her clothes.

"No, you wouldn't."

"He left his wife," Adele told them.

There was silence.

Phil's bit of smile had gone but his face was still pleasant.

"I didn't leave my wife," he said quietly. "She threw me out."

"He left his wife and children," Adele said.

"I didn't leave them. Anyway it was over between us. It had been for more than a year. He said it evenly, almost as if it had happened to someone else. It was my son's tutor," he explained. "I fell in love with her."

"And you began something with her?" Morrissey suggested.

"Oh, yes."

There is love when you lose the power to speak, when you cannot even breathe.

"Within two or three days," he confessed.

"There in the house?"

Phil shook his head. He had a strange, helpless feeling. He was abandoning himself.

"I didn't do anything in the house."

"He left his wife and children," Adele repeated.

"You knew that," Phil said.

"Just walked out on them. They'd been married fifteen years, since he was nineteen."

"We hadn't been married fifteen years."

"They had three children," she said, "one of them retarded."

Something had happened—he was becoming speechless, he could feel it in his chest like a kind of nausea. As if he were giving up portions of an intimate past.

"He wasn't retarded," he managed to say. "He was . . . having trouble learning to read, that's all."

At that instant an aching image of himself and his son from years before came to him. They had rowed one afternoon to the middle of a friend's pond and jumped in, just the two of them. It was summer. His son was six or seven. There was a layer of warm water over deeper, cooler water, the faded green of frogs and weeds. They swam to the far side and then all the way back, the blond head and anxious face of his boy above the surface like a dog's. Year of joy.

"So tell them the rest of it," Adele said.

"There is no rest."

"It turned out this tutor was some kind of call girl. He found her in bed with some guy."

"Is that right?" Morrissey said.

He was leaning on the table, his chin in his hand. You think you know someone, you think because you have dinner with them or play cards, but you really don't. It's always a surprise. You know nothing.

"It didn't matter," Phil murmured.

"So stupid marries her anyway," Adele went on. "She comes to Mexico City where he's working and he marries her."

"You don't understand anything, Adele," he said.

He wanted to say more but couldn't. It was like being out of breath.

"Do you still talk to her?" Morrissey asked casually.

"Yes, over my dead body," Adele said.

None of them could know, none of them could visualize Mexico City and the first unbelievable year, driving down to the coast for the weekend, through Cuernavaca, her bare legs with the sun lying on them, her arms, the dizziness and submission he felt with her as before a forbidden photograph, as if before an overwhelming work of art. Two years in Mexico City oblivious to the wreckage. It was the sense of godliness that empowered him. He could see her neck bent forward with its slender nape. He could see the faint trace of bones like pearls that ran down her smooth back. He could see himself, his former self.

"I talk to her," he admitted.

"And your first wife?"

"I talk to her. We have three kids."

"He left her," Adele said. "Casanova here."

"Some women have minds like cops," Phil said to no one in particular. "This is right, that's wrong. Well, anyway . . ."

He stood up. He had done everything wrong, he realized, in the wrong order. He had scuttled his life.

"Anyway there's one thing I can say truthfully. I'd do it all over again if I had the chance."

After he had gone outside they went on talking. The woman whose husband had been unfaithful for seven years knew what it was like.

"He pretends he can't help it," she said. "I've had the

same thing happen. I was going by Bergdorf's one day and saw a green coat in the window that I liked and I went in and bought it. Then a little while later, someplace else, I saw one that was better than the first one, I thought, so I bought that. Anyway, by the time I was finished I had four green coats hanging in the closet—it was just because I couldn't control my desires."

Outside, the sky, the topmost dome of it, was brushed with clouds and the stars were dim. Adele finally made him out, standing far off in the darkness. She walked unsteadily toward him. His head, she saw, was raised. She stopped a few yards away and raised her head, too. The sky began to whirl. She took an unexpected step or two to steady herself.

"What are you looking at?" she finally said.

He did not answer. He had no intention of answering. Then,

"The comet," he said. "It's been in the papers. This is the night it's supposed to be most visible."

There was silence.

"I don't see any comet," she said.

"You don't?"

"Where is it?"

"It's right up there," he gestured. "It doesn't look like anything, just like another small star. It's that extra one, by the Pleiades." He knew all the constellations. He had seen them rise in darkness over heartbreaking coasts.

"Come on, you can look at it tomorrow," she said, almost consolingly, though she came no closer to him.

"It won't be there tomorrow. One time only."

"How do you know where it'll be?" she said. "Come on, it's late, let's get out of here."

He did not move. After a bit she walked toward the house where, extravagantly, every window upstairs and down was lit. He stood where he was, looking up at the sky and then at her as she became smaller and smaller going across the lawn, reaching first the aura, then the brightness, then tripping on the kitchen steps.

picador.com

blog
videos
interviews
extracts